FLC
S553L

P9-BZR-159
7 3390 00107 6428

DISCARD

The Little Russian

The Little Russian

Susan Sherman

Library of Congress Cataloging-in-Publication Data
Sherman, Susan.
The little Russian / Susan Sherman.
p. cm.
ISBN 978-1-58243-772-9 (hardback)
1. Jewish women—Fiction. 2. Soviet Union—History—
1917–1936—Fiction. I. Title.
PS3619.H4676L58
2012 813'.6—dc23 2011037731

Cover design by Ann Weinstock
Interior design by David Bullen

Printed in the United States of America

COUNTERPOINT
1919 Fifth Street
Berkeley, CA 94710
www.counterpointpress.com
Distributed by Publishers Group West
10 9 8 7 6 5 4 3 2 1

For my father, Lorry

With thanks to my remarkable editor and valued friend,
Dan Smetanka

Blessed art Thou, Lord our God, King of the universe,
Who did not make me a slave.

THE BIRCHOT HASHACHAR

The Little Russian

Prologue

May 1897

THE GIRL STOOD on the platform and stared at the wire that stretched out before her. She was young, not much over fourteen, but the body of a woman strained against her ballet costume. She wore dirty pink tights that bulged at the knee and a cardboard tiara that sparkled in the sun. The tulle skirt was torn in several places, dropping sequins on her tights and slippers. Her mother stood directly below her, cranking a barrel organ that alternated between two popular songs.

"It is time to begin, *maideleh*," she called up. "They're waiting."

It was market day and the air smelled of rotting fruit, manure, and sweating horses. Jewish housewives, still clutching their checkered winter shawls, strolled up and down the aisles of stalls. Over by the rag dealer, women pulled on worn dresses over their clothes. If they liked their reflection in the little mirror hanging on the stall, they kept it to themselves. Better to bargain the price down.

The girl looked out on the crowd that had stopped to watch her. She took a breath and with arms outstretched stepped onto the wire. She paused and waited for the wire to stop bouncing and then took another cautious step. One boy in the back was not fooled by her trepidation. He knew it was all part of the act. He had seen her performance earlier on his way to school and knew she only appeared frightened to win the sympathy of the audience. Soon her confidence would appear to grow as her tricks became increasingly more difficult. In the finale, she would execute a perfect handstand and finish with the splits, her legs delicately balanced on the wire, her arms held high in triumph.

The boy knew he needed to get going. School had let out nearly an hour ago and he was expected at the Chernyi Griaz, a billiards club on the edge of the shtetl that filled with officers from the Zhitomir regiment during the summer months. He went there to play chess and satisfy the bets of those who chose to put their money on him. They called him the wonder boy.

Nobody knew how good he really was. He was always throwing games to keep the odds interesting and the opponents coming. In truth, there was only one man in town who could legitimately beat him, and that was his father. The rest he simply managed, but always in a believable way. It was important to give the impression that he was fallible, a mere human being, although he didn't believe it for a minute. At fourteen, he was anything but humble. Even so, he hid his pride well, knowing that it could get him into trouble. It was important to hide his light under a bushel, as his mother would say. This was an American saying that the boy's older sister had written in a letter home. *You don't have to hide your light under a bushel in America*, she wrote from Rice Lake, Wisconsin. *Here you don't have to be afraid to stand tall.*

Stand tall was another American saying. But Rice Lake, Wisconsin, was a long way from Little Russia. "In the Pale, if you are a Jew, it doesn't hurt to slump a little," his mother would caution. *A kluger gait tsu fus un a nar fort in a kareteh*, she would say in plain Yiddish. A wise man walks on foot and a fool rides in a coach.

The girl took halting steps forward and backward, gradually becoming more graceful, more self-assured, extending a leg out behind her, holding the difficult pose with nothing but air beneath her. The crowd clapped and several peasant boys hooted and whistled. When she appeared to lose her balance, they gasped and froze in disbelief. In the next instant, she steadied herself and there was a great sigh of relief. The boy knew this too was part of the act.

During the finale, the girl executed a perfect handstand, her legs extending straight and stiff over her shoulders, her hands firmly grasping the wire. When the crowd pressed forward to get a better view, someone pushed the rope spinner, who stumbled against the shoe peddler, who tripped and fell against a peasant eating a meat pie. The young man had come to town to buy a scythe handle. He pitched forward and spilled the pie all over the blouse that his mother had embroidered for his name day. When he saw what had happened, he turned on the shoe peddler, shouting and cursing at him. The poor man was so frightened he didn't know what to do. He stood there paralyzed, which infuriated the muzhik all the more. Soon the young man was beating the Jew with his brand new scythe handle, unmindful of the blood that mixed with the gravy on his shirt.

There were those who tried to help the shoe peddler, but they were beaten back by the other muzhiki. There were shouts and screams all around. The boy couldn't see what was happening and tried to push his way through, but the throng was too thick. When it thinned, he found the shoe peddler, his shoes still hanging around his neck, lying dead in a pool of blood. The peddler's children were standing nearby, dry-eyed, watching their mother sob over the body of their father. Women from the town had gathered around her, trying to coax her away, but the widow preferred to sit in the road, rocking back and forth.

THAT AFTERNOON the muzhiki sent a delegation to deliver an ultimatum: five thousand rubles by morning or suffer a pogrom. Women panicked when they heard the news, grabbed their children, and ran home. Shopkeepers shuttered their windows and bolted their doors. The men gathered at the volunteer fire station to deliberate. It was a large loft over the butcher shop, with a makeshift stage at one end and a stack of wooden folding chairs at the other. Under the exposed trestles, men rubbed their beards and paced up and down, while they searched in vain for a way to save their town.

The boy sat at the back and watched his father, the *starusta*, the head of the town, conduct the meeting with his usual composure, giving the floor first to the butcher, then to the water carrier, letting everyone have their say without comment.

"I say we fight," said Yankel Schneider, the blacksmith and a well-known hothead. "We have the numbers and we're strong. We could give them at least as good as we get."

"But they have guns," said Dr. Mikhaeli, the town doctor. "We don't. And even if we did, we wouldn't know how to use them."

"What is there to know?" said Yankel, irritably. "Just point and shoot."

The baker wanted to call in the army. But the water carrier laughed at him. Everybody knew the army wouldn't lift a finger to help the Jews. The grain merchant offered a hundred rubles to stop the catastrophe. Others pledged five or ten depending on their circumstance.

As the afternoon faded into night and the kerosene lamps were lit, the boy grew impatient waiting for his father to unveil a plan. He knew his father would have one. He lived life in the same way he played chess, quietly, patiently, taking his time, following clearly laid-out paths to assured ends. The boy was confident that this crisis would be no exception.

But what the boy didn't know was at that very moment the local muzhiki, at least twenty of them, had arrived in the town square with carts loaded with empty potato sacks, brought in anticipation of a rich bounty torn from the shops and homes of the Jews.

There were other men there too, leaning up against the buildings in the dark, mingling with the crowd, talking to them about how the Jews had grown rich off the labor of the peasant, how they had cheated the peasant in ways he'd never even know about, how they bled him dry, and laughed at him behind his back. These men were not peasants. They were outsiders from the north, Great Russians, artel workers, who wore visor caps, belted gray tunics, black leather jackets, and swords at their sides. They were members of the Alliance of Russian People, the Black Hundreds, as they were known throughout the empire, and they had come to organize the pogrom.

Eventually the muzhiki grew bored with them and began talking among themselves, playing cards and passing around a bottle of vodka that was soon empty. They wanted more, but the Jews owned all the taverns and had locked them up. Someone cried out *Chernyi Griaz!* and there were shouts of agreement all around. The crowd rose up as one undulating mass of thirst, filled with excitement and anticipation, and set off down the main street toward the billiards club.

When the proprietor, Joseph Bokser, and his two sons saw the mob coming, they blocked the doorway to the storehouse and shouted at them to go away. But when the mob threatened them with clubs, pistols, and swords, Joseph Bokser ordered his sons to stand aside and opened the door himself.

Cradling bottles of vodka in their arms and stuffing still more into their empty sacks, the mob fanned out into the other streets. Ostap Shevchenko and his three sons tore the shutters off the mercantile store and smashed the windows with the handles of their rakes. When he hopped over the jagged glass and stepped into the store, he found racks of greatcoats, heavy boots, fur hats, and work gloves—everything he had always wanted but could never afford. He shouted to his sons to start stuffing the potato sacks with everything they could find.

Shloime Lazar, the proprietor of the hardware store, was cowering in the dark behind his shuttered windows. He had been expecting this for years. He had invested in new shutters reinforced with iron bars and gone all the way to L'vov to see Rabbi Levi Israel, a miracle rabbi, who had blessed his prayer shawl and told him that it would keep him safe from the Cossack sword. When he heard his shutters give way to the axes of the muzhiki, he went out to meet the pogromists with his own axe in hand. They surrounded him and cut off his right arm with one tremendous blow. His axe clattered to the floorboards along with most of his forearm and hand. As he lay bleeding to death, his last thought was for his wife and three daughters, who were upstairs hiding under their beds.

With the first screams of the pogrom, the men in the volunteer fire station clamored down the narrow staircase, pushing and shoving one another, frantic to get to their families. "Stay with me," the boy's father said to him as they ran out of the building. "Stay close."

Outside, people were running in all directions, women screaming and clutching their children, shots fired, the sound of shattering glass. The boy saw a muzhik throw a screaming baby out of Judah Altman's second-story window. At the corner, he saw several figures run out of the main shul and down the wide steps carrying half-empty sacks. One of them was Tadeusz Zawadski, a boy from his form at school, who held a Torah crown and a silver candelabrum. Their eyes met in the dim light of a street lamp. A ripple of shame crossed the other boy's face before his eyes went dead and he moved on.

In front of the bakery they found the battered body of the baker and his wife. The old man's skull had been caved in. His wife's face had been laid open and one eye was missing, the socket black with blood. The sight made the boy's legs wobble and his stomach turn. He gaped at the hole where the eye should have been and turned away to vomit. His father pulled him into the shadow of a doorway, put a protective arm around his shoulders, and said, "Listen to me. We will get your mother and head for the woods. I know a place. We will be all right. But I need you . . . do you understand? I need you tonight."

The boy wiped the vomit away with the back of his hand and returned his father's gaze. His face was a mask of endurance. "Yes, Tateh," was all he said.

Before they had gone a dozen steps the boy heard more shots; this time they were closer, maybe even in the next lane. They ran on, taking shelter first in one doorway and then in another. They stuck to the shadows, relying on the night and their intimate knowledge of every alley, doorway, and basement to stay hidden. A goat ran by with blood streaming down her flank, her swollen udders swinging wildly as she plunged off down the street. A cardboard tiara lay crushed and filthy in the gutter. Up ahead, three or four peasants in the middle of the road came toward them. They were shouting and singing a tuneless song. A straggler followed behind, drinking vodka from a bottle, and shooting his pistol through apartment windows. When he ran out of bullets, he crouched in the street to reload.

To avoid them, the boy's father forced open the widow Yehsohua's window and climbed in. The boy tumbled in after him and landed on the floor. When the old woman saw the two figures in her front room she screamed and ran to the back of the house. They ran after her and found her standing in the kitchen, stabbing the air with a butcher's knife, her wispy gray hair standing out in tufts about her head. She screamed in Yiddish, "Get away! Get away or I'll kill you."

"Chainke," the boy's father whispered furiously, trying to quiet her. "It's me. For God's sake, *stop screaming!*"

The old woman stopped. She stared up at them and then burst into tears. "*Ah, es iz ek velt!*" It's the end of the world, she sobbed and sank to her knees. "They're coming. The Cossacks are coming!"

"Calm down, Chainke. It doesn't help to make such a racket."

"I don't want to die."

"Then keep quiet, woman."

He went to the window and looked out on the alley behind the house. It was dark and deserted. Satisfied, he forced the window open and stuck his head out to get a better look around.

"Where are you going?" she cried, struggling to her feet.

"We can't stay here. We have to get home."

"No!" she cried, grabbing hold of his sleeve. "You can't leave me here all alone. You have to take me with you."

"Stop it now!" he said as he disentangled her fingers. "You want to bring them down on our heads? Stay here and keep the lights off and don't make a sound. They won't come for you. You're an old woman with nothing to steal."

But she wouldn't be comforted and kept pleading with him not to leave even after he swung one leg over the sill and lowered himself to the ground. The boy was about to follow when he heard footsteps coming down the alley.

"Stay inside, son. Get down and keep her quiet. No matter what happens, don't move, *farshtaist*?" The boy nodded to show he understood.

The footsteps grew louder, punctuated by the sound of a tambourine, and then, from out of the gloom, a husky voice thick with drink asked, "Hey, who's this? A *zhyd*? It is a *zhyd*. Hey, Yasha, I found a *zhyd*." It was two drunken muzhiki—one of them carried a tambourine, the other a sack of pots and pans thrown over his shoulder.

The boy peeked out through the torn curtains and watched as they circled his father, giving him a little shove and a poke with the tambourine. "It is not a *zhyd*, you horse's ass. It's the *starusta*. Hey, want to join our party, Your Excellency?"

The boy's father shook his head and declined the offer of vodka, but the man insisted. When he refused a second time, the big one with the tambourine grabbed his head and held it while the other one pried open his mouth and poured the vodka down his throat.

The boy slid down below the sill and lay there panting and nauseous. His heart battered against his chest while the room swelled and contracted like a living thing. In the next instant he felt the warm flood of urine, and tears spilled down his cheeks. His gaze fell on the knife that lay glinting on the floor near the prostrate figure of the widow Yehsohua. She moved it away and held a finger to her lips. He didn't argue with her; his hands remained limp at his sides, his legs useless, his eyes fixed on the dull handle of the knife.

Outside a bottle smashed against the building. The two men were arguing about where to find more vodka. When the boy looked out again, he saw them dragging his father off, a tambourine keeping time with their footsteps. As they began to fade into the gloom, the boy thought he saw his father look back once, only once, before they shoved him out to the street.

Part One

THE LADY FROM MOSCOW

Chapter One

September 1903

Everyone knew that if you wanted to reserve a first-class compartment all to yourself, you had to buy four tickets in advance. And since Berta Lorkis had been dreading this long trip for months and months, every excruciating aspect of it from beginning to end, there was some consolation in the fact that four first-class tickets would be waiting for her on the foyer table the morning she left Moscow.

She came down on the left side of the double marble staircase, always on the left for descent, her footsteps echoing off the high ceiling, her hand gliding over the lotus flowers carved into the banister. There wasn't another house in Moscow with a foyer like this one, with its Egyptian columns each topped by a brilliantly colored sphinx. She couldn't be sure, but she doubted if there was another one like it in all of Russia. Even though she didn't design it or build it or even own it, she lived in it. It was the address she gave to cabmen and new acquaintances, the room that greeted her visitors when they first arrived, and that was enough for her.

It was early and the house still smelled of late-night bliny, smoked sturgeon, and cigars from the party the night before. There was a wineglass in the corner behind a chair and one up on a window ledge; a few stray ostrich feathers littered the floor. Under a mass of orchids on the amber table was a cream-colored envelope containing four first-class tickets, a note wishing her a safe journey, and two hundred rubles. The note was from Rosa Davidovna, the matriarch of the Malkiel brood and a second mother to Berta. Berta hadn't expected the crisp fifty-ruble notes.

The coachman in his bottle green caftan opened the front door and announced that the luggage had been loaded and the carriage was waiting. She thanked him and put the envelope in her traveling case. When he was gone she checked her hat in the mirror that hung over the table. She had been right to wear this outfit. The color suited her and the skirt fit her like wax. She checked the back to make sure her belt was straight and fluffed up the flounces on her skirt. She made it a rule never to wear wire in her collars, only whalebone, only lace-trimmed satin petticoats that wouldn't rustle, and only straight in front corsets. She always gave herself nearly a quarter of an hour to put on her gloves, because they fit her that well.

Berta met the coachman at the bottom of the steps, where he had the carriage door open. He took her traveling case and placed it on the seat inside and then took her arm just under the elbow and helped her into the carriage. It smelled of Mendel Afanasrevich's lime shaving soap and the boot wax that his valet favored. There were fur rugs and a leather lap blanket neatly folded on one side of the seat and a newspaper that had been carelessly dropped on the floor. She folded it back along the seams, smoothed out the corners, and laid it in her lap. It would pass the time on the train.

The coachman climbed up on the box, clicked his tongue, flicked the whip, and the coach lurched forward. Soon they were crossing the Bely Gorod, heading down Nikolskaia Street and on through the Garden Ring to the Arbat. Here were many multistoried limestone buildings decorated with black signs in gilt lettering announcing the names of the stores in Russian and sometimes in French. Bells rang out from the numerous churches, proclaiming the hour each in their own way while horse-drawn trolleys clanged up and down the street depositing passengers on nearly every corner and picking up more. They continued on across the Borodinski Bridge, to Berezhki Street and then on to the Bryanski Station, where Berta was to catch the train west to the Ukraine, or Little Russia, as it was called.

Berta, like so many Great Russians, thought of Kiev and the surrounding provinces as a Russian outpost: provincial, backward, but Russified to some extent. She had a respect for both the Polish and the German influences there, but agreed with the authorities that the

Ukrainian culture and language had little to offer. It was banned in the schools and in the government institutions and was thought to be the purlieu of reprobates, lazy slum dwellers, and rustics. Berta was born in Little Russia, a small fact that she never bothered to share with anyone of consequence. She was a Great Russian, as anyone could see by her fierce accomplishments, tasteful dress, and overall refinement.

Throughout the two-day journey from Moscow to Smolensk and Gorbatchovo to Bakhmatch, Tchernigov, and Kiev, Berta spent her days alone in the comfort of her compartment, reading, sleeping, and watching the dark pine forests of the northeast gradually give way to the undulating farmlands in the west. She luxuriated in the solitude and savored the feeling of disconnection, of being suspended between two worlds, a stranger to all, without ties and the expectations that went with them. Then, about 130 versts south of Kiev at a wheat center called Cherkast, an intruder appeared at the door of her compartment. She was a red-faced woman in light-colored muslin, looking hot in an embroidered bolero jacket and high-collared shirtwaist and wearing a hat so enormous, so generously laden with feathers, artificial flowers, and tropical foliage, it was a wonder she got it through the door.

"Sorry, this is a private compartment," Berta said, with a note of alarm when it became apparent that the woman meant to move in with her traveling case, parasol, and numerous packages.

The woman stopped fanning herself with her ticket. "It is?" She shifted her packages to examine her ticket and checked the number on the door. "But this is number five. I'm in number five."

"That is impossible. I booked the whole compartment."

"You did?"

"Of course."

As it turned out, the woman's ticket was marked for Berta's compartment. By rights the railroad should have corrected the mistake and accommodated the lady elsewhere, but the train was full and there was no place else for her to go.

"I am so sorry to intrude," she said as she came back in, taking the seat across from Berta and spreading out her things on the surrounding seats. "I won't get in the way. You're so kind to offer me a place."

Berta gave her a cold, quick smile and tried to ignore the vulgar rustling of the woman's taffeta petticoats. At that point she could've made a fuss, but she was young and the woman was old, at least over forty, and she had learned from experience that waiters, cabmen, and guards on trains always placed age above beauty. She could've chanced it, but in all likelihood she would've lost and then she'd have to spend the rest of the journey with a sullen fat woman not three feet away. So reluctantly Berta accepted her fate with something approaching equanimity.

For the first few hours the two women sat in amicable silence, reading their books and glancing out the window at the passing landscape. There were wheat fields of tawny stubble, haymaking stations, women in garish head scarves raking the tall shafts of grass into carts, farmhouses made of logs covered in plaster, thatched mansard roofs, and horses harnessed under great bowed yokes called *dugas*. Everywhere there was color: lion-colored hayricks, black earth, silver bark, red-belted tunics, embroidered shirts the color of Easter eggs, all set against a hard blue sky.

After a while the woman excused herself, got up with some difficulty, and made her way to the door. There was plenty of room in the compartment, but she was so large and her journey so precarious that she obviously thought it prudent to apologize in advance. When she was gone, Berta took the opportunity to examine the woman's hat, left lying on the seat next to her gloves and a leather-bound book suitable for traveling. Berta knew there was much to learn from a hat. This one looked like it came from the salon of the Allschwang Brothers on the Petrovka, but on closer examination, it was easy to see that it was a well-made imitation, expensive, but not of Moscow quality. Berta didn't have anything against imitations. They weren't for her of course, but they were serviceable for those of a certain class. She wasn't a snob. Quite the contrary, she was modern, forward thinking, and liberal, clearly more suited to the new century than to the last. And besides, she was in Little Russia now and had to expect that kind of thing.

By the time the woman returned, Berta had replaced the hat exactly where she had found it and was sitting back on the horsehair cushions, her feet tucked under the flounces of her skirt, pretending to read her book.

"The porters are going from compartment to compartment," the woman said, taking her seat. "It's never a good sign when they make an announcement in the middle of a journey." She was a nervous sort with a motherly face and an ample bosom that rested comfortably on her midriff whenever she sat down. She kept smoothing her skirt over her prominent belly as if that would make it go away.

"I wouldn't worry about it. It can't be too serious. We're still moving. If it had to do with the train or the tracks, we'd be at a standstill."

A few minutes later there was a perfunctory knock at the door and the porter opened it without waiting for a reply. "I regret to inform you," he said with an officious twitch of his moustache, "that there will be no fish on the menu today."

"No fish?" the woman replied, dabbing at her moist cheeks and upper lip with a handkerchief. It was a hot day and the window was stuck.

"I'm sorry, Madame. The fish in Cherkast did not meet our standards. But we did manage to pick up a fine joint of roast beef."

"Roast beef for lunch? No, I don't think so. That's all right, I'll find something. Please don't worry about me."

The porter withdrew and the woman gazed forlornly out at the Dnieper River flowing patiently beside the tracks. "Can you imagine that? A whole river out there and no fish for the train. And all this time I thought this was the good line."

Fortunately Aleksandra Dmitrievna Tretiakova was a strong woman with a healthy attitude toward life. She prided herself on eating right, getting plenty of sleep, and walking on those rare occasions when the weather permitted, so it didn't take her long to rise above her difficulties.

"So where are you from, my dear?" she asked, plumping her pillow and putting her troubles behind her.

"Moscow."

"I love Moscow. I'd love to live there, but my husband says the wheat is in Cherkast. You have a family? Children?"

"I live with relatives."

"Oh," Aleksandra Dmitrievna's voice slid down an octave in disappointment.

Berta replaced the tooled leather bookmark and closed her book. "The Malkiels, perhaps you've heard of them?" She dropped this little gem as if it were of no consequence.

"The sugar Malkiels?"

"That's right."

"And you're a relative you say?"

"A cousin."

"Oh my, a cousin." Aleksandra Dmitrievna's doughy cheeks flushed with pleasure. "What must that be like? Living in all that splendor." Her eyes were shining.

"It's pleasant," Berta said fanning herself with a cardboard fan decorated with a train, provided to all the first-class passengers by the Southwestern Line.

"Oh, I'm sure it is. Most pleasant. Heaven, I would imagine. You will tell me all about it? You're not one of those absurdly private people are you?"

Berta smiled modestly and sat back in her seat. Maybe she had been too quick to judge this woman. And there was the long train ride ahead of them; and she was nearly finished with her novel; and to be honest, she couldn't think of a more agreeable subject of conversation than herself. So it wasn't long before she was telling Aleksandra Dmitrievna all about her life at Number 12 Leontievsky Street.

She told her about their horses in Petrovka Park, their box at the Bolshoi, and their salon on Tuesdays. She described her former classmates at the girls' gymnasium, Arseniev; their prominent families; and the sensational gossip that no unmarried girl of twenty-three should know much less repeat. It wasn't that Berta was unduly influenced by the awe, excitement, and envy so plainly displayed on Aleksandra Dmitrievna's face—she was simply relating her life as she had been asked to do. True, she omitted a few facts pertaining to her position in that world as a *distant* cousin of the Malkiels'. And to be fair she might have exaggerated her relationship with the more important members of society, but weren't these little transgressions forgivable, especially in light of the fact that she was giving Aleksandra Dmitrievna Tretiakova something to talk about for the rest of her life?

". . . And all the women were wearing décolleté that evening to show off their diamonds." Berta had moved on to the coronation ball at the Hunter's Club in May of 1896. "Luidmila Borisovna wore a branch of them in her hair and Grafina Sergeevna had a rope of them tied around her waist. And you should've seen the roses, a hundred thousand of them. Then at midnight they brought in a huge replica of the Kremlin cathedral made out of red sugar. It was gigantic and took six men to carry it in. It had real doors that opened and everyone who went to the coronation said it was true down to the last detail."

Although Berta included plenty of colorful details in her description of that famous evening, she did leave out certain inconvenient facts. For example, there was that tragedy on Khodynka Field that happened in the early morning hours of the eighteenth, when two thousand people were trampled to death by a panicked crowd of six hundred thousand who mistakenly believed the free beer was running out. When she described watching the fireworks from the club's terrace, she also failed to mention the line of carts rumbling by in the street below and how, in the spectacular flashes of color from overhead, it was easy to see the blue-black bodies, the bloodstained tatters, the smashed noses, the eyes askew, and the many pairs of bare feet bouncing over the cobblestones. She also omitted the fact that the Malkiels were Jews and only invited to the ball because they owned the majority of sugar refineries in Russia and contributed more than three hundred Russian pounds of dyed red sugar.

Soon after that, Aleksandra Dmitrievna opened up her packages and they made a picnic out of biscuits, caviar, and wine. She slathered a biscuit with caviar, and presented it to Berta on a porcelain plate. Berta accepted it graciously, took a bite, and nodded her appreciation.

"And your parents?" Dmitrievna asked, helping herself to another biscuit.

Berta's face clouded. She took a sip of her wine and gazed out the window at a passing farmstead where an old man and his wife were wrapping their house in dried corn stalks as insulation against the coming winter. "They're dead."

"Oh, how awful. Cholera?"

"Typhus."

"We had an epidemic a few summers back. Everyone was boiling water and drinking glasses and glasses of beet juice. Fortunately we were all fine. And so that's why you went to live with your relatives?"

"Yes, they're my family now."

"Of course they are, my dear. And a fine family they are."

Berta's eyes followed a flock of crows rising up in a cloud above a corn field, their shadows making ominous splotches on the corn below. She drained her wine, sat back, and closed her eyes. In a few minutes her lips felt numb and her limbs relaxed. It wasn't a bad feeling, considering.

Late that afternoon the train pulled into a station of no consequence and Berta rose and gathered up her things. Her traveling companion was asleep and snoring into a pillow embroidered with the crest of the Southwestern Line. Berta moved about the compartment as quietly as possible, hoping not to wake Aleksandra Dmitrievna. She wanted to avoid the usual hugging and kissing, exchanging of cards and empty promise making that went on even between strangers when a journey had been shared. She wanted to disappear without a trace, perhaps leaving only a faint whiff of perfume behind. But the train came to such a sudden halt that it woke Aleksandra Dmitrievna with a jerk.

After a blank moment she sat up, wiped away a small puddle of drool from her chin, and looked out the window. "Where are we?"

"Mosny."

She stared out at the dreary station and then noticed that Berta was pulling on her gloves. "You're getting off here?"

Berta nodded.

Aleksandra Dmitrievna took another look at the station, at the barefoot children selling pastries, at the peasants waiting to board, at the muzhik arguing with the stationmaster over a crate of ducks he was refusing to stow in the luggage compartment, and said nothing. There was also a Jewish couple walking down the length of the train searching in every window for someone they had come to meet. She was a small, birdlike woman wearing a dirty head scarf, a plain blouse, and a dark skirt. He wore a visor cap over his tousled gray hair and black trousers with a bulging waistband where his tallis was tied. When they came to Berta's window, the woman's hands flew to her mouth. She elbowed her husband and began to wave excitedly.

"Do you know them?" Aleksandra Dmitrievna asked, looking relieved to be separated from the *zhydy* by a sturdy pane of glass.

Berta glanced up briefly, shook her head, and returned to her gloves.

"But look, she's calling your name."

Berta took another look and this time there was a flicker of recognition. Halfheartedly she waved back. "Oh, that's Rivke. She keeps our poultry. And that's her husband. I guess they've been sent to meet me."

"Why does she keep waving like that?"

Berta shrugged. "They're like children." She leaned over to kiss Aleksandra Dmitrievna on both cheeks. "Now promise you'll come to see me. I'll be back in Moscow by the end of the month. Here's my card."

Aleksandra Dmitrievna tucked it into her pocket and eagerly went in search of her own. "Will I meet the Malkiels, do you think?"

"Of course. We'll have you for tea."

"You really think so?" she asked, taking out a card from an engraved silver case and handing it to Berta.

"I'm looking forward to it."

Berta put the card in her just-in-case bag, where she was bound to lose it. Then she gathered up her things and, after one last good-bye, left the compartment. She could've gotten off right there, but instead she chose to walk through the train and exit at the other end.

The minute she stepped off she felt the full force of the Little Russian summer. She had forgotten how hot they could be, how they weighted her limbs and made her clothes stick to her body. She had to find a way to cut this visit short. She wouldn't last a week in this intolerable hell. Looking past the train station to the dusty road, she thought the heat and flies alone would do her in.

There were several porters leaning up against the little station in the shade and several more sitting on a stone ledge that ran around it. They wore scruffy beards, homespun jackets, dirty aprons, and heavy ropes wrapped around their waists. Berta opened her parasol and motioned one over. They had all been eyeing her, hoping for a little business.

"See that Jewish couple standing over there by the first-class carriages?" she asked, putting a few kopecks in the porter's palm. "Tell them Berta is here waiting for them at the other end of the train." He nodded and strode off to do as he was told. She watched while the couple listened to him then turned to search the crowd. When they spotted her the woman came running over, while her husband followed behind at a more measured pace.

"Berta!" she cried, throwing her arms around Berta's shoulders and holding her tight. "We've missed you. Oh, how we've missed our Berta." She kissed her on both cheeks and hugged her again. Then she held her at arm's length and admired her dress and hair. "Look at her, Chaim. What a lady . . . what a beauty. I would never have recognized her."

"You would have recognized her. You would have recognized her anywhere," said her husband.

"Of course. It's just that she's all grown up now and so beautiful. Look at her, such a *shainkeit*."

When it was his turn, the man took Berta in his arms and held her close. "I've missed you," he said hoarsely.

I've missed you too, she thought, her eyes glistening. He smelled of the grocery, of pickles and axle grease. She could feel his work-roughened hands through the thin muslin of her shirtwaist. She let him hold her a while longer and then gently eased herself free.

"I have a trunk," she said, searching the platform. "Over there by the bench. Can we get the porter to fetch it?"

"A porter? Listen to her, Chaim. The lady from Moscow. Don't be silly, we can manage. Come, we have to hurry. Everyone's coming."

"Everyone?" swallowed Berta.

"Yes, of course, Sonja Zilberstein, Chaya Krasnoy, Pessele and her daughters, Avrum and Zirele . . . they all want to see the famous Berta Lorkis home from Moscow."

"Now?"

"Why not now?"

"But I'm so tired."

"Tired? *A nechtiker tog!* What do you have to be tired about? You sat on a train. Come, you'll eat something, sleep maybe, and then they'll come. Don't look so glum. This is a happy time." She took Berta's face in her hands.

The man struggled with the heavy trunk and finally got it loaded up on the cart. After they took their seats on the bench, he clicked his tongue and flicked the reins and slowly the horse started up the main road into town. Soon they were passing a parade of familiar landmarks that Berta watched go by with a mixture of nostalgia and disgust. There were crooked lanes that veered off at odd angles where sagging wooden houses seemed to tumble in on each other. There were staircases leading up to precarious iron balconies, a roof that seemed to be melting off its house, windows that didn't close, and doors that hung askew. Nothing was plumb in Mosny; no angles met; no corners were crisp. The whole town seemed to be made of candle wax, crooked, malleable, and unreliable in the hot sun.

They passed several boarded-up storefronts, the planks looking like patches over empty eye sockets. The tallis weaver's shop was gone and so was the candlemaker's. Berta remembered playing *going to America* with the cooper's daughter, and now the cooper's shop was gone too; only a few rusty barrel hoops were left, half hidden in the tall weeds. Up on Shulgas Street, the street of synagogues, Berta saw the shul *klopfer*, wearing one large shoe and one small, shuffling along from storefront to dwelling calling the men to afternoon prayers. On a corner three young matrons sat out in front of a secondhand clothing shop. They had placed their chairs up against the building to take advantage of the shade from the overhang. One of them rose involuntarily when she saw Berta coming up the road. They all stared at her. Berta couldn't blame them. They were dressed in dusty skirts, sweat-stained blouses, and dirty scarves, and here she was in her traveling suit and new straw hat with the green band that perfectly matched her parasol. She leaned forward to get a better look at them as the cart went by. Had they gone swimming together, picked strawberries, gone to the heder, the Jewish elementary school? Several seemed familiar, but it had been nine years since she left and she could not tell.

She recognized the *melamedkeh*, the wife of the teacher at the heder, the moment she saw her kneading dough at a long table under an elm in front of the school. Berta remembered the thin little woman, her wispy hair escaping from the confines of her head scarf, her watery blue eyes red rimmed from lack of sleep. She was always frantic with her many businesses. She was either making medicinal bread to kill worms or cooking beans to sell to the students or tending to the chickens and eggs or anything else that would feed her husband and her blind child, whom she loved ferociously.

"Berta Lorkis, what a lady you have become," she said, wiping her hands on her apron and coming over to the cart. She reached up and took Berta's hand. Her hands were like weathered wood. "Learn anything in Moscow?"

"A few things."

"Like what?"

"I read a lot of books."

"Well, I'd expect so. What else have you done? I suppose you speak Russian?"

She nodded.

"Say something for me."

"What shall I say?"

"I don't know. Say, whatever you like. Say *it's a nice day*."

Berta said *it's a nice day* in Russian to the delight of the *melamedkeh*. She clapped her hands and laughed. Her face lit up and for a moment there was color in her cheeks and the fine lacework of lines around her mouth were smoothed away.

THE TOWN SQUARE was dusty and barren, with a town pump in the middle surrounded by rocks to keep down the mud. Limestone buildings, blackened with age, stood on the perimeter of the square and housed the best Jewish businesses, the ones that dealt only in new merchandise. There was Charnofsky's tavern with a picture of a bear painted on the door, and Moesha, the tailor, stitching cross-legged on his cutting table so he could watch the passersby. Gershen's bakery was still located on the corner, where the same dusty plaster wedding cake stood among dead flies in the window.

Chaim pulled the horse up to the front of the store, jumped off, and helped the women down. The Lorkis grocery was located on the northeast corner of the square. It had a fancy sign painted on the window in black letters edged in gold and out in front was a display of farm implements and barrels of tar and kerosene. Two dusty posters hung in the window: one showing a fashionable lady sipping Abrikosov Cocoa; the other, a Muscovite princess praising hygienic Volga soap.

A large woman with small eyes and wide cheeks mottled with a sprinkling of age spots leaned over the balcony where she had been beating a rug and shouted down to them. "Is that your daughter, Froy Lorkis?"

Rivke looked up and beamed.

As Berta watched her mother boast about her beautiful, educated daughter with her trunk full of Paris dresses, it occurred to her that she had missed her parents more than she cared to admit. It came as a complete surprise, especially since she hadn't given them much thought during all those years in Moscow. In fact she had done her best to distance herself from them, from Mosny, from Little Russia and her childhood. She remembered telling Aleksandra Dmitrievna that they were dead and momentarily felt ashamed. It hadn't been the first time she lied about her parents. And she knew that no matter how she felt at this moment, how tenderly she thought of them in the flush of homecoming, it wouldn't be the last.

Berta heard her name and turned to see her sister, Lhaye, flying out the door of the grocery. "You're here!" she exclaimed, throwing her arms around Berta's shoulders.

Any stranger looking at these two would have known instantly that they were sisters. They had the same curly dark hair, which Berta wore piled on her head and Lhaye let fall in thick waves down her back. They were both small with broad, round faces and dark eyebrows over almond-shaped eyes that changed color from green to brown depending on what they wore. They had freckles on their hands and arms that Lhaye ignored and Berta tried to hide with powder, and a full lower lip that covered small white teeth. Berta held herself with an imperious detachment, a regal efficiency of motion. Lhaye, on the other hand, was still growing into her body, a little clumsy, always in a hurry, impatient to get where she was going but not quite sure how to get there.

"We've been waiting so long for you to come home. And you hardly ever wrote. Didn't you get our letters? We were starved for news, starved! You have to tell me everything. Was it beautiful? Remember the night before you left? Remember how we imagined it? Was it like that?"

Berta remembered the day she arrived in Moscow. She had copied a dress off a label of stewed prunes and thought she was the height of fashion. Then she saw what the other young ladies were wearing and realized that the can must've been old. With trepidation she climbed the wide steps under the two-story portico and rang the bell. It was opened by a pretty maid in uniform not much older than she. She asked Berta what she wanted, using the *ti* form ordinarily reserved for informality, children, or subordinates. In that short, seemingly innocuous exchange, Berta knew she didn't belong in Moscow. She felt a chill and went rigid with mortification. What Russian she knew instantly flew out of her head and left her stammering in Yiddish. On impulse she turned and ran down the steps and would've climbed back into the cab, had it not been receding up the drive.

"Come along, it's just as you left it." Lhaye took her sister's hand and pulled her into the store. "We will be sharing our old room. You can have the right side of the bed just like before."

"Wonderful," Berta said without enthusiasm.

She followed her sister into the store, past shelves of dry goods and barrels of flour, barley, and pickles, and climbed the narrow stairs in the back up to the living quarters. The apartment was even gloomier than she had remembered it and stifling hot. The dust-streaked windows kept out most of the light and it smelled of woodsmoke, kerosene, and unwashed bodies. There were no decorations on the walls, not a painting or even a print, only the wedding photograph of Mameh and Tateh that had been hand colored in garish hues. Lhaye led the way down the narrow corridor that had once been painted green but was now an indeterminate color due to the soot and grime from the kitchen stove and the kerosene lamps. Their bedroom was at the far end of the corridor. It was small, with a tiny window that offered no relief from the heat. It was only big enough for a bed, a little armoire, and a straight-back chair that sat in the corner. Tateh had already brought up the trunk, which stood in the center of the room taking up most of the floor space.

"Look at these," Berta said, opening her trunk.

Lhaye came over and looked at the dresses that had been carefully packed away, one on top of the other, each separated by tissue paper. She sucked in her breath, took out the beaded evening gown that was lying on top, and held it up, looking at herself in the armoire mirror. "It's beautiful," she whispered, as if she were in the presence of something truly miraculous. Berta had worn it to Madame Zherebtsova's party. It was in honor of Monsieur Konshin's horse, Avors, who had just won the Grand National. They had brought the champion in for a plate of apples and he had made a steaming mess on the ballroom floor. Valets appeared instantly and scooped up the mess into a sterling silver punch bowl.

Next Lhaye took out an ivory muslin Berta had worn to the Poliakovs' estate just that summer. She almost ruined it when she got her monthly and had to run up to the second-floor bathroom. She was too embarrassed to ask a maid for a rag, so she used several linen hand towels embossed with the Poliakov crest that she found hanging on a silver towel rack.

Lhaye held it up and looked at herself. Her face was flush with heat and excitement. It was such an honest face, so eager and full of wonder. Berta stood behind her and held up Lhaye's hair in a bunch on top of her head. It occurred to Berta that Lhaye wasn't the least bit jealous of her, of her life and of all the opportunities she had enjoyed while growing up. She didn't seem to mind or even notice the injustice of one sister raised in Moscow, the other in Mosny. If the situation had been reversed, Berta wouldn't have been so generous.

"It's yours," she said, kissing her sister on the ear.

"No . . ." Lhaye turned, "you aren't serious?"

"Go ahead, put it on."

"Oh, I couldn't. It's too beautiful."

"Here, let me help you."

Berta helped her off with her clothes and held the dress so she could step into it. Then she buttoned up the back while Lhaye looked at her reflection. "Oh," she breathed, "look at me." She turned this way and that, admiring the gentle drape of the dress over her hips and thighs. Then they heard loud voices out on the stairs and a great many feet shuffling into the front room. "They're here," Lhaye said.

"Go and tell them I'll be out in a minute."

She hesitated. "But they came to see you. Mameh has been talking about this for months."

"It'll be all right. I'll be out soon."

Once she was alone, Berta went over to the nightstand, poured some water into the basin, and splashed cool water on her face. She looked around for a towel, but only found a clean rag and used it to dry herself. Then she stood by the little window trying to catch a breeze. She wanted to go back to her room in Moscow and lie on her down-feather bed. She wanted to take a cool bath and sit on her balcony and watch the children and their nannies in the park across the way. She was hot and wanted to loosen her stays, but Anna wasn't there to help her and she didn't think she could manage without her.

There was a short knock on the door and Tateh stuck his head in. "Your mother is in a state. I've been sent in here to fetch you."

"I'm coming," she said, trying to keep the irritation out of her voice.

"She wants you now."

"Yes, Tateh . . ." she wound an errant strand back into her upsweep. "Tell her I'll be right out."

"All right, but she won't be happy." He started to close the door.

"Tateh . . ."

He turned back.

"Would you be too upset if I left a little early?" She thought she should approach her father first since her mother could be difficult.

"Left where?"

"Here, if I went back a little early?"

"Back where?"

"To *Moscow*, Tateh."

"To Moscow . . . why would you go back to Moscow?"

"I live there," she said in exasperation.

Tateh gazed at her and then came in and shut the door. "So, they didn't tell you, did they?"

"Tell me what?"

His mouth thinned into a straight line. Then he came over and took her hands in his. "Zelda is all grown up now. She's married. She doesn't need a companion anymore. That is why you were sent home."

Berta took back her hands. "You make it sound like I work there. I don't work there. I'm part of the family. They wouldn't *send* me anywhere."

Out in the front room, there were more voices, more people arriving, the clatter of glasses and plates and Mameh's high-pitched laughter. Mameh rarely laughed, except when she was exhausted or nervous.

"There was a letter," Tateh said. "It was in Russian. We had it translated."

"What letter?"

"I have it here somewhere."

While Tateh went off to look for it, Berta sank down on the bed. She was sick with fear. She told herself that there was nothing to worry about. The letter was in Russian. They probably got Ruchel Cohen, the cattle dealer, to translate it. Reb Cohen thought of himself as an excellent Russian speaker, but she had received a letter from him once and knew better.

Tateh came back and handed her the letter. It was short, on Rosa Davidovna's stationery, and she recognized her hand. Berta skimmed the contents . . . *express regrets . . . no longer in need of . . . love and gratitude . . . just like family.* There was a rumbling somewhere down below, the earth was beginning to move, to cave in; rocks were tumbling down the hillsides; there was the sound of rushing water . . . *just like family*. She wasn't family. She was just like family. It was something one would say about a trusted servant or a pet. *We all think so highly of her.*

She is just like family. There was a roaring in her ears. Her stomach was twisted into icy knots. A deep crevasse was opening up, whole trees and houses were sliding into oblivion. Berta lay down on the bed, her head on her arm. Her father was speaking, but she could barely make out the words.

"Is it really that bad being home? You are wanted here. This is where you belong."

She closed her eyes and for the moment she was back in the foyer the morning she left Moscow, her footsteps echoing off the high ceilings, off the brightly colored sphinxes that observed her coolly from atop their columns. There was the amber table and the huge display of orchids, the damp envelope with four tickets and the unexpected money. She didn't know why it hadn't occurred to her at the time. Why it hadn't seemed strange that there was no one there to see her off. No one to say good-bye, to hug her, to kiss her on both cheeks and make her promise to hurry home.

Chapter Two

September 1904

THE BELL on the front door of the Lorkis grocery never stopped ringing. It rang whenever the peasant women came looking for dry goods or pickled fish. It rang when their slow-walking men came in for axle grease or vodka that Tateh sold out of the back room. And it rang for the Jews of the town. The little bell had a cheerful jingle, although it was anything but cheerful to Berta. It jingled when they arrived, when they left, when they forgot something and came back. It jingled all day long, until Berta wanted to rip it off the door and throw it into the river.

It had been a year since she returned to Mosny. The time had passed slowly. At first she hardly slept and thought of nothing but her life in Moscow at Number 12 Leontievsky Street: swimming in the river at Mogolovo; the barges they decorated with fairy-tale characters for Zelda's birthday; Rosa Davidovna tiptoeing into the nursery to say good night before going off to the opera, trailing her scent behind her. For a while, Berta would wake every morning before dawn, hollow eyed and exhausted, wrap up a few pieces of bread, and leave the house. There were few people in the streets at that hour and that was the way she liked it. She didn't want to meet anybody she knew and since the entire town was Jewish, most everybody knew her or at least knew her story. She was the grocer's daughter. She had lived in Moscow in a big house. She had been sent home when the job was done like any factory girl at the end of the season.

For weeks she wandered out of town and walked the rutted cart paths that bisected the fields of stubble and dried corn stalks. The crows came for what was left after the harvest, and clouds of insects rose up off the winter squash that had been left to rot in the field.

She didn't notice the heat and was grateful for the emptiness and the endless expanse of blackened fields fresh from the autumn burning. She was glad to be alone. It felt honest, and there was some comfort in that.

Eventually she started sleeping again and for a few weeks she slept well into the morning, sometimes not even getting out of bed until after noon. Tateh soon lost patience with this schedule and told her she was needed in the grocery. She protested, saying that she wasn't feeling well, that she was too tired, that she needed more time, but he wouldn't be put off.

It was lonely in Mosny. There was nobody to talk to. They were all so irritating in their fanatic adherence to Jewish law and custom, so stubborn and unchanging, without the least appreciation or understanding of culture. No one spoke Russian. They only read Yiddish newspapers and penny dreadfuls. They all dressed badly and bathed infrequently—this being particularly noticeable on hot summer days. No one had ever heard of Balzac, Stendhal, or Goethe or read poetry or listened to a symphony or even a piano sonata.

On some days she would only speak French, even though no one else in town could. On other days she wouldn't speak at all and addressed everybody with a sullen look of disapproval. She often wore her Muscovite silks for no reason, looking especially out of place among the plain head scarves and dusty black skirts. But her worst crime, the one that had won her the enmity of nearly the entire population, was sitting out in the town square under a horse chestnut tree reading a book on Saturday afternoons.

Saturdays were always reserved for the parade of marriageable girls and boys around the town square. There were the girls in their muslin dresses walking arm in arm and the boys standing on the sideline in groups of twos and threes, watching the show and whispering to one another. It was a subtle performance involving ancient social cues: a flick of the eyes past a freshly scrubbed face, a nervous giggle and lingering look from beneath the brim of a straw sailor hat. Because the girls had to look their best, money that had been laid aside for necessities or emergencies was now freely spent on yard goods, gloves, hats, and spools of machine-made lace. It was an investment in the future and as necessary to a good match as a walk around the square, a veiled exchange of glances, and a visit from the matchmaker. It was how courtship was done in Mosny, how it had always been done, that is, until Berta Lorkis came home. Now the boys only wanted to look at her.

Had Berta known the trouble she was causing, she would have picked another bench. She wasn't interested in these boys. Half of them were yeshiva *bocherim*, students from the Talmudic academy in Bogitslav. The rest were apprentices to tradesmen or journeymen. What would she do with a boy like that, especially since they were all younger than she and beneath her in every way?

The people of Mosny didn't know how she felt. They thought she was having fun with them, torturing them by flirting with their boys. The mothers of the girls were incensed, as were the marriage brokers, the tailors, the dressmakers, and anyone else who made a ruble or two off the marriage trade. They all wanted her gone from her bench under the tree. But nobody said anything, so she continued to sit there week after week, unwittingly laying waste to the dreams of mothers and dressmakers.

On this particular hot summer day the store was crowded with muzhiki, peasants who had come in for market day with their carts full of produce. They had lined them up in the town square, fruit here, vegetables there, dairy on one side, honey on the other, and the perimeter filled with livestock. The women left their daughters in charge of the stalls while they came into the grocery to buy staples. Jewish housewives tramped up and down the square, clutching the sweaty arm of a child, fingering the last kopeck, looking for the best potatoes, the firmest beets at the best price. Each side used bits and pieces of the other's language, a price quoted, a counter offer, a sour look of mistrust. Nobody wanted to be cheated. Here there was a tenuous connection between town and country, Jew and gentile, a slender branch built on commerce. But it was also September 1904, exactly one year and five months after the bloody pogrom at Kishinev where forty-nine Jews were killed and more than five hundred injured. So it was no wonder that the Jews were holding their breath, waiting for the branch to snap.

Berta stayed in the grocery that day, waiting on customers, trying to keep her mind far away from Moscow. But there was always something to trigger the memories, a word, a phrase, or a picture of a sled on a can of chestnuts, and she'd be back riding in an open sleigh down Petrovka Street. It was just before dawn and she was bundled up in furs and leather blankets, coming home from a party at the Kokorevs'. Standing there in one of the aisles of the market she could just about smell the signal bonfires at the intersections and hear the sleigh bells and the whoosh of the runners on the hard-packed track. She remembered the way icicles bearded the birdbaths on Leontievsky Street and how it felt to look up to the sky, close her eyes, and let the snow fall on her face, icy and wet, thudding down on her cheeks and lips with the softness of goose down.

"Berta!"

"What?" she asked in annoyance, wrenched from her daydream.

"I am talking to you."

"I know, Mameh. I can hear you. I'm not deaf."

"But you weren't listening. You get that faraway look on your face and a whole mountain could fall on your head."

"What is it?"

"I want you should go over and watch that woman by the ribbons. I think she's about to steal something." Mameh had been born into the grocery business and had a second sight for thieves. At one time her family owned two shops in Mosny, but had to sell the hardware store to pay the bribes that were necessary to keep her brother out of the army. In those days, there was a quota that had to be filled for each townlet. Every year so many Jewish boys were chosen for a twenty-five-year stint in the military. Fortunately, deferments were easy to come by for the right price, but they were expensive. For a time her parents considered dressing their son as a girl for six years and saving the store. But he was skinny and had a prominent Adam's apple, and they were afraid of getting caught. So they sold the hardware store, paid the bribes, and kept the grocery. Eventually Mameh's brother went to the yeshiva and became a popular rabbi though an indifferent scholar. When her parents grew too old to mind the store they gave it to Mameh and Tateh.

Berta spotted the woman her mother was pointing out and had to admit she did look suspicious. She kept fingering the lace and glancing up at the counter where they were standing. So Berta kept an eye on her while edging past the customers and as a result she nearly collided with a young man who was just coming in the door. Their near collision startled her and she swore in French, calling him an imbecile.

"*Je suis si désolé, mademoiselle. J'ai été tout à fait un idiot et prie votre remission,*" he replied hastily, giving her a little bow.

A prick of surprise. She had never heard a word of French spoken in Mosny that she didn't utter herself. In one sweep she took him in. He was Jewish, though not devout, because his hair was cut short and he was clean-shaven except for a dark moustache. He was young, younger than she. His eyes were small like a Tartar's but intelligent. His clothes were shabby; his vest and jacket had come from different suits. Maybe he had learned a bit of French along the way, a few words here and there, but it was clear that he was just another inhabitant of the Pale, unschooled except in the Talmud and the Torah, stolid, unchanging, and ultimately uninteresting.

She went back to the thief and stood there until the woman was shamed into leaving the store. Then she returned to the counter and waited on a young mother with a fussy baby in her arms. When his turn came, the young man stepped up and, after giving her a quick smile, glanced behind her to the shelves where the factory-made cigarettes were kept. "You have Kollis?" he asked in Yiddish, requesting the most expensive brand.

She nodded, got a package down, and laid it on the counter. "Ninety kopecks." It was a ridiculous sum even for readymade cigarettes. She half expected him to walk out. Without hesitation he reached into his pocket, picked out the coins, and gave them to her. Then he picked up his cigarettes, thanked her in French, and left the store to the sound of the jingling bell.

A few days later, just after sunrise, Berta was out walking a track in the fields. She had just come upon a farmstead a few versts outside of town, where the old *bol'shak*, the head of the household, sat with his sons on the porch, eating his bulgur wheat from a wooden bowl. They looked her over with an appraising eye as she passed. They knew her. She was that pretty thing from the grocery where they bought their axle grease and kerosene. She tossed them a look of scorn and quickened her pace.

Not long after that, she heard the groan of wheels behind her and turned to find the same young man from that day in the store riding up in a broken-down cart pulled by an old horse. She had already asked Meshia Partnoy's son, the seltzer man, about him and had found out that he was a wheat merchant from Cherkast. She found out from Meshia Partnoy herself, who put him up in her front room whenever he came to town, that his name was Haykel Gregorvich Alshonsky.

"They call him Hershel. He is very rich, though you wouldn't know it," Meshia said in a conspiratorial whisper when she came in to buy her usual order of Shabbes herring.

"How do you know?" Berta asked.

"He smokes Kollis. I could make a whole meal out of what he pays for those readymades. He can't roll his own like everyone else?"

Hershel Alshonsky pulled up the horse and wished her a good day. "Would you like a ride, Mademoiselle? I'm going into town."

"No, thank you," she replied crisply. "I prefer to walk." It was better not to encourage these boys.

"Suit yourself. But it's a dusty road. Better turn your back when I drive off and cover your eyes."

"I assure you I'll be fine."

He tipped his hat and gave the reins a flick.

A few days later he met her on the same road. When he saw her, he pulled up on the reins and waited until she caught up with him. She was carrying a book, a thin volume, and he asked about it.

"It's poetry."

"What kind of poetry?"

"Good poetry, not nursery rhymes or silly limericks. It's Yeats . . . I don't suppose you've heard of him?"

He thought for a moment. "Can't say as I have. Is he famous?"

"I don't know," she said irritably. "Who cares whether he's famous or not. He's good, isn't that enough?"

"Suppose it is. Maybe I should pick up a copy?"

She shrugged. "Suit yourself. Although, I don't think it would be of much interest to you. For one thing, it's in English. Do you read English?"

"No."

"Well, there you are then," she said primly, with a note of satisfaction.

He regarded her with a half smile. "Are you angry with me, Mademoiselle?"

She reddened. "Certainly not. Why should I be angry with you? I don't even know you. I don't even know why I'm standing here talking to you. Now, if you'll excuse me."

The next time they met he told her to wait as he pulled up on the horse. By the time she decided not to wait, he was already coming around to meet her. "I brought you something. I thought you might like it." He held out another slim volume. This one had a green cover.

She eyed it suspiciously. "What is it?"

"Go on. It's by that poet of yours." He shoved it into her hand.

Reluctantly, she read the title and then looked up at him in surprise. "Where did you get it?"

"In a little shop."

"It's in French. I didn't know there was a translation. I've been struggling with the English." She smiled up at him with something akin to gratitude. He returned her gaze, full in the face, without a trace of embarrassment. She found this disconcerting and not a little annoying, but she kept quiet and turned her attention back to the book. She fingered the title, *The Wind Among the Reeds*, which was embossed in gold above the author's name. When she turned back to the flyleaf she saw his name, Haykel Gregorvich Alshonsky, written at the top in a cramped hand. She looked at him in surprise. "This is your book."

"I may have put my name in it," he said indifferently. His eyes slid past her to a cart rumbling by on a parallel track. A young barefoot girl sat in the back and hung on to the slats, while the cart bucked erratically over the ruts.

She flipped through the pages again and this time found faint pencil notations in the margins in the same cramped hand. "This *is* your book."

His eyes traveled back to her. "Is it?" He gave her a teasing smile.

She studied him for a moment. "You've been playing a trick on me."

He flicked a horsefly off her shoulder. "Well, what if I have? You deserved it, you know."

"I did? And why is that?"

"You haven't exactly been friendly. In fact, you've been pretty rude. And all because you thought I was unschooled and dressed badly and drove around in a broken-down cart. Is that any way to treat a fellow traveler who only wanted to be sociable?"

Of course, she knew he was right.

"And what was I supposed to do? I just wanted to be left alone."

"Is it such a bother to receive a friendly greeting now and then?"

She shrugged indifferently. The fact that she treated everyone in Mosny with the same discourtesy didn't seem much of a defense.

"Look, there's no sense in arguing about it," he said with a generous smile. "The sun is barely up and already it's hot. Why don't you get in and I'll drive you back."

She was still feeling the sting of his reproach. "And why would I want to do that?"

"I don't know. Maybe for the conversation. You might be in need of it just now. I imagine you still think a lot about Moscow. It can't very be easy living here after your life there."

A pang of grief and for a terrible moment she felt her eyes welling up with tears. She looked up into the sky to keep them back and shielded her eyes with a hand even though the sun was still low and not very bright. When the moment had passed and she was once again on solid footing, she said, "I suppose it is going to be hot today."

"Good, then it's settled." He took her hand and helped her up to the bench. As she climbed up she was acutely aware of a hole in her stockings just above her right ankle that she had been meaning to mend.

She didn't want him to see it and was careful to stoop as she climbed up to keep her skirts over the spot.

When she was comfortable, he went around and climbed up beside her. "Do you believe in fairies, Mademoiselle?" It was an allusion to Yeats.

She smiled with pleasure. "Of course I do, don't you?"

He laughed and picked up the reins and gave them a snap. The horse started up and the cart dipped and bounced over the ruts. All the way back they talked about fairies, ghosts, and gods. They quoted passages, sometimes in unison.

A FEW WEEKS later, Hershel pulled up to the store in a new droshky. Berta was the first one to see it.

"Is that yours?" she called out as he jumped down.

"All mine. You like her?" He turned back to admire the carriage.

"She's beautiful. I like her very much."

Berta had to admit that the droshky didn't look all that new; the paint was peeling off the chassis and the mudguards were cracked and needed repair. But the brass lamps had been recently polished and the spoke wheels had been painted yellow and the seats seemed to be in good condition.

"I bought her off a cabman in Cherkast. Come out with me. I have to see a man about a load, but it won't take long. It's a beautiful day."

Berta went up to change into her lavender tea dress. She wore her straw hat with the matching hat band and carried her lace parasol. After she was seated alongside Hershel, he urged the horse on and it trotted out to the clatter of hooves on the hard dirt. She watched her reflection ripple in the shop windows and caught the women at the town pump giving her hard, envious looks. She closed her eyes and it felt like Moscow again, the same heady sense of entitlement, of being special and apart, of being up high where she couldn't be reached.

They drove out on the Cherkast road that led north to the wheat center of the same name. It was a wide ribbon of gravel bisecting the rolling fields of half-reaped wheat, the tawny shafts standing straight and tall in the sunlight, casting straight-edged shadows over the stubble left behind by the scythe. Here and there were one-story houses built of logs and plaster, covered with thatched mansard roofs and surrounded by a variety of defeated outbuildings. The yards were typically littered with years of farm trash: broken-down carts, rusted-out tubs, bits and pieces of old scythes and sledge runners and stacks of moldy crates. There was always a dog or two in the yard that barked as they rode past.

They turned in on one of the back roads, the droshky bouncing along the dusty track, the bells jingling on the harness, the springs squeaking like startled mice. It was one of those hypnotic days, warm and drowsy. There was a hectic surge of excitement inside Berta, an urge to let it all in: the sun, the smell of the black earth, the caress of muslin against her back. Her senses were alive and for the first time in a long while she felt the thrill of freedom—from the store, from the town, from the life she had fallen into since leaving Leontievsky Street.

Hershel pulled into a rutted drive that led down to a farmstead just off the main road. "This shouldn't take long," he said, bringing the droshky to a stop in front of a threshing shed whose roof nearly sagged to the ground. He jumped down. "Want to come along?"

She nodded and held out her arms so that he could help her down. Together they went up to the house, skirting rusting barrel hoops, a dung heap, beehives, and barking dogs the color of parched earth. At the door he stopped and waited. "Why don't you just call out?" she asked.

"It's considered bad luck. We just have to wait for someone to come. But it won't be long with this racket."

A moment later a woman with a baby on her hip appeared at the door and looked at them with suspicion. She wore a faded skirt and a gaudy head scarf and shooed the dogs away with a wave of her hand. Hershel tipped his hat and asked in Surzhyk for the whereabouts of the *bol'shak*. The baby began to fuss so she stuck a finger in its mouth while she nodded over to one of the larger outbuildings.

They found the *bol'shak* and his sons repairing harnesses in the barn, a rambling structure with stalls on one side, battered work benches on the other, and a hayloft in the back. The boys had the same light hair, flat wide face, rounded nose, and suspicious mouth of their father.

At first Hershel and Berta stood at the barn door, aware that they hadn't been invited in. Hershel wished them a good day and said he'd come to buy their wheat. He was speaking Surzhyk like a muzhik and this seemed to lessen the tension. They knew he was a Jew, but a Jew who had taken the time to learn their language. Berta may have been reading into it, but it seemed to her that he had gained some respect for his efforts, especially with the *bol'shak*, who motioned them in.

Berta could barely speak the language, a mishmash of Russian and Ukrainian, but she had picked up enough working in the store to get the gist of what was being discussed. Hershel was saying something about a cow and their neighbor, possibly calling into question their neighbor's skill at husbandry, and this they found uproariously funny. They talked about beehives. Hershel complimented the *bol'shak* on the hives they had seen on the drive. The old man took it in stride. After that she lost the thread of the conversation until the *bol'shak* invited them into his home for bread and salt.

The house was well kept for that part of the country, although the walls, which had been whitewashed once, were nearly black with soot and grime. They sat at a long farm table and ate bread slathered in lard topped with stout granules of salt, which they washed down with kvass served in jam jars. The men smoked their pipes filled with the foul-smelling *makhorka*. They weren't in a hurry to get down to business and the conversation meandered over taxes, the purchase of a new horse, and the design of a new steam-powered threshing machine from Germany.

After the bread was consumed and several more glasses of kvass were drunk along with some vodka, Hershel and the *bol'shak* finally got down to talking about money. At first they started out far apart, but over time Hershel was able to bring the price down. He didn't do it by belittling the man's wheat as other merchants would have done. He did it by praising all the wheat in the region and implying that if he didn't get his price here, there would be plenty of other places he could go. Finally, when they got down to haggling over two kopecks a pood, Hershel excused himself and went out to the carriage. He came back in carrying a sack of coins, which he emptied out on the table. Hundreds of shiny new kopecks spilled out over the worn planks and rolled through specks of salt and the sweat from the cold glasses. There were two- and three-kopeck coins, some five-kopeck, and a few *grivenniki*, ten-kopeck coins, all sparkling in the light that poured in through the open doorway. When the *bol'shak* saw the mound of coins he grinned and Berta saw that he was missing several teeth.

After the deal was struck, Hershel shook the man's hand. The *bol'shak* walked them out to the droshky while his sons and daughter-in-law watched from the porch. Berta climbed up and brushed off the bench with her gloved hand. Then Hershel climbed up beside her and, after saying good-bye, signaled the horse and started up the rutted lane.

"Once I figured out they'd rather have a sack of kopecks than a piece of paper with the czar's picture on it, the rest was easy. I never cheat them. I always give them a fair price, but it's my price. Next spring I plan on managing six more silos. I already talked to Knoop and he's happy to give them to me. He knows I get the best wheat and nobody gets my price. And after that I thought I'd ask for a piece. They won't turn me down. They can't. They know I'll go over to the competition if they do."

She looked at him from under her hat. It was a look of admiration, not coy, but openly admiring, and he took it in with pleasure. "You're good at this, aren't you?" she asked.

"Am I?" he said, barely suppressing a smile. The horse trotted past wide swaths of ripened wheat. "This is Adamovich's," he said with a wave of his hand. "I own it. All of it. I bought it when it was only seed." He didn't mean that he actually owned the fields, only that the consortium in Moscow had bought the wheat. But he was so connected to his work that these lines were often blurred. "Already it looks to be one of the highest yields in the district. He's used a new seed from America. And he's got the best soil. You can taste it."

"You taste the soil?"

"Of course."

She made a face and he laughed carelessly. He had a nice laugh. They rode back under the trees, the sunlight spilling through the leaves and tattooing the ground. It was quiet with only the clip-clop of hooves and the occasional thrum of a steam-powered thresher far off in the fields to break the calm. When the road got rough she had to hold on to the side of the box for support, but even so, her shoulder swayed into his, creating a stir of desire.

She asked him where he grew up and he told her about the shtetl where he was born and about the gymnasium where he went to school.

"It's called Leski. Not far from here. On the way to Cherkast."

"And what about your parents? Do they still live there?"

His smile faded a bit and he looked away. "They're dead."

"Oh. I'm sorry. How did they die?"

"They just did. Sometimes people die for no good reason."

She thought this was an odd answer. She felt awkward after that, like she had committed some breach of etiquette, and didn't know what to say.

They rode on in silence for a while, until he said, "Her name was Sophie. She was very beautiful, my mother. She had long fingers. She used to say they were her secret when she played Rachmaninoff. She had great plans for me. She wanted me to grow up to be a famous doctor, not the kind who sees patients. She said anybody could do that. She wanted me to do research and make discoveries and get my name in the history books."

"Is that what you wanted?"

"No. Or rather I didn't know what I wanted. I suppose I just wanted to make her happy."

"And what about your father?"

"He was an educated man. He read to me when I was little and taught me to play chess and told me scary stories."

She laughed. "What kind of stories?"

"Mostly ones about dybbuks and golems and vampires."

"Weren't you frightened?"

"Of course, but that was the point. I wanted to be frightened. Once he told me about the blue man who lived under our house. I used to dream about him. I remember he had sharp teeth and an evil smile. I wasn't sure what he wanted, but I was pretty sure he was up to no good. After that I wouldn't go to sleep without a lamp. My father took me under the house to show me there was no one there, but it didn't do any good. I still wouldn't go to bed without the lamp."

"And what happened to him?"

"The blue man? I expect he's still there."

"Under the house?"

He looked out across a field where peasants in belted tunics were moving up the furrows in careless concert, their long-handled scythes cutting swaths of ripe wheat, their heads bent to the task.

"Under every house."

THAT NIGHT, Berta stood by the window brushing out her hair and looking down into the street. There was a peddler coming home from the road. He wore a shabby overcoat and carried a bundle on his back. The torn lining of his overcoat dragged on the ground behind him. Usually the peddlers stayed out until Friday afternoon, when they came home for Shabbes, but this one was coming home early, exhausted, shoulders slumped against his luckless life. She stood there not really seeing him, but thinking of Hershel, of his parents, and wondering how they died.

She put her brush on the nightstand and climbed into bed next to Lhaye, who was already asleep. She closed her eyes and soon she too was asleep—dreaming that she was a little girl playing in the yard behind the grocery with a caterpillar on a stick. She was sitting in the dirt watching it inch up to one end of the stick and then turning the stick upside down, watching it inch back up again. Someone called her name and she looked over at the crawl space under the building. There she saw a face grinning back at her from out of the darkness. It called her over. She didn't like the look of its teeth. They were sharp and very white against the gleam of its blue skin.

Chapter Three

December 1904

WHEN BERTA arrived at the women's bathhouse, she knew that it was silly to hope for clean water. The water was rarely changed and always an unusual shade of green. In fact, the whole place smelled of the fecundity of a healthy swamp. Even the little foyer smelled of over-ripe vegetation.

Berta climbed the steps of the raw-boned building, opened the door, and stepped inside. The bath keeper's wife was sitting on a chair in the overheated foyer with her knitting on her lap. She was making a blanket for her grandchild, and although it wasn't even finished yet, it was already dirty from the coins she handled all day long.

The old woman looked up at the door and frowned. "It's not closed all the way," she said, drawing her shawl up around her shoulders.

Berta turned back to the door and slammed it shut. Then she stepped forward, dug into her pocket for the ten-kopeck coin, and handed it over. "Is the bath clean today?"

"Of course it is clean. It is always clean. I clean it myself." Her eyes were the color of the bathwater and her mouth was a line of disappointment sunk into the cavity between her cheeks. Berta didn't argue. Instead she took the towel that was offered, so thin it was nearly transparent.

In the summer Berta bathed in the river at a spot reserved for women where a spit of land curled around a tiny backwater and trees and bushes grew up into a privacy screen. Here the water was cold and clean, and afterward there was a little beach where she could lie out in the sun and dry off. But now it was winter and the snowy drifts made cushions and mounds out of the bushes and fence posts. The Dnieper flowed under a thick layer of blue-green ice and the beach was covered in snow. In the winter there was only the bathhouse.

Berta walked into the bathing area, undressed, and laid her clothes out on a bench. She took off her stockings and shoes last so she wouldn't have to stand barefoot on the moldy tile and stepped gingerly into the bath. It was a tile pool filled with murky water, big enough to accommodate eight or ten bathers with steps at either end. She tried not to think about the marble bathroom she left behind on Leontievsky Street. It did no good to think of these things. They were gone and were not coming back. Instead she waded down the steps, plunged into the fetid water, stood, soaped, and plunged down again to rinse off. Then she climbed up the steps, the water cascading off her body, and went over to a barrel of water that stood in the corner. She dipped a small bucket into it and poured the river water over her head and shoulders, gasping from the shock of the melted snow.

"That will kill you dead, Berta Lorkis."

Berta felt blindly for the towel and dried her eyes. It was Meshia Partnoy, Hershel's landlady, spreading out her things on a nearby bench.

"You're going to catch your death with that freezing water." She had begun to undress, seemingly quite comfortable with her surroundings. Her flesh was pale and moist and seemed native to this steamy swamp. "I don't see why you just don't sit in the bath like everyone else. It's very refreshing."

"It's green and it stinks."

"*Nu*? A little green never hurt anyone. It's a mineral bath from the springs under the ground. That is why it smells so bad. But it's good for the joints. Ask anyone around here, these baths are very healthy."

Meshia Partnoy climbed into the pool and lowered herself into the water with a sigh and crouched down, displacing a gentle current that circled her dimpled thighs and rose up over her breasts and shoulders to her chin. She closed her eyes. Without opening them again she said, "I'm coming to see you tomorrow. I want some yard goods. I am going to make myself a new dress."

Berta looked over at her. "What's the occasion? It must be something special." A new dress was an event in Mosny. Why make a new one when a used one was just as good and could be bought from the rag dealer for a fraction of the cost?

Froy Partnoy opened her eyes. They were glittering buttons in the half-light of the bath. "You haven't heard? We are going to America. My brother has sent us the money and we are off in a week."

"To America? Mazel tov. I hear it's a wonderful place. You should be very happy."

"Of course I should be happy. What is not to be happy about? My brother owns a pickle factory there in the big city. He has fifty men working for him and an ice box and a toilet right in his house."

Berta liked Meshia Partnoy and her son, but frankly she could not have cared less if they went to America or to the moon. It was the woman's lodger she was thinking about.

"And what about Hershel Alshonsky?" she asked casually.

During the last of the summer she and Hershel had gone out for rides together, played chess in the tearoom, and picnicked on the spongy moss that grew alongside the streams. They had become friends, or so she had thought, but then the leaves began to fall and he started to come less frequently. Now it was winter and she hadn't seen him in two months and eighteen days.

"Who?" asked Meshia Partnoy.

"Your lodger."

"Oh him . . . I guess he will just have to find another place to stay, although it can't be very easy this time of year. Still, he could look in Bogitslav. He might have some luck there. I know a place or two." Then she stopped and looked at Berta, a slow smile of recognition spreading across her face. "Oh, I see how it is."

"How what is?"

"Well, he's not exactly handsome, but they say he's a real *macher*. Real smart, if you know what I mean. And he knows how to make a kopeck or two."

"I don't know what you're talking about. I was just making conversation."

"He is educated. And they say he has a real nice house in Cherkast. You could do worse."

"I don't see what that has to do with me. I was just curious, that's all."

"Of course you were," Meshia Partnoy said, with an exaggerated look of solemnity.

Berta buttoned up her blouse, tucked it in, and gathered up her things. "Good-bye, Froy Partnoy," she said coolly.

"Good-bye, Berta, and good luck."

Berta left the women's bath without bothering to say good-bye to the bath keeper's wife or even stopping to put on her hat. After a short walk home she arrived at the grocery door with a helmet of frozen hair.

The next day was the *yarid*, market day, and Berta was working the counter. The grocery was crowded with muzhiki, women mostly, who came in with a rush of cold air, the snow melting from their hair and sheepskin jackets, stamping their felt boots on the wooden floor that was soggy and bowed at the door from years of traffic. Berta should have been tending to the customers, but her mind wasn't on the task. Instead her eyes kept straying out the window to the shoppers in the square and to the rows of sledges where the horses dozed under their *dugas*.

"Where are you going?" asked Mameh when she saw Berta taking her coat off the hook.

"I have to go out. I'll be right back." She pulled a scarf out of her pocket, fit it over her head, and tied it under her chin.

"But it's the *yarid*. You can't just leave."

"I'll only be a few minutes, Mameh. Lhaye is here. She'll help and there's always Tateh."

"We have customers. I need you here."

"I said I'll be right back."

Berta opened the door, stepped outside, and closed it even though she could still hear her mother talking to her. She stood on the step, putting on her gloves and surveying the square. Her eyes moved from the stalls, to the stack of folding chairs leaning up against the tearoom, to the horses marking the frigid air with their breath. She walked up a row, moving in and out of the crowds, looking at the men leaning up against the tavern wall, at the porters huddled around a fire in an old drum, at the muzhiki playing cards around a bench that had been cleared of snow. Then she moved back down another row, searching out the faces, the dark corners, and the storefronts.

"Looking for somebody?" It was the shul *klopfer*, the old man who called the men to prayers. He held a bloody handkerchief in his hand. His face was white, drained of all color, and he kept moistening his cracked lips with his tongue.

"No, no one."

"Maybe I can help?"

"No . . . but thank you."

She liked the little shul *klopfer*. He had always been kind to her. She wanted to say more, maybe ask about his health or his family, but before she could say anything, he doubled over, coughing up blood into his handkerchief.

By closing time she knew Hershel wasn't coming. She thought he had probably found a place in Bogitslav and she would never see him again. Even though it was dark and the square was empty, she took one last look around as she brought in the rakes and hoes and rolled in the barrels. She turned the sign, closed the door, and locked it with the brass key that was smooth with wear. Then she pulled down the shades and, after blowing out the lamps, climbed the stairs, only half listening to her parents, who were arguing about money in the kitchen.

They often argued about money, so it was a surprise to find Lhaye on the steps listening to them. When Lhaye heard Berta coming up the stairs, she turned and held a finger to her lips and motioned her to sit down beside her.

"He is not coming to ruin my daughters," Tateh was saying. "He is coming to buy wheat. And while he is at it he's going to stay in our house."

"For what? For ten rubles? You are willing to ruin the reputation of your daughters for ten rubles? Do you know how people will talk?" Mameh had a love for *news*, as she liked to call it. She knew what constituted good fodder for gossips, especially since she was known to indulge in it herself.

"Nobody is going to ruin anybody's reputation. He will be a lodger, that's all. People will understand. He'll stay in the linen closet."

"And how will he stay there?"

"I'll take out the shelves."

"And where will we put the linens?"

"What linens? A few towels. Put them somewhere else. Rivke, *ten extra rubles*!"

"Who are they talking about?" whispered Berta.

"Reb Alshonsky."

Berta stopped and shifted her gaze back to her parents. From where she was sitting she had a good view of their feet. Her mother's solid shoes planted implacably on the smooth planks, her father's worn boots shifting the weight of his body first to one foot and then to the other as he sought relief from the pain in his lower back. She had heard them argue before, only this time she was keenly aware that they were arguing about her future. She had decided some time ago that her future lay with Reb Alshonsky. And now fate, if she believed in fate, which of course she didn't, was bringing him to her. But she was also aware that it hinged on her mother doing something that she had never done before, an act of capitulation that was completely out of character for her: Her mother would have to concede to her father and let him win an argument. This seemed inconceivable to Berta as she sat on the stair, listening to their every word and whispering an urgent prayer to a God she feared did not exist.

HERSHEL ARRIVED during the last of the great storms. Berta was just closing up when he appeared out of the swirling snow wrapped up in a greatcoat and wearing a *papakha* on his head. He told her that he had been away on the Black Sea and gave her a little box covered in red and orange cockle shells. They stood by the stove talking about his travels, about a trip to Moscow and another one to Petersburg. He didn't explain why he had been away so long and she didn't ask.

"So, is my room finished?"

"It is. But my mother doesn't want you staying here."

"I thought she liked me," he said, removing his gloves and holding his hands up to the dying fire. He hadn't yet taken off his coat. Melted snow circumscribed a neat circle of damp on the floor beneath him.

"Not since she found out you'll be sleeping in our linen closet. She thinks you're going to ruin our reputation and come into our room at night and have your way with us. She calls you a *mazzik*, a demon, so if you want to stay here, you'll have to win her over. Although, that won't be easy."

"I think I can manage. I'm usually pretty good at that sort of thing." He didn't look the least bit concerned.

Berta knew it would be this arrogance that would prompt her mother to send him packing. She would see his swagger, cheeky grin, and charming manner as a direct assault on the good name of her daughters. She thought about warning him, but she knew it would do no good. She had learned that about him over the summer months. He would do it his way, no matter what anybody said.

That night, supper was served at the table in the front room. Tatch had just returned from evening prayers and had taken the time to comb his hair with water and put on his good Shabbes coat. It still had a torn piece of cloth affixed to the lapel from the last funeral he had attended, the wife of the cattle dealer who had died of a woman problem. He sat at the head of the table when Hershel came in and greeted his guest with a stiff formality. "You're over here, Reb Alshonsky," he said, indicating the chair next to him.

Hershel nodded and took his seat across from Lhaye. She was wearing one of Berta's Moscow dresses. It was a midnight blue satin with bugle beading and lace sleeves, much too fancy for a simple meal at home. She also took the time to pile her hair on top of her head and even added an ostrich feather that she found at the bottom of the trunk. Hershel complimented her on her appearance and she thanked him, the feather bobbing with determination as she lowered her head and blushed.

Mameh made no special effort for her guest. She wore her old apron at the table and kept the lace runner that she used for holy days in the drawer. Instead she used the everyday tablecloth that was stained and yellowed and torn in two places.

At first there was an uncomfortable silence lasting through the blessing, which of course was proper, but also through much of the bread and soup.

"It's very good, Froy Lorkis," Hershel said, finishing up his bowl.

She gave him a tight-lipped smile, rose, and gathered up the bowls. "Berta, help me in the kitchen."

Berta and Hershel exchanged a look as she reached for the soup pot.

"Do you have to be so rude to him, Mameh? It's embarrassing," she whispered, after carrying the pot into the kitchen and setting it down on the counter. "Can't you say something nice? Ask about his health? Anything . . . ?"

Mameh was at the stove scooping out the last of the boiled potatoes into a bowl with a rusty slotted spoon. "It is not enough that we have a *mazzik* staying with us? I have to make nice to him too?" She made no effort to keep her voice down. She reached into the salt box and took a pinch between her thumb and forefinger and sprinkled it over the potatoes. As an afterthought she took another pinch and dropped it into the pocket of Berta's apron.

"Oh, Mameh," she said with annoyance.

"Hush now. I know what I'm doing. And take this." She took off an amulet from around her neck and put it around Berta's. "Keep it on and don't take it off, no matter what anybody says."

Berta examined the amulet. It was the ugliest thing she had ever seen. "What do you think he's going to do to us?"

"Just wear it. Tateh has invited a demon into our house. So you will excuse me if I take a little precaution."

Berta gave her mother a look, picked up the bowl of potatoes, and carried it out to the front room. Mameh came out a few minutes later with the fish, and the meal continued on in silence.

"So where are you off to?" Tateh asked, seemingly unaware of the tension in the room.

"To Chewnyk's and Kedzierski's," Hershel replied. "I thought I'd pick up a load or two if the price is right."

Tateh knew these families. They came into town for supplies. They had large farmsteads to the west of Mosny with many *desyatins* in cultivation. "I would also try Babzak," he said. "They say he uses the *scientific approach*. He already paid off his debt, so he must have done well. Of course, he is always bragging about this so-called approach. But if you can stand to listen to him, I'd give him a try."

"Thank you, I will."

Tateh helped himself to a piece of fish and passed the platter to Lhaye, who eyed it suspiciously and passed it on. She didn't like fish. "Will you be back tomorrow?" she asked, helping herself to the potatoes.

"No, I go on to Bogitslav."

Tateh's jaw clicked as he chewed. "I have a cousin in Bogitslav," he said between bites, "maybe you have heard of him, Mottel Royzen?"

Hershel thought for a moment. "I know a Zevi Royzen from Medvin."

Tateh considered this and shook his head. "No, never heard of him."

"Still, tragic story, Zevi Royzen," said Hershel, carefully removing the skin from his sturgeon before sticking a fork into the white flesh.

Mameh kept her eyes on her plate.

"What happened?" asked Lhaye.

"Excuse me?"

"To Zevi Royzen. What's the tragic story?"

"Oh, very sad. His wife died. Beautiful woman and a fine housekeeper. A real *balebosteh*, they say."

"How did she die?"

"She was cleaning a chicken and she cut her finger on the neck bone. It was nothing, a little cut, some blood, nothing to fuss about. But then the finger turned all red and her hand blew up like a balloon and she started to run a high fever. Her husband called in the best doctors, a whole team of them, but it was too late. Three days later she was dead."

Mameh looked up.

"Just like that?" asked Lhaye.

"Just like that. And that's not the worst of it. He remarried. The daughter of a rope spinner, so of course there was no dowry. Not that he cared. He was a rich man. Well, not rich exactly, but he had money, could go out for a meal once in a while and take in a play. He made fine saddles and sold them to people who could afford them. Anyway, as marriages go, this one was a disaster." He stabbed a potato with his fork and stuck it into his mouth.

"How come?" Lhaye asked.

Hershel chewed, swallowed, and shook his head. "Not such a nice story. You don't want to know."

"But I do," she said, her feather bobbing emphatically.

Tateh said irritably, "What difference does it make? He's not my cousin. We don't know him. I'm sorry for his troubles, but it's got nothing to do with us."

"But I want to know, Tateh."

"Go on, Reb Alshonsky. It's all right. We're all grown-ups here," said Berta.

Mameh poured herself another glass of wine and glanced briefly at him from over the rim.

"Well," Hershel continued a little doubtfully, "Let's just say that a young girl gets ideas in her head. Maybe she starts to think she doesn't want to be with such an old man. Maybe her eyes wander over the fence where the grass is greener. Maybe they linger a little too long on the glazer's son." His voice trailed off and they sat there in silence, mulling over the implications.

After dinner they moved across the room to the settee and chairs. Hershel declined Tateh's offer of the wing chair and pulled over one of the chairs from the table. "You know a Rabbi Liebermann from Dunivits?" he asked his host, once they were all settled.

"I think I've heard of him. Is he famous?"

"A little famous." His eyes flicked over to Mameh, who was mending one of Tateh's shirts. There was a rust-colored rip on the sleeve as if stained by old blood. "So you haven't heard about his son?"

"I didn't know he had a son."

"Oh yes, he had a good son. A promising scholar they say, until the trouble started. All out of the blue like that. Without warning. Shocked everybody. No one could understand how one day he could be himself, a good, obedient boy, and the next . . . disrespectful to his mother, shouting out obscenities in shul. And you have to remember this was from a boy who never did anything wrong in his whole life."

"How old was he?" asked Lhaye.

"Thirteen, fourteen. He was already promised to the daughter of a rich textile merchant. Of course, his father didn't want the girl's family finding out about it and calling off the wedding. He tried beating the boy, but the outrages only continued. Soon he was laughing at funerals and once he molested the serving girl, a shikse no less, and was even suspected of stealing money from the owner of a ribbon factory. Naturally the rabbi was at his wit's end. He was just about to give up and send the boy to an asylum, when it came to him."

"What?"

Here he paused for effect. "That his son was possessed by a succubus."

Silence.

Mameh held the needle in midair. Lhaye stared at Hershel, her lips slightly parted. Berta burst out laughing.

Tateh straightened. "Berta . . ."

"You don't believe in this nonsense."

"Reb Alshonsky is our guest."

"But he doesn't believe in it either. He's just having fun with us. It's ludicrous, and he knows it."

"No, she's right. I didn't believe it at first. I thought the boy was bad or crazy or had eaten something that made him sick or some other perfectly rational explanation. But then I was there in Dunivits on the night they performed the exorcism and I saw it all with my own eyes."

"Oh, please . . . there's no such thing as a succubus. It's a fairy story to scare children."

Mameh turned on her daughter. "Listen to you . . . such a *maivin*. You would be wise not to laugh at such things, my girl. You do not know everything." Then she turned to Hershel: "Please excuse my daughter. She speaks out of turn. It's one of her many faults." These were the first words she had spoken to him all evening. When Hershel's eyes flicked over to Berta with an unmistakable look of triumph, she realized what he had been up to and sucked in a smile.

THAT NIGHT she lay next to Lhaye, listening to Hershel tossing and turning across the hall, the straw mattress rustling under his body. She pictured him, bare chested, rolling to one side then the other, pulling up the covers and throwing them off again.

Finally she fell asleep and woke up sometime in the middle of the night to the sound of an animal whimpering in pain. At first she couldn't place it. She thought it might've been the little whistle Lhaye made when she slept, but then she heard it again. It was Hershel groaning in his sleep. When the groaning grew louder and threatened to wake the household, she rose and put a shawl on over her night-dress, her hair hanging in a thick braid down her back, and went out into the freezing hall. She shivered in her bare feet, her breath visible in the frosty air. When she pulled back the curtain she found him asleep on his side. She reached out and shook his shoulder. "Wake up . . . Hershel, wake up."

He opened his eyes and grabbed her arm. For an instant, he didn't recognize her.

"Sorry," he said.

"You had a dream."

"I know. I'm fine."

"Are you sure?"

"Yes. Go back to sleep."

She went back to bed and wanted to think about what she had just seen, but soon she too was drifting off. She was still aware of the bed and Lhaye sleeping next to her but also of a swirl of shapes behind her closed eyes. The shapes soon merged and became recognizable objects: a chair, the kitchen stove, a country road.

HERSHEL CAME back a few weeks later and told them a story about a miracle rabbi who had saved a town from a pogrom by casting a spell on the pogromists. That night Mameh served chicken and it wasn't even Shabbes. The lace runner was proudly displayed on the table. Mameh listened to the story with slightly parted lips, her eyes fixed on her guest, her pupils dilated in the dim light, listening to every detail while her chicken got cold. Mameh was a great believer in miracle rabbis.

After dinner she invited Hershel to sit with her on the settee. "Here. On this side," she said, plumping up the one pillow. Tateh was no longer wearing his good coat. He sat in his armchair and quietly nodded off. The girls were in the kitchen.

"Shall I tell you about the pauper who died in Esther Churgin's shed?" he asked. He sat back on the pillow, propped his elbow up, and dropped his chin on his hand.

"I knew Esther Churgin when I was a girl," Mameh said, picking up her mending. The light behind her threw a halo around her untidy hair and softened the lines around her mouth. The lighting and her eager anticipation made her look almost like a girl. "She married my cousin's half brother. I heard they went to live in Kiev. But then he died and I haven't heard another thing about her."

"Then this should interest you."

He told her a story about a pauper who had come to Esther Churgin begging for a place to stay. She let him have the shed in the back and even gave him a few sticks of wood for the stove. "Apparently, his heart gave out during the night, for when she went out to get him for breakfast, she found him dead on the straw."

Mameh tsked as she continued to sew.

"But that's not the end of it. When the porters came to take him away, guess what they found in his pockets . . ." Here his voice dropped to a conspiratorial whisper. "A big pile of rubles."

She looked up. "Big? How big?"

"More than you ever saw in your whole life."

"Was she allowed to keep them?"

"Of course. It was her shed, wasn't it? And her pauper. The man had no family. No one to leave them to. It was only right and proper that she should get the money, especially when you consider that she was kind enough to give him a place to die. In fact, to this day, they say that because of her generosity she is now the richest woman on Slavyanskaya."

"I had no idea."

After that there was a story about a witch who turned babies into bats and more stories about angels, magic, and mayhem, a sudden turn of fortune, and a miraculous healing. Soon Mameh was looking forward to his visits and making the dishes he liked best. If he didn't come, which often happened for two or three weeks at a time, she'd ask Tateh if he had heard from Reb Alshonsky, was he held up by business, would he be coming soon? She often said that she was worried about him, but really she was worried about missing *the news*.

"I WAS THINKING, maybe I could come live with you once you're married?" Lhaye asked. She was stretched out the bed next to Berta. It was late and they had blown out the candle to save the wax. Outside the night was still and the square was deserted. A mockingbird was protesting some disturbance, running through his repertoire of songs in hopes of attracting a mate even at this late hour.

"Who says I'm getting married," Berta said.

"Don't be silly. You're getting married." Lhaye propped her head up on her palm and looked over at Berta. "Do you think his house is large? Do you think it's a mansion?"

"How would I know?" Berta rolled over and closed her eyes.

"I think it's a mansion. I think it has a turret and lots of servants."

Usually Berta enjoyed talking about these things, girlish dreams of weddings, of her escape from Mosny and the life that awaited her once she and Hershel were married. Yet even in the happiest times these dreams were tempered by niggling doubts. After all, there hadn't even been a proposal. Hershel hadn't talked to Tateh and nothing definite had been said, although much had been hinted at. "You're going to like Cherkast," he had said to her on more than one occasion. Sometimes he talked about traveling together and how he wanted to show her Petersburg and Paris. Once, out of the blue, he asked her if she liked rubies. When she said she did, he nodded with satisfaction and fell silent as if he were filing it away for future use.

While he was in Mosny it all seemed possible. He was attentive and affectionate, brushing the hair out of her eyes when she worked at the sink, nibbling the back of her neck, stealing kisses even when her parents were in the house. But when he was gone and she didn't know where he was or when he was coming back, the doubts would begin to surface, making it increasingly hard for her to believe that there would ever be a wedding or a life with him in Cherkast.

That spring he stayed with them for several weeks while he traveled the countryside buying wheat. One day, he invited Berta to come along, and soon after that she was accompanying him on most every trip. Typically, they would start out early, just after sunrise, and not be back until late in the afternoon. Sometimes they traveled great distances before they came to a particular farmstead that Hershel had marked on the map that hung over his bed. They both enjoyed these outings in the sunshine and under the new leaves, especially since Hershel was good at finding dry roads and staying out of the mud that plagued the other travelers.

Whenever he pulled into a drive, she would ask: *chaver* or *prostak*? A *chaver*, a friend, meant that she could go down with him. It meant that the *bol'shak* wouldn't be offended if he brought a female onto the property. A *prostak*, an uneducated boar, meant that she had to wait for him up on the road. If he brought her with him, there would be too many questions and it might jeopardize the sale.

That afternoon they stopped at the top of a drive overlooking a small farmstead below. A line of clothes was drying in the hot sun and a woman bent over a washtub on legs. She straightened to look at them, sheltering her eyes with her hand and shushing the dog that had begun to bark.

"A *prostak*," replied Hershel to Berta's question. "So you better get out here and wait for me." Berta looked disappointed, but gathered up her parasol, book, and blanket and climbed down.

When Hershel came back up nearly an hour later it was already getting late. The ride back was a long one, but he knew a shortcut that would get them back before dark. They rode out under a tunnel of glittering leaves, emerging now and then into the brilliant sunshine. Somewhere along the way they came to a crossroads marked by a signpost where numerous signs for peasant villages and townlets were posted in Russian. They were just passing the sign when Berta cried out to stop and Hershel pulled up on the reins.

"Did you see that?" she said turning back. She was nearly shouting in her excitement. She didn't even wait for the carriage to come to a stop, but jumped down and ran back to take a look at the signs. "Hershel look, it's Leski! It's only three versts from here."

Beside them was a freshly plowed field of sweet-smelling earth. There were women in the field moving up one row and down another, sowing handfuls of seeds from sacks hitched over their shoulders. Their attention kept getting drawn away from their task to the two people in the new droshky who had stopped at the crossroads. They were strangers who were probably lost and arguing about which way to go. They were far more interesting than the seeds.

"I know. Get in. It's late. We have to be heading home." He suddenly sounded very tired.

"But it's so close. Don't you want to see it?"

"No."

"But it's where you were born."

His expression hardened. "Berta, get in the carriage."

"Why?"

"Just get in." He kept his eyes on the road.

She shook her head and climbed back into the carriage. She adjusted her skirts and held on to the side as it lunged forward. Even though it took over an hour to get home, they rode in silence.

THAT SUMMER Hershel came often, his visits sometimes stretching into weeks, and it seemed to Berta that he was with them more than he was away. It was calming and exciting to have him so close, to meet him in the hall in the morning, to sit across from him while they ate their bread with wild blackberry jam that she had made the summer before. Many mornings she woke up with a luxurious feeling of contentment, knowing that her doubts were trivial, that she had nothing to worry about, that she could dream about a new life and not be afraid.

One night after supper, she and Hershel went out walking down the main road into the countryside. There was a full moon and their shadows glided along beside them, over the ruts in the road, over the piles of dead leaves still smelling of hot dust. They walked on until they came to the tavern on the outskirts of town, where a blind man sat with his son at an outdoor table. He wore a long coat of homespun wool, beside him was a wooden staff propped up against the table, and in front of him was an empty shot glass. He looked up and stared sightlessly at Hershel and Berta as they walked past. His son, who was sitting beside him, raised his head from the table to see who was going by. His hair had been hacked into uneven waves that nearly covered his ears. His beard was ragged and mostly gray. His blind father asked him about the strangers.

"Only *zhydy* from town," his son told him. He dropped his head back down on his arms and closed his eyes. He was more tired than drunk. "The grocer's daughter and the wheat merchant."

They walked on until the only sound they could hear was the clacking of the bare branches in the wind, the snuffling of horses in the pasture, and the crunch of their feet on the gravel. Hershel stopped by a small collection of gravestones and leaned over to kiss her. He paused just as his lips touched hers. His movements were unhurried and even a little playful, nibbles on her upper lip, his mouth covering hers, until finally what had been innocent became more urgent. When he was about to let her go, she drew him back, reaching up and pulling him closer.

Afterward, they stayed in each other's arms, her breasts against his chest, their bodies so close that she could feel his belt buckle pressing into her stomach. They began to sway together, ever so slightly, dancing without music. He whispered in her ear. "I'm going away soon."

She pulled away from him. "Again? Where?"

"All over. Odessa mostly."

"For how long?"

"Don't know. Depends. Could be a while."

"Why didn't you tell me before? I could've prepared for it."

He laughed. "And how would you have done that?"

"I don't know. I would have thought about it and gotten ready. As it is, you'll be off and I'll still be getting used to it."

"I'll write if I can."

"If you can? They don't have pen and paper in Odessa?"

"I don't know. I haven't been there in a while."

She looked at him and burst out laughing. "What am I going to do with you? You're thoughtless and cruel, and I seriously want nothing more to do with you."

"Well, if you're sure about that."

"Of course, I'm sure."

He slipped his arm around her shoulders and she leaned into him. They walked on, happy to be in each other's company. For the moment there was no past or future, only the two of them, the night, and the road back home.

Chapter Four

March 1905

THE JEWISH intellectuals of Kaminits-Podolsk were like the Jewish intellectuals everywhere in Little Russia—frequently unemployed and always on the lookout for a way to pay the rent. For the lucky few who had a formal education, there was law, medicine, or engineering. The rest sought a position in an office or in a school where the work wasn't too taxing and they had time to pursue their real interests, be it scholarship or politics. Eventually, certain offices became known for their concentration of scholars and radicals. The Office of the District Chief was known as the Conservatory of Arts and Letters, the Municipal Waterworks became the Academy of Sciences, and the Podolia Trade Bank was the Yiddish Literary Society. The society was famous in certain circles as the place to go if you were Jewish and looking for small firearms.

Hershel had spent this last trip traveling first to Odessa and then up to Moscow and back to Odessa on consortium business. He had seen buyers, met with shippers, and in one case supervised the loading of tons of wheat into the hold of a cargo ship bound for Great Britain. Once he was finished with the consortium's business he was free to go off on his own. When a series of pogroms broke out in Podolia Province, the General Jewish Workers' League, the Bund, sent him and a brickyard worker named Scharfstein to see what could be done.

It took them nearly three days by train to get from Cherkast to Proskurov, where they hired a sledge and set out for Kaminits-Podolsk, a small city located on the Bessarabian border. After the long train ride Hershel was too tired and cold to appreciate the scenery. Scharfstein drove the horse up into the mountain passes, past woods of jumbled undergrowth and half-frozen streams, through rich valleys stilled covered in snow.

By the time they reached the town it was late and all the shops were closed. They didn't bother to look around for the best room but took the first one they found, which happened to be in a respectable family hotel run by a Jewish widow and her daughters. The girl at the desk showed them the room, which only had a bed, a dresser, and a washstand.

Once she had gone, Hershel and Scharfstein eyed the bed and decided it was too small for two no matter how they positioned themselves. Hershel offered to flip a coin, but Scharfstein declined. He insisted that Hershel take it. "You're paying for it. Why shouldn't you have it?" Scharfstein had a wife, five children, and no money for train tickets or hotel rooms, so it was understood that Hershel paid for everything.

The next morning Hershel walked into the Podolia Trade Bank looking for Mendel Kramer. At first glance, the place looked like any other bank: neoclassical columns holding up a vaulted ceiling, heavy oak counters, and an immense safe in the back, all sturdy and well built to give the impression of solidity and permanence. But this was no ordinary bank. One only had to look at the clerks to know that; their beards were untrimmed, their collars yellow and limp, their shoes too comfortable and in need of a shine.

Mendel Kramer met him at the door and shook his hand. "Monsieur Alshonsky, it's so good of you to come by on such short notice. If you'll step over to my desk, I'll explain the problem with the loan." He said this in a loud voice for the benefit of anyone who might be listening. Lately, there had been talk that the Literary Society had been infiltrated by members of the Okhranka, the czar's secret police. Although there was no concrete evidence of this, precautions had to be taken.

Kramer was a large man with a thick moustache that covered his entire upper lip. His face was shaped by his large, slightly protruding eyes and the dark hollows beneath them. Hershel had met him on several occasions in private homes and once in Kiev at a concert. He had gotten the impression of a man who was dedicated to the party but not a fanatic, measured in his actions, judicial, a thoughtful man that could be trusted.

After they sat down Kramer took out a file from his desk and showed it to Hershel. Hershel noticed that it was a mortgage written on a warehouse for a man named Joseph Blank. He pretended to look it over while they talked.

"They were supposed to arrive last week, so we are all pretty worried," Mendel Kramer said, as he pointed out a clause to Hershel. "We think they may have been confiscated in Chernivtsi, but not by the authorities. We would have heard otherwise. Somebody has them and it looks like they want to keep them. Still, you never know. They could turn up. Or maybe an offer will be made and we can buy them back. How soon are you going?"

"Now."

"Then you have a problem, my friend."

"You don't have any here . . . a few revolvers, a rifle or two?"

"Everything we have is up in Frampol. There's been a lot of trouble up there lately. I know this isn't good news, but there's a chance the shipment will turn up."

Hershel shook his head. "I'm not going to wait."

"You might want to think about it. Otherwise you'll have to cross the border yourself. It's not so easy up there. I can't think where you can buy them safely. It might be wise to wait."

Hershel knew he was right. The sensible thing would be to wait and see if the arms arrived. Otherwise, he would have to send Scharfstein across to Austria, and there would be no guarantee he would find what they needed or be able to smuggle them back across the border. He admired men like Kramer, thoughtful men who lived lives of measured calculation. He often thought he'd like to be more like him. But his nature was otherwise and there didn't seem to be much he could do about it.

"I won't wait. There isn't time."

"Yes. I understand," Kramer murmured. And he did too. They chatted for a while longer, mostly for appearances' sake. Then Kramer got up and walked Hershel to the door, where they shook hands. He stood there watching while Hershel climbed up on the sledge next to Scharfstein, picked up the reins, and snapped them once.

THE TOWN of Smotrich was located north of Kaminits, about sixty versts east of the Austrian border. It was built on the edge of a forest and named after the river that flowed through it. On the right bank was the town, and on the left, across the town's only bridge, was a sugar beet factory owned by a rich family who lived in Kiev. Beyond the factory were great stretches of snowy sugar beet fields, broken up here and there by peasant villages, which were merely a line of huts on either side of the road. Smotrich was a real town; it had a proper square, a firehouse, and a collection of shops including a tavern and a tearoom. There were several heders, a yeshiva, eight small synagogues, and a hundred Jewish families. The pride of the town was the Great Synagogue, which was said to be "world famous" for its elaborately decorated ark.

"Call out again," said Scharfstein. "There has to be someone around."

"I called out twice already."

"Well, call louder. Maybe no one heard us."

They had arrived in the town square late in the afternoon just as the sleet was turning to snow. They had found the town deserted and locked up tight. They drove around the square looking for the *starusta*, but so far no one had appeared, only a yellow dog picking his way down a snowy lane. Before Hershel had time to call out again, the door to the butcher shop opened and a man clutching a greatcoat over his round belly poked his head out and called to them.

"You Reb Alshonsky?" he asked. He had graying red hair and wore a visor cap.

Hershel prodded the horse and she ambled up toward the man. "Yes. We're looking for the *starusta*."

"I'm Yudel Polik, the butcher. We have been waiting for you."

"Is there some place for the horse?"

"Don't worry about the horse. They will come for her." He held the door open.

They jumped down, grabbed their bags from the sledge, and followed the butcher inside. The shop smelled of meat and was nearly as cold as it was outside. The glass case was empty, but hanging above it were a dozen sausages.

"It's gotten worse," Polik said, his voice dropping to a whisper. "Much worse." He was leading them back behind the counter to the staircase. "The *babas* in the village are saying a Christian girl has been raped. They're saying it was a Jew."

Hershel exchanged a look with Scharfstein. The old women in the peasant villages were always starting rumors. And it was always about the next village over and about girls no one knew. "Where is everybody? Did they run away?"

"No, they're hiding."

"Well, you better call them out."

"Now?"

"Right now."

He thought about it. "Yes, all right." Then he lowered his voice as he labored up the stairs. "Just don't say anything in front of my wife. She's frightened enough as it is. She doesn't know about the rumor."

From up above they could hear his wife calling down to them. Her voice was brittle with fear. Reb Polik called back, assuring her that everything was all right. Everyone would be safe. The strangers had arrived.

When Hershel walked into the firehouse that evening, he had only to glance around to understand the politics that divided Smotrich. On one side of the room were the shopkeepers and officials in folding chairs. These were the Zionists, the righteous men, who longed for a homeland in Palestine. On the other side, sitting on benches or leaning up against the wall, were the workers from the sugar beet refinery and the tannery. They were Bundists and believed, like the Mensheviks, in revolution and a new socialist order. Usually the Zionists went to synagogue and the Bundists to the tearoom, both taking pains to avoid the other. But last week a pogrom broke out in Frampol and twenty people were murdered. Today there were no Bundists or Zionists in Smotrich, only frightened men desperate to protect their families.

Hershel didn't have the words for an inspiring speech, nor was there time. The best he could do for them was to give them a job to do. The carpenters were told to make pikes out of ash wood, and the blacksmith was ordered to make spearheads for them. The roofer was sent to help households reinforce their doors and windows, and the locksmith was told to replace flimsy locks with strong ones. He ordered sentries to stand guard day and night on the road leading into town and on the bridge. He ordered night patrols for the town. He picked men at random, often pairing a Zionist with a Bundist. Nobody seemed to notice. Then he told the rest to meet him in the morning for target practice.

THAT NIGHT they went back to Yudel Polik's apartment and sat down to supper with his four young sons and his wife. She was a plump woman, twenty years younger than her husband. She had a round, pleasant face, but her features were still with fear. After the blessing, she put a bowl of beets and potatoes on the table and passed around a platter of beef. While Reb Polik helped himself to an enormous slab, she asked Scharfstein about his wife and children. Her voice was strained and her eyes kept straying to the window at every sound. Once she stopped midsentence and looked up, alert, tense, perhaps listening for something beneath the wind.

"What is it?" whispered her eldest son.

"Shush!"

The boy looked like his mother, big round eyes set far apart, his mouth a nervous line of worry.

Her husband patted her hand. "It's nothing, Hannah. The wind," he said patiently.

His wife listened for a moment longer, then got up, went to the window, and, leaning over a side table crowded with porcelain figurines of shepherdesses and court ladies, peered out through the glass. "Did you bring up the knives?"

"You asked me that three times already."

"Well, did you?"

"*Yes!* Now come, sit down, Hannah. You have to eat something. You're going to worry yourself to death."

She did as she was told and they ate in silence. When they were done, Froy Polik got up without saying good night, left the dishes on the table, gathered up her children, and took them to her bed.

IT SNOWED all night and by morning the clouds had drifted away. It was a fragile dawn softened by a swirling mist. Hershel stood on the road and watched Scharfstein in the sledge gliding over the bridge, past the sugar beet refinery, heading west for the Austrian border. Since there were only four handguns in the town, one of them misfiring and probably dangerous, they decided that he would have to leave as soon as the sun was up.

Hershel shivered despite his greatcoat and wished he could've been the one to go. He and Scharfstein had been doing this together for five years, since he was sixteen, and they had never been in a situation like this before, without arms or seasoned comrades to help. With growing apprehension, he watched Scharfstein's retreating figure disappear over the hill. Overhead a wavering line of crows, black stains on the white counterpane, flew over the sugar refinery and landed in the linden trees that grew on the river's edge.

Without warning, and with a sickening chill, he recalled an image from one of his nightmares—the body of an old woman lying on the ground with a mutilated face. He quickly swore out loud to dispel the image and shoved his trembling hands into his pockets. He and Scharfstein had come up with a plan, but he didn't think much of it. Given more time, he liked to think he would've come up with something better. He stood there a moment longer, watching the crows and thinking of Berta, missing her, thinking of the spot on the back of her neck that he liked to nuzzle, remembering what she smelled like and wondering if he would ever nuzzle that spot again. Then, with an enormous effort of will, he turned away from the bridge and started back to town.

He checked on the carpenter and the blacksmith. He made sure the sentries were in place and the houses were being secured. Then he gathered up the rest of the men and took them out into the forest for target practice. He had his doubts about teaching them how to shoot and suspected that he might just be wasting bullets. If threatened, he knew they would most likely panic and fire wildly, if they fired at all. Even so, he found a clearing on top of a small hill not far from town and hung several paper targets on the trees. He had the men gather around while he showed them his revolver, a Rast-Gasser from Vienna. He taught them how to use it, and one by one they came up to a line in the snow to shoot. There weren't enough cartridges to allow them to fire off more than a few rounds, but at least everyone got a chance to sight, squeeze the trigger, and feel the recoil.

They hadn't even gone through half the cartridges when they heard a shout from below and saw Yossel Feisis, the water carrier, yelling, waving his arms, and running up the hill. "They are coming!" he shouted as he struggled to climb the hill in the snow. "They are coming into the town."

"How many?"

He fought to breathe, his breath coming in ragged gasps. "Ten sledges. Maybe more. I didn't wait to see. I saw the first one though. A pile of potato sacks."

Instantly, some of the men turned and ran down the hill. Others held back and looked to Hershel with panic in their eyes. "All right," he said quietly, making his voice even and calm. "We'll get ready. We'll be all right. But we have to hurry, there's much to do."

When they got back to the square, he took the best shots aside and gave them the guns and what cartridges he had left. He called them the naturals, to build their confidence. In reality he knew they couldn't hit anything, but at least they wouldn't shoot each other. He told them to go to the firehouse and put on the uniforms, including the brass helmets. He told them to then go up to the rooftops. He pointed out spots along the roofline that took in the entire square. "There and there, one there, and two over there. When I give you the signal you start shooting. You won't hit anything from that distance, but it doesn't matter. Just empty your barrels, but don't do it all at once."

"What is the signal?" asked the tailor.

Hershel thought for a moment. "I don't know yet. But you'll know when you see it."

The little tinsmith looked up at the snowy rooftops and paled. "How are we supposed to get up there?"

"Get the roofer. The rest of you get the axes from the firehouse and barricade yourselves in your homes."

"There aren't enough to go around," someone called out from the back.

"I have some in my store," offered the grocer.

"Good. Now go."

The men ran off in all directions, some to the firehouse, some to the grocer's, the rest to their homes. Hershel found a spot between two buildings that had a good view of the square and took in most of the roofline. He stood there among soggy newspapers, a rusted-out skillet, and rotting garbage and listened for the bells on the harnesses.

He soon heard them in the distance, ringing out in a variety of pitches, sounding all the more unnerving for their childish gaiety. Soon the square was filled with sledges, packed in so tightly that it was easy for a man to hand a bottle of vodka to his neighbor. Hershel looked up at the rooftops and willed the naturals to hurry.

A peasant stood up in a sledge and addressed the crowd in Surzhyk. He wore a filthy *tulup*, a long sheepskin coat, and *valenki*, long winter felt boots. His head was bare and his hair was straight and thick. He was drunk, but that didn't stop him from standing up and addressing the crowd.

"Friends," he said, swaying slightly on his feet. "Every day the *zhyd* cheats us, and what do we do about it? Every day he charges us more for sugar and tobacco. He takes our beetroots and pays us practically nothing. He says he doesn't set the prices. Well, I would like to know who does. Do you? Does your neighbor? Maybe Baba Yaga sets the prices?" The crowded hooted at this and several men clapped.

Hershel kept scanning the rooftops. It was taking them too long.

"And now the *zhyd* wants our daughters," continued the peasant. "He wants to use them as whores. To dishonor them and humiliate us." His gestures were grander, his voice louder as he grew bolder on the approbation of the crowd. "He has taken an innocent and fouled her with his filth. Does anyone here doubt that she is as good as dead?"

Finally there was a figure on one of the rooftops. He had climbed up from the other side and was crawling over the icy shingles to the peak. There he rose cautiously to his feet, balancing in the bank of snow.

"It is time we got our own back. It is time for justice. They need a lesson. They need to know what happens to a *zhyd* who ruins our daughter." The crowd was on its feet. There were shouts of agreement from all around. One man fell out of his sledge and the others laughed at him, calling him a castrated ass and other obscenities. He was too drunk to be offended.

Another figure appeared on a roof across the square from the first. He was more comfortable with heights and walked easily into place, straddling the snowy peak, keeping an eye on the square, looking for the signal.

Someone shouted from the back of the crowd: "Kill the *zhydy* and save Russia and the czar!" The crowd roared. Someone else picked up the cry. *Kill the zhydy and save Russia and the czar!*

Hershel saw two more figures get into position, their brass helmets blazing in the noonday sun. Then he saw the last figure, the tinsmith no doubt, crawling through the snow on his belly across the roof to the chimney piece, where he wrapped his arms around the bricks and clung on for dear life.

By now the crowd was stirred up from the chanting. Hershel knew that in a few moments the men would take up their axes and smash the doors down. They would hack to pieces anyone who got in their way. They would take what they wanted, including the women, kill the children, and set fire to the town.

When he stepped into the square he didn't know exactly what he was going to do. He only knew that it all depended upon his performance and so he concentrated on that, on pacing, on slowing everything down. He slowed the way he walked into the square, the way he stepped up on the bench.

He studied the crowd while they studied him. He was a stranger and they were curious. When they had quieted down, he began to speak. He said in Surzhyk: "I am a Jew." He looked into their faces, into their eyes. He wasn't in a hurry and they saw that. "And you have come to kill me. But I can tell you right now that you won't."

A man muttered to his neighbor. Another straightened and stood up in his sledge. Someone reached for his axe and stepped out into the snow. Others stood their ground and waited to hear what the mad Jew would say next.

He saw all of this and continued. "And why won't you kill me?" he asked the crowd. "Why wouldn't you just cut my head off or my arm and watch me bleed to death?"

There were shouts of *Yes, why don't we? Why not?*

"You won't," he shouted back. "And the reason is not because I'm such a good fighter. Or that you are such good men that you wouldn't kill an unarmed man. The reason is . . ." and here he paused as his eyes swept the crowd. "The reason is very simple, my friends. You value your families. You value your farms and your homes. What you don't know is that at this very minute there is a man at every barn and at every house with a bottle of coal gas, a long rag, and a match waiting for my signal to burn your farms to the ground."

For a moment the crowd stood there in silence. Then someone shouted, "He is lying!" And another bellowed, "He is bluffing!" There were cries of fear and disbelief that soon turned to fury. The crowd began to surge forward.

"You don't believe me?" shouted Hershel. "You want proof?" He looked up at the rooftops and nodded. Instantly shots rang out from every side of the square.

There were screams. The crowd dropped to the ground in the snow and covered their heads. Some looked up to see where the gunshots were coming from and found avenging angels straddling the rooftops wearing golden helmets all aglow, like a crown of fire.

More shots and the crowd scattered. Some leaped into their sledges and flew off down the road. Others tried to quiet panicked horses but were trampled to death as the terrified animals galloped off, dragging their overturned sledges behind them.

It took less than five minutes, but when it was over the square was empty except for the dead. The sledges were gone. Some pogromists could still be seen on the road chasing after their horses through the snow. The only sound was the tinsmith, still clinging to the chimney, calling for help because he was afraid to let go.

Chapter Five

July 1905

THERE WERE always little dramas in Gershen's bakery on Friday mornings. What with the women standing in line for their Shabbes loaf, impatient, irritable, their appetites sharpened by the smell of baking bread coming from the two ovens in the yard, there was always some incident to break up the monotony. On that morning, a small clot of women had just stepped inside the bakery, anticipating an end to their long wait. They each carried a lump of braided dough wrapped up in brown paper, and from time to time looked up from their conversation to see how far they had to go before they reached the counter. They were all dressed in black, for each had lost a loved one and was still in mourning.

There were two among them whose skirt and blouse were a deeper shade of black. These garments belonged to the two professional mourners in Mosny, whose job it was to be the embodiment of sorrow, hopelessness, and despair. They were dedicated mourners, blessed with all the requisite talents: a pallid complexion, a sorrowful expression, and an all-black wardrobe.

"What are you talking about?" snapped Aviva Kaspler. She had kneaded her challah the night before because she had an early funeral that morning. "He has not been here since Tisho be-Av. If he had been here, I would have known it. You think I don't know who comes and goes around here?" She was a tall woman, with broad shoulders, a jowly face with heavy features, and a booming voice, perfect for keening above a crowd.

"*Draikop!*" said Yael Schlaifer, her partner and the only other official mourner in Mosny. "He was here right after Reb Shtarker's funeral and in that droshky of his with the yellow wheels. How could you have missed him? And her in those fancy clothes. They went out riding. She was carrying that parasol of hers, the one with the lace. I ask you, who puts lace on a parasol?" She had a small, pointed face that was engulfed by dark-rimmed glasses. Her greatest asset was her pinched mouth that could effortlessly convey heart-wrenching sorrow for as long as was required.

"She calls *me* a *draikop!*" exclaimed Aviva. "And who is the *draikop*? You're thinking of the bookseller. He was the one who came by that day."

"You don't think I can tell the difference between the wheat merchant and the bookseller?"

Since cholera and typhus were frequent visitors to Mosny, these two enjoyed a thriving business, albeit a rocky partnership due to the stresses of their success and their strong personalities. Although they argued about most everything, when it came to mourning, to crying as if their hearts would break, none were better. They worked themselves into a frenzy, playing off each other like seasoned opera singers. They were crowd pleasers and knew how to get a funeral off to a good start.

"Either way, he hasn't been here since before Shabbes Chazon, that's for sure," said Nessie Laiser, the wife of the roofer. She was careful not to take sides. Nobody in Mosny wanted to take sides when it came to the official mourners. They had sharp tongues and they knew how to use them.

"And you know what that means?" added Yaffa Hamerow, the tavern keeper's wife. "She'll end up a spinster after all. Her poor mother must be brokenhearted."

"I would not like to be Rivke Lorkis." said Aviva. "To have a daughter like that? And speaking French when you least expect it." She was about to say more, but Yaffa elbowed her when she saw Berta pushing open the door of the bakery.

Berta stepped inside and edged past the line on her way to the counter. "*Gut* Shabbes," she said in their general direction. She didn't like coming to the bakery, especially on Shabbes, when it was crowded.

"*Gut* Shabbes," they said nearly in unison.

She stepped up to the counter and asked the baker if there was any challah left. "Of course there's challah left," he replied irritably. He was a busy man and had no time for foolish questions. "There's the line, Your Highness. You'll have to wait like everyone else." Berta shot him a look and turned back to the line. *God, how I hate Mosny and everyone in it.*

After Hershel's last visit, it became apparent to Mameh that he was going to ask Berta to marry him. Since Berta had similar thoughts of her own, she didn't bother to deny it and instead chose to keep quiet on the subject. Mameh took this reticence as confirmation, which gave her license to tell anybody who would listen about the fine wedding they were planning. Women who had nothing good to say about Berta Lorkis were making nice to her in hopes of securing an invitation. Esteem for her rose among the housewives and their daughters. She was going to marry Reb Alshonsky, live in a big house in Cherkast, and ride around in a practically new droshky. She would have store-bought dresses and jewelry and go to parties where an orchestra played and exotic food was served at midnight. There was even talk of indoor plumbing. But as high as their opinion of her was in those heady days, it plummeted after Hershel failed to reappear nearly four months later. One day she was to be the bride of a successful wheat merchant, the next she was jilted and disgraced, the humiliation of Moscow all over again. Now, nothing awaited her but spinsterhood and the consensus was that it couldn't have happened to a more deserving girl.

"So, how's your lovely mother?" asked Yael Schlaifer, as Berta passed their little group on the way to the end of the line.

"Well."

"And your father?"

"Also well."

As she walked on, she could hear them giggling and whispering behind her back. *The greedy pigs*, she thought, *passing judgment on me, rooting around for every detail—the* yachnehs, *the* yentehs, *the loudmouthed gossips*. She was halfway out the door when she nearly collided with the milkman's wife. She ignored the woman's murmured apology and walked on to the end of the line. She blamed her mother for this. If her mother hadn't told everybody she was marrying Hershel, then she would've been free to suffer in peace. No one would've known what she was feeling. Now everyone knew and they were reveling in it.

At first when Hershel didn't return, Berta thought it was just business that kept him away. It wasn't hard to explain away the absence of letters. He wasn't a writer. Then one Tuesday, when it was Lhaye's turn to open and Berta was out for her customary walk, the thought struck her that he was with another woman. She hadn't even been thinking about him. She had been standing by a stream using a low-hanging branch to keep her balance, while she dangled first one shoe in the rushing water and then the other in an effort to wash off the mud. The thought came to her like a sharp intake of breath and she sank down on the bank and stared at her shoes still dangling in the rushing water. Her limbs felt detached. She wasn't even aware of the icy water seeping in through the cracks around the soles. Of course he had other women. Why hadn't she seen it? A successful wheat merchant like that? A *k'nacker*, a bounder, he would have plenty of women.

On the way back, she pictured him out with a woman in his droshky. They might visit the same spots that she and Hershel had visited, laugh about the same things. She would be sophisticated, a worldly woman; perhaps she had been to university. Maybe he would tell her about the little grocery clerk in Mosny, the one who was still waiting for him. She would be another story in his repertoire along with Esther Churgin's beggar and the succubus who claimed the rabbi's son.

After that Berta's thoughts grew even darker and she stopped sleeping. Then she was sleeping too much and later she was back to wandering the fields in the early morning. Furious, indignant, wretched, and lost.

It was a warm day and Berta was down at the river, although the water was still too cold to stay in for long. Soon she was wading back out, her toes avoiding the rocks and digging into the fine sand, her body wet and nearly numb, her clean hair streaming down her back. She reached for her towel before lying down on the beach and closed her eyes. She could hear the women by the water who had come down to wash their clothes. Their chatter mingled with the jays fluttering in the oak trees. Off in the distance she heard the low chug of a barge traveling down to the docks, and from the cemetery that lay between the river and the town she could hear the wailing of the mourners at a late-afternoon funeral.

Even though the wailing was faint compared to the lap of the water over the rocks and the distant roar of the rapids farther downriver, it still seeped into her consciousness, soon becoming a prickly source of irritation, a hard bright reminder of her own hopelessness. When it was all she could bear, she got up, put on her clean clothes, tucked the dirty ones under her arm, and followed the path up the slope.

The path led around the perimeter of the cemetery, where she could see the funeral party assembled at the gravesite. They were burying the shul *klopfer*. There were a few mourners in attendance along with the rabbi and the beadle. The shul *klopfer's* son was there too, watching the plain pine box slip into the ground, looking a little lost with his wife's arm around his waist. A little girl stood next to them toeing the dirt and looking around at Berta, for no other reason than there was nothing else to do.

On the road back to town, Berta met Froy Salanter, the proprietress of the tearoom. Froy Salanter was something of a rebel with her wild frizzy hair and her high-heel lace-up shoes bought special in Kiev. She could afford to be because she had a successful business that sold only new items and a very good string of pearls that secured her place among the best people. For this reason she often spoke to Berta Lorkis, flaunting her friendship with the outcast, disdainful of the gossip that it would undoubtedly encourage.

"*Nu*, maybe now you will come back to my shop and play a little chess? Now that your partner is back."

"Excuse me?"

"Your chess partner. That nice young man. Didn't you know?"

"No, I didn't know."

"Well, he is here all right. Arrived about an hour ago."

Berta was glad she had been forewarned, because now, when she walked into the square and saw Hershel's droshky tied up outside the grocery, she was able to maintain an air of disinterest. This was fortunate because the shoemaker's good-for-nothing son, who was planted outside his father's shop in his usual chair reading a Yiddish paper, actually put it down to watch her. The women at the well, their hair shiny with kerosene, turned in her direction, and the porters playing cards on the bench under the trees looked over at her with interest. With all these eyes on her it was important that she maintain her composure as a quick succession of emotions washed through her: first icy apprehension, then relief at his return, and finally a knotted ball of anger in her stomach.

"He's back," Lhaye said in a hurried whisper, when Berta walked through the door to the sound of the jingling bell. "He's come back to you."

A yelp of incredulity. "To me? Oh, that's rich."

"Shush, he'll hear you." She flung a worried look up the stairs. "He asked about you right off. He even wanted to go looking for you, but Mameh said you were bathing. Do you want me to fix your hair?"

"What for?"

"Oh Bertenka . . . don't be like that. He really wants to see you."

"And that's why he stayed away all this time."

"I'm sure he has an explanation. Don't be angry with him."

Berta looked at her sister and batted away a circling fly. "You don't understand," she said turning to the stairs. "He's come to buy wheat, that's all. I'm just a sideline."

She didn't expect the jolt she felt when she saw him standing in the front room with a glass of tea and a plate in his hand, awkwardly searching for a place to set them down. He left them on the side table and came over to her with a look of eagerness that was unmistakable. "Berta . . ." he said, holding out his hand for hers. There was nothing guarded about his greeting.

Ignoring his hand she said, "Reb Alshonsky."

Her chilly reply produced the effect she wanted. His smile faded and he slowly dropped his hand. The samovar went on bubbling in the corner, giving off its comforting smell of charcoal, while her mother served poppy seed cake on the good plates, of which there were only three left.

She held one out to Berta. "Come have some tea with us, *maideleh.* Reb Alshonsky was just asking about you."

"Another time. I have a headache."

"*Nu*, a little tea will do you good."

"I don't want tea. I want to be alone."

"Stay with us. This is your favorite."

"I told you I don't want any. I'm going to my room." She turned and left before her mother could object any further.

That night over supper, Hershel told them about a stage show he had seen in Odessa featuring Wondrous Wisarek, the human snake. "I don't know what kind he was supposed to be. A big one, I suppose . . . maybe a python or an anaconda. He had on a leotard that was covered with glittering scales and he slithered across the stage and up a tree trunk and wound around and around the branch. I don't know how he did it. It was as if he didn't have any bones at all. It was really quite amazing." He took a sip of wine and tried to catch Berta's eye, but she kept her expression neutral and her eyes averted.

Mameh kept fussing over him. She filled his glass the moment it was empty and gave him the best piece of fish. It infuriated Berta to see her mother behaving like that to a man who had treated her daughter so badly.

After supper, while Lhaye and Mameh were gathering up the dishes, Hershel took Berta aside and asked her if she wanted to come out with him.

"I have to help. I have dishes to do."

"No, you don't," said Mameh, clearing away the plates. "Go with him. It's all right."

"Stop nagging me, Mameh. If I wanted to go, I would." She picked up a platter, pushed past her mother, and went into the kitchen.

Mameh gave Hershel a wan smile. "She's not herself tonight, Reb Alshonsky. Girls have their days, you know." She didn't like discussing monthlies in front of a man, but she was desperate to explain why her daughter was such a *meshugeneh.*

Later when Mameh and Hershel were settled on the settee and Tateh was in his chair with his Yiddish paper, Hershel told Mameh a story about a man who had goat's hooves for feet and was cured by a miracle rabbi. She pretended to listen, but she couldn't keep her mind on the story. For the first time, news from her own house seemed more *tragical* than anything she could hear from the outside world. Everything was going wrong. Berta was determined to ruin them and drive them deeper into poverty and there was no reasoning with her. Like most young people, she had a head full of chicken feathers and didn't know the first thing about common sense. Why she didn't jump at the chance of marrying such a boy, so accomplished and well-mannered, such a *choshever mentsh*, was baffling to her.

THAT NIGHT Berta woke to what she thought was the sound of the mourners in the cemetery, until she realized that it was in the middle of the night, during a rainstorm. She lay there listening for the sound and when she heard it again she knew that it was Hershel having another one of his nightmares. She didn't want to go to him. She wanted to ignore him and go back to sleep, but she could hear him struggling with something awful. So she swung her legs out of bed and walked on tiptoe across the damp floorboards to the door.

Out in the hall the roof was leaking in several places and the water was dripping into the pots her mother had placed throughout the rooms. For an instant the hallway was bathed in a cold blue light and a second later a crack of thunder shook the house.

"Berta . . . ?" He was calling to her from behind the curtain.

She hesitated. "Yes."

He sat up and shoved aside the curtain. "I was dreaming again. I'm sorry."

"It doesn't matter. Go back to sleep."

"No, wait." He reached out a hand for her and caught her wrist. "Stay with me for a while."

"I want to go back. I'm cold."

He pulled her over to the bed. "Just for a minute. Here, sit here." He moved over to give her room. "Put your feet up on the bed. It's warm."

She stood there on the cold floor uncertain what to do. The water was dripping steadily from the ceiling, splashing out of a nearby pot and seeping into the floorboards. The air was damp and smelled like mildew. After a struggle she sat down on the straw mattress and lifted her feet up off the floor. "What is it?"

"I want to explain about not writing and staying away for so long."

"What's there to explain? You have other friends. I don't need to know anything else."

"Friends? You mean women?"

"It's none of my business."

"It is your business and you're wrong. There aren't other women."

"Then what?"

He watched the water drip into a nearby pot and then pushed himself up on the pillow. "I was in a shtetl."

"A shtetl?" Her forehead crinkled in confusion. "Why?"

"I was helping people."

"In a shtetl?

"That's right."

"All this time?"

He nodded.

"And what were you doing in this shtetl?"

He pulled the blanket up over his chest. "Educating them, I guess you could call it."

"A school?"

"Of sorts."

She stared at him in the dark. Then she shook her head. He was playing with her and she didn't like it one bit. "I have no idea what you're talking about and I'm cold. I'm going to bed." She stood up.

He grabbed her hand again. "No, don't go yet?"

"Why not?"

"Look, I can't tell you what I was doing there, but I can tell you why I went."

She took her hand back but made no effort to leave.

"Please," he said, "sit down. Give me a chance."

She looked across the hallway through her bedroom to the little window framed by the white curtains she had made herself. It was a blank square in the dark until another burst of lightning lit it up with the same blue light. Without looking at him, she slowly sank down on the edge of the bed, as far away from him as possible.

He began his story with the girl on the tightrope. He told her about the shoe peddler; his father, the *starusta*; and all the events that followed. When he had finished she sat there looking at him for some time and then slowly moved into his arms. At first he seemed surprised that she was even in the room with him. His mind was still on that night long ago and it took him several moments to come back to her. When he did, he kissed her and buried his lips in her neck. In a rush of relief she believed that she knew him, that he was a good man, and that she loved him. These were simple thoughts, uncomplicated, but so immense, so grand, that they threatened to overwhelm her. As close as she felt to him, she had to get closer. So she picked up the blankets and climbed in beside him. He rubbed her shoulders and drew her close to his bare chest. His feet found hers and he rubbed them with his instep to warm them. She had entered the nest of a wintering animal. It smelled of sleep and country roads.

They lay with their arms wrapped around each other, listening to the rain and the bony scratching of the bare branches on the roof. He kissed her again and this time his tongue searched out hers. His hands were flat on the small of her back gently guiding her up on top of him. With their breath all around them, they began their nearly silent lovemaking. The fact that they could be caught at any moment and had to stifle the sound of their pleasure only heightened it. Even the quick pain of her first time didn't dampen the extraordinary sensation of having him inside her, all around her, enveloping her, absorbing her, until she was only vaguely aware of the storm outside and the rustling straw beneath them.

THAT FALL they were married in the *groyse* shul, the grand synagogue, the largest and most elaborate shul in Mosny. Since Hershel hadn't asked for a dowry, most of the money the Malkiels had sent to Tateh—what was left after the odd emergency—was put into the wedding. There were flowers, fancy foods, famous musicians from Kiev; even the invitations were printed on linen, with two envelopes, one inside the other and tissue paper separating the pages. Everyone was invited, all the relatives, Aunt Sadie and Uncle Sol, the Rosenthals and the bunch from Smelo: all their friends from the village including the official mourners Aviva Kaspler and her business partner, Yael Schlaifer.

The procession started at the grocery door and proceeded on through the town and down to the Street of Synagogues to the main shul. Old women danced in front of the bridal couple, the klezmor band played a march, and children made a game of running through the crowd to keep up. As the crowd followed the bride and groom into the synagogue, there were audible sighs of relief, since it was a hot day and the interior of the stone shul was cool. The center aisle was decorated with swags of roses that looped from pew to pew. Nobody in Mosny had ever seen anything like it. Aviva Kaspler whispered to Yael Schlaifer that she thought it looked Christian and Yael Schlaifer was inclined to agree. They were both wearing their customary black, although, as a concession to the wedding, they each wore a bunch of silk flowers at their waist.

That night everybody gathered in the *shalash*, the three-sided enclosure that Tateh had built against the side of the store where the banquet and dancing were to take place. There was a platform built on one side for the orchestra and another on the other side for the bride and groom. All around the perimeter were tables and benches for the guests. There were delicacies on the banquet tables that no one had ever tasted in their entire life. Little bits of heaven they said, although some refused to touch them and whisperings of *traif* moved from table to table, especially among the older guests.

Moses Kumanov and his *klezmorim* had not been hired to play at the wedding. Once the guests had gathered in the *shalash*, the musical duties were turned over to a small orchestra that had been brought all the way from Kiev. Reb Kumanov was philosophical about it and was heard to say that it was perfectly fine with him. "A bride has a right to choose her own music." But then in a stage whisper he added, "Although, what kind of music these fellows are playing is anybody's guess. You can't dance to it. No *froelichs*, no *volochel*, no *bolgar*. Certainly no *kazatska*. Forget Jewish," he said with a dismissive wave of his hand, "it is not even Russian." Some said it was from Germany, and like everything from Germany, it was well put together but lifeless.

The oddest thing about the evening was that there was no *badchen*, nobody to tell funny stories and jokes and make up rhymes about the guests and the presents they brought. Nessie Laiser, Yaffa Hamerow, and the milkman's wife were disappointed by this and were complaining to the official mourners when Berta drifted over. Ordinarily, they would have a few choice words to say about her too, once she was out earshot. But this time they were so taken by her radiance, her beatific smile, and the love that poured out of her for Hershel Alshonsky, for the guests and musicians, even for them, that it left them speechless.

Yaffa Hamerow watched Berta glide over to the next table. Nessie Laiser said nothing and shifted uncomfortably in her chair. Aviva Kaspler murmured something about how in love they were and wasn't that fine. Yael Schlaifer said nothing. A memory had percolated up from her own wedding and took her by surprise. It was just a fleeting image of her hand in Yakov's as they walked out of the synagogue into the sunshine. Pausing at the top of the steps for a kiss, he whispered something that she couldn't quite remember. Maybe he told her they would always be together or they would have many children or he would always strive to make her happy. It didn't matter, because two years later there was a cholera epidemic and she buried him in a plot overlooking the river. It was her first funeral.

Part Two

The Wheat Merchant's Wife

Chapter Six

December 1913

To THE casual traveler, Pavel Ossipovich Lepeshkin looked relaxed. He was seated in the dining car at a table laid for tea. Just inches from his fingertips stood a small, three-tiered silver tray of forgotten finger sandwiches and pastries. A cold cup of tea sat on a sturdy saucer stamped with the crest of the Nord Express. The cream in the cup was congealing, the sandwich bread was growing stale, and the pastries were looking decidedly gray.

Staring out the window at the Alexandrovo station, Pavel looked like a young gentleman dulled by train travel on his way home from school for the holidays. But his face was beaded with sweat and nearly the color of the tablecloth and his hands were trembling. His blond hair was swept back off his forehead, his nose was flat and led down to a pointy chin, and his intense brown eyes hardly seemed to blink as he stretched to look up and down the track. He resembled a burrowing animal caught halfway out of his den by the screech of an owl and the thunder of flapping wings.

The trains from Berlin on their way to Kiev and Moscow always stopped at the Alexandrovo station when first crossing the Russian frontier. After changing trains to accommodate the wider-gauge track, second and third-class passengers were expected to line up, their baggage and passports at the ready, and wait their turn in the customs office. First-class passengers were allowed to send a porter with their passports and remain in the comfort of their compartment. But recently there had been an incident and now the authorities were asking to see their luggage as well. Pavel wanted to go with his traveling case but was told to wait in the carriage so as not to draw attention to himself. So he waited, and had been waiting for nearly an hour, wondering if in the next moment the gendarmes would appear or, worse, agents of the imperial secret police.

Pavel didn't want to speak to anyone. The last thing he wanted was a friendly passenger chatting him up, so he kept his face turned to the window and his arms crossed over his chest hoping in this way to keep away any interlopers.

An elderly woman seated across the aisle took no notice of these precautions. In a voice that was a little too loud, she declared in barely accented French, "My, what a wait. We've been sitting here for nearly an hour. You'd think they'd get on with it." She was a wisp of a woman with a visible line of powder at her throat and long knobby fingers, who seemed lost in her fur wrap and enormous hat. "I dislike these long delays, don't you?" she went on, undeterred by his reticence.

A diamond and ruby brooch winked at her throat and reminded him of a similar one his mother owned. Even though he had just been there a few months before, he longed to go home again. He wanted to be back in the nursery, eating bliny and sour cream with his Slavic nanny, Mariasha, to be gathered up in her arms and held to her abundant breasts, to be fussed over and pampered, to be told what a good boy he was and how he would always be loved and, above all, *kept safe*. The fact that he had outgrown his nanny and the nursery years ago did little to ease the ache he felt now.

"You haven't touched your cakes, dear. Aren't you hungry?"

"Guess not," Pavel said, swallowing hard.

"On holiday, then? Coming home from school?"

Pavel nodded.

"University?"

He nodded again and mentioned the name of the university he attended. It was a fashionable one, favored by the aristocracy and the *kupechestvo*, the wealthy merchant class.

"Ah yes, my nephew went there. But of course that was a long time ago. You wouldn't know him, Nikolai Aleksandrovich Chaliapin?"

Pavel shook his head and hoped she'd go away. Instead she chatted on about her nephew at the ministry, her trip to Paris, and the impeccable service at her hotel. Instead of listening he kept his eyes on the crowd outside his window, hoping to see the porter returning with his case. Surely, there must've been some trouble. How long could it take? In his mind he saw a gendarme riffling through his suitcase, his big hands pawing through the fine linen shirts his mother had bought at Muir and Mirrielees, digging underneath, past his trousers and vests to the hidden compartment below. There the officer would have no trouble finding a stack of *Brdzola*, the Struggle, a seditious newspaper started by a former Theological Seminary student turned revolutionary named Iosif Vissarionovich Djugashvili, later to be known as Koba, and later still to adopt the underground *klichka* of Stalin. Next to the papers the gendarme would find five semiautomatic Browning pistols. After that, there wouldn't be much left of Pavel's life—a speedy trial and an exile order. By Christmas he'd be in Siberia, where the temperature typically hovered around sixty below. How many winters could he survive there? Two? Maybe three?

Pavel was Jewish. More than that, he was a socialist and a member of the Bund, the General Jewish Workers' League. He attended most of the Bund meetings at the Kleinmikhels' or at the coffeehouse where he learned about organizing the Jewish worker and about melding the socialist rhetoric into a palatable concoction that promised civic rights and freedom from the anti-Jewish laws of the czar. The particular branch of Bund activity that interested Pavel was forming the self-defense units to protect the townlets and *shtetlekh* against the ravages of the pogroms that had been increasing dramatically since the October Manifesto of 1905. Factions loyal to the czar blamed the Jews for what they saw as a threat to the autocracy. The day after the czar announced the manifesto granting a constitutional government to the people, these factions launched pogroms in more than three hundred cities across the Pale, beating thousands to death, destroying homes and businesses, and orphaning thousands of children. That was five years ago. Now Mendel Beilis, a minor factory official, had been accused of killing a Christian boy for ritual purposes—the old blood libel from the Middle Ages revived to stir up trouble. The trial had begun in September. It was now December and the Jews were holding their breath.

During the day, Pavel was a second-year university student, but at night he became a revolutionary, an organizer, a protector of those who had never thought of protecting themselves. His dedication to the Bund had nothing to do with Inessa Zenzinova—even though Morris Eiger, his boyhood friend from his years at the gymnasium, insisted that it did. Morris was also a Jew and an exasperating cynic and the only person in the world, aside from Mariasha, who could call him Pavlech.

Morris was dead wrong about his feelings for Zenzinova. It was absurd to think that Pavel was only there for her. True, her smooth thighs, ample breasts, and fascination with free love were a draw. Yes, she was older and could offer him excursions into unexplored territory heretofore only imagined in adolescent fantasies. But how could one think that the afternoons in her apartment on Amsterdam Street, even with her mouth firmly planted around his cock, his tongue assailing the portals of her perfumed crotch, the full-length mirror in the corner reflecting their coupling, while brilliant in every way, could be the real motivation behind his socialistic zeal? It was nonsense. He was a dedicated radical, willing to sacrifice everything, even his life, for the laboring masses.

A couple of weeks earlier they were seated in the Kleinmikhels' faded living room. Everyone was there: Antokolsky, Dobroliubkov, Lliodor, and the rest. Mariya Kleinmikhel had just brought in tea and vodka and Pavel was in the middle of one his "florid expostulations," as Morris liked to call them. "Ever meet a worker, Pavlech?" asked Morris, with mocking interest. "I mean aside from that one time you visited your father's factory. Ever actually sit down and talk to one?"

Pavel generally ignored Morris's puerile attempts to humiliate him in front of Inessa and the others. But on this occasion, when everyone was laughing at him and even Inessa was suppressing a smile beneath the lip of her glass, Pavel had no choice but to fight back. When Antokolsky asked for volunteers to smuggle newspapers and pistols over the Polish border, his hand shot up. Nobody laughed at him after that. He wasn't just talking in the safety of the Kleinmikhels' parlor; he was acting—which was more than could be said for the others. For one glorious week Pavel was a hero. Even Morris had to grudgingly allow him his glory.

Now sitting on the train, waiting to be arrested, he couldn't believe he let his pride drive him to this precipice. Yes, he wanted Inessa's respect and even more her glorious thighs wrapped around his back, but to die for it? Why didn't he see then what he saw so clearly now? There had to be a traitor in their circle. He had been betrayed. Soon there would be an arrest, followed by a short trial and a long death, and the worst of it was he had brought it all down upon himself.

When the porter arrived a few minutes later with his suitcase and passport in hand, Pavel nearly collapsed with relief. He gave the man a large, ludicrous tip and sent him on his way. After that he ordered fresh tea and turned his full attention to the Duchess Milista, listening to her account of her problems with her head gardener and the coming-out party for her niece. Suddenly he was a charming and loquacious traveling companion. The transformation was no less than miraculous. Soon he had moved over to her table and was offering her slightly off-color anecdotes about student life, not enough to offend her, but enough to get her to wag her handkerchief at him and pretend to blush.

When Pavel arrived at the Vienna station in Warsaw he took the junction line to the Kovel station, where he was to catch the express to Moscow. He didn't have much time. He found the bench where he had been instructed to sit, put the suitcase down at his feet, and waited. There was to be an exchange; that's all he knew. Someone was to come and take away the case and leave an identical one in its place. He opened a newspaper and tried to read it but ended up reading the same two sentences over and over again without comprehension. He found himself watching the passersby, searching their faces for a subtle look, a nod, a sign. But they passed him without a glance. His stomach churned. He wondered what he would do if no one came. He wanted to leave the case and walk away, but what if someone saw him and ran after him or, worse, called a gendarme?

Then he noticed a well-dressed man with a neatly trimmed black beard and a long cashmere scarf standing near the archway that led to the platforms. At first, Pavel had the notion that he might be the one. His heart beat faster, there was a cold seep in his stomach, and for a moment he was convinced he'd been saved. He had fleeting thoughts of returning to his life, to the monotony of classes, to Inessa's breasts, when he noticed that the man wasn't carrying a traveling case and was giving him one of those looks he had seen in a public toilet once and a couple of times in a club. He gave the man a frosty look and let his eyes slip away. It was enough to make an end of the business. The stranger shrugged it off and moved on.

There were only a few minutes remaining before the train departed when a large, red-faced gentleman with thinning ginger hair and a silver-tinged moustache, accompanied by his wife, four young children, and their exhausted nanny, walked through the large double doors that separated the terminal from the town outside. To Pavel's consternation, the family found their way to his bench and before he knew it had spread out their belongings, driving him to the very edge of his domain. Even with the nanny in attendance there were just too many runny noses, too many sweaters to remove, and fights to break up. The clamor of their voices filled the terminal and drove the other travelers to vacate the vicinity and seek refuge in other parts of the station. Pavel wanted to join them but he had his orders. He couldn't leave his bench.

He watched the father trying to cope with his brood and then turned away in disgust. The man's sanguine attitude toward the piercing voices, the whining and crying over hats and toys, made him prickly with irritation. Obviously the man loved his children too much to be an effective disciplinarian. He wondered if a man like that ever had real cause to worry. True, he had responsibilities, a household to maintain, a wife to please, and an exhausted nanny, but he didn't have five semiautomatic pistols in a suitcase at his feet.

A stuffed camel sailed through the air and glanced off Pavel's shoulder. Pavel turned to the child who threw it and gave him a cold look of reproach. The nanny dove for it and gave it to a smaller child who stopped screaming once he realized the coveted thing was back in his lap. Pavel sat there brooding, bearing it as best he could, while silently willing the family to leave. It seemed to work, for soon after that, the patriarch stood and announced that they were off again. After a flurry of activity and an anguished cry over a missing doll that was soon found, the father, carrying a child in one arm and an array of suitcases in the other, led the way across the terminal and out through the arch to the platforms.

Pavel waited on the bench a few minutes more until the last whistle blew and the station master called out his train to Moscow. Then he picked up the suitcase, hurried out to the platform, and boarded the train. He told himself that it would be all right. He would dine in his compartment and leave only when necessary. In this way he would get to Moscow undetected, deliver the suitcase himself, and thankfully get on with his life.

Once he was in his compartment with the door locked, he relaxed a little and gradually closed his eyes. He didn't wake until much later, when his eyes opened with a start and he found the train at a standstill. His first thought was that they had reached Kiev. But it was too quiet, and they weren't scheduled to arrive before morning. He looked at his pocket watch—it was half past three.

He lay there listening for sounds, trying to ignore the hard knot of fear in his chest. His mouth was dry, his legs felt weak and shaky. Occasionally the train would belch and hiccup. Aside from that, the night was quiet. Far off he thought he heard shouting, but it may have been the wind. That uncertainty worsened his fears and made him restless. He got up, threw on his clothes, and went to the door. He opened it soundlessly and peered out into the corridor. It was empty and silent. It smelled faintly of cigars and clean clothes. He went to the carriage door and looked out at the platform. The sign over it said LUBLIN. They were still in Russian Poland. A soft rain had begun to fall and a locomotive standing on a nearby track glistened slick and black like a slug in the night.

The platform was lighted by one electric bulb and standing directly beneath it were two gendarmes and another man wearing baggy wool pants, a visor cap, and a black leather jacket. They were all smoking hand-rolled cigarettes through cupped hands while huddling together under the covered platform to keep out of the rain.

Pavel watched them for a few minutes more until he was certain they were Okhranka, the czar's secret police. It was simple, someone had given him up and now they were coming to arrest him. He saw it all: the questions, the freezing cell, a swift trial, his mother weeping, his father in anguish, and then the long train ride to Siberia. For one queasy moment he stood frozen at the carriage door, staring helplessly into his future. Then he flew back to his compartment, slammed the door, and locked it with trembling fingers.

His first instinct was to escape. He went to the window and tried to open it. It was stuck. He pounded on the frame, no longer worried about the noise he was making until the wood gave a little and the window opened. But the opening was too small for him to crawl through. He thought about sneaking out the carriage door until he heard footsteps down the corridor coming toward his door. He grabbed his suitcase and flung it open. All thoughts of heroism and revolution, of laying down his life for the new social order, vanished as he dove into the suitcase and hunted for the latch that would release the false bottom. His hands were trembling so badly that he couldn't find it. He tore at the material with his fingernails, but it remained intact. The footsteps were getting closer now and he could hear loud voices. Frantically he searched for his pocketknife until he remembered loaning it to Morris who, as usual, had failed to return it.

Then he stopped and stared at the shirts that he had flung about his compartment. They weren't his linen shirts from Muir and Mirrielees. They were cheap homemade cotton shirts. The pants were too short and the boots were too small. He slammed the lid. There had been a child's gold star on the spine of the case that his nephew had stuck there last summer. It was gone. This wasn't his case. These weren't his things.

When a knock came at the door he panicked and shoved the suitcase under the bed.

"Are you all right, sir?" It was the *provodnik*. "We heard a noise. Do you wish some assistance?"

"No, no. I'm fine," he said breathlessly.

"You sure?"

"Yes, leave me alone."

"Yes, very good, sir." And then the footsteps retreated down the hall and he heard "Says he's all right." "Maybe he's drunk?" Then a deeper voice: "Didn't sound drunk." The first voice: "Probably just out of his head. They're all out of their head."

Pavel sank down on the bed and waited until his heart slowed and his breathing became more regular. Then he crept out of his compartment and padded down the hallway to the carriage window. The men were still smoking under the electric light. The rain was still falling. Then in a huff of steam and smoke the train pitched forward and started to pull out of the station, going slowly at first, but soon picking up speed, plunging faster and faster into the gloom, a juggernaut of iron and fire. With a great sigh Pavel went back to his compartment and lay down on the cramped bed.

After a while he let his mind wander back to the Kovel terminal, to the man with all the children. He saw him picking up a child in one arm and an array of suitcases in the other . . . suitcases of all sizes and colors, suitcases like his own, stuffing them under his arm and in his hand, striding through the platform archway, while trailing his brood behind him. Then just before he disappeared under the arch, Pavel remembered that he turned back and glanced at him. At the time it barely registered. But now Pavel realized that it was more than just a random glance in his direction: It was a look of gratitude for a job well done.

Chapter Seven

December 1913

"IT'S TIME to begin, *maideleh*," she called out. "I'm waiting."

Berta broke an egg on the edge of the bowl and dropped the contents into a hollowed-out onion full of water. She swirled the mixture around with her finger while chanting a spell she made up on the spot.

"What is it, Mameh? What do you see?" asked Sura, running over and peering into the onion beside her mother.

"I see a long life, *maideleh*. A long life with a handsome husband and lots of children."

"I don't want children. I want horses."

"And lots of horses."

"Arabians?"

"Of course. A whole pasture full of them."

"Where?" said the child, peering into the onion.

"There," she said pointing. "Where the yolk swirls into the water."

"It tells you all that?"

"And much, much more."

"Like what?"

"Like you must eat your breakfast and get ready to go out."

They were sitting at the children's table near the stove in the nursery. It was an elaborate affair with its own kitchen and music room outfitted with downsized instruments, a schoolroom decorated with maps of the world, several closets full of clothes, and a wall of shelves lined with toys. All this magnificence, this extravagance of color and mechanical contrivances that whirred into life simply by winding a key, were placed there solely for the enjoyment of two children: Sura, a fearful five-year-old with tiny, nervous hands, darting eyes, long brown hair, and a rare smile, and Samuil, a precocious seven-year-old, whose insouciance and careless way of addressing adults made him seem much older.

"I don't want to go out, Mameh," Sura murmured, her large eyes staring out the window at the brilliant sun and its reflection on the billowy mound of snow that leveled the landscape outside their window.

"But you need fresh air and exercise. It'll be fun."

"It won't be fun at all. It's cold out there and I'll hate it."

"Where is your hairbrush, my darling?"

"Dunno."

"Where did you put it?" She hunted around and found it on a bookshelf. "Here, let me brush it out for you." She stood behind her daughter and began to brush out her thick curls while breathing in the comforting smell of her hair, of soap and starched linen.

"What if I get lost out there?" Sura fretted, her brow making a furrow under the fringe of hair.

"You won't get lost," Berta told her. "You're only going out into the yard."

"What if they don't find me and I freeze to death like that squirrel we saw the other day. Ow, Mama!"

"Sorry."

"And what if my hands break off and I melt and become all squishy and turn into a puddle."

"Galya won't let that happen. You say this every day and so far you're still here and you have hands and feet and you're not a puddle at all." Berta looked up when her son came in and watched as he collapsed in the chair opposite his sister.

"Why do they even come if they don't like the music?" he said sulkily. He grabbed a roll and began to butter it. Every Thursday Berta hosted a musical salon and Samuil was already anticipating the intrusion.

"How do you know they won't like it?" Berta asked.

"Because I heard them talking the last time they were here, Olga Nikolaevna and that other one, that friend of hers, the one with the big horse teeth."

"You mean you were spying on them."

"They said what a bore it was. And they wondered when it would end. Stupid women, why do you ask them? I wouldn't have them, not on a bet. I'd only have you and Tateh and Galya."

Sura ignored her brother and went on with her worries. "But Galya is always talking to the maids, Mameh. She could easily lose me and then I'd end up like the squirrel."

"No one is getting lost," Galya said, coming into the room with a basket full of laundry. The nursery was presided over by Galena Okorokova, a busty potato of a woman who spent her off days in her room conversing with the dead.

"See, darling? Galya wouldn't lose you. She'll never take her eyes off you."

"You don't know that. You're not even there. How do you know?"

"You're not getting lost, my little chicken," said Galya with a smile. "Galya is there and she watches you like a hawk. You're never out of her sight."

Samuil went on: "Why do you like them, Mameh? They only come to show off their diamonds and they're so boring and never have anything interesting to say."

"Then why do you spy on them?"

"I want to."

"You shouldn't spy on people. It isn't right and you know it. Nobody likes a spy."

"I don't care."

"Well, you should care. You have to get along in this world. And anyway, it's wrong."

"I don't think it's wrong," he said, buttering another piece. "I think it's educational. I learn all sorts of useful things." He took another bite and washed it down with warm milk.

"Not for a seven-year-old."

"And besides, I'm good at it," he said, putting down his glass. "It's my calling. Tateh says it's important to find your calling early in life and here I am only seven and already I've found mine." He was proud of the fact that he could hide almost anywhere, spy on the servants and guests, and then sell his tidbits to Galya for candy or extra time at the stables.

Berta held her daughter's chin in her hand and turned her head first to the left and then to the right. "There now, don't you look lovely?" She kissed her daughter's nose and Sura scowled and rubbed it. "Go on now," Berta said turning her daughter around and giving her a little shove. "It's time to get your coat and boots on. You're going out."

She watched the children put on their things at the front door. Samuil threw on his coat and hat and stuffed his gloves in his pocket, flung the door open, and, after calling back a halfhearted good-bye, raced down the steps and across the drive. Sura pulled on her gloves, pushing the wool down around each finger until they fit perfectly. She was like Berta in that way, taking her time to do things right. When she was done she put on her hat and followed Galya out the door. Berta stood in the doorway and watched her pick her way through the snow, following in Galya's footsteps, leaping from footprint to footprint to keep her boots dry. Berta had a sudden urge to run after her and scoop her up into her arms. She was such a small thing in a big world. It was heartbreaking to see her little figure struggling through the frozen expanse of snow and frost.

When Berta stepped back inside and closed the door, she heard Petr the valet and Vasyl the porter in the breakfast room chatting about a horse race that Petr had bet on and won. Apparently Vasyl hadn't followed his advice and was kicking himself for being left out of the winnings. She strode in and wished them a good morning. It was hardly morning. The sun was already high in the sky, throwing brilliant shafts of light against the damask wallpaper, washing out the color to a pale yellow.

Petr bowed slightly. "Good morning, Madame."

Vasyl wiped his hands on his pants and gave her a nod in deference, his eyes dropping to a spot on the floor.

"I see you've been busy," she said, looking around at the room.

"Yes, Madame," said Petr in his usual brisk way. "We will need two extra rows at least. Did Vera tell you? We thought we would use the breakfast chairs."

She thought for a moment. "Yes, good idea."

Since it was Thursday the breakfast room was being transformed into the music room. All the furniture had been cleared out except for the yellow tile stove in the corner and the piano that stood in front of the tall windows. The men had been setting up the chairs and now she could see what it was going to look like with the semicircle of folding chairs filling the room.

She wandered over to the window and looked out on the little park beside the house. It was blanketed with glittering snow. Galya was sitting on a bench bundled up in a beaver coat, gossiping with the nanny from across the road. The nanny's charges were sledding down the baby hill, as Samuil called it. Sura wasn't playing with them. She was sitting next to Galya, clutching her arm, looking anxious and bored at the same time. Samuil wasn't in sight and must've been around the back sledding down the big hill that led to the frozen pond.

Across the park on the road she saw a sledge whir by and turn into her drive. It was the boy with the ice sculpture. Once, a rearing horse had been delivered with a melted tail and hooves that were barely more than puddles. It had been delivered too late to send back. Berta thought it had probably been rejected by another house and sent to the Jews as an afterthought. After that she insisted that the sculpture be delivered early and that she inspect it herself.

Preparations had been going on since early morning. The floors had been washed and polished, the rugs swept, cupboards emptied of china and linen, and the chandeliers lowered and dusted. The flowers had been arranged in vases and now stood in the hall waiting to be placed throughout the house. Although the servants bustled from parlor to dining room, from upstairs to downstairs, from breakfast room to library, arms full, faces glistening with sweat, brooms and dusters at the ready, no room was more filled with commotion and anxiety than the kitchen. Berta usually avoided it on Thursdays. The cook was an irritable Slav from Kiev with a ferocious sense of entitlement and tolerated no interference in her domain. Unfortunately the ice sculpture was in the pantry and there was no way to get there except through the kitchen or outside and around the back. So rather than risk disturbing the cook, Berta wrapped a coat around her shoulders, put on her boots, and stepped out the front door.

The sun had just risen above the tallest trees and was shining down out of a flawless sky. The steps down to the drive had been cleared from last night's storm, but there were still traces of snow in the corners and a sheen of water over the marble made them slippery. Berta had to hold on to the hand rail, which was still covered with a sharp-edged pile of snow. Her gloved hand cleared it as she went down the steps, the moisture turning the fawn-colored leather a dark brown.

Berta's house sat perched on one of the highest points in the Berezina, on a little hill that overlooked the city of Cherkast. From there she could see the smoke from the chimney pots and the steam rising up from the rooftops. Further down she could just make out the ice fishermen's shanties on the frozen river and a line of moving dots that had to be the ice cutters coming down with their sledges to haul away great blocks of ice.

These people, along with their brethren in the factories, were peasants of the *chernozem*, the black earth: illiterate, superstitious; plagued by lice and tuberculosis, often landless, hungry; they came in from the countryside to earn a few rubles a day for ten hours of hard labor. They slept by their machines or on filthy cots in barracks. Most of them were zealous believers in miracle cures and in Russian Orthodoxy. Always their future had lain in a short life of hard work for the good of Mother Russia, but now they were raising their voices against the hard labor, the poverty, and the fines that were levied against them for the smallest infractions. Strikes were breaking out in Moscow and Saint Petersburg, over two thousand of them in 1912 alone. Men in visor caps, black leather jackets, and knee boots had come to Little Russia to organize and the workers were listening.

Berta came down the last few steps and followed the circular drive around to the side of the house where the snow was deeper and the going more difficult. The ground had been trampled by a jumble of footprints and sledge tracks left by the vendors who had been coming and going all morning. She took advantage of the tracks and walked in them, following them around to the back of the house. While she was making her way she idly examined the confusion of footprints at her feet and out of them identified her son's small boot print. She could tell they were his by the size, the short stride, and the shallow depression.

She tracked them down the drive and was surprised to find that they didn't lead her to the sledding hill but to the pantry door. She had a knack for picking out her children in a crowd—a glimpse of hair, a brown arm, the back of a head. She could find her children anywhere.

Vera, the maid, and Zina, the cook's helper, were busy polishing silver at the harvest table and jumped to their feet when she walked through the door. The delivery boy stood in deference, whipped off his cap, and kept his eyes on his shoes.

"No, please, it's all right. I've just come to look at the sculpture."

Zina said, "It's over here, Madame. Here, I'll get it for you." Zina had a wide, pleasant face with a broad nose and a space between her two front teeth. She often suppressed a smile, pretending to be shy and to know her place despite the spark of mischief in her eyes. Samuil said she occasionally stole away to meet a trolley conductor under the big elms over by the bench. When she would come back and tell Vera all about it, he'd be hiding nearby and listening to every word, which he would then sell to Galya for more time with his horse.

The ice sculpture was sitting at the other end of table wrapped in burlap to keep it cold. Zina untied the sacks and they fell away, revealing an arch of wheat shafts over a nest of birds. "Ah . . . look at that. So pretty," Zina said, examining it. "Clever too. And them is ducks, I suppose. Little ducks in a nest."

Berta had ordered robins, but she didn't mind the ducks. She told the delivery boy that she would keep it and that his employers could bill her. He nodded but didn't leave right away. Instead he glanced at the hot cup of tea that he would soon be leaving.

"Go ahead. Finish it. Nobody minds."

He looked up at her and nodded gratefully. And for a moment nobody moved while they waited for her to leave.

"Yes, well, that's it then." She looked up and addressed the room. "Samuil . . . time to go."

The others gaped at her. "He is not here, Madame," Zina said.

And then to the shelves that lined the walls, to the dry goods, canned goods, cooking utensils, and the great wheel of cheese that sat up high on the top shelf, she called out again, "Come along, Samuil. I mean it."

"If we see him, we will tell him you are looking for him."

"That's just it, you'll never know he's here." This time she tried a different tack. "If you come out right now, I'll take you to the concert next week."

Silence . . . and then a muffled voice from the top shelf, from behind the cheese: "What are they playing?"

Zina looked at Vera in alarm. She was probably wondering what the boy had heard and more important what he would repeat.

Berta thought. "I don't remember."

"Then how am I supposed to know if I want to come?"

"Samuil . . ." she said wearily.

He peeked out from behind the wheel and then reluctantly climbed out of his corner and down the shelves, jumping the last few feet to the ground.

THURSDAYS RAN smoothly for the most part, but there were always problems along the way. Sometimes the wrong flowers would arrive, once the poultry man ran out of game hens, and another time there were no quinces in Cherkast. Any number of things could go wrong on Thursday. But nothing as catastrophic as the phone call she received that afternoon.

"I'm so sorry to be calling this late," croaked the pianist from the other end of line. "I thought I could play for your guests, but the doctor says I'm not to go out. I have a horrible cold as you can hear. I hope you will forgive me."

Berta struggled to hide her annoyance. "Of course," she muttered. "Don't give it another thought." She wanted to say something about canceling this late, but the girl was a rising star in the musical circle and she couldn't afford to alienate her. So she forced herself to sound solicitous, wished the girl well, and even offered a few home remedies that included teas made of mullein flower and yarrow to draw out the fever.

During the next hour, Berta telephoned every pianist, violinist, and cellist she knew in Cherkast. There weren't many. While she pleaded and cajoled, flattered and bribed, she scratched a widening chip of paint off the Chinese lacquer table. It was unusual to have a telephone alcove this elaborate in the Berezina. The houses in the neighborhood were large but nothing compared to the Moscow mansions. The Alshonsky house was the exception. It wasn't larger than the rest, but it had been furnished at great expense. The house had once been owned by a fish merchant who had lost his business due to bad luck and the high cost of debt. Hershel often reminded Berta that it was about to do the same to them, especially if she didn't stop throwing money away on furniture and draperies.

By the end of her fruitless search, she had chipped away a whole corner of the table. She was cleaning the paint out from under her fingernail when Galya happened to walk by carrying a tray for the children. Berta looked up and brightened with a sudden idea. "Galya . . . who is that famous medium you're always talking about?'

"Marfa Gorbunova?"

"Yes. Is she good?"

"Very good, Madame. The best in all the Russias."

"How do I get a hold of her?"

Galya put down the tray on the hall table. Her lips puckered in thought. "I know a woman who knows her. I could go around and see if she knows where to find her."

"Good, could you do that for me?"

"Of course."

"I mean right now. I'm in a bind. I need her to come here tonight."

Galya stiffened. "You want her to come to your party?"

"What's wrong that? I think she'll be very entertaining."

Galya pulled herself up and cradled her breasts in her arms. "I am very sorry, Madame, but Marfa Gorbunova does not entertain guests. She does not do party tricks. She communicates with those who have passed over to the other side."

"Don't worry. She'll be treated with the utmost respect. Now go ask your friend where to find her. We don't have much time."

Galya hesitated. "She might not know."

"Well, ask her anyway. And when you find this woman tell her that if she comes to us we'll be very grateful. Tell her we understand money is of little value to a spiritualist of her standing, but still there will be a generous compensation."

Galya shook her head doubtfully, picked up the tray, and started up the stairs. She groaned occasionally and stopped frequently to catch her breath. Berta wanted to hurry her along, but knew that if she said anything, there would be a long-winded complaint about aching legs and a weak back, and that would take much longer than if she didn't say anything at all.

BERTA REALIZED, with a pang of disappointment, that Hershel wasn't coming to her party. She was sitting at her dressing table while Vera pinned the last silk rose in her hair. He would be missing another party and she would once again have to make excuses for him and pretend it didn't matter. A brief spasm of irritation crossed her face as she stared vacantly at the little porcelain box filled with hairpins.

"Madame is not pleased?" asked Vera.

"Uh?" She looked up briefly. "Oh no, it's lovely. Perfect."

"More roses perhaps?"

"No, it's fine. It's done, Vera. You've done a wonderful job. Thank you."

They paused to listen when they heard the first guests arriving downstairs. "Well, that's it then," Berta said. She rose with a sigh of resignation and checked her reflection in the full-length mirror. Not even the yards of chiffon and the girdle of beading at her waist could lift her spirits now.

On the way down the stairs she reminded herself that it did no good to be angry. It only got in the way of her duties as a hostess and made her party a miserable chore. And besides, she had no right to object. They had made their bargain a long time ago. In exchange for her lovely life Hershel had the freedom to come and go without question. He never stayed away for more than a few weeks at a time and he always came home greedy for her company. She never begrudged him his good works in the *shtetlekh*, until now, when he had begun to miss her parties. No one said anything of course, but she knew his recent absences were beginning to stir interest.

Downstairs, she pushed open the double doors leading to the parlor and fixed what she hoped was an optimistic smile on her face. Inside she found her first guests, the Tretiakovs, struggling to their feet to greet her. "My two early birds," Berta said, meeting them halfway among the palms and ferns and heavily fringed furniture.

Aleksandra Dmitrievna kissed her first on one cheek and then on the other. "That's just it. Who wants to be the first? Just for once I'd like to be a little late." She looked pointedly at her husband, Aleksei Sergeevich.

"What difference does it make?" he grumbled, taking Berta's hand. He had no patience for his silly wife. He was a short man with a moustache resembling a furry creature that had stretched out under his nose and died. He looked directly into Berta's face and gave her hand a gentle squeeze. "Madame Alshonsky." She liked Lenya and he liked her. It was an odd sort of friendship because they rarely spoke, at least not directly, but there were often moments like this.

"Doesn't she look lovely, Lenya."

Without taking his eyes off her, he said, "Of course she looks lovely. She always looks lovely." This was not a compliment. Aleksei Sergeevich did not give compliments, as he saw no use for them. It was merely the truth as he saw it.

Aleksandra Dmitrievna and Berta had become friends since that day they met on the train to Mosny. Berta hadn't lost Alix's card but kept it as a memento and looked her up when she arrived in Cherkast. She thought their friendship would be an entrée into Alix's world, but Berta soon found that the society in Cherkast was even more closed to Jews than the one in Moscow. In fact it was something of a mystery to Alix's friends why the Tretiakovs socialized with the Alshonskys. They were Jews and, worse, Jews of an indeterminate origin. Hardly the social equals of the Tretiakovs.

When Berta realized that she wouldn't be included in Alix's set, she made up one of her own. In contrast, her circle was made up almost entirely of mongrels. Her guests were castoffs of the prominent families: disinherited black sheep, progressive thinkers, radicals, and artists. There was a Jewish textile mill owner and a few Jewish wheat merchants, but mostly their set was young, smart, and chic. This was the draw for Alix. While she was not young, she thought of herself as spirited and every bit as modern as Berta and her crowd.

Soon after the parlor began to fill up, Olga Nikolaevna, the painter, arrived with a new lover in tow. She was small with a pixie's face and the first in their circle to wear her hair in a bob, which she secured by a satin headband and an ostrich feather. Her new lover was older than his predecessors and acted as if he were used to better company. Olga introduced him only as Valya and added in a loud conspiratorial whisper that he was extremely rich and had a wife and a whole herd of children.

Poor Pavla arrived next, looking grim and out of place. Everyone called her poor Pavla because her husband had been sent to Verkhoyansk, a remote outpost in eastern Siberia, for hiding a few SRs, social revolutionaries, at his summer estate. Now, in order to survive, Pavla had to sell off everything. Everyone pitied her, but no one wanted to spend much time with her.

Yuvelir arrived after that with a few of his friends and introduced them around as the new wave in poetry. Yuvelir was a poet, a vegetarian, and a hypochondriac and often complained about his cruel childhood to anybody who would listen. His family owned several mills in the region; he was poor because he refused to come into the business. He considered himself an artist and above the concerns of the material world, that is, until he had to pay the rent. Then he would go to his mother, who had money of her own and no qualms about supplying her son with all the material comforts he so proudly eschewed.

Mademoiselle Zuckerkandl and her brother, the writer David Zuckerkandl, arrived with Valentin Guseva, the son of the textile manufacturer. Valentin was pretty like a girl with a full feminine mouth, long lashes over dark eyes, and delicate fingers. They called him *Her Majesty* in school and he never got over it. Although it nearly destroyed his academic career, it also drove him to shooting, which is why he became a crack shot and famous all over Cherkast.

After that, a whole crowd of odds and ends arrived: a sculptor, a doctor and his wife, a minor composer, and the Rosensteins. When

Berta saw the Rosensteins her hand flew to her mouth and she gave a little gasp. She had forgotten to tell them of the change in program. They had lost their daughter to consumption some years back and she thought they might not be comfortable with a séance. But Madame Rosenstein assured her that it would be all right. "We don't believe in such things, my dear," she said in her breathy voice. She was one of those hectic little women who spent their life seeing to the needs of others. "We've been invited to three this year already."

Petr came in with a calling card on a silver tray. Since nobody in Berta's set bothered with such formality, she picked it up with interest. It belonged to Marfa Gorbunova and she had written a message on the back: *I must see you out in the foyer. Your evening depends on it.*

Madame Gorbunova had very definite ideas on how Berta could best secure the success of her evening. They all had to do with making sure that Madame Gorbunova was comfortable and her needs were met. After she introduced herself and her assistant, a correct little man named Monsieur Fevrier, she launched right into the list.

"First, I never see the guests before I perform a communion. Next, I'll need a small table with a tablecloth and two candles. I'll need two whiskeys, no water, no ice, and a linen napkin. In addition, I'll need a comfortable chair and a small footrest that will fit under the table. A lap blanket of pure wool is essential and a little pillow for my back is preferable. Monsieur Fevrier will see to everything, but we will need to be shown to the communion room as soon as possible and provided with all my necessities."

At first Berta was a little put off by this speech. She thought that since she had hired Madame Gorbunova for the evening, the medium would treat her with a certain amount of deference. Now she could see that she had been wrong. Since she didn't want to jeopardize her party over a question of pride, she agreed to everything on the list and even showed them into the breakfast room herself.

On the way, Madame Gorbunova took her time to look around. She stopped to finger a pair of brightly colored majolica parrots on a perch. "You have a lovely home here, Madame Alshonsky. I have never been in a Jewish home before. I didn't think they were so nice and clean."

Berta did what she always did when faced with comments like that: She kept her expression neutral and said nothing.

Later, after everyone had filed into the room and found a seat, Monsieur Fevrier turned off the lights. The only remaining light, apart from the firelight that escaped through the cracks around the grate and door of the tile stove, came from two ruby red globes that stood on either side of the little table at the front of the room. They glowed and threw blood red patterns on the walls and on the ceiling.

Madame Gorbunova waited for a few minutes to let the tension build. Then she entered the room, walked over to the little table, and greeted her audience. Her gestures were a little too large and her words a little too deliberate. Berta guessed that she finished off the two whiskeys and hadn't bothered to share with Monsieur Fevrier. In a prepared speech Madame Gorbunova requested that the audience remain quiet throughout the communion. She said that while she could not promise anything, her spirit guide, Prince Pietro Cribari, had told her there were spirits asking to be heard. She explained that she could not be responsible for anything that was said during the communion, that she was just a vessel, a human telephone, if you like, and nothing more.

Then she took her seat behind the table and closed her eyes. Slowly she relaxed; her chin slumped forward until it came to rest just above her large bosom. After a while her breathing became deep and regular and her hands fell out of her lap and hung by her sides. She appeared to be in a deep trance.

"You may sit up now," Monsieur Fevrier said quietly.

Madame Gorbunova sat up and opened her eyes. She stared straight ahead, seemingly blind to the twenty or so people who sat in their chairs leaning forward, holding their breath.

Nothing happened.

The audience sat waiting, growing bored, whispering among themselves, and fidgeting in their seats. Berta was beginning to worry. But soon Madame Gorbunova's eyes began to flutter liked moth wings and she started to speak in a husky man's voice. It was the voice of Prince Cribari, an Italian who always spoke Russian, a fact that nobody bothered to question.

"There are three of us here tonight," the Prince said through Madame Gorbunova. She shifted her position in the chair, crossing one arm over her stomach and using it to brace her other arm. She held an invisible cigarette between her fingers and occasionally took a puff.

"Can you describe them?" asked Monsieur Fevrier.

A long pause. "A soldier with medals on his chest. He is angry because he wasn't supposed to be shot. He says it was a mistake. It was supposed to be the other fellow who ducked to light his cigarette. He is looking for his wife. He sees that she is not here tonight, so he has agreed to step aside."

Another long pause. "A foundry worker from Moscow. He is upset because he says he is late for work and they will fine him if he doesn't hurry. He cannot understand why he is so cold, since he works in front of a furnace all day long. He doesn't know he is dead. The others have been trying to explain it to him, but he refuses to listen."

She sat up and craned her neck as if trying to see something at the back of the room. "I see a little girl over there with brown curls. She is coming over. A sweet little thing. She has something to say."

"What is her name?"

Madame Gorbunova took a long puff on her invisible cigarette and blew out invisible smoke. "Eva."

There was urgent whispering in the room. The Rosensteins huddled together, speaking in low intense voices.

"May we speak to her now?" the assistant said, quietly.

Madame Gorbunova's head slumped down on her chest. Then, after a moment or two, she slowly raised it again. This time she uncrossed her legs and twirled a finger around an imaginary curl. Even though she was well over forty with baggy cheeks and thinning dark hair, she had transformed herself into a little girl.

"Mameh, I didn't hide Bobbeh's teeth."

"Oh my God." Madame Rosenstein rose from her seat.

Monsieur Rosenstein grabbed her arm and pulled her back down again. "Sit down," he whispered fiercely. "You're making a spectacle out of yourself. It's only a trick."

"It wasn't me, Mameh."

"It's Eva!" Madame Rosenstein cried out in a hoarse sob.

Her husband said, "It's not Eva. She is dead and in the Garden of Paradise."

"I was just looking at them. I wasn't going to hide them."

"I know, darling. She's not angry with you."

"They fell, Mameh."

"I know. We found them. They were behind the bed."

"Bobbeh is angry with me."

"No, she's not angry, my precious. She loves you." Her voice broke and tears spilled down her cheeks.

"Bobbeh is angry because she can't find her teeth."

A mist began to form over Madame Gorbunova's head. A shock rippled through the audience followed by a cry from Madame Rosenstein. Monsieur Rosenstein's hand shook as he took hold of his wife's arm. "We're leaving," he said firmly. But when he tried to get up, his legs buckled out from under him and he sat down.

A hand reached out for Berta's shoulder. "Madame . . ."

She jumped, turned, and found Vera standing behind her. "What is it?" she hissed.

"A telegram."

"Not now, Vera."

"It's from His Honor."

"For God's sakes, we're right in the middle of—"

As she said these words the mist evaporated. After a moment of darkness, Monsieur Rosenstein led his sobbing wife from the room. Madame Gorbunova opened her eyes and watched them leave. Then she looked around at the crowd and asked Monsieur Fevrier what had happened.

Chapter Eight

December 1913

HERSHEL stepped off the train and screwed up his face against the cold. Behind him the train was belching and spewing out a curtain of steam that evaporated in the cold air. The snow blew in sideways under the platform roof and blanketed the worn boards, piling up against the benches and hurrying the passengers inside. Clutching his hat with one hand and his suitcase with the other, Hershel ran for the station door, slipping on a patch of ice and catching himself on the back of a nearby bench.

The station was stifling and smelled of burned butter and pickled vegetables. There was a railway restaurant on one side of the terminal with its display of blue mineral water bottles stacked in a pyramid. He caught his reflection in the glass partition that separated it from the rest of the station. Flakes of snow still clung to his beard and he brushed them off, reminding himself that it needed trimming.

Hershel strode to the ticket counter where he called over the stationmaster and gave him his suitcase to watch and a ten-kopeck coin. On his way out through the big glass doors he checked his pocket watch and found that it was half past seven. He had left instructions in Kherson that morning that he wanted a telegram delivered to Berta at this time so she would think he was still there. He knew she wouldn't be happy with him when she read it and that he would have to make it up to her when he got home. He pictured her in the foyer, dressed for her salon, tearing open the telegram, reading it, crumpling it, and handing it back to Vera. He knew after that she'd take a moment to compose herself before returning to her guests, adopting that strained half smile that she reserved for public disappointments. He didn't like disappointing her, but there was nothing to be done about it. His presence in Poltava was unavoidable.

Out on the sidewalk his eyes teared from the cold, but he didn't mind. It woke him up. He'd been on the train since early morning, traveling up from Kherson, following the Dnieper past Elisavetgrad and finally on to his destination. He couldn't tell Berta that he was in Poltava, because it was only about fifty versts southeast of Cherkast and she would expect him home for her party. So in the telegram he wrote that he was still in Kherson meeting a buyer for supper.

A young couple ran past him, holding hands and skipping around the slower-moving pedestrians. They ran over to a tram that sat waiting on the tracks. Hershel walked over to the same tram and followed the couple up the steps. He paid the conductor and sat at a window seat looking at his reflection in the glass. The tram was mostly empty except for a small group of soldiers in the back. They were passing around a bottle. They had probably just started drinking since they weren't even half drunk.

The tram started up the hill, passing dimly lit streets and shops. All the way along the horses strained against the steep grade, steam rising off their flanks, their hooves crunching on the snow, their breath whitening the air. On Tzarskaya Square the shops were still open and brightly lit. There were Jewish shops of quality: the Dochman Stationery shop, the Aronheim and Cohn Department store, and Albert Baum's grocery shop. There was a shop that sold baskets and another that sold hats and another for gramophones and English bicycles. On one corner a small band was playing and a few couples were dancing in the street.

Hershel got off at the corner of Petrovskaya and Ulitza Kotlyarevskago in front of the bronze statue of the Little Russian poet I. P. Kotlyarevsky. He stood on the corner to get his bearings and started down Petrovskaya in the direction of the Jewish district. They were paving the sidewalk on that side of the square and the workman had left piles of wooden blocks along the curb. He had to avoid them and step down into the snow to make his way along, avoiding the slippery ice wherever he could.

The Yiddish Art Theater was located on the street of bakeries. It was in a converted warehouse, a drafty building with blacked-out windows, a rough stage, a dusty curtain, and row upon row of salvaged theater seats. The house was full that night because a new play, one direct from America, had just opened that weekend and the word in town was that it was a three-handkerchief performance. Hershel sat in the middle of a row in the orchestra section among noisy couples, whining children, and picnickers sitting in their coats eating their supper out of a basket. There was no attempt made to quiet down even after the curtain was raised. Instead they continued to talk loudly, calling to one another across the theater and passing food around as if they were at their kitchen table. Fortunately the plot was simple and the acting was so broad that it was easy to follow. Not that Hershel cared about the performance.

He looked around at the people sitting next to him. To his right was a prosperous-looking fellow, his wife, and five children; to his left was an elderly couple eating chicken and kasha from covered bowls. A row of yeshiva students sat in front of him and beside them sat several widows wearing black dresses and heavy winter shawls.

At intermission he got up and followed the crowd into the lobby. He went outside for a smoke along with three other brave souls. The gusts were so violent that the snow seemed to fall upward into the black sky. A dog ran by with a muzzle covered in ice. Across the street a figure hurried along the snowy sidewalk wearing a greatcoat and clutching a blanket around his shoulders for warmth. Hershel found a sheltered spot against the building and after several attempts managed to light his cigar. It was a waste of a good cigar since he couldn't possibly finish it before intermission was over, but he hadn't had one all day and the urge was strong. While he puffed away he studied his fellow smokers huddled against the building. None of them returned his interest. Instead they kept their eyes averted, taking long pulls on their cigarettes and filling the night air with plumes of white smoke.

The audience quieted down for the second half of the performance. There was too much going on even for this garrulous bunch to ignore. The hero, who had escaped the army and fled to America in the first act, was never heard of again. The heroine kept waiting for a letter that never came. When word finally reached her that her fiancé was killed in an accident, she was forced to marry another man. The dead hero came back in the final scene to speak through her mouth, vowing to love her forever. Women wiped away their tears and blew into handkerchiefs. Men grew quiet and children stopped fidgeting. Only Hershel seemed unmoved. He kept looking at his watch and wondering when it would be over. Finally the bride killed herself and the curtain came down. After numerous curtain calls, the house lights came up and the audience filed out.

Hershel kept his seat until the theater cleared. He looked around at the empty rows of seats and wondered what he should do next. Should he give up and leave? It was possible that his contact never showed. Maybe he sensed some danger of which Hershel wasn't aware. Maybe he had taken the money and left town. It wouldn't be the first time Hershel had been cheated. But then he thought to look under his seat and then the seat next to him, where he found the suitcase. As he picked it up and walked up the aisle to the door, a child's gold star on the spine of the case caught the stage lighting and winked.

It was late. He didn't expect to find a cab in this district, so he wasn't surprised to find the street empty. Most of the theater crowd lived in the vicinity and had already hurried home. He knew it was going to be a long cold walk down to Tzarskaya Square. As a stranger carrying a traveling case in the deserted streets, he was more concerned about standing out than getting frostbite. He finished pulling on his gloves, picked up the case, and started down the hill. Fortunately the wind was at his back. He took care not to slip on the ice, navigating his way down the dark street.

Just before the square he saw two gendarmes smoking on the corner under a lamppost. They took the smoke deeply into their lungs and let it out in billowy puffs while they talked. When one of them spotted Hershel, he nudged the other and together they watched him struggle down the slippery hill. He knew Poltava well. He had met "friends" here many times and knew the streets, especially the ones around the square. So without hesitation he stopped to talk to the police officers.

"I think I'm lost. I have a warm room and a bed waiting for me somewhere around here. You know where I can find Gogolevskaya?"

The one with a fat neck that spilled in rolls over his collar nodded and gestured down the street. "It is on your right. You are headed in the right direction, just keep going." Hershel thanked him and walked on. When he came to Gogolevskaya, he turned in, just in case they were watching. He kept walking, knowing that the street curved back to the main road farther on.

By the time he got back to the station the restaurant was closed, which was too bad, because he was hungry. He retrieved his other case from the stationmaster and found a bench where he could doze while he waited. Of course the train was late but not hours late, as it usually was. It arrived in a cloud of smoke and a hiss of steam, coming to a clamorous halt of grinding iron and screeching brakes. Most of the windows were dark and the shades were drawn. Hershel walked down the platform and boarded the train somewhere in the middle.

He was hoping for an empty compartment but found it crowded with sleeping army officers, their greatcoats thrown over their bodies for warmth, brass buttons gleaming in the subdued light, braids, epaulettes, and knee-high boots of fine leather. A few stirred when he walked in but soon closed their eyes and went back to sleep. He hoisted the suitcases up onto the overhead shelf and settled down in the last empty seat for a watchful night. But he was too exhausted to stay awake and soon closed his eyes. After the train fell into the easy rhythm of the tracks, he drifted off.

It was a gray dawn when he stepped out of the railway station in Cherkast. The outlines of the buildings, trees, and sledges were slowly coming into focus, their edges hardening against a lightening sky. He waved over a sled and put his cases in first and then climbed in beside them.

"Number 237 Lubiansky Street," he told the cabman. He was telling him how to get there when the driver interrupted him. "Alshonsky. I know where it is. Go up there all the time. You are an early one. Never had one this early before."

He flicked the reins and the little horse trudged on through the snowy streets. Hershel sat back and closed his eyes. There was something satisfying about living in a house that the cabmen knew, a house that wasn't just a structure, but a landmark.

Occasionally, he'd look back at the journey from Leski to the top of the Berezina and marvel. He knew luck had a lot to do with it and never fooled himself into believing that it was all due to his talent alone. As the sled took him past the warehouse district and up to the nicer shops, past the comfortable homes to the larger houses in the Berezina, he managed to forget about all the money he owed, the debt that was woven into the upholstery of every chair, rug, and drape. Instead he remembered his first job with the consortium, unloading sacks of wheat from the barges. From the barges to the Berezina, what would his father have said? He would've cautioned his son to look for the tip of the blue tail, the gleaming teeth, and the claw. *He'll be under there*, he would have said. *The blue man always is.*

The sled pulled into the drive and deposited him at the door. He paid the cabman and carried his suitcases up the front steps to the carved oak door and inserted his key into the lock. When he walked into the foyer he heard snoring coming from the parlor. He followed it and found Yuvelir sleeping on the sofa with a blanket tossed over his shoulders, his head buried in a pillow, his blond hair streaming over his face. Hershel thought about waking him and sending him home but decided against it. It would have meant a conversation, and besides, he was used to finding a stray guest sleeping in his parlor after a party.

He carried the cases upstairs and stopped off in his office. He fumbled in the dark until he found the desk lamp and switched it on. The lamp only lit a small portion of the room, leaving the rest in semidarkness. There was a staircase to one side of the desk that was decorated with carved devils and demons from the Faust legend. The small puddle of light elongated their features and cast eerie shadows on the wall behind them. Hershel went to his desk and pulled out the top drawer. He emptied out the few contents and turned the drawer over. Taped to the underside was a small key. He took the key and went into a closet full of winter coats, left over from past seasons. He moved them aside, revealing a small door near the baseboard. He used the key to unlock it and pushed it open. Then he went back to retrieve the suitcase and quietly unloaded the revolvers and the newspapers into the hidden cupboard. Once the case was empty, he closed the little door, locked it, and returned the key to the underside of the drawer and slid it back into place. Then he turned off the light and walked down the hall to Berta's bedroom.

They called it her room even though he always slept there, except when he came in late and didn't want her to know. It was a comfortable room filled with feminine things that he found endearing: several wardrobes stuffed with dresses and shoes, a dressing table laid out with silver brushes, combs, and a silver bowl filled with hairpins, and buttons, broken chains, and objects he couldn't name. There was a Chinese screen in the corner that she had bought at auction for a ridiculous sum and a large porcelain vase filled with peacock feathers that made him sneeze. The fire in the porcelain stove was fresh as was the fire in the fireplace. He pulled off his boots without the help of Petr and set them down on the floor. Then he pulled his shirt over his head without bothering to unbutton it.

"What happened to you," she asked without opening her eyes.

"Didn't you get my telegram?" He dropped his pants and stepped out of them.

"I thought you said you'd be home for my party."

He came over to the bed and lay down beside her. "Sorry, *mishka*. I wanted to come. I really did."

"Sometimes I think you don't like my parties." She reached out a hand and drew him closer. He put his head on her breast and could hear her heart beating.

"And how am I supposed to answer that? If I tell you the truth, you'll be angry with me, and if I do not, you'll accuse me of lying."

He let his fingertips trail down her sternum between her breasts and over her belly, moving down to the cleft between her legs. His fingers were in no hurry.

"So you couldn't lie in a believable way?" she said, pushing him away and pulling the sheet up over her body.

"I like the idea of your parties." He slowly pulled the sheet back down again. This time he kissed her breasts, brushing her nipples with his lips the way she liked, teasing her with the conversation.

"Well, you would've liked this one."

"Why?"

She sucked in her breath. "There was a séance."

He stopped what he was doing and looked up at her. "A séance?"

"No, excuse me, a communion."

"With ghosts and mist and tambourines?"

"No tambourines. I think there was mist. It was all very dramatic. Madame Gorbunova," she breathed.

He slid down between her legs and parted her thighs. He was home in his den now, safe from the world, hidden deep underground. Her scent welcomed him, sweet and loamy with a hint of perfumed powder. "Who's Madame Gorbunova?"

She sucked in her breath. "Galya's medium. The one she always goes on about."

He looked up at her and burst out laughing.

"What's so funny?"

"Now, that, I would've liked to have seen."

"I know. You would've been amazed."

"I thought you didn't believe in that kind of thing."

"You should've seen it. It would've made a believer out of you."

"I doubt it. They use all kinds of tricks, you know."

"I don't think so. Not this time. It looked too real."

He shook his head and looked at her with affection. "*Mishka . . .*"

"What?"

"I missed you."

She gave him a little laugh, scrunched down under the covers, and took his penis in her hand. When she put it into her mouth, words left him; syntax became meaningless; the world began to fade. She stretched her body over his belly and chest and sat up over his pelvis, guiding him in. Slowly, methodically, she began to rotate her hips, leaning forward until her nipples just brushed his lips. Her eyes remained half open and glittering in the firelight.

Hershel was a lucky man. He was in love with his wife. Other men had mistresses and dalliances of all kinds, but he never did. He still liked having sex with her. She thrilled him. The events in his life were often so chaotic and uncertain that he needed something he could count on, a place to come home to, and Berta provided him with that. Yet, she, herself, wasn't predictable. He knew her to be capricious, moody, and even trivial at times. She could be exasperating and still he adored her. He couldn't help it. Their relationship was one of his many contradictions. He needed certitude, a quiet routine, possession, and belonging, but he also loved a challenge. And Berta was all of that.

"TATEH . . . Tateh . . . wake up."

Hershel opened his eyes and found his daughter's face not three inches from his own. "What is it?" he mumbled, turning over and closing them again.

"You have to tell Galya that she can't put Masha out into the snow."

"Who's Masha?"

"*Masha*, Tateh!" she said with exasperation, her eyes filling with tears. "She had her kittens last night and Galya wants to put them out into the snow. You have to get up." She shook Hershel and bounced on the bed. "You have to tell her she can't do it."

"Yes, all right. Only let me sleep now."

"*No, Tateh!* She won't listen to me. You have to get up and tell her *now*!" She pulled on his arm and tried to drag him out of bed.

"All right, Sura. All right, my darling, I'm getting up." He sat up and wiped his face with a hand. "Where's your mother?"

"Looking for Samuil."

Just then the door opened and Berta came in. "Sura, I told you not to wake your father."

"I want him to tell Galya she can't put Masha out."

"I already told her. She's making a proper place for Masha."

Sura jumped up and ran for the door. "Did you tell her to use the laundry basket? Galya," she shouted out in the hall. "Use the laundry basket!"

Hershel collapsed back down on his pillow. "What time is it?"

"It's late. Nearly teatime. Why don't you get up and help me look for Samuil."

"Where is he?"

"If I knew that, I wouldn't be looking for him. I think he's in your study."

Hershel's smile faded. "My study? I don't want him in my study." Hershel swung his legs over the edge of the bed and stood up.

"I'll go see if I can find him," she said.

He found his clothes laid out on a chair and started to dress. "No, I'll go."

"We'll both go."

"Berta!" But she was already out and calling down the hall.

Hershel heard her by the door of his study calling out Samuil's name. He tucked in his shirt and buttoned his trousers. He wanted to put on his boots, but more than that he wanted to get his wife and child out of his study. So he left the boots and went barefoot out into the hall. There were the usual sounds of the maids chattering downstairs and the clatter of pots and pans from the kitchen. He found the door to his study closed. When he tried the knob and found it locked his apprehension began to grow.

"Berta, open the door," he said quietly.

He listened for footsteps and heard them crossing the room, first muffled by the rug and then loud on the hardwood floor and then muffled again. The door opened and Samuil stood there nearly in tears.

"I'm sorry, Tatch. It was just a game. I won't tell anybody, I promise."

He looked past his son to his wife, who was sitting on the floor in front of the closet. In her lap were two revolvers and a German pistol.

She looked up. Her face was stiff with shock. "Hershel?"

He ignored her and took his son's hand. "Samuil, come here." He sat down in his desk chair and drew his son over. Then he put his hands on his shoulders and looked into his face. "I'm going to tell you something very important and I want you to listen."

Samuil began to cry.

"There's no need for that. You're not in trouble. But I need you to understand what I'm about to tell you." Samuil nodded and stifled a sob. "In Russia, Jews are not allowed to own guns. Do you know what that means?"

He nodded again and brushed away his tears.

"What does it mean?"

"They shouldn't have guns."

"That's right. So those guns shouldn't be here. And if anybody ever found out, we'd all be in serious trouble."

"I'm not going to tell anybody, Tateh."

"Nobody, not Galya, not anybody."

"I know. I won't tell a soul." The little cords on his neck stood out as he tried to catch a sob.

"I know you won't." Hershel pulled his son to him. His hair smelled of mothballs from the closet. "We just have to be very, very careful. There are people out there who want to do us harm. Not Mameh and me, necessarily, but other Jews in the towns and *shtetlekh*, understand?"

Samuil nodded.

"They do terrible things to them. And the Jews have no one to protect them, not the police or the army. So they have to protect themselves and that's what these guns are for."

"Yes, Tateh."

"So now you understand."

He nodded.

"Good. Now go find your sister. Help her with Masha's kittens."

Samuil nodded and walked slowly to the door. When he had gone, Berta got up from the floor and went over to the sofa and sank down on the cushions. She grabbed a pillow and held it to her chest, wrapping her arms around it for comfort.

"What are they doing here, Hershel?" Her voice was even and cold.

He picked up a gun and examined it. "They're called spitters," he said, casually fingering the trigger. "As if all they'll do is spit at you."

"You think this is a joke?"

"I'm just keeping them for a friend."

"A friend. What friend?"

"A friend, Berta. You don't need to know."

"Is he a Jew? What kind of a friend asks you to keep guns in your house?"

"They'll be gone by tomorrow."

"By tonight, Hershel."

His eyes narrowed. "I don't take orders."

He stooped to gather up the guns and walked into the closet. He put them back in the hidden cupboard, locked it, and came back out with the key. He went over to the desk, pulled the drawer out, and taped the key to the underside.

"And what if you get caught?"

"I won't."

"But what if you do? You'll be sent to Siberia. You'll die in a Siberian labor camp."

"I'm not going to get caught. You're getting excited over nothing."

"Nothing, he says! Our life, is it nothing? Our children, our house, our home?"

"That's enough, Berta."

"Why are you doing this? Why are you jeopardizing everything?"

"I said that's enough!"

He turned his back on her and looked out the window. He could see her reflection in the window pane, sitting on the couch on the other side of the room, her lips pursed in disapproval. He was aware of the cold floor under his bare feet and the draft coming in through the French windows. He suddenly wanted his boots. He wanted to be dressed. More than that, he wanted to be away from her. He turned and walked purposefully past the couch to the door.

"Where are you going?"

"I want to get dressed."

"But we haven't finished yet."

"This conversation is over." He walked out the door.

She jumped up and ran after him. "Hershel . . ."

He kept on going.

"Hershel!"

"I'd advise you to stay away, Berta." He walked into the bedroom and shut the door a little too hard.

At first he was too angry to think. He sat down on one of her fancy chairs, then realizing where he was, grabbed his boots and went across the hall to his own room. It was freezing in there, so he rang for Vera. She didn't have to be told what he wanted. She appeared at the door with a basket full of wood and promptly got the fire going in the stove. While he waited to warm up he poured himself a whiskey and sat down on the bed to drink it. When he was finished he poured another and this time sipped it more slowly. After a while he set the glass down, lay back on the pillows, pulled the comforter up to his chin, and closed his eyes. He fell asleep and when he woke he was still angry, still didn't want to talk to Berta, but lying there in the darkening room, with the whiskey taking the edge off his anger, he had to admit that it might be time to quit. Not that she was right. Not that she had any say in the matter, but last night's journey on the train had told him something that he could no longer ignore: He wasn't afraid of sharing his compartment with the army officers, and he should've been. He should've been on high alert, tense, aware of every detail, straining to hear snatches of conversation, making notes in his head. Instead, he was tired and bored and even dozed. Mistakes happened when you were that comfortable. He'd seen it in other men.

Sometimes he wondered why he didn't quit. He had been helping Jewish families for years now and maybe it was time to stop. He often wondered why he'd traded his safety and that of his family for people he barely knew. He didn't have an answer. Sometimes he thought it was because the nightmares faded whenever he did this kind of work. Whole nights would go by and not one mutilated body; not one decapitated head; no corpses with empty, bloody eye sockets; and no blue men. Other times he thought it was about honor or duty or even redemption. As he sat on the edge of the bed looking out at the fresh snow falling silently in the park, he wondered if he really needed an answer. Or if the answer was so large and bright, so infused in his fundamental nature, that he would be forever blind to it.

Chapter Nine

January 1914

THERE WERE too many revolutionaries in Moscow. At least that was the opinion of Pavel Ossipovich Lepeshkin, who had come to stay with his family for the holidays in the Arbat district. Because he couldn't help bragging about his exploits on the Russian-Polish border, word got around that he was a hero who had narrowly escaped arrest. Soon friends and even some acquaintances came to him with requests to smuggle arms and comrades in disguise across one border or another. How could he explain that his days of daring exploits were over? That he had learned his lesson and would now fight for the rights of the oppressed Jewish worker solely from the safety of Kleinmikhels' parlor? He couldn't, not if he wanted to remain a hero of the laboring masses. So, at the first opportunity, he hopped a train to Cherkast to spend the winter holidays with Morris's family.

"Pavelech . . ." Morris shook him awake. "Pavelech, wake up. It's time to go." It was freezing in the guest room. The fire had nearly gone out in the stove and the girl hadn't come by to get it going again. Morris was dressed and ready to go. He poked at the fire and put on another log. "Are you getting up or not? My father is waiting for you."

Pavel was in bed with the quilt pulled up around his face. He lifted his head and looked at the window, where the first threads of dawn were struggling through the curtains. "What time is it," he croaked.

"Early, let's go. You said you wanted to come."

"I was being polite."

"Well, it's too late now. You have to come. He's counting on you. He says he's going to make a real *tsaddik* out of you. I told him to forget it. Such a *shmendrik* doesn't deserve his time, but he wouldn't listen."

The log caught fire and soon the stove began to crackle in protest. "How long will it take?" he asked, sitting up.

"You've never been to *davenen*?"

"Morris, you know my family. They live in the twentieth century."

"An hour . . . maybe a little more. But hurry. You don't want to make him angry."

Pavel dressed, refusing to hurry, and went downstairs to the sounds of morning in the Eiger household. The laundresses were chattering among themselves as they moved through the bedrooms gathering up the dirty linens. He could smell breakfast cooking in the kitchen. Above him on the landing he could hear Morris's sister calling to their mother. He had never been up this early in his own house and had no idea what it sounded like. In this house it sounded efficient, upstanding, infused with a moral certitude that he found irritating, much like Morris himself.

When Pavel joined the father and son at the front door he found them already dressed for shul with their prayer shawls around their shoulders, holding the tefillin in their velvet pouches.

"You didn't bring your tallis?" Reb Eiger asked.

"I didn't think . . ."

"No, you didn't think. But lucky for you I have an extra one." He said this with a grudging paternalistic affection as he handed Pavel a velvet bag embroidered with gold thread. Pavel thanked him, unbuttoned the bag, took out the prayer shawl, and started to put it on. Then he remembered, muttered the prayer for putting on the tallis, and wrapped it around his shoulders.

Reb Eiger raised his eyebrows and briefly looked pleased. "Maybe not so much work after all."

Once outside they joined the other men going to morning prayers. They moved like black specters in their long coats, caps, and heavy fur gloves, their feet creaking on the snow as they walked up the short hill. At the end of the street was the simple wooden synagogue that Reb Eiger had attended his whole life. The first story was squat, broken up with little windows, and covered in peeling plaster. The next story was made of unpainted wooden planks and lined with seven small windows on every side. Above this was another tier of taller windows that nearly looked new. Pavel followed Morris and his father up the one step and across the covered porch to the door. There he followed the others and recited the Mah Tovu, touched the mezuzah, and kissed his fingertips before entering.

The darkened interior was lit by only a few candles and bitterly cold. There was a stove in the middle of the aisle between the pews, but the fire had gone out. Around it on the wooden floor lay several transients who were just waking up as the congregation filed in. They muttered to one another in sleepy tones, sitting up and stretching, pulling their coats on with yellowing fingers. One was a cigarette maker who smoked most of his profits. The others were a porter who slept with his head on his rope and a beggar with a stained yellow beard and a coat of rags. They were all waiting for the beadle to come back with a load of wood to revive the fire.

Pavel sat with Morris and his father along the eastern wall. This was a place of honor. Reb Eiger was a rich man, the owner of a brickyard, but more than that, his good works and contributions to the synagogue and other organizations had earned him the coveted place among the righteous. An ancient prayer book was shoved into Pavel's hand. It was yellowed and brittle with dirt and age.

The men shuffled into their places in the pews and opened their prayer books. The rabbi stood among them facing the Torah ark, his prayer shawl pulled up over his head and shoulders, his fingers fumbling with the pages of his prayer book, stopping when he had come to the right place. Without preamble or even calling out the page number, the prayer began. First the Adon Olam, then the Yigdal, then the Birkat HaTorah and Birchot HaSachar.

Blessed art Thou, Lord our God, King of the universe,
Who gave the heart understanding to distinguish between day and night.

Amen

Blessed art Thou, Lord our God, King of the universe,
Who made me an Israelite.

Amen

Blessed art Thou, Lord our God, King of the universe,
Who did not make me a slave.

Amen

The Rabbi chanted the words while the men said them silently to themselves or sang them in a cacophony of discordant notes, rocking back and forth on the balls of their feet, praying to God in their own way. Pavel stood apart and watched the men chanting the words, the Akedah L'Olam, Yehei Adam, and the rest. His lips moved silently, but no sound came out.

His grandfather had brought him to a prayer house when he was little that reminded him of this shul. His father was busy running his factories and had little time for his son. So his grandfather took him by the hand and walked with him on Mondays and Thursdays and let him stand beside him to watch the proceedings. He promised Pavel that on his thirteenth birthday he would give the boy his prayer shawl. Pavel waited patiently for that day, but his grandfather died before he was ten and the old man's shawl went to another relative.

He didn't know whether it was the memory of his grandfather, the singsong of the prayer, or the smoke from the stove, but something took hold of him in the half-light of the shul. Even cynical Morris seemed to be affected by the rhythms of the prayers, the power of the words, and the community of the ancient tribe. Pavel wanted to join them. He wanted to feel their connection with God and talk to Him as they did . . . as his grandfather did. But when he tried to recite the prayers, his reedy voice embarrassed him. He felt awkward davening with the others and his thoughts kept wandering away from God. He tried to focus on the Almighty, but he kept thinking about breakfast, a hot cup of coffee, Inessa's breasts, and wondering how much longer this would take. When he looked at Morris, who seemed so engrossed in the service, so a part of the congregation and comfortable with God, he couldn't help but envy him.

Later that afternoon, Pavel and Morris were enjoying schnapps by the fire. The snow was drifting down in a silent mass. He was thinking it had been a supremely satisfying afternoon when the clock downstairs struck the hour.

Morris looked up from his book. "Is that four then?"

Pavel checked his pocket watch. "Half past."

Morris sighed and closed his book. He got up and stretched. "Well, that's it then. We have to be going."

"Going? Where are we going?"

"Didn't I tell you? We're meeting old friends for tea."

"No, you didn't tell me. Who are these friends?"

"You don't have to come. I just thought you might be interested. They're factory workers, Pavlech. Members of the Bund. I thought you might want to meet real workers for once in your life."

"I've met real workers. Plenty of times. I don't need to meet more."

"But I already told them about you. They want to meet the big hero who eluded the Okhranka at the Polish border."

"I told you, I made that part up. There was no Okhranka. And in any case it was Lublin and not the border."

"Still, they want to meet you. Come, you'll like these men. They're good comrades, the real thing. And besides, if you stay here, you'll have to go to *maariv* with my father."

"Who says?"

"I happen to know he's going to ask you. And you won't say no."

"How do you know?"

"Because you won't. You never do. You're too much of a coward. So what'll it be, evening prayers or tea?"

An hour later they walked into the tearoom located on a miserable little street in the factory district. Inside, the air smelled of sweat and rotten eggs since it was across the street from a sulfurous paper mill. There was a young girl working the place, who didn't look to be much over nine or ten. Too short to reach the counter, she had to drag over a wooden crate to take the orders and then drag it back to the stove to fill them.

Morris ordered a pot of tea and two cups and they took it to the reading room in the back. It was nearly empty except for a woman who sat reading a tabloid, looking suspicious and sullen, with a bruised arm still showing the shape of the fingers that had grabbed it. Behind her were two *babas*, old women, who sat hunched over their tea and coughed into twisted handkerchiefs wrapped around their fingers.

When Morris's friends arrived, he rose to greet them, hugging them and clapping them on the back. "Pavel, meet these savages. This is Zolman and Yosele. They work in the brickyard. And this wild man is Yankele." Morris grabbed his friend in a headlock and rapped his head with his knuckles. "He's a danger to life and limb, so better keep your distance."

Yankele tore himself free. "*I'm* the wild one. Hardly. You should've seen this boy. A holy terror. Had the whole town waiting to thrash him."

Morris feigned surprise. "Me?"

"Dyeing the water carrier's horse green?"

"That was Zolman."

Zolman was dragging over a chair. "Horseshit . . . that was you, Morris. That was your idea."

These men didn't look very wild, nor did they look much like men. They were boys, no more than nineteen, but already exhausted from marrying young and having too many babies to support. Zolman had been the best of them at the heder and everybody thought he'd have a bright future as a scholar or a teacher. But when his father broke his leg in three places, Zolman had to go out and earn a living. He was thirteen at the time and lucky to get a job at the factory loading bricks into the kilns. Yosele's entire family was wiped out in a cholera epidemic when he was six. He came to Cherkast to live with his aunt. Unlike Zolman he wasn't disappointed with his life in the brickyard, because there had never been talk of anything else. Yankele was the youngest of three and the happiest because he had a wife he still liked to look at, only two children, and a trade, tailoring. There were so many tailors in the Pale that he considered himself a lucky man to have a job at all, even if it did entail laboring in an airless room for twelve hours a day stitching army uniforms on a pedal-driven sewing machine.

Morris said, "Come, sit down. I'll get us some tea. And I brought a little schnapps."

Zolman said, "Who can say no to that? And get some cakes too. You're the rich man."

Morris came back with tea and cakes and passed around the flask. Soon everyone was eating and getting drunk. At first the talk was innocent enough and centered on their childhood exploits. Loud arguments broke out over details that were of great importance to them but meant nothing to Pavel. Their talk reminded him of his brothers. Pavel was the baby of the family, years younger than the others, and was never included in their adventures or their late-night talks. Here too he seemed to be an outsider and once again he envied Morris.

"So, tell me what you've been up to?' Morris asked.

The young men exchanged glances and at first no one spoke up. "What do you mean?" asked Zolman. He glanced at Pavel.

Morris screwed up his face in annoyance. "I told you he's all right. I've known him almost as long as I've known you. He's the hero of Lublin."

Yankele took a pull on the flask and handed it to Yosele. Yosele passed it on to Zolman without taking a drink. Zolman didn't take one either and let it sit there.

"We're moving out in a circle," he said, keeping his voice low. It was an unnecessary precaution since they were speaking Yiddish in a Russian tearoom. "We're moving out from Cherkast. Training them in the *shtetlekh* and the towns. Sometimes we can arm them, but it's getting harder to buy guns."

Yankele leaned in and fingered a lump of sugar from a bowl that sat in the center of the table. "Have you heard of Medvin?"

Morris shook his head.

"A real success story, that one. You know the shtetl? It's not far from here. We gave them a few pistols once and a little training. Not much. Then not long ago the peasants started bragging about a pogrom. This was"—he thought for a moment—"last spring, I think." They showed up at market saying they were coming back to wipe out the town."

"The whole town?"

"That's what they said. The next day they came down the main road in their carts. The Jews hid in the bushes on either side of the road and waited for them. They had maybe three pistols between them and not much ammunition. They started firing when the carts came into range. And as soon as they'd fire off a round, they'd toss it to the next man. He fired off a round and tossed it on. Soon it sounded like an army out there in the bushes. The muzhiki got so scared they ran off without a second thought. Some didn't even bother to turn their carts around. They just left them and ran off into the woods."

They drank some more while Yosele told them the story about hiding under the floorboards in Odessa during the pogrom. Morris told them about their group in Switzerland. When Pavel told his story everyone was impressed. He only exaggerated a little to give the story color. As the evening turned into night, they talked about their plans for the future: schools and a hospital, the establishment of *kehiles* and other self-governing bodies, Yiddish as the primary language, and an agenda of national-cultural autonomy. Pavel looked into their sweaty faces around the table and saw the same kind of fervor that he had seen on the faces in shul that morning. In shul the ardor had been for the love of God and His laws. Here, it was for social justice, empowerment, and dignity, but the feeling was the same, the intensity of purpose borne out of thousands of years wandering in the Diaspora.

And he felt it too. It may have been the whiskey, the talk, or the late hour, but whatever the reason, by the end of the evening he felt like a brother to these men. He had never felt this way before, not even to his own brothers. They were all comrades in the struggle. He would've done anything for them. So, when Zolman told them about their plan to break into a police warehouse to steal guns and asked for their help, Morris agreed without a moment's hesitation. Pavel agreed too. Afterward he joined in when the flask was passed around even though he didn't particularly like whiskey.

PAVEL FELT nothing but disgust for Morris when he came into his room on the morning of the break-in and found him lying in sweat-soaked sheets, his face flushed with a high fever, his hair plastered to his forehead, and a deep rumbling in his chest whenever he took a breath. "What's wrong with you?" he asked, not bothering to hide his annoyance for the malingerer.

Morris opened his eyes and with some effort managed to focus them on his friend. "Pneumonia," he whispered. He was propped up on pillows to make it easier to breathe. His room was a study in gloom. The heavy curtains were shut and the only light came from a small lamp on a table beside the bed. There was a white enamel inhaler beside the lamp emitting a lazy trail of steam out of its funnel that smelled of eucalyptus oil.

Pavel pursed his lips and shook his head. "For God's sakes, Morris. I know what this is about. You don't want to go tonight. All right, so we won't go. You don't have to put on this show."

"I'm sick, Pavel. Ask my doctor. I'm running a high fever."

He snorted. "Right."

A coughing spasm caught him by surprise and when it was over he lay back on the pillows, panting for breath, wiping his hands on the sheets.

Pavel's lip curled up in disgust. "Can't you use a handkerchief?"

"In case you haven't noticed, it isn't pleasant having pneumonia. I may have to go to hospital."

Pavel looked pained. "Well, what about tonight then?"

"You're going to have to go it alone."

"I don't want to go it alone. It's goddamn freezing out there."

"What choice do you have? They need a lookout."

"They'll just have to postpone it."

"They can't. The guns might be moved any day. You'll only be a lookout."

"*Only . . .*"

"Not much can happen to you. You'll be standing out on a corner. The others will do the rest. You can't back out now. I think even you can see that."

"*Even me?*"

"You know what I mean." Morris closed his eyes and lay back.

"Oh fine. You're really a load of horseshit, Eiger, and I'm never forgiving you for this."

"I know," he said with a faint smile.

That night Pavel waited out on Potemkinskaya, down in the factory section, hoping that Zolman and the others wouldn't show up. It was so cold that the snot froze in his nose and it hurt to breathe. He was standing in front of an old factory building across the street from the police warehouse. The factory was deserted, with missing windows like broken teeth and a front door secured with a flimsy padlock. It used to be a textile mill. He could see that by the likeness of a loom carved into the lintel over the doorway.

Although it was a snowy night with an icy wind blowing in off the river, there was some light coming from the Nicholas Sugar Refinery located at the eastern end of the street. It had one enormous smokestack that belched flames and burning cinders into the black sky, and the yard was lit because the refinery doors were open. As he stood on the corner trying to see the hands on his pocket watch, knowing that it was late and hoping that it was called off, an electric tram rumbled by, pulling cartloads of beetroots on the icy tracks in the middle of the road. He watched the tram pull into the refinery yard, where he could see men silhouetted against the light of the open doorway. When the tram had come to a stop, the men tilted the carts to spill the tubers out in the snow and started loading them onto a conveyor belt.

Looking down the other way, he saw Zolman and the others walking toward him out of the flurries. There were two other men with them that he didn't recognize. One was expensively dressed and seemed out of place like Pavel. The other one was a laborer like the rest. With a pang of regret he walked down to meet them. There was a nod between them, no introductions or explanations, none of the joviality from that night in the tearoom. The new men were older and seemed to be in charge. The shorter of the two, the laborer, the one they called Scharfstein, took Pavel aside and told him where to stand so that he could have a good view of the street and the surrounding buildings. It was on the corner directly across from the police warehouse in front of the deserted factory. Pavel took his sentry post and watched the others cross the street and disappear around the back of the warehouse.

For a while Pavel saw nothing except the whirlwinds of snow and the men working the carts at the refinery. Then, after a short while, he saw the play of electric torch beams through the dark windows of the police warehouse and knew they were inside. He tried to keep his attention on the street. He knew that any trouble would come from down the street, not from the refinery or from the steep ravine behind it, but from the west, from the town, so he kept his eyes mostly in that direction. It was so icy out he began to shiver and curse Morris, blaming him for the cold and the fear that felt like something died in his stomach. After a strong gust of wind drove him back into the doorway of the deserted textile mill, he thought that if Morris survived the pneumonia he would kill him.

He began to take shelter in the doorway. He told himself he would only stay there for a little while. He reassured himself that it would be all right; besides, no one would be out on a night like this. He tried to limit the time he spent in there, but it was such a relief to be out of the wind. He could have stepped inside the building. It would have been easy to pry the padlock off the door. He probably would have done it if he hadn't heard voices behind him.

At first he thought his comrades were coming back and very nearly hurried out to the street so they wouldn't know he had abandoned his post. But then he realized the voices weren't coming from across the street, but from down the block, from the direction of the town. He froze. He peered out from his hiding place and saw two gendarmes coming his way. He jumped back and flattened his body against the wall. His heart was racing. He couldn't think. His mind was a jumble. He wanted to run to the warehouse, but it was too late for that. Instead he tore off his glove with his teeth thinking that he would whistle. But he was never very good at it and now his lips were numb. In any case, the wind was too loud.

As the two policemen approached, he fell to his knees and held his breath. He could hear the crunch of their feet on the snow and even made out most of their conversation above the wail of the wind. One of them thought he had heard a noise in the warehouse and wanted to investigate. The other wasn't for it. He argued that they ought to go to the sugar refinery to get warm and have a cup of tea. More was said that Pavel couldn't hear, but the first one must have prevailed for they never passed him by. When he got up his courage to look out again he could see them crossing the tracks and trudging through the snow up to the warehouse windows. They brushed off the snow and shined their lights inside. Then they went on to the next set of windows and then around to the back.

Pavel waited in the doorway trying to get up the courage to run over to the warehouse and warn the others. At first nothing happened; he thought maybe they had heard the gendarmes and were hiding somewhere inside. Then he heard shouts and a couple of shots and before he knew it he was running blindly up the street toward the refinery, slipping on the ice, catching himself on a rusted beet cart and racing on past the boarded-up shacks and broken-down outbuildings that lined the street. He didn't stop until he came to the edge of the ravine. Looking over the ledge he saw only a sheer snowy rock face and a black void beneath it. He turned back and this time ran to the refinery yard, where the men were still loading the beetroots onto the conveyor belt. Without a word he stooped to join them, piling the roots onto the belt, keeping his head down and ruining his fine calfskin gloves on the dirt that encrusted the tubers.

When the police ran by he looked up with studied unconcern and in doing so caught the eye of the other workers, who were watching him. There were three of them, dirty, careworn faces, wearing patched coats and felt boots. They stopped their work and studied him. Then the one with the raggedy beard took Pavel's gloves right off his hands. The other one took his fur hat and the last one took his coat. In exchange the flat-faced little man gave Pavel his coat, a filthy assortment of mismatched patches. Pavel took it without a word, and put it on. It was too small. After that the men returned to their work, and Pavel did the same.

He was just beginning to wonder how long he would have to stay there, in the cold, with his back beginning to ache, when a new contingent of police arrived and approached the workers.

"See any suspicious men around here?" asked the captain.

Pavel's heart began to thump in his chest. The workers shook their heads.

"Some men run past here? Maybe they headed off into the gulley or down over there," he said, pointing to the edge of the ravine.

A sullen silence.

The captain looked at them and shifted his weight from one leg to the other. Then Pavel saw his eyes flick to the new gloves, to the fur hat and the coat.

"There is a reward, you know." he said, shoving his hands in his pockets and hunching his shoulders against the wind.

They looked up.

Pavel's heart stopped.

"A reward?" asked the one wearing Pavel's gloves.

"How much?" asked the one wearing his hat.

"Twenty rubles."

Pavel looked at them, silently pleading with them. But they knew he was a Jew. A Jew owned the corner store. Jews did business with the devil and some even had horns and a tail. The shame of it was that Pavel could've easily outbid the police for his life. He could've offered them any amount they wanted. But it was too late. His options had just run out and all he could do now was slump down on a pile of roots and watch his end unfold.

Chapter Ten

January 1914

IT WAS nearing dawn and only the members of Berta's inner circle were left lounging about on the settees and chairs, among the ferns and orchids, with their ties loosened and shirt collars unbuttoned, tiaras and ostrich feathers lying where they had dropped them. Olga and her lover, Valya, were on the floor sitting on cushions. She was using her considerable talents as an artist to paint his toenails. Her bobbed hair fell around her face as she leaned over his bare foot resting in her lap. There was a bottle of nail varnish wobbling precariously on the rug next to her.

"Stay still," she said impatiently. "How am I supposed to do this if you keep moving?"

"I hope you know this is ridiculous."

"Oh, stop being so dull."

"It's going to spill."

"It's not going to spill. Not if you stay still and let me ply my trade."

"You've already got it on your dress."

"Olga . . ." Berta said with annoyance. "Do you have to?" She was standing by the window watching the horizon turn from black to a deep blue. She had been expecting Hershel to walk through the door all evening. He told her that he had to go out and wouldn't be home for her salon. Still, she didn't expect him to stay out all night.

"I'm almost done," Olga replied. "But he keeps moving."

"I'm not moving. You're drunk."

"I am not drunk."

"Yes, you are. It's so like you to think that it's the world that's swaying and not your own body. She's drunk," announced Valya to the assembled. "Let the world know that the great painter and love of my life, Olga Nikolaevna," he took her chin in his hand and leaned over to kiss her lips, "is nothing but a common drunk."

Valentin Guseva was stretched out on the sofa, his arm thrown back supporting his head, his girlish mouth plump and slightly open. Across from him on a matching sofa was Aleksandra Dmitrievna, bundled up in a blanket, her arm resting on a pillow beside her, the rings on her fat fingers winking in the firelight. Yuvelir was seated in a chair at the edge of their little circle with his bare feet propped up on a hassock. His toenails were painted purple.

Valya looked down at his blood red toenails and wiggled his toes. "I actually do like them."

Olga laughed. "Told you," she said triumphantly. "And you put up such a fuss. You never listen to me."

"I always listen to you. I have no choice. You never stop talking."

She ran the brush up from his toe to his ankle, leaving a line of varnish on his leg. "Olga!" he said, pulling his leg back.

"Yes, my darling?" she said feigning innocence.

"Such a child." He took out a handkerchief and tried to wipe off the varnish, but it smeared all over the hair on his legs.

"I'm bored. What should we do now?" Yuvelir said.

"Something fun," said Olga, returning the brush to the bottle with the deliberate concentration of a drunk. "Something dangerous and morally reprehensible. Maybe we should kidnap someone."

"Who shall we kidnap?" asked Yuvelir with growing interest.

"Someone helpless. Someone who couldn't put up much of a fight. A child perhaps. I know, a Christian child. We'll make matzos out of his blood. Berta will show us how."

Berta turned back from the window. "You seriously think that's funny, Olga?"

"We're just having fun, *zaichik*. Don't be such a sourpuss."

Berta wandered back to the little circle and took a seat. "It's late. I want to go to bed."

"Why don't we all go to bed?" said Yuvelir. "I'm sure there's one around here big enough for all of us."

"Now that's an idea," said Olga, standing and stretching her little body and nearly falling over.

"Even for me?" asked Alix. She had persuaded Lenya to go home without her. Now she could stay up with the young people and get into all kinds of mischief and he couldn't do a thing to stop her.

"No, not for you, *maya krasavitsa*," said Valentin with a yawn. "You're much too refined for that."

"You mean old and fat," she replied glumly.

Berta was bored with her friends and wished they'd go home. She wanted to go to sleep. She wanted Hershel by her side, safe and warm in their bed. She wanted him to curl up behind her and wrap his arm around her waist.

It had been three weeks since she found the pistols in Hershel's office and since then everything had changed. Now she was always on edge, anxiously awaiting the next calamity. He had tried to reassure her, telling her that it was only the one time, a favor for a friend, but she didn't believe him, not really. She kept hearing boots on the front steps and watched for the Okhranka at the door. She couldn't sleep and when she did she had nightmares of blue men galloping across frozen landscapes.

"I know," Olga said with a childish clap of her hands. She ran to the drapes and pulled off the tieback cord. "I'll go and hide and whoever finds me can tie me up and do whatever they want to my body."

Yuvelir said, "Now, that's a wonderful idea."

"Yes, I'm all for it," Valentin chimed in.

"I thought you only played that game with me," Valya said sulkily. He wasn't having much luck with the varnish.

"*Tryn-trava*, darling," Olga said with a wave of her hand.

Berta hated that phrase. Loosely translated, it meant that everything was going to hell anyway, so what did it matter? But it did matter. Her life mattered; her family and home mattered. They mattered very much.

"It's late," she said to the others. "It's time for all of you to go home. I'll call a cab."

"Oh, don't be like that. We're just having fun. You could hide with me," said Olga.

"Doesn't sound like much fun to me," Alix said, rolling over and pulling the blanket up over her shoulders.

Yuvelir said to Berta, "I'd find you first, I promise. You wouldn't have to bother with these lice." He nodded in Valentin's direction.

"I'm not playing your stupid game," Berta replied. "I'm tired and I want to go to sleep."

"Then we'll just have to play without you," said Valentin.

Olga said, "Yes, we're very sorry, Berta, my sweet. But we won't let you kick us out. We're here to stay. It's for your own good. We can't let you waste your life sleeping away your days." With that she grabbed the cord and ran from the room shouting, "Give me to the count of thirty. No fair cheating. Count to thirty."

Yuvelir and Valentin counted out loud in unison, then ignored her wishes, skipped to thirty, and ran after her. Valya sat back on the cushions and looked over at Berta with half-closed eyes. "I've played that game one too many times with her. Now, if you were to play . . ."

Berta shot him a look and walked back to the window. She could see fragments of the cold dawn through a jumbled tracery of ice crystals on the window. The tracks from the sleds were nearly obliterated by the last of the storm. The only evidence of her guests' comings and goings were faint definitions under the new snow in the road.

Alix sat up with a heavy sigh and swung her feet to the carpet. "Poor Berta. I'm afraid we haven't been very good guests tonight. Well, I'm going home. I'm exhausted." She stood up and leaned her fingertips against a little table for balance. "I'll probably have to ring up for the car. I can't imagine Lenya remembered to send it back for me. That would be his revenge. Keep me waiting for it."

A sleigh glided up the road and pulled into the drive. At this hour Berta knew it had to be Hershel and hurried to the front door. Stepping outside she stood under the portico, shivering with her arms clasped over her chest while she watched him climb out of the cab. "Hurry up, it's freezing out here," she called to him.

The horse stamped his feet and shook his head, jingling the bells on his harness. When Hershel straightened she saw in the growing light that his coat was stained black in the front, that he wasn't wearing a hat or gloves, and that his hair was wet and matted against his scalp.

"Where have you been?" she asked, once he had joined her at the door.

"When we get inside."

"What's that stain? Is it blood?"

He didn't answer her but led the way into the house. Alix was in the foyer putting on her coat. "There you are," she said. "Everybody was asking about you. I hope you told that cabman to wait. Lenya took our car and stranded me here. Isn't that just like him?"

"You'll have to call your own cab," Hershel said, striding past her to the stairs. "I'll need that one."

"You're going out again?" Berta asked.

"Come up, I have to talk to you." His tone was flat and chilling.

The two women stood there a moment watching him climb the stairs. "I'm sorry, Alix," she said without taking her eyes off her husband.

"Don't be, *milochka*. They want what they want. What's the point of arguing? Go up to him. I'll be all right."

"Are you sure?"

"Of course. Go on, I'll ring you tomorrow."

Berta kissed her on both cheeks and hurried up the stairs.

She found Hershel in his bathroom with his shirt off and the hot water running in the sink. Steam curled up and clouded the mirror. He was using her good scissors to cut his beard close to the skin. There were curly black hairs on the counter, more floating in the water, and even more stuck to the blades.

"What's the matter, Hershel? You couldn't give Alix the cab? That's not like you."

"No, I suppose it isn't." He applied a thick layer of shaving soap over his face and chin.

"Why are you shaving off your beard?"

There was a knock on the door.

"That'll be Vera," he said. "Tell her to bring up three suitcases. Not the big ones. I want them easy to carry."

Her stomach churned. "Are you going somewhere?"

He dipped his razor into the hot water and then, leaning forward to get a better look, scraped a swath off his cheek. The beard made a crackling noise as the razor wiped it away. "Please, Berta. Just do as I say."

She opened the bedroom door and found Vera standing there wearing her nightdress with a shawl thrown over her shoulders. After Berta explained what she wanted, Vera asked, "Shall I pack them for you, Madame?"

The question threw her for a moment. It hadn't occurred to her that she might be going somewhere. "No, that's all right. Sorry to bother you this early."

"S'all right, Madame. No bother."

Back in the bathroom, Berta found a stranger standing in front of the mirror, dabbing at a dribble of blood on his chin. With his beard gone, Hershel's face was pink and vulnerable like the underbelly of a newborn animal. The oval forehead was familiar, as were the dark eyebrows, the Tartar's eyes with the long lashes and the high-bridged nose. But the mouth was new, a surprise, a complete stranger, and it changed his whole appearance. She had never seen it before.

"Why did you shave?" she asked him again. She stood at the bathroom door, the steam hot on her cheeks, her back cold from the unheated room.

He rinsed off his hands and face and then splashed water over his chest and under his arms. He grabbed a towel off the rack and dried himself, smearing it with the blood from his shaving cut. Then he stuck a little tissue on the wound to stem the flow and when he was satisfied he looked over at her. His eyes were black and cold like pebbles. "We broke into a police warehouse tonight."

Her face went flat. "Why?"

"They had guns and we needed them."

"But I thought—"

"I know what you thought." He pushed past her and left the bathroom. She followed him into the bedroom and found him searching through the armoire. "There was a boy. Not much over eighteen. We thought he was experienced. We were told he was reliable and would make a good lookout, so we stood him outside, across the street from the warehouse." He found a shirt and put it on, squaring his shoulders to make it fit better, and then started buttoning it up.

Down below in the alcove off the foyer the telephone began to ring. They stopped when they heard it. Hershel went to the door and listened. He left her standing in the open doorway and called down: "Who is it, Vera?"

Vera had been taught never to shout and ran up the stairs to deliver her message properly. "He didn't say, Excellency. Only that he wishes to speak with His Honor. He said it was urgent."

Hershel glanced back at Berta and then followed Vera downstairs. Berta waited for him in the hallway, while her heart began to pound. She had no idea what was happening, but she knew it was something awful, something to be feared. Her world was under assault, that much was clear. Her beautiful house in the Berezina, her family, her friends, and all her precious things were vulnerable and could be taken away. Hershel had gambled with them and, judging by his behavior, had lost.

When he came back to her he was carrying a small suitcase. "What is it? What's happening?" she asked.

"It's Scharfstein."

"Who?"

He went back into the bedroom and she followed him inside. "They've arrested him. There's no time to pack now. Get the children ready. We're leaving in ten minutes." He was fumbling with the button on the back of his stiff collar.

"Leaving? Where?"

"To America."

She stared at him. "I'm not going to America."

He draped his tie around his collar and looked at himself in the armoire mirror while he tied it. "You have to come. You have no choice."

"I'm not leaving my home, Hershel. Everything is here. My life is here. You expect me to walk right out the door on a moment's notice?"

"Yes, I suppose I do. Now, hurry, we don't have much time."

"Well, I won't do it. I just won't."

He sat down on the bed and began pulling on his boots. "You're going to have to, Berta. We can't stay here. If we do, I'll be arrested."

Berta couldn't believe this was happening. Everything seemed so unreal, slowed down, as if underwater. He was telling her that her life in Cherkast was over, that everything that was important to her was gone and there was nothing she could do about it. "Then you go," she said firmly. "I'll come later."

He stopped and looked over at her. Then he stood and stamped his feet, working his toes into the boots. "I'm not going without you."

"But you have to."

The door burst open and Olga raced in on bare feet, laughing and squealing. Berta turned on her. "Get out!" she screamed. "Get out of this house."

Olga stopped and stared at her, momentarily shocked into silence. She held up her hands and patted the air. "Yes, *kotik*, now don't get excited." She backed out of the door. "I'm going. We're all going. Calm down."

Berta slammed the door after her. They could hear her down the corridor telling the others that Berta had lost her mind and that they all had to leave immediately. There was a clamor of voices, questions and answers that faded down the stairs and out through the parlor door.

"Berta, listen to me." Hershel tried to take her into his arms, but she pushed him away. She took a seat in the chair near the armoire and dropped her face in her hands. He sat across from her on the bed and leaned in. "There's no need for this. There's a new life waiting for us in America. We'll stay with my sister. I hear Wisconsin is a beautiful place. It's true we won't have much at first, but I'll find something."

"What will you do there?" she asked through her tears.

"I don't know. It's a big country. Plenty of opportunity. It could make our fortune."

She shook her head slowly. "I know how people live there, Hershel. You're not fooling anyone. Is that what you want for us? For your children. To live like that?"

"There are all kinds of people and they live all kinds of ways."

"I saw pictures of those horrible tenements in a magazine."

"That was New York City. This is Wisconsin. It's different. Now come, get up and tell Galya to get the children ready."

She watched him through a haze of tears as he threw some clothes into the small case. She had heard about the tenements in New York City. She knew how people lived there. She wondered if Wisconsin was any better. Maybe it was worse. Maybe they'd be hungry and cold and crammed into a few filthy rooms like the pictures in the magazine.

"Berta . . ." he said, slipping on his jacket.

"What?"

"We have to hurry."

She drew a breath. Then she sat up and wiped her face with both hands. "I told you I'm not going," she said grimly.

"Don't be ridiculous. You are coming with me."

She shook her head.

"Then I'm not going either."

"But they'll arrest you."

"Undoubtedly."

She was about to argue with him when they heard the sound of sleighs coming up the road. "Hershel . . ."

"Shush!"

The horses turned in at the drive and soon they were pulling up to the front door. He looked at her and smiled. It was the bitter half smile of defeat. "Well, it seems it's too late now," he said quietly.

"Oh my God. You have to hide."

"I don't think that would work. I'm not Samuil."

"What are you going to do?"

Someone knocked at the bedroom door. "Go away," Berta shouted.

"Madame . . ."

"Tell them to go away, Vera."

"Who, Madame?"

"The men at the door."

"It is only the cabs."

"What?"

"For the guests, Madame. The cabs to take them home."

And then, as if to confirm this fact, they could hear excited chatter and laughter in the foyer. There was a high-pitched squeal from Olga and a girlish shout from Yuvelir. Berta ran to the window and looked out on the drive. Hershel came over and stood beside her. From where they stood they could watch the guests make their way down the snowy steps and pile into the cabs.

"Go now, Hershel," she whispered. "Please, what are you waiting for?"

"Are you coming with me?"

"No . . . not now."

He gave her a level look. "I could insist, you know."

She held his gaze. "I know."

He looked at her a moment longer and then down at his hands. "I always knew you were like this. But I thought if ever the time came . . ."

"Hershel, please, it happens all the time. You know that. Men go first and the women and children follow."

He stood there a moment longer and she thought he was going to say something, but instead he picked up his traveling case and left the room.

At the front door she watched him put on a clean coat and pull a fresh pair of gloves from the pockets. "Where will you be?" she asked.

"Does it matter?"

He put on the gloves then a *papakha* and stepped out into the frosty morning. The towering black clouds on the horizon were lit from beneath by the rising sun.

"Hershel . . ."

"I'll write," he called back over his shoulder. "If you need money, see Levy. There isn't much, so be careful. I'll send you more."

"I'll miss you."

He ignored her, threw his case in the back, and climbed in after it. Once he was settled in with the leather rugs on his lap, the driver urged the horse on and the sled plunged forward. She stood at the top of the stairs and shivered in her evening dress waiting to see if he'd turn around. When the sled disappeared beneath the crest of the hill, she came back into the house and shut the door. Her legs gave out and she slumped into a nearby chair. She hugged her chest and trembled. There was a glossy spot of red on the floor, hard and smooth. She bent down to touch it and found that it was nail varnish.

Chapter Eleven

May 1914

It was hours before dawn when Berta first heard knocking at the front door, not knocking exactly, more like tapping, so soft that she couldn't even be sure she heard it at all. Then, after a short silence, it started up again, only this time it grew louder, slow beats, evenly spaced, until they tapered off into silence. At first she thought it might be a branch in the wind. But there were no branches by the front door, and it was a still night with hardly a breeze. Then she thought it might be some kind of prank, but certainly not by children. Not this time of night.

She'd been in bed for hours and hadn't yet slept. Falling asleep was difficult now that Hershel was gone. She usually stayed up alone most nights worrying. He had been gone for four months and still she hadn't received a letter: not a card, nothing, not even after she found his sister's address among his things on his desk and had written to him several times. Not knowing was becoming more and more intolerable with each passing day. She'd made inquiries with friends who would have known if he'd been arrested, but nobody had heard anything. He wasn't in any of the prisons or hospitals. He had simply disappeared.

The tapping began again, only this time it was so faint that she could barely hear it. She considered ignoring it, trying to get some sleep. Then it grew louder. She sat up and threw back the covers. She put on her dressing gown and found her slippers. She thought about ringing for Vera or Petr, but for reasons she couldn't explain, she didn't want them to know about it.

By the time she walked out into the darkened hallway, it had stopped again. She stood there listening, her eyes settling on a puddle of moonlight that had formed on the landing. When she reached the top of the stairs, she could see an irregular patch of light jutting out over the parquet floor. She followed it across to the front door.

"Who's there?"

Her voice sounded muffled, tremulous, like it was coming from a wax cylinder for a phonograph player. She tried to peer out through the windows on either side of the door, but the angle was too sharp. She could only see a portion of the doorstep.

"Who's there?"

She hesitated, then turned the latch and heard the bolt retract. After a moment she turned the handle and slowly opened the heavy door. From where she stood, the front step looked deserted, but she couldn't be sure. She opened the door a little farther and peered out until she could see the whole portico, the wide steps, and the drive beyond it. Nobody was there. It was quiet except for the crickets and a gentle rustling in the trees overhead. The moon was full, shadows flitted across the drive, and the branches of the trees were silhouetted against the black sky. She was about to close the door when she noticed something in the drive. She thought it might be a dead animal lying half hidden under the box hedge that lined the gravel. She thought of Masha the cat. Poor little Masha had been left out all night and had disappeared. Now, here was her body, killed by some wild animal. She hurried down the steps and strode out across the drive. Maybe it wasn't too late to save her. She couldn't imagine how she would tell Sura that Masha was dead.

When she got closer she could see that it wasn't an animal, but an old traveling case, half buried under the hedge. She would've left it there, if there hadn't been something familiar about it. She couldn't be sure in the dark, but it looked a little like one of Hershel's traveling cases. She picked it up gingerly, and holding it away from her night dress, she brought it back inside and carried it up the stairs, a litter of dirt and leaves trailing behind her. She went down the hallway to her bedroom and put the case on the floor before turning on the lamp. It smelled of mold and leaf rot and seemed to be more like a living plant than a manufactured object. There were trails of snail slime on the lid that glistened in the lamplight and attached to the handle were old spider's webs encrusted with leaves and bits of insects. The locks had been pried open and the hinges were rusty. Even with these insults to its integrity, Berta could see that it had once been a fine case. It was made of leather and although there were no engraved initials on the backing plate, it most likely had belonged to someone who knew quality. She tried to remember if all Hershel's cases had initials on them.

When she opened the lid she found that it was empty, as were all the interior pockets, except for one that contained the stub of a train ticket to Kiev. Even though it had been a good case, it was a common one. There had to be thousands of them in Little Russia. How could she say with any certainty that this one had belonged to Hershel? How absurd to think there was even a remote possibility that it was the one he took with him. And yet as she lay back in bed and closed her eyes, she tried to picture him packing, throwing his shirts into the case, closing it up, grabbing the handle, and walking off with it down the hallway. She tried to picture the case as he threw it into the sled and then climbed in after it, ignoring her, adjusting the lap rugs before signaling the driver.

A FEW DAYS later Berta took the children down to the shops. It was such a warm and inviting day that she decided not to take the motor but walk down the hill. The Berezina was busy that afternoon. Gardeners and their helpers stooped over hillocks of bare earth, shoving bulbs into the ground, while nannies kept an indifferent eye on their charges and gossiped with their colleagues in the private parks. Samuil was excited and wanted to run down the hill. Berta told him he could only go to the corner but then must wait for her before crossing the street. A motorcar sped past, belching black smoke from the exhaust pipe, and startled everyone with an explosive backfire. Berta had promised Samuil a new trick from the magic shop and he had pestered her all morning, until she gave up trying to enjoy her breakfast.

"What if I find two tricks, Mameh?"

"What if you do?"

"Could I get both?"

Sura, who had no interest in magic, was cranky and complaining about the walk even though they had only gone a few blocks. She wanted to go back and get the motor. As a compromise Berta agreed to wait on the corner for the next tram.

Among the passengers waiting at the tram stop was a well-dressed woman in a large hat making a list in a little book with a pencil. There was a gentleman reading a paper with a headline proclaiming STRIKE! in large black letters. There were several girls in plain skirts and white blouses, servants most likely on their day off, and several young men, also servants, who eyed the girls and whispered among themselves.

Samuil stood on the curb and when the tram appeared up the hill he shouted, "Mameh, it's coming!" The gentleman glanced over from behind his paper.

"Not so loud, darling. I can see."

The horse-drawn tram came to a stop in front of the passengers. The metal wheels screeched in their tracks and sparks flew out from under the carriage. Samuil tried to rush up the steps, but Berta put a hand firmly on his shoulder to hold him back. "Let the lady go first," she whispered.

"Do we have to go at all?" Sura whined.

"Of course we have to go. Why did you bring her, Mameh?"

Berta took Sura's hand. "Don't you want to go to the magic shop?"

"No," she pouted.

They started up the steps. "You'll see lots of interesting things."

"It's scary in there. There are dead animals and it smells like old people." She was referring to a stuffed fox in the window with a frozen snarl on its face.

"We'll have a wonderful tea afterward. With cake and everything. Wouldn't you like that?"

"S'ppose."

At the top of the steps Berta handed the change to the conductor and was given three tickets. She led the children to the back of the tram, where they found seats by a window so Sura could feel the breeze on her face and not throw up.

Samuil said, "So, what about it, Mameh? Can I have two tricks? Two would be much better than one. You know how quickly I master them. Two would last longer and we wouldn't have to go back right away."

"We'll see."

While the driver was still waiting for the new passengers to take their seats, an artel worker, wearing a black leather jacket and knee-high boots, ran over from across the street and climbed aboard. He reached into his pocket, handed over a coin, and took his ticket. The tram lurched forward and bumped over the cobblestones. Using the top of the seats to steady himself, he made his way to the back, and slid into a seat directly across the aisle from Berta.

Soon they were picking up more passengers and the carriage became crowded. Every seat was taken and people were standing in the aisles holding on to the leather straps. Samuil was explaining to Berta how a card trick worked. It was an old one that he didn't care about anymore, so he didn't mind parting with its secret. She knew he liked playing the role of expert, so she let him go on while she pretended to listen, her gaze traveling from her son's eager face to the artel worker's reflection in her window.

For a moment she thought she recognized the man. She may have seen him in the neighborhood, possibly out of the corner of her eye or in a quick glance on the street. His appearance wasn't distinctive. His hair was closely cropped and thinning, so it was possible to see his pink scalp through the stubble at the back of his head. He had a wide forehead; small, deeply set eyes; and no beard. He wore a black visor cap and kept wiping his nose with the back of his hand. It may have been that he worked in the area or maybe she saw him once or twice down at the shops. What caught her attention was that he was watching her too.

Berta stood and rang the bell. "We're getting off here."

"But this isn't our stop," Samuil said.

"It's all right. We can walk from here."

"Why, Mameh?" Sura asked. "I don't want to walk."

"It's a beautiful day. It'll be good for you."

The tram stopped in its tracks and Berta herded the children down the steps. "Why do we have to walk?" she whined. "I hate walking."

Berta stood on the curb, with her hands on Sura's shoulders, watching the tram move on down the street. She wanted to see if the man got off and was relieved when he didn't. This reassured her but not enough to keep her from glancing nervously at an unemployed factory worker slouched in a doorway, at the butcher's boy unloading a cart in a nearby alley, and at a cabman smoking a cigarette by his carriage. She didn't notice any of the women on the street. They were an inconsequential blur.

"What are we waiting for, Mameh?" Samuil asked, impatiently. He wanted his magic tricks.

They walked on and turned in at the nunnery. After a few blocks more they reached Bessarabka Square. There was an accordionist in the little park playing "Song of the Boatman." A woman sat on a bench nearby and started to cry. At the other end a young man was eating pirozhki from a greasy newspaper. He looked over and considered the crying woman for a moment and then returned to his food.

Berta and the children crossed the square and turned into a dark lane lined with second-rate shops. She kept glancing behind her. She wasn't sure what she was looking for, perhaps a man like the one on the tram. She had been seeing men like that from time to time, or at least she thought she had, watching her from the other side of a street, through a shop window, or following her with their eyes from a doorway.

"What are you looking for, Mameh?" asked Samuil impatiently.

"Nothing, darling."

"You keep turning around."

"I was just wondering if this was the right lane. They all look alike, that's all."

"Of course it's the right lane. Look, here's the shop."

The magic shop was located between a tobacconist and a junk store in the middle of the lane. It sat back from the street and was half hidden by an elm, whose sickly branches struggled upward toward the light. In the display window was a round table covered with a white tablecloth. On a shelf above it sat the stuffed fox with yellow glass eyes snarling down at the passersby. Spread out on the table was a deck of cards and next to it a magic wand and a crystal ball. They had been coming to this shop for well over a year now and the display had never changed.

Instead of a bell, the door groaned when Samuil pushed it open. Sura hated the groan and groped for her mother's hand. The shop was long and narrow with a counter on one side and shelves behind it. There were many strange objects on the counter and on the shelves: a dismembered hand in a bottle that looked almost real, a stuffed raven on a perch, a two-headed snake in a jar, and boxes and boxes of magic tricks.

"Master Alshonsky. Your Excellency . . ." Reb Rubenstein bowed with a flourish for Samuil's benefit and gave him a hard candy that miraculously appeared out of thin air. Then he found another one behind Sura's ear and gave it to her. "And what can I do for His Honor today?"

He was an older man with a wide, jowly face, drooping eyelids, and a prominent belly. But he hadn't always been like that. There was a poster of him as a young man hanging on the wall by the door. It showed a well-built man dressed in a cutaway tuxedo with a black cloak hanging over his shoulders. He held a black wand over a scantily dressed woman who was floating above a coffin. The caption read NOTHING SHORT OF A MIRACLE!

Samuil told Reb Rubenstein that he was interested in card tricks today and Reb Rubenstein agreed that it was an excellent choice. While they looked through boxes marked THE HINGE COLOR CHANGE, THE FINNISH CONUNDRUM, AND THE RISING FAN, Sura examined the curios in the bottles, all of which she had seen a dozen times. Berta kept glancing out the window, watching the few shoppers hurry by with sacks of vegetables from the green grocer down the street.

"And how is Monsieur Alshonsky?" Reb Rubenstein asked as he wrapped up the two tricks that Samuil had chosen.

Berta hesitated. "He's fine. Just fine," she said with a thin smile.

Monsieur Rubenstein looked up at her and held her gaze. "I am glad to hear it." He went back to the string that he had been tying around the package. He tied it into a firm bow and used a pair of rusty scissors to clip it free from the ball on the counter. Then he handed the package to Samuil. "Do not rush them. Take the time to do them right. You'll be happy that you did." Samuil nodded with childish solemnity and took the package as if he were taking a Torah scroll.

Berta handed Reb Rubenstein the few rubles that he had asked for and he reached into his cash box for the change. When he gave it to her he said, "Take care."

"Yes, thank you."

She turned to go, but before she could, he put a hand on her arm. She looked back at him.

"He is very resourceful, you know. I wouldn't worry."

She stared at him for a moment longer. She didn't like this sudden familiarity, his hand on her arm, the sympathetic tone. She murmured something about an appointment and hurried the children out of the shop.

All the way up the street Samuil chattered on about his new tricks and how he would first try them out on Vera and Galya because they were so easily taken in. Berta wasn't listening. Her mind on was Reb Rubenstein. She was trying to remember how they came to patronize his shop. Then she remembered an afternoon that Hershel had spent with Samuil, just the two of them. They had come back after the outing with a sack full of magic tricks. She and Hershel were happy to encourage Samuil's sudden interest in magic. They thought it would distract him from spying on the servants and their friends.

After that they stopped at the glove shop, where Sura got a new pair of white gloves embroidered with violets. "I want a long pair like yours, Mameh. Like the ones you wear when you go out."

"Those are for ladies, darling. When you're older you can have a pair like that. For now you're going to wear these."

Their last stop was the English Room, a small but popular lunchroom just off Davidkovo Square. They sat in a little alcove by the bay window with a good view of the street. At that hour it was crowded with commodities traders from the exchange on the corner, who sat in the back drinking colored vodka, eating smoked fish, and arguing about the best way to maintain the protective tariffs. Up in the front sat older ladies with their daughters and granddaughters sipping tea and peeling off the fingers of their gloves so they could pick up the tea sandwiches. Tartar waiters with white aprons tied around their waists threaded their way between the tables, refilling teapots and delivering three-tiered silver servers of tea sandwiches, scones, and tarts to the center of the tables.

Samuil sat with his back to the window and unboxed a magic trick. He spread out the instruction sheet on the table and took the cards out of the box. With the cards in his hand and his eyes on the instructions, he attempted to mimic the diagrams that illustrated each step of the trick. Periodically he stopped to take a bite of a sandwich or a tart and then went right back to work.

Berta watched him master the trick. He was like that with learning. He pounced on the unknown with energy and enthusiasm, tearing it apart, examining each piece, until he knew just how it worked. Her gaze shifted to her daughter, who was sitting quietly in her seat looking mournfully at the sandwiches on her plate. Even though there was smoked salmon on white bread, her favorite, she didn't take a bite. Berta knew she had been missing her father. She kept asking about him: When was he coming home, where did he go? She wrote letters to him that Berta pretended to mail but really hid in the back of a drawer in her nightstand.

"Don't you want a sandwich?"

"No."

"Aren't you hungry?"

"Yes."

"Then why don't you have one?"

"I don't want to get my new gloves dirty."

"Then take them off."

"I want to wear them."

"Then use your knife and fork."

"To eat a sandwich?"

"Why not?"

There were two men sitting nearby talking over a tiny table, leaning in over their teacups with a quiet intensity that seemed out of place among the ladies at tea. One of them was a big man, dressed in workingman's clothes, a gray tunic, wide black belt, and loose trousers. He held his cup by the bowl instead of using the handle and finished his tea in two gulps, his prominent Adam's apple working as he swallowed. His companion was a student, a Jew most likely, with a thick moustache that he kept smoothing with two fingers. Berta couldn't hear what they were saying, but the attentiveness of the worker and the avidity of the student, the way he kept making little jabs in the air with a stiff hand to make a point, caught her attention.

A moment later the door opened and two men dressed in leather coats and visor caps sauntered in. When the student looked up and saw them coming, he lowered his eyes and hunched down in his seat. He picked up his cup, murmured something to his companion, and took a sip. His companion stiffened too but didn't turn around. They sat there quietly, pretending to drink their tea, as the men passed them without a glance.

Berta watched the reflection of the men in the window as they strolled to the long banquet table in the back where platters of *zakuski* were set out on display. As she watched them move up the table, picking up an olive or a pickle, she was aware that the student was also following their progress in the glass. He got up, threw down some money, and grabbed his satchel and books. His companion got up as well and followed him to the door, where they took their coats off the rack and left without bothering to put them on.

Outside, before they had a chance to walk on, another man in a peacoat came up behind them and grabbed the student's arm. They were standing right outside the restaurant, directly in front of Berta's window. The student tried to pull away; he was arguing with the man but getting nowhere. The other two men came out of the restaurant and joined them. One of them put a pickle in his mouth to free up his hand as he reached for the student's other arm, which he held in a tight grip, high up, directly below his shoulder. It was then that the man in the leather jacket turned in Berta's direction and she saw his face for the first time. With a shock of surprise she recognized the artel worker from the tram.

The entire altercation lasted less than a minute. Several ladies turned around in their seats to see what was going on outside. A waiter stopped by Berta's table because it had the best view in the house. As the men led the student off, he dropped his satchel and books on the sidewalk and tried to go back for them but was pulled away. The worker was left standing there in front of the window, watching them go. It was impossible to tell what he was thinking. His features were bland and expressionless. He stood there for a moment longer and then stooped to pick up the satchel and books. After that, he walked off in the other direction. The patrons in the restaurant soon returned to their conversation. It was a testament to the frequency of this sort of thing that in a few minutes no one was talking about it.

"Come, we're leaving," Berta said, gathering up her gloves.

The children looked over at her in surprise. "But we're not finished yet," Samuil said.

"It doesn't matter. We have to leave." Berta reached into her bag, pulled out several rubles, and put them down under her plate.

"I haven't had my tart yet," Sura complained.

"You'll have one at home. Come along. We have to go . . . *now*." She stood, took Sura's hand, and pulled her up. Samuil started to gather up his cards. "I don't see what all this fuss is about." He sounded like Hershel and for a moment Berta felt a pang of longing.

"Leave them," Berta said holding the door open for him.

"What? My magic tricks?" He dove for the cards and shoved them into the bag. "I can't just leave them." He grabbed the stray ones and the instruction sheet and rushed for the door.

Out on the street Berta searched for a cab and found that they all had fares. "We'll have to find a tram," she muttered, more to herself than the children.

Samuil looked up at his mother in annoyance. "What is *wrong*, Mameh?"

"Nothing is wrong. It's just late, that's all."

She hurried up the street to the tram stop, but it was empty. It had come and gone and they would have to wait a long time for the next one. "We can always walk from here."

"From here?" Sura moaned miserably. "All that way?"

"It won't be so bad. If we hurry, maybe we can catch a tram farther on."

"Why can't we just wait here?" Samuil wanted to know.

Before Berta could answer a man leaned in and said: "I have something to show you."

A sudden icy chill. "What is it?" she asked breathlessly.

"Come over here, out of the way of the crowd. You will like it." He motioned her over to the doorway of a small hotel. She followed him reluctantly. He had a round head and ears that stuck out on either side. The glare on his glasses obliterated his eyes.

He opened a leather case and showed her the contents. "Are they not beautiful?" The case contained rows of rings, watch chain fobs, and gold watches neatly displayed on a blue velvet mat.

She waved him off. "Oh no, I'm not interested."

"Why don't you at least take a look? A pretty lady like yourself?"

"I said I'm not interested." She was about to push past him when something caught her eye. It was a white gold pocket watch with an ornate face and an intricate engraving of vines and flowers on the case. She reached for it. "Where did you get this?"

"Now if I told you that you could just—"

"It looks like my husband's watch."

He grabbed it and snapped the case shut. "I think you must be mistaken." He turned and started to walk away.

"It looks just like it."

"A very common watch."

"It's white gold."

"Still, very common."

"I just want to know where you got it."

He shook his head and picked up his pace. She tried to follow him, but Sura slowed her down. "Please," she shouted after him, "do you know where he is?"

The man ducked into a side street and when she reached the corner she found that he had disappeared. Now all she wanted to do was get away. She saw a tram across the street and took hold of Sura's hand. "Hurry, we can catch it."

"But it's going the wrong way, Mameh," Samuil told her.

They ran across the street, avoiding the carriages and a few noisy motorcars, and hurried to catch up as the tram doors were closing. Berta waved to the driver, who opened them again and waited for them to climb aboard. She shoved the necessary coins into his hand and took the first seats by the door.

"I'm going to be sick here," Sura said.

"We're not going far."

"Still, I'm going to be sick."

"Where are we going, Mameh?" asked Samuil.

"I don't know."

"Shouldn't we get off and find a cab? We're going in the wrong direction."

"I know, Samuil. You don't have to tell me."

"Why did that man have Tateh's watch?"

"It wasn't Tateh's."

"You said it was."

"I was wrong."

"Why did you say it was?"

"I made a mistake. Samuil, please, I have to think."

After a few stops they got off on Dulgaya Street, the street of butcher shops, in the heart of the Jewish neighborhood. It was crowded with housewives and their children and street vendors pushing carts of secondhand goods: shoes, books, and clothing, any bit of rag or piece of furniture that somebody might want to buy for a kopeck. There were several butcher shops on the street with slabs of beef hanging in the windows.

"Why are we here?" Samuil asked. He wrinkled his nose against the smell of blood on ice. He was about to say more when he spotted three boys playing goose in the street. They stopped to watch the strangers go by. The leader eyed Samuil and whispered to one of the smaller boys, who giggled.

"We're here to see Mumeh Lhaye."

Samuil was amazed. "They live here?" he asked. The children had never been to Lhaye's apartment. She always came to them, so they never knew how their aunt and uncle and cousins lived.

Ten years ago Lhaye met a young factory worker named Zev Rosenbaum in a poultry market on Dulgaya Street. She was visiting Berta and had come to Dulgaya Street to buy a kosher chicken since Berta didn't keep kosher and Lhaye refused to eat *traif*. As she stood at the counter and waited for the poultry man to wrap up her bird, she asked Zev for directions to the tram that would take her back up to the Berezina.

"Oh ho, the Berezina. You work there?"

"No, my sister lives there."

"Is she rich?"

"Yes, but I'm not."

"Well, in that case, I'll walk you to the tram stop. It's easy to miss."

Although he wasn't pious, his father was and that was good enough for Mameh, who gave Lhaye her blessing. They were married in Mosny. Then she went to live with him in Cherkast, where they had three children in quick succession. He had contacted poliomyelitis from the local baths when he was a child and walked with a heavy brace on his left leg. But that didn't slow him down. He had a reputation for being responsible and smart, a hard worker despite his infirmity, so it didn't take him long to work his way up at the Nicholas Sugar Refinery, where he operated the vacuum pans and was popular with the workers that he helped to organize. Lhaye had recently given birth to a fourth child and now they all lived in the one-bedroom apartment over one of the butcher shops with no running water, a shared commode out back in an overgrown field, and several troublesome neighbors. Berta had offered her a nicer place to live, but Lhaye always refused, saying that she liked to be in the neighborhood, by which she meant the Jewish neighborhood. Berta suspected the real reason was that Hershel and Zev often fought over politics. Zev was a hothead Bolshevik and wouldn't accept help from Hershel, the Bundist, if his life depended on it.

At the end of the block Berta entered through a dark doorway and climbed up the steep wooden staircase. She and the children walked down the hallway, past a line of clothes drying overhead and several bags of garbage that gave the building its characteristic smell. When she reached Number 5 she stopped and knocked on the door. Receiving no answer she knocked again and this time she heard a voice asking her to be patient. A moment later the door opened and Lhaye was standing there holding her sleeping baby.

"What a surprise! Come in. Come in. Please excuse the mess. Oh, don't you look lovely, Sura. New gloves?" She kissed the children and Berta as they came in. "Sit! Sit! What can I get you?"

"Nothing, we just had tea. I have to talk to you."

"Of course. Children, why don't you go outside and play."

"No," Berta said.

"Vulia is outside. He can watch them." Vulia was only a year older than Samuil, but seemed so much older from all his years in the neighborhood.

"No, please, Lhaye." She didn't want to insult her sister's neighborhood, but on the other hand, she didn't want her children going out there and catching some disease.

"All right. You know best." And then to the children she said, "How about some honey cake, yes? I made some delicious cake." She gave the sleeping baby to Berta and took the children into the kitchen.

While she was gone Berta held the fat baby in her arms and kissed his downy hair. It smelled like milk mixed with lotion and cornstarch and it reminded her of her own babies. She could hear Lhaye putting the kettle on and setting out the plates while she hummed a tune Mameh used to sing. If Berta closed her eyes, she could almost believe that she was back in Mosny upstairs over the grocery—the same smells, the same noise outside in the street, the same scratchy furniture. It brought back the old feelings of her adolescence, of familiarity and alienation, of inclusion and entrapment. It was both disconcerting and comforting.

In fact, the furniture was Mameh's from the grocery. After Tateh's heart gave out, she decided she wanted to follow him. Her family and friends told her that she was too young to die, that she should learn to live with her loss, perhaps make a new life for herself near her grandchildren. But she wouldn't listen. Instead, she sat down and wrote a long letter to her daughters. In it she explained that while she loved them both equally, she was giving everything to Lhaye since Berta had married a rich man. Then she sold the store and waited. It took two years.

"I think the Okhranka is following me." Berta said, barely above a whisper, once her sister had returned to the front room and settled down in the chair across from her. They were speaking Yiddish. Berta had tried to teach her Russian, but Lhaye never wanted to learn. Lhaye preferred the old ways, the Jewish cycle of observances, keeping kosher, bringing to Cherkast the life she once had in Mosny.

She looked worried. "Why?"

"I don't know. It must have something to do with Hershel. When he left I thought they wouldn't be interested in me, but I think I was wrong."

"Are you sure?"

Berta kissed the baby again and handed him back to Lhaye. "I don't know. That's just it. I don't know what's real and what's not." She got up and went to the window. She could see Vulia playing hoops with his friends in the street. "Last night someone was knocking at the door."

"Who?"

"I don't know. When I went down to see, no one was there. I found an old suitcase in the bushes. I thought it was Hershel's. The one he took the night he left."

"How could that be?"

She shrugged and came back to the sofa and sat down.

"Have you heard from him?"

She shook her head. "I think he was arrested." She kept her voice down so the children wouldn't hear.

"You don't know that."

"There was a man in the magic shop."

"What magic shop?"

"He asked about Hershel. I think he was trying to tell me something. But I don't know what it was. I don't know, Lhaye. I don't know anything." She started to cry.

Lhaye moved over beside her and put her free arm around her shoulder. "Oh, Berta, you're all worked up. Look at you. You're seeing things that aren't there. Listen to me, sometimes when people go to America they don't want to write at first. They don't want to write until they have good news to share. That's probably what Hershel is doing. He's waiting until he has something good to say."

Berta didn't answer her. She wrapped her arms around her chest and hugged herself even though it wasn't cold in the apartment.

"If you're so worried about him, why don't you go?"

She looked up. "To America?"

"Why not?"

"What if I can't find him?'

"He's at his sister's."

"What if he's angry and doesn't want to see me? What if he's done with me?"

"Berta, such silliness. He loves you. You're everything to him. Why would he leave you? He's a good man. Good men don't leave their families."

She laughed a little. Sometimes she grew impatient with Lhaye's innocence.

"What? You don't think I know a thing or two? You think I'm so simple I'd believe anything, is that it? Well, I've got news for you—everything isn't all black either. There are bright spots too."

THAT NIGHT Berta lay in bed and tried to recall the face of the man on the tram. She remembered the leather jacket and the way his pink scalp showed through the stubble on the back of his head. She remembered his deep-set eyes. Then she tried to recall the man in front of the restaurant. She tried to picture that moment when he turned toward the window and she saw his face. But was he really looking at her? Could he actually see her through the glass, or was it too bright outside? Maybe he was only looking at own his reflection. Maybe he could only see the things around him on the sidewalk, the passersby, and the traffic in the street. And did he really look like the man on the tram? True, he was clean-shaven with short hair, but his hair was thick and blond, his jaw jutted out, and his chin wasn't right. He couldn't have been the same man.

After that she began to relax under the covers. She rolled over on her side and brought her knees up to her chest. The rest seemed ridiculous too, the suitcase in the hedge, the watch, even Reb Rubenstein, a harmless shopkeeper asking after a valued customer. Lhaye was right about seeing things. She was on edge. In the morning she would write and tell Hershel she was coming. She would wait for his answer, pack up her things, and walk away from her house. The thought of being with him again made her feel light and sleepy. She closed her eyes, letting the knot in her neck ebb away. Vague images of a sparkling lake came to her in the dark behind her eyes: a beach, a boat, a tree-lined shore.

Then she heard it: faint tapping at the front door.

Part Three

The House Jew

Chapter Twelve

August 1914

BERTA SOLD the motorcar and gave notice to Karl the driver because she could no longer afford him. He couldn't have been very surprised—she had already let Vasyl and Petr go. There were no more salons or dinner parties or ice sculptures. When she wanted flowers for the table she picked them from her garden or stole them from a neighbor. Hershel had been gone for seven months.

It was late morning and she was standing at the window in the breakfast room watching Karl and the new owner lean over the open hood and inspect the engine. Karl had brought out his special tools and was showing the young man how to use them. He had been washing and waxing the motor all morning, as if he were laying out a corpse for viewing.

That afternoon Berta took the children down the hill to the Iliuziia Theater to see *Cossacks of the Don.* Usually she would've sent Galya, because she didn't like to be seen in such places, but she wanted to spend time with the children and they had been pestering her all week to take them even though they had seen it many times before. As they walked down to the tram stop, Samuil chattered on about the film, describing all the scenes and getting so tangled up in his descriptions that eventually she stopped listening.

"If you've seen it so many times, why do you want to see it again?" she asked.

"It's wonderful, Mameh. You'll see. The riders stand on their hands in the saddle even when they're galloping really fast. And they do other tricks too. They turn around so they're facing the wrong way and then they stand up and let go altogether and hold their arms out like this." He held out his arms and pretended to lose his balance.

"They sleep in tents, Mameh," added Sura. "And eat from tin plates. And they sit around fires and tell stories."

"What kind of stories?"

"I don't know. It's silent. You can't hear what they're saying. You can only see their lips move and read the words at the bottom of the screen. But I can't read that fast and Galya can't read at all and Samuil won't tell me, so I don't know."

"Why should I have to stop and explain every two minutes," grumbled Samuil.

"I'll tell you, *maideleh*," Berta said, smiling down at her.

Sura looked up at her mother and beamed and then took her hand.

They walked on to the tram stop and waited in the shade of a lime tree. Berta was glad there were no others there. Even though she hadn't seen anything unusual in months, she still kept an eye out. She looked at the men who passed her. She was always on the watch for strangers who held her gaze a little too long or looked at her from out of the corner of their eyes. At night, she always listened for tapping at the front door. For this reason, she rarely went out, so it felt good that day to feel the sun on her back.

The Iliuziia Theater was nothing but a storefront on a little side street in the factory section. Berta paid the few kopecks at the door and she and the children walked into the darkened room. There were folding chairs lined up in rows in front of a screen. A few people had already taken their seats. A young girl came down the aisle and lowered the gas lamps that lined the walls. When it was dark, the projector hummed into life and men with leathery faces were shown trekking in the Caucasus. They carried bulky packs on their backs and wore lambskin hats with earflaps and laughed and talked directly into the camera on their way up the steep trail. After a newsreel, *Cossacks of the Don* came on and for nearly half an hour the children sat transfixed by the flickering images on the screen.

When it was over they left the theater and stood out on the sidewalk, dazed and blinking in the afternoon sunshine. They walked past a shoe factory, where Berta could hear the workers tapping nails into the soles of boots. The sound reminded her of the nocturnal tapping at her front door and for the moment it threatened to darken her mood.

When they got closer to Davidkovo Street, they heard shouting and singing and the roar of a large crowd. Two women hurried out of a milliner's shop and ran up the street to see what was happening. Shop assistants from the confectionary shop of Brassov and Sons stuck their heads out of the door and a boy ran past carrying toys for sale on a tray. "What is?" Berta asked the boy.

He shouted back over his shoulder. "It's war! We're at war!"

"With whom?" Berta shouted back. But he was gone before he could answer.

When they reached the boulevard they found it filled with throngs of people, some hugging each other as if there had already been a victory, others shouting out blessings for the czar and Russia. Storefronts and cafés were emptying out. The big brass doors of the commodities exchange swung open wide and traders and secretaries ran out in twos and threes. Everywhere strangers kissed each other on both cheeks. There were sporadic shouts of "God save the czar!" Someone began singing the national anthem and instantly others joined in. A boy raced past with newspapers under his arm, shouting "It's war! It's war! We're at war!"

Berta stopped a waiter who was running by. "Who's at war?" she asked.

"We are, *mamushka*! Russia is! We are all at war."

"With whom? With America?"

"No, silly woman," said an advanced-courses girl with several books under her arm. "With Germany! With the bastard Hun! The kaiser has declared war on us. He woke up the sleeping bear."

A young man with a bowl-shaped haircut was calling up to another young man, who was hanging over a balcony waving a Russian flag. "You know Leo?" he shouted up.

"The one with the English mother?"

"He signed up."

"Already?"

"He is there now."

"Wait for me. We can't let him beat us to the front."

Russian flags began appearing in more windows. Two horse trams stopped in the middle of the street as the drivers leaned out and shouted to one another. "Now they'll get what's coming to them. God bless Mother Russia!"

"God bless the Little Father!"

Berta took the children in hand and turned onto Malo-Vasilkovskaya Street to get out of the crowds. "Where are we going, Mameh?" asked Sura. "I want to see." She tore her hand away.

"Can't we stay, Mameh?" pleaded Samuil.

"No, I have to take you home," she said, reaching for Sura's hand.

"Will there be fighting?" asked Samuil, his eyes glowing with excitement.

"Yes, but we won't be here to see it."

"Why not?"

"We're going to America."

Samuil looked up at her in surprise. "To see Tateh?"

"Yes. But first I have to buy the tickets."

"I want to see Tateh," Sura said, suddenly excited.

"When are we going?" asked Samuil.

"As soon as possible."

"Can't we stay for the fighting?"

"No, it's too dangerous."

"Even if we watch from the rooftop like we did when they had fireworks?"

"No."

Samuil looked disappointed, until he had another thought. "Are we going on a big ship?"

"Yes."

"Will I be sick?" asked Sura.

"Maybe at first. But you'll get used to it."

"And we can have our own cabin?" asked Samuil.

Berta nodded.

"Will Masha be sick?" Sura asked.

"Masha will stay here with Vera."

"We can't take Masha?" Sura said, her eyes filling with tears.

"No. Cats don't like the ocean."

She started to cry. "I don't want to leave Masha."

"Sura, please, just walk with me. I have to get to the steamship office."

"Masha is going to be very sad."

"Masha will get over it. And so will you. When we get to America, I'll get you two cats."

Sura looked up at her mother and wiped her eyes. "Can they be kittens?"

By the time Berta came back down the hill the crowd had swelled to thousands and was overflowing into the surrounding streets. The steamship office was located in Davidkovo Square directly across from the little patch of grass where the Merchant's band had set up their instruments to play patriotic songs. The recruitment center was also on the square and crowded with young men, their eyes shining, their heads erect because they were following God's will and pledging their lives to Mother Russia. Berta watched these able-bodied boys with their broad shoulders, strong backs, and blond hair. These were the heroes of the black earth. Their mothers clung to them and begged them not to go. But how could they not? It was the adventure of a lifetime. They would go fight and come back heroes. They would do their part for the Little Father. As she watched them from across the square, their eyes glazed with the fervor of the newly converted, she thought how easy it was to convince them to give up their young lives . . . and for what? For a flag and an indifferent czar who, if he considered them at all, thought of them only as a burden of an office he never wanted nor was qualified to occupy.

SHE COULDN'T book passage until late October on a ship departing from Odessa, bound for Liverpool and then on to New York. She was not happy about the delay, but at least it gave her time to wrap up her affairs. Over the intervening months she let go of the staff, closed up the house, and said good-bye to her friends. On her last day in the city, she stood on the bluff overlooking the river, shrinking into her coat, shivering and stiffening against the wind. She had come down to the shops to pick up a few things for the trip and was grateful when she found that they still carried sewing kits, lambskin caps with earflaps, and yarn. As she stood there watching the barges pull into the docks she brought her muff up to cover her mouth and nose and smelled the perfume on the fur mixed with the clean, cold smell of the river. Below her on the little beach by the docks were lines of brightly colored rowboats that had been hauled out of the water and turned upside down, proof that winter had come. She remembered hiring the blue one on a bright, hot Sunday afternoon with Hershel and the children. There were a dozen boats for hire on the river that day, bobbing in the water, looking like pieces of colored licorice in a glass bowl.

Now that she was about to leave for Odessa, there was nothing to distract her from her worries. She still hadn't received word from Hershel and didn't know where he was or how to find him. She had his sister's address and would start there, but she worried that his sister had moved or didn't know where he was or, worse, that it was the unthinkable. The thought that something had happened to him rarely left her mind. It gnawed at her during the day, and at night it robbed her of sleep. Now, on the eve of her departure, she steeled herself against these thoughts. She had to keep going. She had to find him.

She walked in the park along the bluffs for the last time. She passed the merry-go-round that was shuttered and dark and the Merchant's Club where the brass band used to play in the flower garden before they were sent off to the front. The park was deserted of course. The ice cream girls in their white aprons and blond hair were gone, as was the man with the monkey who begged for coins. The kvass sellers were gone and so was the old lady who sold hats and Russian flags: They were all gone. Soon she would be too.

She crossed the street, her feet creaking on the snow, and walked down to Svetlanskaya. There she passed the Niklolaev IronWorks factory, a brooding hulk with grimy windows and smokestacks jutting up into the sky. On the other side of the street were the neglected apartment buildings that housed the workers, cold water flats without heat or gas, surrounded by empty lots full of trash and horse manure.

She jumped when the whistle blew and a minute later two guards in company uniforms pushed opened the great iron gates. Soon a crowd of women poured out of the factory floor dressed in heavy coats, woolen hats, stockings, and boots. Berta wasn't surprised to see that all the workers were women. She knew that the men had all gone to the front and many were now in their graves. In the past three months these women had taken their places, making cannons instead of farm machinery. They stared at her as they passed. They looked her up and down with envy etched in every line of their work-worn faces. They took in her furs, her gloves, and her expensive boots, whispering and giggling to each other, even once or twice jostling her on purpose. They were menacing enough to make her want to turn up the first side street.

Back on Davidkovo Street, she passed shops she used to frequent that were now shuttered for lack of goods. Here and there were burned-out buildings, blackened timbers littered with broken glass and twisted iron. These were once German shops. The war was going badly and Russia had suffered terrifying defeats. A whole army was lost at Tannenberg; army corps turned into divisions, brigades into regiments. There were hundreds of thousands if not a million Russians dead on the battlefields only three months into the war. Hatred of the Germans was running high. Everyone with a German name was suspected of being a spy; even the empress, who was German, was suspected of treachery.

The war had changed so much in Cherkast. Supply trucks parked in the streets were waiting to go to the front. Curtains were drawn over many of the windows, garbage left to rot on the stoops, a sure sign that a son or husband had just been lost. The air was acrid with the smell of smoke—not the smoke of factories, but of burning fields. Berta told herself that it was only the muzhiki burning what was left of the summer wheat, but it made her nervous all the same. She thought she could smell burning villages. She imagined the war was coming closer, even though she knew it was still hundreds of versts away.

It was growing dark and because the motor had been sold she had to walk home. There weren't many cabs left because most of the motorcars had been requisitioned and the horses too, so the trolleys weren't running either. Before trekking up the hill she decided to warm up with a cup of coffee. Fortunately the English Room was still open, so she stopped in there. The lunch trade was over and since no one had the time or money for a formal tea, the place was empty. The waiters in starched white aprons sat in the back eating their lunch at a long table and smoking hand-rolled cigarettes. They looked over at her when she came in, but no one made an effort to greet her. Eventually a heavyset waiter with a round, oily face sighed deeply and got to his feet. He sauntered over with a look of indifference.

"Good afternoon, Madame," he said patiently, taking her coat and hat.

"Just coffee, please," she said, following him over to a table by the window. It was covered in a white tablecloth and decorated with a red carnation. Overhead was a clumsy painting of Red Square and another of the czar and his family. She sat down and put her things on the empty seat beside her and looked out the window at the street traffic. There was a group of soldiers, deserters most likely, standing on the corner in front of the restaurant, selling cigarettes and sunflower seeds.

"So I say to him, it is not my war, it's his war. Let him fight it," grumbled a waiter from the back table.

"That is what I say," echoed his colleague.

"Why should I go?" said another. "I do not even know this kaiser. Why do I have to go and die in a trench because the czar does not like his cousin?" These were all the older men who hadn't been called in the first wave but would certainly be called now that Russia had suffered such heavy losses.

"Did I tell you about old lady Demianova?" said the first. "The one who lost three sons? She went crazy after that and now she wanders around the village looking for them. I nearly jumped out of my skin one night when I looked out the window and found her looking back at me with those crazy eyes. My mother says they ought to take her away and lock her up, but I think she's suffered enough. 'Let the old lady be,' I told my mother. Anyway, she will freeze to death by winter's end. You can be sure of that."

Her waiter brought over a silver pot of coffee, poured a cup, and set it down in front of her. She was about to thank him when the door opened and a frigid blast of cold air came in along with two officers dressed in greatcoats and lambskin hats. One of them had a paper under his arm, the other a small bundle. Both of them noticed Berta right off but were too polite to stare at a pretty woman sitting alone.

"We'll have a table," said the first one, smoothing his carefully trimmed beard. Like so many others he looked like the czar. He gave his coat and hat to the waiter.

"And two brandies," said the other, adding his things to the pile. The waiter handed their things to the girl at the hat check counter and showed them to a nearby table.

"They're not all like that, you know," said the shorter of the two, taking his seat. "I had a lieutenant in my unit once and he was downright decent. A good man and I trusted him. We all did." He crossed one leg over the other and Berta noticed that his boots had been outfitted with heels to make him appear taller.

"That's just like you. You're such a child. You'd trust anyone," said the other.

"I'm telling you he was honorable."

"How would you know?"

"I know, that's all."

"And suppose you're right. That makes one. One good Jew out of how many, five million?"

"I don't know about the others and neither do you. You accuse me of being gullible and yet you seriously believe they cut the phone lines and reconnect them to the Austrians."

"Why not?"

"Impossible, for one thing. Do you know anything about telephone lines? *Baba*'s yarn. Old crones making up stories to stir up trouble."

"So maybe it isn't true, but everybody knows that 90 percent of them are traitors and the rest are spies. If they didn't do that, then they did something else. I'd bet my life on it."

Berta pretended not to hear their conversation. She stared blankly into her coffee cup and then looked up out the window at a passing convoy of army trucks that belched out clouds of blue smoke from their exhaust pipes. She had heard the rumors of Jews hiding gold in corpses and sending them to the Germans, of floating messages in bottles and signaling the German artillery with lanterns and flags in the trees. Everyone was convinced that Jews were collaborators. Nobody thought to question otherwise.

Whenever she was confronted with something like this she pretended not to hear. Over the years she had perfected a look of disinterest, as if it had nothing to do with her, as if she had no thoughts on the subject. In truth it had everything to do with her. It filled her with humiliation for being a Jew and for not defending them. She was angry at the anti-Semites but also angry at the Jews for holding themselves apart and making themselves so conspicuous. It made her miss her parents. Sometimes she thought she ought to do something, say something, but she never did. Instead she kept quiet and justified her cowardice by reasoning that it was important to get along and not make a fuss.

"And I suppose they had something to do with Odessa?"

At that Berta looked over at them.

"Could be, hadn't thought about it."

"Absurd. Now you're really stepping over the line. I wash my hands of you."

"Blaming me for the truth?"

"What happened in Odessa?" she asked, not bothering to make an excuse for interrupting.

The two men looked over at her, obviously pleased by her question. "It was in the papers tonight, Miss. The Turks shelled the city and sank a gunboat and blocked us in."

"A blockade?"

"So it seems. There were two German battle cruisers."

"And there's no way out?"

The officers exchanged a look. "Well, no, that's the idea of a blockade, you see."

"So we're trapped here?"

"I suppose you could put it that way."

The officers wanted her to stay and tried to entice her with details of the event, even though she had no interest in any of it. When the waiter came by, she gave him a ruble without glancing at the check, gathered up her things, and left. Out on the street she went first in one direction and then another, knowing that something had to be done but not knowing quite what.

IT WAS after midnight when Berta arrived at the Cat Gut Club, located in the cellar of a warehouse on Podkolokony Street in the heart of the Lugovaya Market. It was a popular gathering place for artists and poets and scions of wealthy families out for an exotic evening of poetry readings and music. On special nights the dancer Marianna Golitsyn dressed as a gypsy and performed on a mirror sometimes wearing underthings, sometimes not, depending on her mood. Mostly it was a place for all the classes to come together and drink "pineapple juice" from teacups. It's what they were calling vodka since the czar outlawed it at the beginning of the war. It was also the place for paying bribes, selling information, and buying cocaine.

When Berta came down the steps the first thing she noticed was the smell, which only grew steadily worse as she descended into the club. Despite the vases of flowers that lined the wall, the whole place stank of faulty plumbing. It was worse in the lobby, so bad she had to keep her gloved palm over her mouth and nose until she managed to weave through the crowd and enter the main room.

The club proper was a cavernous space built beneath the street. The ceiling and walls had been covered with rough patches of gray plaster to give it the appearance of a cave. Berta stood on the bottom step and scanned the crowded room looking for Yuvelir. It was packed with a rowdy crowd of officers and enlisted men, their women drinking alongside them, smoking cigarettes right out in public. Everyone was singing and clapping while in the center of the room enlisted men were dancing the *kazatska*, their arms folded across their chests, their legs shooting out from under their torsos as they jumped up and down.

Berta was surprised by the gaiety in the room. How could they be in such high spirits with a war going on? Didn't they realize that hundreds of thousands of their compatriots were dying at the front? She looked at their drunken faces—at the young officer grabbing a woman and pulling her down on his lap, another falling backward into the crowd, a girl with smeared lip rouge squinting through a haze of cigarette smoke—and realized it wasn't gaiety that filled the room that night, but a desperate attempt to deny the inevitable. These were officers about to lead thousands of untrained peasants to their death. These were enlisted men about to meet the enemy without guns or bullets. Since there weren't enough arms to go around, they would be expected to *earn* their rifles by prying them out of the hands of their dead comrades. Looking around at the singing and dancing and drunken lovemaking, she understood that it wasn't a party she was witnessing, but a last supper.

Berta spotted Yuvelir seated in the back with five young officers and walked over to join them. He jumped to his feet and reached out for her hand. "Madame Alshonsky," he said with mock formality. "What is the world coming to when Berta Alshonsky graces us with her presence in a hole like this?"

"I'm sorry to interrupt your party. I really can't stay."

"Nonsense. Come sit with us." He kissed her on both cheeks and pulled over a chair. "Gogochka, get Madame Alshonsky a pineapple juice."

The talk was all about war: stories of horror and heroism, who was gone and who wasn't coming back, of the government's mismanagement, the crumbling supply lines, and the faltering munitions factories that were struggling to keep up with demand. The usual spy rumors came up, but thankfully no one mentioned the Jews. They all knew she was Jewish. No doubt they were raised to be anti-Semites, but civilized ones, who kept a check on their views when in the company of Jews of Berta's class.

She waited for as long as she could and then she leaned in. "I have to speak to you," she said to Yuvelir. The waiter had just come and put down a platter of *zakuski* in the center of the table.

"What now? Can't it wait?"

"No, it can't."

He'd been turned down for service when he tried to sign up during the initial flush of wartime patriotism. The army said his politics were too radical and they didn't want him. With all his friends gone he had nothing to do but help in the various wartime charities and write his memoir, which he thought was interesting enough to be published. But tonight a few of his closest friends were back and the last thing he wanted was to be pulled away from them.

She rose and the gentlemen got up in deference. She said her goodbyes and then turned to Yuvelir. "Come along, Misha, you're going to walk me home."

It was late and Podkolokony Street was shrouded in thick fog. It had snowed while she was in the club and now the wind swirled the snow into drifts around the lampposts and up against the buildings. Every now and then a candle appeared in a window, but mostly the street was dark and deserted. Occasionally, a figure materialized out of nowhere, a leering face in the gloom. There was a distant screech of laughter, then a man's drunken cry. Someone was calling for help. They passed an old woman sitting on a curb with a baby in her arms. She held out her hand for a coin. Berta ignored her and walked on. Everyone knew where these beggars got their babies—they rented them by the hour off the nursing mothers, hoping for a little pity and a few kopecks to buy lodging for the night.

"I have to get to Vladivostok and you have to help me," she said. Up ahead they could just make out the lights on the bridge that spanned the ravine. Once they were across they would be out of the market and the neighborhood would gradually get better.

"Why?"

"I'm going to America."

"It's too late to go to America."

"Not if I leave from Vladivostok. But I need you to get me a travel permit."

"Do you know how far that is?"

"I don't care."

"Nine thousand versts."

"Will you help me?"

"It'll take you a month, maybe more. It's hard traveling. What about your children? Berta, be reasonable. It's impossible."

"Don't tell me what's possible. I want you to talk to your father."

"I'm not even speaking to him. I can't ask him for a favor."

"Misha . . . I need this."

"He makes me grovel. He can be awful."

"Then ask your uncle."

"What makes you think I'm on better terms with him? He's just like my father. They even look alike. People are always getting them confused."

"Then ask somebody."

"I don't even know where to begin. Berta, I love you, but you're asking too much."

"Do I have to list all the things I've done for you? Is that really necessary?"

Yuvelir took in a deep breath and let it out in a rush. He shook his head in consternation and kept his eyes on the ground in front of him as he walked beside her. "Sometimes, I don't know how you get me to do these things."

She laughed and took his arm. "My poor *dorogoy*."

"And I suppose you're going to need rail tickets?"

Yuvelir walked her all the way back up the hill and slept on the sofa in her parlor. The next morning he had breakfast with her in the kitchen because the breakfast room had been closed up. She sat with him at the long worktable in the center of the room and watched him sip his tea and butter his scone. He wasn't used to getting up in the morning, so he wasn't very talkative and didn't even complain about missing a night with his friends.

THE CHERKAST train station had been donated by the rich merchants of the city as a testament to their wealth and good taste. It was supposed to rival Iaroslavl Station in Moscow. It had a medieval spire on one side, an elaborate rotunda of glass in the middle, and two round moderne turrets on either side of the large double doors. It was costly to build, but it gave the people of Cherkast a beautiful railroad terminal and the merchants a sense that they were every bit as wealthy, as cultured and as worthy of respect, as their Muscovite counterparts.

That was before the war. Now when Berta walked in through the massive double doors, carrying her bundles and trailing her children and Mitya, the gardener's helper, whom she had hired to see her safely on the train, she found that most of the expensive tile floor, the one that had cost thousands and thousands and months of negotiation, was covered with men, women, children, and all their belongings. There were families, old couples, and wounded soldiers who had been treated and released; most were stretched out on blankets on the cold floor, napping, smoking, and playing cards. Against the north wall were recovering cholera patients who had been dumped there because their beds were needed by the wounded. Children made a game of leaping over them, until their mothers saw what they were doing and screamed at them in panic.

Berta had expected this. She had heard what the train stations were like and had prepared for a long wait. But when she walked in that day and actually saw it, smelled the multitudes, heard the hacking coughs, and saw the mass of bodies stretched from one wall to the other, she had to force herself to enter.

"I don't want to go in, Mameh," Sura said, holding on to the folds of Berta's skirt.

"I know, darling," said Berta, "but remember, I said there would be lots of people. And you said it would be all right, because they were just like us. Just people who wanted to take the train, remember?"

Sura nodded wordlessly but kept clinging to Berta's skirt. Samuil spotted a boy with a bird in a cage and went over to investigate. "Don't go far," Berta called after him, but he didn't need his mother to tell him not to get lost.

When Berta looked around for a place to put her things, nobody would meet her eye. They all ignored her and let her stand there with her bundles and her frightened child clinging to her skirt. She had to step over several old men, peasants who grumbled at the intrusion but made no effort to give her room. Then a young woman in the crowd motioned her over. She was a mother too and had a daughter about Sura's age sitting next to her on a mat. She was a peasant in a rumpled skirt and felt boots, who looked up with puffy, sleepless eyes. Berta and

Mitya moved forward on tiptoe, stepping over several people before getting to the little place that the woman had made for them by gathering in her bundles.

"Thank you. I don't know what we would've done," Berta said, spreading out a mat.

"That's all right," the young mother replied in broken Russian. "An old man gave me this spot two days ago. He said he'd had enough and went home. Funny thing was a train came shortly after that, but he wouldn't have gotten on anyway. He was too old and not very strong."

Berta and Mitya made a little encampment by arranging the bundles in a circle around their mats and blankets.

"Mameh, I want to go home," Sura whispered, her round, frightened eyes soon filling with tears.

The woman's little girl watched her, glancing at Sura's doll. She was a pretty girl, dark like her mother, with soft eyes and a full mouth that looked as if it had been stung by a bee.

"Why don't you show this nice little girl your doll?" Berta said to Sura.

Sura looked over at her and shook her head.

"Why not, it might be fun."

The little girl got up and took a cautious step forward. "No," Sura said, clutching the doll to her chest.

"That's not very nice," Berta said.

"I don't care. I don't want to be nice. I want to go home," said Sura, tears spilling down her cheeks.

Berta shrugged helplessly. "I'm sorry," she said to the little girl. "Maybe another time."

"That's all right," the woman said, drawing her daughter to her. "She's shy too. We understand."

Berta suddenly sat up. "Samuil?" She jumped to her feet and Mitya did the same. "Samuil!" she cried out, looking in every direction.

"Here, Mameh!"

She whipped around and found him over by the boy with the bird in a cage. "Oh," she sighed in relief. "Well, don't go far," she called out. He ignored her and went back to the bird. "It's just like him to get lost.

He's always wandering off." She sat down, ignoring all the exhausted faces that were glancing over in her direction.

"They are such a worry, aren't they?" said the young mother. "They like to keep us worrying from one minute to the next." Her daughter lay in her lap and she stroked her long hair, rocking her back and forth like a baby. "We almost lost this little one last winter . . . she had a high fever. I thought she was going to burn up."

"Sura had a fever like that two years ago. The doctor said she was lucky to survive."

"Lucky to have a doctor, I'd say. There was an old woman in our village who came whenever there was sickness, but I never believed in her spells. She cut a length of Olga's hair and wound it around a knife and put it under her bed. That was supposed to cut her fever."

"Couldn't you get a real doctor?" Berta asked.

"I wanted to, but my father-in-law was against it. He said the old woman was just as good. I suspect he didn't want to pay. I can tell you when Olga grows up she will go to school. She won't be like her mother. She'll be able to make her own way. She'll be smart and maybe even have a trade."

Sura got up and came over to Olga and held out her doll. Olga sat up and took it tentatively. She fingered the delicate lace collar and the velvet dress and moved over so that Sura could sit down beside her.

After Kata Chaneko introduced herself and took out her embroidery, their little encampment began to take on the flavor of a domestic scene. "So, what have you heard?" Berta asked, watching Kata's deft fingers move the needle back and forth through the yoke of a child's blouse.

"A train is coming. They say it's a big passenger train, big enough to take us all, but I wouldn't count on it. I've seen lots of trains come and go since I've been here, but all of them were going the other way, to the front. Troop and supply trains mostly, hardly any passenger trains. Once I saw one of those special trains, the kind with the red curtains. It whizzed by here like a lightning bolt. People said it was the czar and the czarevitch, but who can tell?" Kata tied a knot and cut the thread with her teeth. "So where are you going?" she asked, looking up briefly.

"To Vladivostok and then to America."

"Such a long way. Why are you going there?"

"My husband."

"He is not in the war?"

"No, he was in America when it started."

"This is good, yes? You still have a husband. Mine is dead."

"He was in the war?"

Kata nodded. "The Jews killed him. They tell the Germans where to bomb. They have a lotion, you know. The Jews I mean. They put it on and it makes them safe from the bombs."

Berta stared at her new friend, then let her eyes travel to an old sleeping couple lying nearby. After that she let the conversation slip away. She would've liked to look for another place to sit, but Sura was too comfortable with Olga and she didn't want to make her move. So instead she lay back on her bundles and closed her eyes. Vladivostok was so far away. America was halfway around the world. What would she find when she got there? Would she find Hershel? Would he be alive? And what would she do if he weren't?

Berta thought she would never get to sleep in the crowded room. There were people all around her, coughing and snoring and talking in loud whispers. The wounded were groaning and there was a cholera patient who kept calling out for a nurse. But she must've fallen asleep because sometime in the middle of the night she was awakened by an approaching train whistle. She got up along with the rest of the crowd and started to gather up her things. She could hear the blasts of steam from the locomotive and the clanking of wheels as it changed tracks and pulled into the station. Soon the crowd was on its feet, lumbering forward in an insomnious haze. She called to Mitya, who was already behind her with the bundles. Berta picked up Sura, ignoring her sleepy protests, and took Samuil's hand.

At first the crowd was hardly moving, inching forward to the platform, a human tide at Berta's back, pushing her along onto the heels of the people in front of her. A shout from the platform alerted the crowd that the train was boarding. After that they became more insistent, jostling one another for a better position, pushing forward with growing impatience, unmindful of the belongings of others that they trampled under their feet. A shriek was heard in the crowd. It sounded terrified and put everyone on edge.

"It's the bird, Mameh," shouted Samuil over the tumult. "It's only the bird." And to prove him right the bird screamed again, but this time his scream was answered by another across the room on the other side. It was the scream of a terrified woman, followed by shouts of men. Then, more screams.

The crowd began to panic. It surged forward, carrying Berta and the children along, trampling everything in its path, an insensible mass of humanity that threatened to eat itself alive. Mitya soon disappeared as the crowd closed in around him and Sura began to cry. In an instant Samuil's hand was torn from Berta's. "Samuil!" she screamed. "Samuil!"

"I'm here, Mameh," he shouted back, and then miraculously his hand found hers.

She saw an old man trip and fall and heard him screaming as the mob crushed him. His wife tried to help him up, but she went down too. Her shrieks were ignored until they were cut off. Kata and Olga were ahead of them. Kata screamed as Olga was torn from her arms. She bent down to pick up her child and was knocked off her feet by the oncoming throng. By the time Berta reached the spot where they had gone down she thought she could see a blue black arm barely visible beneath the tramping boots.

"Don't let go!" she shrieked, holding tight to her children while she frantically searched for a way out. They were trapped in the howling blanket of people that stretched from one wall to the other. People were screaming and clawing at one another, struggling to stay on their feet. Clothes were torn from victims' bodies, their faces misshapen, teeth broken, limbs at odd angles. The floor was sticky with blood and vomit.

Then she saw that even in their panic the people were avoiding the cholera patients. They were going around them as if they were surrounded by a solid wall of fire. Inside, the patients lay on mats breathing their infected air, sweating through their bedclothes and watching the desperate crowd with feverish, glassy-eyed stares. The crowd skirted their perimeter, sometimes tripping over the invisible line, but always leaping back, choosing the possibility of being crushed into a bloody mass to shitting themselves to death.

Berta allowed herself to be carried along, but she kept edging closer to the north wall. A woman to her right tripped and screamed. She was trampled despite her husband's efforts to fight off the crowd. He fell too and a man tripped over them both, several more went down, and for an instant she could see a way to the wall. She didn't hesitate. She got a good grip on Sura and held on to Samuil's hand and, leaping over a crushed body, she pushed her way through the crowd. At one point she nearly lost her footing but regained her balance and made one last effort to get through, until, at last, she succeeded in breaking free and came stumbling into the north wall and the relative safety of the infected area.

A patient looked over at her as she crumpled to the floor next to his cot, hugging her children, crying and thanking a god that may or may not exist. He tried to say something to her, but his voice was too feeble. It was lost in her tears and the chaos all around them.

Chapter Thirteen

January 1915

THE MORNING was brilliant and bitterly cold after the snowstorm. The snow was so deep it nearly covered the first-floor windows. A boy arrived in a sledge and handed Berta a note through the kitchen door. It was from Hershel's attorney, Mendel Levy, and in it he requested to see her in his office as soon as possible. *No appointment necessary.* It was that phrase, more than anything, that made her feel queasy. After her first fearful thoughts she reasoned that it couldn't be that bad or Mendel Levy would have come up to see her himself. It might even be good news. He had heard from Hershel and everything was all right. There was money she didn't know about. He had figured out a way to get them out of Russia. They were going to America. She knew it could be dangerous to think like this. She could be disappointed or worse. It was such a long-held belief in the *shtetlekh*, thinking too positively invited disaster, that she just accepted it without question.

Since she had to go to her bedroom for suitable clothes, she put on a heavy coat and gloves. She and the children had been living in the kitchen all winter because she couldn't afford to heat the rest of the house; now, whenever she had to go out to the other rooms, she had to bundle up as if she were going outside. She pulled on gloves as she walked through the butler's pantry to the dining room, where the table and chairs sat huddled together under sheets. All the furniture in the house had been covered in white sheets and now the interior seemed to merge with the white snow outside, as if the house had turned itself inside out.

Later that morning, Mendel Levy met her in the reception area of his office and took her hand in greeting. He ushered her down the hall to his private office, all the time chattering about how lucky they were that they lived in Cherkast and not in Moscow, where the shortages were bad and the lines were impossible. "I hear they have to be up before dawn just to get a can of kerosene. They're even burning the fences," he said, showing her into his office. It was an overheated affair stuffed with leather furniture and the Matisses he was fond of collecting.

After they were settled and tea had been offered and declined, he told her the bad news: The bank was repossessing her house. She stared at him and for a moment didn't know what to say. Even though she knew the mortgage hadn't been paid in months, she still couldn't quite believe it. Staring vaguely at a bronze bear on his desk, she said, "I thought you were going to say you found a way out of Russia for us."

"Berta, we've been through all that," he said, with a note of impatience. "There is no way out."

"Not even through Finland?"

"I told you about Finland. It's impossible. It's all impossible. Now it's time to put away these ridiculous notions and start thinking about how you're going to make it through the war. It won't be easy and there's no telling how long it will last. That's why the first thing we must do is sell your furniture."

She looked up in alarm. "All of it?"

"I don't think you understand your circumstances. Your accounts have been wiped out. You have no more money. That's why it's important to start living within your means. Fortunately, I know a little apartment not far from the Berezina. You and the children will be quite comfortable there. It's a nice apartment. A friend of mine had it for years."

With the mention of friends she thought of her own and how, in a few weeks, everyone would know that she had been thrown out of her own home. She thought of poor Pavla, whose husband had been sent to Verkhoyansk. Soon everyone would be feeling sorry for her, giving her advice, and calling her poor Berta behind her back. It would be intolerable. "Does everyone have to know?"

"They'll be a notice in the paper."

She closed her eyes.

"It's the law. But don't worry, I'll handle it. It won't be nearly as bad as you think."

Mendel Levy was able to convince the bank to post the foreclosure notice on a Friday, in the late afternoon paper, where it wouldn't draw much attention. After that he saw to an auction house to oversee the sale of the furniture. Of course there had to be advertising to bring in a crowd. Berta stayed home that day and received no one. Alix came by the house afterward to tell her all about it, not that Berta particularly wanted to know. This didn't stop Alix, however. She eagerly relayed all that had happened at the auction: who was there, what they had bought, and how much they paid for it. She even admitted to buying a few things herself and hoped that Berta wouldn't think she was being disloyal or callous.

Berta was glad when Alix left so she could mourn the loss of her home in solitude. She spent the afternoon wandering through the empty rooms, cold as ice caves. That night she made a fire in the stove in her bedroom and spent one last night on a mattress on the floor. She lay down under the quilts and listened to the wind rattling the windows. She watched the firelight cast long shadows over the walls as she tried to remember the name of the cellist who had come to play a few years back. The Bach cello suites. A small girl from the academy with long, beautiful fingers. Berta remembered that she had trouble lugging her cello around. Anna Vasilevna, that was it. Good, now she could sleep.

The apartment that Mendel Levy rented for her was on a tree-lined street not far from the shops on the corner of Sretensky and Kiyevskaya. It wasn't what she was used to, but it was a pleasant place full of light in a respectable neighborhood and her neighbors were quiet and well-mannered. There was a professor of languages, or maybe it was literature, living in the apartment above her. He wasn't old, but his body was bent and he walked with two canes. She talked to him on several occasions because Masha didn't get along with his cat. The two felines even fought once or twice on the steps outside the building. They agreed over a cup of tea in Berta's apartment that there wasn't much they could do about it.

During the winter of 1915 the news was encouraging. The army had achieved stunning successes against the Austrians in Galicia and in the Carpathians and even the impregnable fortress of Peremyshl had been taken. With money in her account from the sale of her furniture and the good news from the front, she and the children settled into their little apartment. Now that there were only four rooms to heat, the apartment was warm and comfortable. She even managed to save some of her furniture, two settees from the parlor and a carved oak library table that she put in the bay window in the front room and covered with masses of ferns and orchids that she had kept alive in the kitchen while the rest of the house froze.

Samuil was enjoying spying on the tenants. Vera stayed on at a reduced salary, as well as Zina, the scullery maid, who was cheap and said she could cook. That part was a lie. But Berta gave her a cookbook and encouraged her to learn on the job. Since Zina had been born in Moscow to a pair of textile factory workers and spoke Russian, not Surzhyk like the other domestics, she had the kind of self-confidence that it took to reach beyond her station. She could read and write and thought herself too good for the boys in Cherkast. For all these reasons, Berta got the idea that she could learn how to cook. And she did. In fact she got so good at it that she began to take on airs. Vera complained that she was becoming temperamental, telling the other servants in the building that she was an artist with food.

By early spring, speculation and the resulting inflationary prices had absorbed most of the furniture money. The war was going badly again. The Germans had swept into Russian Poland and occupied most of Lithuania and there was even talk of losing Riga and maybe even Petrograd. Berta cut back on kerosene. The house grew colder because the price of wood began to climb and now they could only afford to heat one room at a time. To save money Berta made a point of shopping for the food herself. Zina often complained about the quality and even threatened to quit on a few occasions.

On this particular night Berta had taken a candle to her room and was sitting at the ebony Chinese table, the one she salvaged from the telephone alcove. She ran a finger over the spot where she had scraped the paint away and for a moment she took time away from her account book to remember that night when the pianist had canceled at the last minute and she had to hire Madame Gorbunova to take her place. It was hard to imagine that there had ever been a time in her life when her greatest worry was finding someone to play at her salon. Now everything had changed. Hershel had been gone for nearly a year and a half, and she doubted whether she would ever see him again. She was trapped in Little Russia and running out of money and no amount of cutting back was going to change that fact. If they were going to make it through the war, she would have to earn more.

The next day she got up early, and after a cup of tea and a stale bun in the kitchen she went off to the House of Baranov to sell her jewelry. She had all her pieces in her just-in-case bag tucked into the pocket of her coat. She didn't feel safe carrying it around with her. To make sure that it wasn't stolen by the many pickpockets and thieves who were roaming the streets, she kept her hand in her pocket firmly clasped around the purse as she hurried down Sretensky Street to Davidkovo Square, past the old men playing skittles on the little patch of grass in the center, to the great brass and glass door of the House of Baranov.

The shop smelled of almonds because there was a little alcove off the main gallery where customers sat on damask sofas and sipped almond tea while they looked over the jewelry set out on velvet-lined trays. Today the shop was empty except for a pretty saleswoman who stood behind a bank of glass cases at the back of the shop. Berta had never seen a woman behind the counter before and guessed she was only there because her male counterparts had been slaughtered on the battlefields.

"May I help you?" she asked, with an inquiring look. She had black hair that was swept back off her face and thick eyebrows that had been plucked into submission.

"Is Monsieur Baranov here?"

"Which one?"

Berta thought for a moment. "Either one."

"May I say what this is about?"

"I have jewelry to sell," she said, trying to sound offhand. She could feel her cheeks flushing and was grateful when the girl turned to the back room.

Both brothers came out and greeted her in a friendly fashion, for she and Hershel had long been good customers. These two brothers looked remarkably similar. They both had long faces, bald except for a swath of hair at the back of their heads, and they both wore jeweler's loupes hanging by a cord around their necks. Not much time was spent on pleasantries and soon she had her jewelry displayed on a velvet tray. The brothers examined the pieces through their loupes, exchanging them back and forth until they had examined every one. Then Vladimir P. Baranov, the spokesman of the two, looked up and said, "I remember these."

"You sold them to us."

"I know. Fine pieces, every one. But I'm afraid we can't give you even close to what they're worth."

"How much?"

The two brothers looked over the lot quickly and then after exchanging a look, Vladimir P. Baranov said, "Five hundred."

Her eyebrows flared. "For all of them?"

"I'm afraid so."

"But they're worth three times that amount."

"Probably more. Problem is the war. Times are uncertain. There isn't a lot of demand for fine jewelry these days."

"You can't do any better than that?"

"Afraid not. You can try the other houses, but I expect you won't get much more. And there is the danger of walking around with them in your pocket."

After a brief hesitation Berta parted with everything except for the diamond and pearl bracelet that Hershel had given her when Samuil was born. That she would keep forever. Folding the rubles into her just-in-case bag she left the shop, muttering to herself as she walked back up to Sretensky Street. She kept going over the figures in her head. When she became aware that she had been talking to herself, she colored and looked around to see if anybody had noticed. A soldier leaning up against the edge of a bank building looked over at her and said, "No matter, Madame. I do it all the time myself."

Berta found that no matter how careful she was with money there was always something unexpected that came up. Samuil needed school supplies and a new uniform. Sura got sick and needed a doctor. The rent was raised. There were shortages and everything went sky high: kerosene, bread, vegetables when she could find them, and eggs and butter, which generally she could not. All these extras devastated her budget, so much so that by a year later in the winter of 1916, she found herself worse off than before and nearly three months behind on the rent.

One night she and the children were at the little table in the front room having supper by the light of only one kerosene lamp. Now kerosene was only available to those who got up before dawn and stood in line for most of the morning. The dining room was cold and they were bundled up in coats and hats and holding their hands over the bowls of hot soup for warmth. Berta had set the wick too high on the lamp and smoke curled out of the chimney and rose up to the ceiling in lazy circles.

There was a crash in the kitchen, the sound of a smashing plate and a string of swear words in Russian. A few minutes later Zina appeared in the dining room with her suitcase in her hand and a hat on her head. She was flushed with frustration and her lips were quivering with emotion.

"I am a cook," she cried. "That's what I do. I am an artist. But how am I supposed to do my work when there is nothing to cook? No vegetables, no meat, no chicken, nothing, nothing but green potatoes and bad fish and long lines. And it stinks here. The whole town stinks and I am sick of it. I am going back to Kiev."

Berta didn't try to stop her. She couldn't afford her anyway. She apologized for not having the money to pay her but told her to be patient and she would send her the money soon.

"Why? What will be different?" asked Zina, not bothering to hide her irritation at not being paid what was owed her.

"I'm going to find work."

Zina barked a laugh. "You? You working?" The proper deference a servant paid a mistress had all but eroded away after several empty paydays.

"Yes, and why not? I thought I'd find some work in a dress salon, provided the clientele is of my class . . . my former class, that is," Berta said, her voice trailing off.

Her honesty had an effect on Zina. She gazed at the smoking lamp and then back to Berta. Softening, she said, "*Da*, I can see that. You would do good in something like that. You know how to dress. You have beautiful things."

It was true. She did have excellent taste and an eye for fashion. She could put together ensembles and had done it for Alix and a few of her closest friends. And she could bring in the customers. She knew them all personally. They had been her friends.

THE FIRST dress salon Berta tried was S. A. Konovalova Dress and Costume Company. The shop was empty, except for a few shop assistants and a live model who sat in a gilt chair by the door, reading a magazine and waiting for customers to request her. The girl looked up when she saw Berta come in, straightened quickly, and put down her magazine. A shop assistant came over and asked her if she needed help. Berta thanked her and said she was there to see Madame Konovalova. The girl went off to find the proprietress and left her standing at the window, watching a religious procession in the street. The crowd was led by a priest in a black robe carrying a cross. Directly behind him were several women holding up icons, more people, more icons, and then a surprisingly large crowd.

After Madame Konovalova heard Berta's request for work she said, "I'm not surprised, Madame Alshonsky. I heard about your misfortune, about your house and your things being sold off. I was sorry to hear of it."

"Yes, well, I'm sure there are those who are worse off. But now you can see why I need the work."

"I would like to hire you, I really would. But orders are down and yard goods are hard to come by. If I wanted to make gowns out of wool and cotton I wouldn't have a problem. But try finding voile or crepe de Chine these days. The truth is, Madame Alshonsky . . ." and here she let her voice drop to a whisper, "I've even been thinking of letting some of the girls go."

A short while later Berta was back on the street, grateful that her first interview was over. She hadn't found work, but at least she hadn't been humiliated. She tried three more salons without luck before she came to the S. I. Brodsky Dress and Fur Company, located across from the opera house in the best part of town. Monsieur Brodsky was very particular about his girls and dressed them all in black skirts and white shirtwaists with a coat of arms, a *B* intertwined with vines and tiny birds, over the breast pocket. There were several girls waiting for customers in the elaborate shop that day and a live model in the window wearing a fur coat. There weren't many customers though—the war had weeded out the pretenders. But there was always money among the *kupechestvo*, and there would always be a season and dresses that went with it.

Monsieur Brodsky brightened when he saw Berta at the door. She had been a valued customer once and they had enjoyed something of a friendship. She knew all about his mother, whom he doted on, and who had recently lost her foot to diabetes. She thought if anybody would give her work it would be S. I. Brodsky.

"Madame Alshonsky, we were so worried about you. We haven't seen you in such a long time, and now here you are again and looking more beautiful than ever." Monsieur Brodsky was a small man, very correct in a stiff collar and dark suit with his coat of arms embroidered over the pocket. She happened to know that his father was a Jew. Although he didn't consider himself a coreligionist, it still brought a certain ease to their dealings. "Fortune has smiled on you. This is good news. So tell me what can I do for you."

"Actually, I'm not here to buy anything."

"Oh, you say that, but I bet we could entice you. We have such delicious new designs. Have you seen this one yet?" he said, pulling out a black satin decorated with braiding and jet beads.

"Monsieur, you don't understand, I've come looking for work."

"Here? You want to work here?"

"I have a fashion sense. You said so yourself. And I know everyone. I'd be valuable. And I don't think I'd be wrong in saying that we were friends once."

Monsieur Brodsky waved to a well-dressed woman who had stopped to look at the model in the window. She waved back and motioned to him that she liked the coat. He put his fingers together and gave her a little bow. "That's Tatiana Tikhonova, do you know her? A lovely person. Her husband fell off a mountain before the war and died. Lucky for her, I hear he was impossible."

Then he took Berta's arm and led her to a secluded spot in the back of the store. "I want you to know that we're still friends, Madame Alshonsky. And that's why I'm not going to make an excuse and send you on your way. I'm going to tell you exactly why I can't hire you. Why you would ruin my business in a week if I did."

"But, Monsieur—"

"No, let me finish. You need to hear this. You need to know how things are. It's very simple. You're a Jew and nobody wants to buy from a Jew, especially not now, not with the war and the talk of spies. A peddler maybe, a window washer, but not a shopgirl in a fine salon. Nobody wants a Jew getting that close to them, seeing them in their underwear and touching them. It wouldn't do. Wouldn't do at all. I wish I could help you, and if it were a different time, you're right, I would hire you."

She nodded slowly, thanked him in a small worried voice that she hardly recognized, and left the shop. She knew he was telling her the truth. He would have no reason to lie; he was just trying to help her. But she couldn't let him frighten her. She had to keep going. Something would come up. She would meet someone who knew someone who was looking to hire and she would hurry over and get there before anyone else. That's how it would happen. All she needed was a bit of luck and so far, up until now, she had been very lucky in life.

She spent the rest of the afternoon trying every shop on Davidkovo Street, big and small, dress shops, milliners, a department store, even the green grocer on the corner. No one would hire her. Eventually the shops began to close, the wind came up, a light dusting of snow began to fall, and still she wouldn't go home. So she walked down to the river. It was frozen solid and even though it was nearly dark, there were still ice fisherman hunched over their holes in the ice. Several of them were following the footpath up the bluffs with a catch of silvery fish dangling from a line.

When it got too cold to stand out on the bluffs, she turned back to the city and followed one of the main streets back into town. She walked through what was left of the German neighborhood and on past the Cherkast Agricultural Academy on Skakovaya Street. Slowly the reality of her situation began to sink in: She was alone with two children in a country at war. She had no money and no skill that could earn her a living, nothing of value left to sell, and there was no end to the war in sight. If her children were to grow up, it would be because she found a way to keep them from starving. If they received an education, she would have to pay for it. It was all up to her now, no one else, just her.

She kept going, not wanting to turn back and face the responsibilities that waited for her at home. The snow fell harder driven by the wind. It was wet and it ruined her hat, soaked through her clothes, and crimped her hair into frizzy ringlets about her face. She was shivering and her hands were starting to cramp despite her gloves. She kept thinking of the beggar woman on Podkolokony Street in the Lugovaya Market begging for kopecks with a rented infant. A phrase began to circle through her thoughts like the tail of a kite. *Beg, borrow, or steal. Beg, borrow, or steal.* It became like a tune in her head that wouldn't leave. *Beg, borrow, or steal. Beg, borrow, or steal.* But she would not beg and she could not steal, so what did that leave her? Borrow. She would borrow the money. She stood in front of a burned-out shop that had once been a German bakery and looked up into the black sky, letting the snow fall on her cheeks and lips while she thought it over. She opened her mouth and the flakes landed on her tongue and melted instantly. She thought about where she would go, whom she would ask, and the more she thought, the more it began to look like a simple solution to a dreadful problem.

The next morning Berta went to see Aleksandra Dmitrievna and was told by her maid that she was still asleep. Berta would not be put off and pushed passed the girl, saying that it was all right, Madame Tretiakova had asked her to come around and get her up early. She went up the stairs, her hand gliding over the marble balustrade carved to look like waves on an ocean, and opened Alix's door without knocking. She found her friend asleep under a mound of quilts and down-feather pillows and shook her awake.

"Berta, *milochka* . . . so early?" she croaked. "What time is it?"

"It's time you were up."

"But it's still the middle of the night." Alix never got up before noon, sometimes not even before two or three in the afternoon. She never went to sleep before dawn. She was fond of saying that she kept Moscow hours, even though she had never lived a day in Moscow or anywhere else except Cherkast and the little village near Kiev where she was born.

Her father had been a cotton mill owner. He had nine children, most of whom he didn't like very much, but Alix was the baby and he loved her dearly. He always treated her like the baby until the day he died and that was fine with her. So fine, in fact, that even after she had five children of her own and had reached middle age she still couldn't see why she should be treated any differently.

"I have to talk to you. It's important," Berta said, opening the drapes and letting in a rush of sunlight. Alix's room was a great lagoon of green satin. The whole house was built around an ocean theme. It had a wavy iron fence out front and a wide frieze of shells and fantastic sea plants just under the roofline. The floors were decorated with inlaid shell patterns and seahorses made of exotic woods.

"So bright," Alix complained. The light was reflecting off the snow outside and filling the room with a blazing white light. She put her hands over her eyes and the rings on her fingers threw off a thousand tiny rainbows over the satin-lined walls. "It's a good thing I love you," she said, pulling the sheet over her face. "Now go away."

Berta came over and sat down on the edge of the bed. "Alix, you have to wake up."

"I want to sleep. I was up all night on the telephone. Things are bad. Very bad. The cities are starving. And who will plant in the spring? All the boys are dead and buried, poor things. I'm very worried, Bertochka. Very worried indeed."

"I need to talk to you."

"Olga Fedorovna says there is going to be a revolution. Her husband wants it. Can you imagine that? A revolution here in Russia. Of course we always talked about it, but I never thought that it would actually happen."

"Alix . . ."

"Did you know they tried to kill Rasputin?"

"*Alix!*"

"What? What is it?"

"*Will you listen to me?*"

"You're scaring me. Is it the children?"

"I need to borrow five thousand rubles."

She sucked in her breath and sat up. "*Milochka* . . . my God, that's a lot of money."

"I know. But I'll pay it back."

"I'm sure you will. I don't doubt it for a minute. It's just that—" There was a knock on the door and the maid came in. "The house Jew is here, Madame."

"Why is everyone coming so early?"

"Can't we finish this, please?" Berta asked.

"Yes, of course. But first I must get up." Alix sighed and swung her legs out of bed. The maid hurried over to help her on with her dressing gown. "Come down with me. It won't take a minute. He brought me some bracelets. I have to choose one so that Lenya doesn't get me something awful for my name day." She was heading for the bathroom and expected Berta to follow.

"I can't stay, Alix. I need to know if you're going to loan me the money."

"It's so much, *milochka*. I hate to bring this up at a time like this, but do you know how you're going to pay it back?"

She followed Alix into the bathroom. "Hershel . . . who else?"

"You said he wasn't answering your letters."

"It's the mail, Alix. And the war. Everybody knows that. He probably already sent the money. It was held up by the blockade. It'll get here when it's over."

"Yes, of course it will. But just in case . . . not that it would ever happen this way, but let's just say, Hershel doesn't want to repay the loan. What if he has other plans for the money? How would you pay it back then? I know I'm being overly cautious, but it's just that Lenya will ask me these questions and, naturally, I have to have an answer. You know how he is."

"Of course I'd pay it back. I'd find work or sell something, I'd find a way. But it won't happen like that. Hershel always pays his debts."

"I know. I'm just being foolish. And you are so dear to me. I couldn't deny you anything." She thought for a moment and then brightened. "I have it. I won't tell Lenya. Why does he have to know? I have my own money."

After that the two women hugged and kissed and Berta left her in the bathroom splashing icy water on her face, which, as everyone knew, was good for the liver and circulation.

Once it was all settled Berta seemed to uncoil; every muscle in her body relaxed. She was flush with relief. On the way down the stairs she had an urge to talk to someone, to chatter about nothing, to be frivolous and flirty. Which explains why, when she saw the house Jew waiting in the little office off the foyer, she stopped to talk to him. He looked up nervously at her approach, a little man in a shabby tweed wearing a jaunty bow tie that seemed out of place with his grave expression.

"She'll be down in a little while," she said in Yiddish.

"Yes, thank you," he replied, also in Yiddish. He seemed a little surprised at finding a young woman in this house who spoke to him in his mother tongue.

"What kind of jewelry did you bring?"

"Pearls."

"She wants pearls?"

"Pearls with diamonds. She says she has a friend who has a bracelet she has always admired and I'm supposed to find her one just like it."

Berta laughed and wished him good luck. She fingered the coveted bracelet on her wrist as she swept out the front door. It was a cold, bright morning and she took a deep and freeing breath. She hurried down the steps and stopped at the bottom to turn her face up to the sun and catch a little warmth before setting out for home. After that she stopped off at the butcher's and the bakery and went to the produce market in search of the freshest potatoes, onions, and beets. At last she could open her purse without that familiar dread that came with every kopeck she spent. Now that the threat had been lifted, she could see how frightened she had been. She had contracted into a hard nut, shunning company, avoiding anyone she knew, not even wanting to get out of bed in the morning. But as she walked home at her customary clip, stopping to talk to shopkeepers and even smiling at a soldier who was selling sunflower seeds, she felt whole again, safe. She had pulled herself through.

When she got home she met her upstairs neighbor, Professor Bardygin, on the stair and stopped to invite him over for tea and pastries.

After that she climbed the last few steps to her door and was about to insert her key into the lock when Sura opened it and gave her mother a disapproving frown. "Where have you been? We were expecting you hours ago."

"Well, I'm here now."

"What's all this?"

"If you help me in, I'll show you."

Vera hurried over to help. "So much, Madame?" she said peeking into a bag. "Butter," she exclaimed.

"Did you get something for me?" Sura asked. Berta held up a pastry box. "What is it?"

"A surprise."

Sura followed them into the kitchen, where they put the packages down on the butcher-block table. It was a small kitchen with a brick stove in the corner. Most of the shelves were empty except for a few dishes and glasses. Vera had her pick of shelves when it came to putting away the dry goods.

"Can I have some now?" asked Sura.

"No, you must wait for tea."

"Are they little cakes?"

"We'll see."

"You must have found work," Vera said, dumping the onions into a basket on the counter. Then she found the package of meat and her eyes widened. "Meat, Madame. You must've found a treasure."

That afternoon they were in the kitchen preparing the stew. Vera had peeled the onions and Berta was chopping them. Her eyes were tearing so badly that she had to stop and splash them with cold water. The whole house smelled of frying onions, meat, and woodsmoke. The boy had delivered a bundle and now nearly every stove in the apartment was going and it was so warm that Berta had to take off her sweater.

"What if Professor Bardygin wants a chocolate one?" Sura asked. She was following her mother from table to sink and back again. She had stolen a look at the cakes and now she was intent on securing a chocolate one for herself.

"He won't."

"But what if he does?"

"We won't let him."

"But he's our guest. We'll have to let him."

"Then you can have the other one. There are two chocolates."

This seemed to satisfy her for the moment until she remembered she had a brother. "But what if Samuil wants it?"

"We'll give him the lemon."

"He doesn't like lemon."

There was a knock at the door and Vera went to see who it was.

"Then he can have the apple."

"He'd rather have the chocolate."

"Then you can share it with him."

"But it's so small, Mameh."

Vera hurried back in and whispered, "It's Aleksei Sergeevich Tretiakov. He wants to see you."

Berta stared at her without blinking. "How did he look?" she asked, untying her apron with trembling hands.

"Stern."

She went out to the front room, where she found him standing at the window, looking out on the street, with his hat in his hand, still wearing his overcoat. There was a red halo around his head from the setting sun. The potted ferns she had brought from Lubiansky Street cast leafy shadows on the walls and furniture and turned the little room into a jungle of chiaroscuro. Even with his back to her she could see that he was stiff and uncomfortable. When he turned at her approach he barely looked at her. She saw the firm set of his mouth under his moustache and the hard glitter in his eyes and her stomach dropped. She knew what he was going to say even before he opened his mouth. It was all over. She had lost and now they would be out on the street.

"Aleksei Sergeevich, how nice of you to call." She was surprised at how calm she sounded.

"Yes . . . yes," he said, not bothering to hide his impatience. Alix was always joking about how she managed Lenya, but nothing was further from the truth. Aleksei Sergeevich ruled his household the same way he ruled his export business: with a keen sense of propriety, moderation, and thrift. He didn't inherit his fortune—he made it with hard work and his wife's small inheritance. He was a Slavophile. He liked to collect Russian paintings, admired all things Russian, and had no patience for any schemes that he considered to be out of the bounds of common sense. Moreover he cared little for the sentimental wishes of his silly wife and long considered her money his.

"May I offer you some tea?"

"I'm not staying. I'm sorry, but I'm going to have to get right down to it. My wife made you a promise this morning that she cannot possibly keep."

"I see."

"Although it is not my intention to add to your troubles and I am naturally sorry for them, I'm afraid you will have to look elsewhere for the loan. You see, my wife is not in control of *her money*, as she calls it, and has no right to make you such an offer."

"I understand."

"Yes, well, I'm very glad you do," he said, casting his glance about him to see that he hadn't forgotten anything. "I hope you are well . . . considering."

"Yes, thank you, Aleksei Sergeevich. Very well."

On the way to the door he asked about her children and about her new apartment and how she was getting along. Her answers were all positive and she seemed quite normal. She gave no indication of the storm raging inside her head, of the panic that froze her thoughts and the heavy weight on her chest that was making it hard to breathe. She had no idea what she was saying. Fortunately these little pleasantries were so much a part of her that they didn't take any thought at all. After she closed the door, she came back into the kitchen and told Vera she was going out and not to wait tea for her.

"What about Professor Bardygin?" asked Sura, as she stood at the door and watched her mother put on her coat.

"Tell him I had to go out."

"And what about the cake?"

"You have it without me," she said putting on her hat.

"A whole chocolate one?"

She stopped and laid a hand on her daughter's cheek. Then turning back to the door she said, "Whatever you like."

She walked down Sretensky Street, ignoring the crowd all around her and keeping her eyes on the ground in front of her so that she wouldn't have to speak to anyone. She didn't go down to the bluffs or up to the Berezina; she avoided the streets where she might run into someone she knew and headed straight for Dulgaya Street.

There she found it crowded with refugees from Galicia and Lithuania—whole families huddled around fires built in metal drums with their belongings scattered around them, bundles of clothes and wheelbarrows filled with household items that they managed to save. It was so crowded that she had to walk down the middle of the street, skirting a mound of horse dung still steaming in the frosty air. Everywhere there were Jews who had been expelled from the towns along the front. There were old men and women; mothers with children; sick, starving people staring at nothing, seeing nothing, waiting for something to happen: death, disease, for somebody to tell them what to do now that they had lost everything—their families, their homes and businesses—everything that had once given their life meaning.

Berta glanced over at a group of children, orphans most likely, huddled together over a fire. They looked hardened and defiant as though they had been on the street for a long time. A boy of about ten looked up as she came closer and for a moment there was a glimmer of recognition in his eyes. She might have looked like his mother in the murky twilight. He might have thought he recognized the quick step or the hair or the figure. He was wearing a man's overcoat with the sleeves rolled up and held a cigarette between his fingers. But in that instant the hardness left his face and hope returned, and for a moment he looked like a child again. Then he got a good look at her in the gaslight and his eyes went dull with disappointment. He shoved the cigarette between his lips, stuck his hands in his pockets, and hunched his shoulders against the cold until he looked to Berta like an old man.

She turned in at Lhaye's apartment and walked up the steep flight to the musty hallway. She edged past the barrel of water on the landing with its collar of ice.

"What is it? What's wrong?" Lhaye asked, when she opened her door and found her sister standing there, wet and cold, a lost look in her eyes, her features smooth with fear. Lhaye was holding the baby on her hip and stepped aside to let her in. "You look horrible. You're shivering . . . are you sick? Here, sit here. Let me get you a blanket."

She shooed her older children into the kitchen and gave the baby to Vulia and went to get Berta a blanket. She came back in and tucked it around Berta's legs and shoulders the way Mameh used to do when they were little and the winter winds were blowing outside. After that she went into the kitchen to make a glass of hot tea, brought it back, and sat down across from her. "So, tell me. What is it? What's wrong?"

"I don't have any money."

Lhaye laughed with relief. "Is that all?"

"All? I have no money for rent or food. We're destitute. I tried to find work but no one will hire me. I sold my jewelry. I even tried to borrow, but it's hopeless . . . all hopeless. We're going to be out on the street like the people out there." She burst into tears and buried her face in her hands. The children stuck their heads out to watch their aunt cry. Lhaye waved at them to go back into the kitchen. Then she put her arms around her sister and held her, rocking her like Mameh used to do.

"First of all, Bertenka, you will never be out on the street," she said. You'll stay by us."

"Here?"

"And why not?"

Berta looked around at the water stain on the wallpaper and the dirty lace curtains. There was a basket of yarn beside her on the floor with a pair of rusty scissors sticking out of a skein. There were bedrolls against one wall where the children slept when it wasn't too cold. "What will Zevi say?"

"He will be happy to have you. And he can find you work at the factory."

She thought of the factory girls coming out of the ironworks that day, hard, sullen, eyes swollen with exhaustion, misery stamped on their dirty faces.

"Don't be frightened. It won't be so terrible. It's not like some of the factories you hear about. The workers are organized. Zevi will take care of you."

Berta took a sip of the tea and then another and soon color began to creep back into her cheeks. She was beginning to see that moving in there was her only real option and that she was lucky to have it. "Are you sure about this? You wouldn't mind?"

"Of course I wouldn't mind. To have you and the children here with me? What more could I want? And besides, you're my sister. Where else would you go?"

A few days later Berta and Vera packed up the apartment. Professor Bardygin made room in his section of the basement so she could store her furniture there. The rest, clothes and a few toys, she packed up in the suitcases. She and Samuil loaded them into a wheelbarrow that she had borrowed from the green grocer down the street. Vera wanted to help her down the hill, but Berta said no. "You can't do for me anymore, Verochka. I'm on my own now. I'm going to have to get used it."

She hugged Vera good-bye, picked up the handles of the wheelbarrow, and started down the hill with the children in tow. It was heavy and hard to maneuver, especially when she came to the corner and had to let the wheel bounce down over the curb. It tipped over, and the suitcases spilled out onto the cobblestones, but fortunately an old porter and a soldier were there to help her put them back again, and they even helped her across the street and up on the opposite curb. Eventually, with Samuil's help, she got the hang of it and was able to maneuver it down the streets and through the crowds. She didn't want to meet anyone she knew, so she kept off Davidkovo Street and took shortcuts through the alleys and courtyards whenever she could. Samuil was excited and thought of it as an adventure. Sura wanted to know when they could move back home and be with Masha again, who would now be staying with the professor.

That night Berta, Lhaye, their children, and Zev all crowded around the little table in the front room and ate a supper of soup, bread, and boiled beets. There were three adults and six children in the two rooms, three if you counted the tiny kitchen. Berta's things were piled in a corner of the front room. This would be her place for now, a corner of an apartment on Dulgaya Street in the Jewish neighborhood.

"No matter what, just know this is your place too, Bertenka," her sister said as they were clearing away the dishes. "It is not much, but it's a place of your own and it cannot be taken away from you. So you can stop worrying. You have family that will take care of you. You are not alone."

Berta squeezed her hand and managed a smile. She looked at her suitcases piled up in the dark corner and at the brown water stain on the wall above them. She thanked her sister, but really she was thinking about the roof and wondering where she could find a bit of canvas to protect her belongings.

Later Lhaye spread out some blankets on the iron stove top so that she, Zevi, and the children could sleep over the dying coals. She offered the spot to Berta, but she declined it and instead made a bed for herself and her children on a pallet in front of the stove. For the first few hours she lay there watching the glowing coals through the cracks in the stove, trying to ignore the scratching and scurrying in the walls all around her. Then she closed her eyes and tried to sleep. After a few hours she gave up and went into the front room. There she put on several layers of clothing and wrapped herself in a blanket. She brought a chair over to the window and wiped off the lacy pattern of ice that formed on the inside of the glass so she could watch the snow fall through the circle of lamplight across the street. It was deserted now. The refugees had been ordered out. Some went on to an uncertain future in the provinces, others to camps in Siberia or northern Russia. The people were gone, but bits and pieces of their belongings were left there: an old straw mattress lying in the gutter, a bundle of old clothes, a handcart with a broken wheel, a pair of shoes frozen stiff in the snow.

She saw an animal race through the gaslight, casting a long shadow on the building behind it. It was small, a weasel or perhaps a sable, something wild in the middle of the city. For some reason it reminded her of Hershel and she ached to be with him. She closed her eyes and remembered what it was like to lie next to him, to smell his hair, taste his lips, to feel his body against hers, the way his muscles worked, the way his pleasure came with hers, and the tranquility they shared afterward.

She tried to send him a thought. She pictured it like a flowing tendril of hoarfrost moving out from Cherkast, to the rest of Little Russia, to Russian Poland, Germany, and on to the western front. It moved west to France, to England, out across the Atlantic to New York and then to Wisconsin, which she pictured as a city like Cherkast. There an icy tendril moved across the cobblestone streets until it found him asleep in his sister's house.

Are you there?

It would come to him in a dream. He would wake and remember it.

Are you there?

And then he would reply. He too would sit by the window and send it off. She wondered if it would take the same path or come back to her by a different route.

And then she had it, clear as clean water.

Are you there?

But it was only her own thought back again, lonely and lost: It had traveled all across America, across the Pacific Ocean, across Siberia to Russia, to Little Russia. And finally back to the room on Dulgaya Street.

Chapter Fourteen

March 1916

On the morning before Purim, Berta found the can of kerosene outside the door with a note attached to it: *For Madame Alshonsky*. She and Lhaye had been up late the night before embroidering gifts for the children and as a consequence had used far too much of it to light their work. Since Lhaye would be spending most of the day baking and preparing the meal to break the fast for Queen Esther, it was up to Berta to rise before dawn and go down to the market for more. It was still dark when she left the apartment that morning and so she nearly tripped over the can on her way out the door.

"No signature?" asked Lhaye. She was rolling out the dough for the hamantashen. The *mohnelach* was already hardening on the cookie sheet. "Who could've left it? Did you do a kindness for somebody?"

"I've barely left this apartment, you know that."

"Maybe it's for Purim?"

"Kerosene for Purim? And who would give me a present? I don't even know anybody."

Lhaye picked up the baby before he had chance to crawl toward the hot stove and handed him to Berta. She took him in her lap and entertained him with a bunch of measuring spoons.

"Maybe somebody thinks they know you?"

"Here? Who knows me here?"

"Maybe they know Hershel?"

"Why should they know him?"

Lhaye took a bite of the *mohnelach*. "It's good. Nice and sweet. Know what that means? Going to be a good year." She went back to her rolling pin. "It's a mystery, that's what it is."

"And even if they knew him, why would they leave me a can of kerosene?"

"Maybe he helped someone and now they're helping us. Why should we question it? *Ven dos mazel kumt, shtel im a shtul.* If fortune calls, offer him a seat. Here, give me the baby. I'll get Vulia to watch him. You pluck the bird."

That night the neighbors came in to read the Megillah, the book of Esther, and break the fast. They brought noisemakers so that every time Haman's name was mentioned they could spin the handles and make a loud racket. The men stamped their feet and the children spun their *graggers* until there wasn't an apartment on the street where one could find peace and quiet. When the people upstairs came down to complain they were invited in to stay. Soon the little apartment was filled to capacity and people were spilling out into the hallway and even into the street. The crowd stood around, talking over each other and eating *mohnelach* and hamantashen and washing it down with good strong tea.

The next day Berta and Lhaye cooked all day for the celebration that night. Zev should have been in shul reading the Megillah for a second time, but instead he went to work. He was a Bolshevik and had nothing good to say about the ritualistic nonsense of his forebears. It was a sore subject between him and Lhaye. She nagged him to go to shul and to stop lighting his cigarettes on the Shabbes candles. In turn he begrudged her the few kopecks for a Shabbes goy.

That night the Purim players came to their courtyard and put on a play about King Artaxerxes, Haman, Mordecai, and Esther. There were songs; a man dressed as a woman; three-cornered hats made out of brightly colored cardboard; and *kozeh*, the goat, a man dressed in a goatskin decorated with beads, coins, and little bells.

Berta and the children stood on the sidelines and watched the play, clapping and singing at all the appropriate parts. After that came another play about Joseph, more songs, and even some pathos. To lighten the mood, *kozeh* came bounding into the circle, leaping into the air, twirling and shaking until all the bells, big and small, were ringing. He sang a nonsensical song that made the children laugh and even Sura forgot her shyness and joined in.

IT WASN'T long before Berta's money was gone and she had to rely on Lhaye and Zev for her most basic needs. To their credit they never complained or even mentioned the work that awaited her down at the factory. They didn't have to. She knew where she was headed and so did they. She had even begun to wake up before dawn to the sound of the factory whistle.

She hadn't thought of another line of work until she went to Alix's house, one afternoon in late March, to sell the pearl bracelet. She thought she might get a better price from Alix than from the Baranov brothers. She purposely made an appointment on Thursday, because the Tretiakovs always went to the Melgunovs' for a late supper after the theater on Thursdays and she knew Alix would want to wear it that night and be more likely to accept her price without question. So at half past four she arrived at Alix's house and was shown into the sea green parlor.

Berta had been counting on tea at Alix's all day long. Since she had to rely on Lhaye for her food, she had taken to eating less and that day had eaten nothing in anticipation of a proper Russian tea. She was not disappointed. There were cakes and tea sandwiches and a large plate of scones. When Alix left the room to have a word with the cook, Berta scooped up several sandwiches and four scones and put them into her just-in-case bag. She had a fleeting notion of regret, that she was not only manipulating her friend to get more money out of her, but also stealing food from her as well. Then her stomach rumbled and all thoughts of regret evaporated.

When Alix returned, Berta took out the velvet pouch and removed the bracelet. She had no feelings about it now. It was no longer the bracelet Hershel had given her when Samuil was born. Now, it was simply food.

"Put it on," Alix said eagerly, holding out her wrist.

For a moment Berta was worried that the bracelet wouldn't fit. She put it around Alix's wrist and tugged on it a little to make the clasp lock. "Perfect," she said, thinking that if it had been a millimeter shorter, she would've gone hungry that night.

"It's not too small?" Alix asked, moving her hand this way and that so she could see it from different angles.

"No, it's a little snug, but they're wearing them like that."

Alix looked at her doubtfully. "You sure?"

"Absolutely."

"How much? Give me a bargain. I'm your best friend."

Berta quoted her a price that was twice what the Baranov brothers would give her.

"It that a good price?"

"Of course. You think I would take advantage of you?"

Alix apologized for doubting her and went to a cabinet decorated with carved shells and seaweed and got the money out of a little box. Berta stuffed the bills into her bodice, kissed her friend twice, once on each cheek, and saw herself out. On the way down the hill she stopped off in a little public square and sat down on a bench to eat her tea sandwiches and scones. There she surveyed her feelings and found that she was relieved and happy to have the money, but saddened by the change in her friendship with Alix. Alix was no longer her best friend. In fact she was no longer a friend at all. Alix was a customer.

After that, she sold a brooch to Maria Gerasimovna Melgunova, who had no problem doing business with Berta Alshonsky as long as she came to the back door like any other tradesman. When Berta ran out of jewelry to sell she borrowed some from the Baranov brothers, who were happy to give it to her at a steeply discounted price. Their discount plus a modest markup kept her out of the factory and her children fed. After that she acquired other customers, some strangers, some former friends. Soon she was branching out into furniture, shoes, clothing, whatever was wanted. She knew where to get the best merchandise at a discount and how to make profit.

By the summer, Anna Mikhailovna Vishniakova had heard that Berta Alshonsky could find anything at a good price, even with the war, and ordered a gilt mirror of good quality. Berta had such a mirror stored in the professor's basement. She wrapped it in burlap and took the train to a station that was several versts from Anna Mikhailovna's estate. Since she didn't have the money to hire a cart, she had to walk all the way with it. It was hot and her shoes hurt and she was worried about breaking it. A small convoy of trucks passed her loaded with supplies for the front. Their heavy tires left a choking cloud of dust in their wake, which stuck to her sweaty face and made it hard to breathe. There was a family of muzhiki at a haying station near the road, an old man, his wife, and several young girls, who stopped by their cartload of hay to watch the pretty woman, with arms like sticks, carry the heavy gold mirror down the dusty road.

Finally she reached the country estate, limped up the stone steps, and knocked on the door. It was opened by Olya, the maid from Moscow, a bony Slav with a faint moustache and prominent cheekbones. She stood there, taking Berta in, while wiping her hands on her apron.

"Who is it, Olya?" called her mistress from somewhere inside.

"It's the house Jew, Madame," Olya called back, keeping a wary eye on Berta. "She's come with your mirror."

"Tell her to go around to the back," called out Mikhailovna.

"Yes, Madame. You heard her," the maid grumbled, blocking her way. She nodded to a path that led around to the back and then shut the door.

Berta stood on the steps and looked out into the yard, to an oak and birch stand just beyond the grass that was ablaze with the color of autumn. The fallen leaves formed choppy waves at the base of the trees and dead branches poked bony fingers up through them like the skeletal remains of fallen soldiers. She was not the house Jew. She would never be a house Jew. She was Berta Alshonsky, temporarily reduced in circumstances. She had no doubt that her situation would soon right itself. There had been a mistake. She was not meant to live like this. She was meant for her former life and soon it would be returned to her.

She picked up the mirror and went down the steps. The sky was a cloudless expanse of white and somewhere in the stand of oaks she heard the monotonous drone of a woodcutter's saw. For the time being she would have to ignore the unsavory parts of her life, the little terrors, the slights and insults, the injuries to her pride and the bitter uncertainties of the future. She had room for only simple thoughts now: keep going, turn a profit, bring food home, and extract the most out of the least. All the rest was a distraction that kept her from a good day's work. She decided to add a surcharge on to the price of the mirror: 5 percent for the journey, 5 for the heat and dust, and another 5 for having been mistaken for a house Jew.

THERE WAS a one-story house of weathered wood and peeling plaster that shared a courtyard with three similar houses. It was just off Davidkovo Square near the *zemstvo* building and directly across from the Church of the Resurrection. It wasn't a very fashionable neighborhood. These weren't fashionable people. The owner of the house was the assistant manager of a textile plant owned by Yuvelir's family. In the past Berta wouldn't have known these people. It wouldn't have occurred to her to stop and speak with them, to exchange a pleasantry or ask about their children. Now everything was different. Now they were her customers and she couldn't afford to be picky.

It was January 1917 and the country had been at war for nearly two and a half years. Everyone was talking about revolution. The consensus was that it was only a matter of time. Bread was scarce in the cities. People had to wait in long lines for it, only to find that the bakeries had run out of flour. Food shortages were everywhere. The factories were on strike. The war was going badly: inexperienced leadership, wholesale desertion, and the rolling stock had proven inadequate to supply the front. There was a stench of decay in the air. Russia was festering. Everyone knew it was going to be bad, but no one imagined how it could be much worse, with people dropping everywhere of disease, of starvation, of war, young and old and even children, the bodies piling up like hayricks after the autumn harvest.

Berta stepped off the curb and crossed in front of a sledge that was being pulled by its driver. The man had a harness over his shoulder and he trudged through the snowy street pulling his heavy load, his face screwed up with the effort. She jumped over a mound of snow in the gutter and landed up on the other side, ignoring the taunts of three soldiers who were standing over a fire in an old drum. One of them was roasting chestnuts over a grate and selling them in paper cones.

She followed the little walkway around to the back of the house where the *dvornik* was shoveling out the courtyard. He looked up briefly when she passed but said nothing and returned to his work. She tried to knock on the door, despite the heavy bundles in her hands, but soon gave up and kicked it several times instead. She didn't want to put the packages down because it was hard to pick them up again. She was wearing men's gloves that were too big for her and made it difficult to hold things. She wanted to take them off but knew she would be risking frostbite. There was a sharp wind, and the sun, a dull orb in the sky swaddled in clouds of frost and snow, hung over the domes of the Church of the Annunciation.

She heard a voice from inside: "Nastya! It's the boy with the wood."

It was the cook. Berta recognized her voice. Then she heard quick footsteps crossing the kitchen and the door opened with a gentle gust of warm air and the cloistered smell of baking bread. The housemaid looked her over. "It's only the house Jew," she called back over her shoulder. She stood there dressed in her starched white blouse and black pinafore. Her cap was a large black bow.

"Well, bring her in," said the cook, bristling with impatience. "You're letting in the cold air."

The maid stepped aside to let Berta in but made no move to help her with the bundles. Berta nodded a greeting and edged past her into the kitchen. The cook looked up from her worktable. She was stuffing a bird with bread crumbs, dried apples, and cranberries, and Berta caught the velvety perfume of cloves and cinnamon.

"I'd appreciate it if you didn't kick our door," the cook said, shoving another handful of stuffing into the breast. "We have better things to do then paint our back door every time you come to call."

She was a trim woman wearing a starched white cap and apron. Her hands were glistening with grease, and bits of berries and apples were sticking to them. "Well, just don't stand there," she said to the housemaid. "Show her into the parlor and tell Miss she's here." And then to Berta she added, "I expect you brought the boas?"

Berta nodded.

"Well, go on then," she said, nodding in the direction of the parlor. She wiped her nose with the back of her hand and went back to stuffing the bird.

The parlor was damp and smelled of mold and wet carpet. It was crowded with gilded pine furniture, flimsy sticks of wood covered with cheap fabric. After the maid had gone Berta unpacked the boas and laid them out on the settee. Then she went over to the porcelain stove that stood in the corner and tried to warm her hands. They were frugal with wood in this house and the fire had been allowed to go out. Still there were a few lingering coals in the grate and she bent down to gather in what warmth she could.

"Have you been waiting long?" asked the girl, breezing in through the double doors. She hardly gave Berta a glance as she hurried over to the boas hanging over the back of the settee. "Oh, these are lovely." She was the youngest of five daughters and the only one still left in the house. The others had made suitable marriages long ago and were scattered all over Little Russia. All of her brothers were dead except for the one who was in the tubercular hospital in Poltava.

"What do you think? This one?"

She held up a garish one, the only one of the five that was too big for her. She was a short girl with a thick waist and the last thing she needed was more bulk hanging around her neck. But she had chosen the ostrich feathers, the most expensive one, the one that would bring in two extra rubles.

Berta could smell her unwashed hair. "Yes, it's absolutely perfect for you. It looks wonderful."

"Really? Not too much?" She threw it around her neck and looked at herself in the mirror that hung over the mantel.

"No, it's very flattering. It even goes with what you're wearing."

A moment later her mother walked in and brushed past Berta without a word. "The house Jew is here and no one tells me?" grumbled Pelageia Iakovlevna. She had a pasty face with heavy, mannish features and thick lips that turned down at the corners. "Here, let me see that." She looked at her daughter and slowly shook her head. "No, no, no, it's too long. It's too thick. It's not at all what you should be wearing."

"But I like it."

"It's not right. I'm telling you it looks terrible on you." She looked over the choices and picked up a modest one made of chiffon ruffles. "Now here, try this one." She unwound the offending boa from around her daughter's neck and replaced it with her choice. She took a step back and studied the effect. "Much better. There, see? What did I tell you? Go have a look."

The girl looked in the mirror and made a face. "But I like the other one. Why can't I have that one?"

"Because it's too big for you. It looks ridiculous. You want to look ridiculous? Now, if you stayed away from the pastries . . ."

The girl took off the chiffon boa and put back the feather one. Then she glanced over at Berta. "The house Jew likes it. Go on, tell her. She said it was perfect."

"It's what they're wearing, Madame," Berta said, sounding a little bored. She found that an attitude of detachment worked best in these situations, especially with women of this class. They expected to be overlooked and when they weren't they grew suspicious. In reality she was anything but bored. She was thinking about the extra rubles and the meat it would buy for Sura. She hadn't been well lately and the doctor said she needed a strong beef broth.

"I sold one just like it to Nadezhna Gerasimovna and she's a large woman and everybody said how wonderful she looked in it. And besides, everyone knows that when you wear your hair up and your shoulders flat against your sleeves you need something fussy around your neck."

Pelageia Iakovlevna took a long look at her daughter: "But so fussy?"

"It's her color and with her eyes and hair . . . it's what they're wearing."

She turned her head to the side and then to the other side and studied her daughter closely. "I don't know. I don't think so. It doesn't look right."

"Oh, Mother," the girl said in despair.

"I'm telling you it's just not right for you. Stop pouting. I know about these things."

A hard silence.

Berta watched mother and daughter gaze reflectively at the line of boas. She could see that a compromise was eluding them. "It's terrible about Nadezhna Gerasimovna, isn't it?" she murmured.

Iakovlevna turned to her with sudden interest. "What is?"

"About her husband, I mean?"

"I haven't heard a thing."

"Well, you know, he's so much younger than she and handsome in his own way. Everyone said it was bound to happen." Berta let her voice trail off. She looked deliberately at the young girl and said nothing more.

"Maria," her mother said, "have you completed your lessons?"

"Of course."

"I think cook baked a cake. Why don't you go get a piece?"

"You're always telling me I shouldn't."

"I think one piece wouldn't hurt."

"What about the boa, Mama?"

"Go have your cake."

"Not until I know about the boa."

She paused. "Yes, all right. If it means so much to you."

"Oh, Mama," She kissed her mother and danced out of the room with the feather boa still wrapped around her neck.

When berta left the house that afternoon she tucked the folded rubles in a bag she kept in the inside pocket of her skirt. She had sewn the pocket there for just this reason. It never occurred to her to feel guilty for steering the girl in the wrong direction. She knew her customers relied on her for honest answers, confiding in her, asking her advice on all sorts of matters, but she had children to feed. She glanced up at the darkening clouds blowing in from the north, great primordial monoliths rising up over the sun. It had begun to snow and she still had to go up to the Berezina.

She wrapped her hands in the rags she had used to protect the boa and picked up her bundles. She started up the hill, avoiding the dark icy patches on the sidewalks, hugging the buildings for protection against the wind and taking shortcuts across the courtyards whenever she could. In one courtyard a maid ran out without a wrap to scoop up an armful of wood. In another the *dvornik* was stacking wood for the night and watched her with suspicion as she walked by. In yet another she could smell three suppers cooking in the three kitchens that bordered it.

Soon she was on Vladimirskaya not far from the Church of the Rising Cross, passing the shops she used to frequent when she lived there. There was a tearoom where she used to take the children for treats. That afternoon it looked deserted. Only the steamy windows and the palm fronds flattened against the sweating glass were proof that it was open. She was just passing when she heard someone calling her name and turned to see Yuvelir pulling up in a motor car. It was an American-made Ford, thick and black like a piece of coal.

"Berta, silly girl, where have you been?" She had not seen him in nearly a year. He didn't know she had lost her apartment and was living on Dulgaya Street.

"What are you doing out here?" he asked. "It's brutal. Come and sit in my new motor. What do you think of her? Isn't she a beauty? She'll do twenty-five versts an hour, more if the road is good."

"Where did you get a motor car?"

"My cousin. He's off killing Germans, so he gave her to me. Of course they'll requisition her as soon as they see her, but so far I've managed to keep her safe. Don't suppose you have any petrol?"

"What would I be doing with petrol?"

"Just asking. Come along, get in. I'll take you where you want to go."

"I can't, I'm meeting a friend."

Yuvelir looked genuinely disappointed. "All right, throw me aside. You've obviously replaced me with better friends. How come you never ring me up anymore?"

"I've been gone."

"Where?"

"Kiev, if it's any of your business."

"Kiev, how boring. Why would you choose somebody from Kiev over me?"

"I haven't. Look, Misha, I can't stand here and chat. It's cold and I'm late."

"Someone said you were selling things. You're not poor, are you? Everyone is so poor nowadays."

She laughed. "I really have to go. I'll ring you up soon, I promise."

"Yes, yes, go on with you. Desert me like the disloyal friend you are." He turned back to the wheel, but saw that a sledge was blocking his way, another one being pulled by its driver. "Oh look at this." He shouted out the window, "You going to move that thing?"

The driver of the sledge glanced over at him and glowered.

"Like to go on if you don't mind."

The driver wasn't in any hurry. He took his time going around to the front of the sledge. There he picked up the rope with a deliberate motion, and after giving Yuvelir one last look of contempt, pulled his sledge out into the street. The last Berta saw of Yuvelir he was waving to her as he pulled out. He shouted something out the window, but it was lost in the curtain of falling snow.

ELIZAVETA SHAPOSNIKOVA was one of Berta's best customers, not because she was generous or easy to get along with, but because she was no longer young. Her arthritis was always worse in the winter, making it impossible for her to go out and shop on her own. She lived in a gothic mansion on Kropotkin Street. It had been built by her husband, a banker, an old believer, who thought a house should be substantial, made out of stone, and have at least one crenellated tower. This one had three.

It was late afternoon by the time Berta knocked at the side entrance. She stood there in the cold, shivering and waiting for the maid to answer the door. Her stockings were damp because the soles of her boots were starting to give out and water had begun seeping in through a hundred tiny cracks in the leather.

The door was finally opened by the housemaid, a small woman with precise gray hair under a starched cap. "You're late," she grumbled, stepping aside to let Berta in. "She doesn't like it when you're late. She's got her nephew in there with her now and I expect she'll turn you out when she hears you're here."

Berta was used to being treated like this by the household staff. Recently she had come to the conclusion that housemaids were a miserable lot. She thought this was probably due to the fact that they had no life apart from their employers, had to be on call twenty-four hours a day, could have no family of their own, and weren't paid nearly enough. At the same time she noticed that scullery maids seemed happier by comparison. This was odd because scullery maids were at the bottom of the heap; only house Jews and peddlers were below them. She reasoned that this probably had something to do with their proximity to food.

Berta said nothing and followed the woman down a little hallway to an office where Shaposnikova met her tradesmen. There they found a fire in the fireplace, dirty tea things on the desk, and a samovar bubbling in the corner. "Look at this," the maid grumbled as she gathered up the plates and piled them onto a tray. "Never gets any better. Always up to me. She hires the young ones from the countryside because they're cheap and then I have to do all the work."

Berta saw that there were little tea sandwiches left on the silver tray and an unmolested lemon tartlet. The maid picked up the tray and turned to the door. "I'll tell her you're here, but she won't want to see you."

"Tell her I brought the candlesticks."

"Won't make a bit of difference. She's got her nephew in there. She won't want to be disturbed."

"Just tell her about the candlesticks."

"Yes, yes," she said impatiently, shifting the weight of the tray to her left hand so she could reach for the door handle. As she did a smoked salmon sandwich slid off the tray and fell to floor. A moment later the lemon tartlet suffered the same fate. Berta looked at them lying on the floor, the meringue flecked with dust but the filling still good and looking firm and sweet in its flaky crust.

The maid said, "Are you going to stand there? Go on, pick it up. Put it on the tray. I haven't got all day."

Berta bent to pick it up and tossed it on the tray. It landed in a cup of cold tea. Then she retrieved the sandwich and did the same. After the maid left the room, Berta could hear the purposeful clip of her retreating footsteps and pictured the lemon tart, soggy with cold tea, sinking to the bottom of the cup.

A few minutes later she heard Elizaveta Shaposnikova's uneven gait coming down the same hall, the rhythm of her heel on the stone floor punctuated by the dull thud of her cane. The old lady appeared at the door, muttering a greeting as she limped over to the desk to examine the candlesticks.

"This is it? Where are all the others?"

"These were the best I could find, Elizaveta Shaposnikova. They're Naidenov's from Petersburg." The Baranov brothers had given her a good deal on them, because she had threatened to go elsewhere if they didn't. She had no intention of passing on the savings to Shaposnikova. She picked up the best one and laid it into Shaposnikova's twisted hand. She was careful not to stare at the old lady's fingers. They were bent away from the thumb, like the trailing fins of tropical fish. The knuckles and joints were twisted into knots of hard bone. "Here, look at this detail. Isn't it beautiful? So delicate. All the best families buy their silver from Naidenov."

Shaposnikova cradled the candlestick between her forearm and claw and stared at the intricate beading and engraving. Then she looked at the others. After a few moments she looked up at Berta. "Go down the hall and fetch my nephew. He'll know which one to choose."

Berta nodded and left the room to do as she was told, but she didn't know the house and didn't know where to find the parlor. The first door she opened led to the sitting room with a soaring cage of parakeets standing in a corner. Then she found the music room and finally the main parlor. There she saw a young man standing by the French doors watching the snow blanket the little park outside; his back was to her, pale hair curled over his collar, his delicate fingers hung by his side. When he turned she saw it was Yuvelir.

"Berta, what are you doing here?"

Berta forced a smile despite her thumping heart. "I think I'm looking for you. I've been sent to find Elizaveta Shaposnikova's nephew."

"She sent you?"

"She wants you to look at the candlesticks."

"What for?"

"She can't decide and she thinks you have good taste."

"Of course I have good taste. I have the best. But what are you doing here?"

"I brought them."

"Why?"

Berta's face went blank and then she forced a smile. "A charity, why else?"

Yuvelir followed her down to the office. "Don't you women ever get tired of charities? What would you do if there were no war widows and orphans?"

She laughed and it sounded false to her. "We'd invent them, of course."

When they got back to the little office they found Elizaveta Shaposnikova still cradling the candlestick. "I think I want this one. What do you think, Misha?"

"I don't know." He looked them all over. "I guess I like it."

"Guess? Misha, I want your opinion."

"Yes, all right. Get that one."

The old woman studied it a moment longer. "You're right, I do like this one. Yes, all right," she said to Berta, "bring me six of these. And I'll need them by Saturday. Bring them in the afternoon. Don't be too late. I'll need them for dinner."

"Are we done now? May I have my drink?" asked Yuvelir with exaggerated patience.

"Yes, of course."

He held the door open for her. "Berta? Won't you join us?"

Berta's face flamed and she tried to protest, but Elizaveta Shaposnikova cut her off. "What are you doing?" she asked her nephew in surprise.

"I'm inviting Madame Alshonsky to stay for a hot drink."

"I can't stay, really," Berta said, hurrying to wrap up the candlesticks.

"Misha, have you gone completely out of your mind?"

"What's wrong, Tante?"

Berta said, "That's it then. I'll be going."

"You're inviting the house Jew for a drink?"

She wanted to run out the door but forced herself to stay, standing there motionless, the mortification pulsating like a bright, white star.

"She's the house Jew, Misha. Who did you think she was? She came here to sell candlesticks." Shaposnikova shook her head and limped to the door. "Not a brain in his head," she muttered. "Hopeless. If he weren't my sister's child . . ."

Once she had gone Berta stole a glance at Yuvelir. He was gazing at the bubbling samovar. "I thought you said it was for charity."

"Yes, well, I lied, didn't I?"

"Misha!" his aunt called from down the hall. "Are you coming?"

"Yes, Tante," he called back. He glanced at her briefly and then headed for the door. "Well, good luck to you," he said vaguely. Then without waiting for a response he strode out the door and disappeared down the hall.

After he left she held on to the edge of the desk and waited until her heart stopped racing. Then she straightened and picked up the bags. At the back door she stood on the threshold watching the snow flurries in the shaft of light. Beyond the light there was nothing but blackness and the piercing cold. It was as if the universe ended at the bottom of the steps. Finally she took a deep breath and stepped into the arctic night.

Chapter Fifteen

March 1918

IT WAS COLD in the apartment. In the morning, the dregs in the bottom of the glasses were frozen, the laundry hanging in the front room was brittle, and there was ice on the inside of the windows. When it was cold like this Zev's leg ached. Pain shot up his thigh, spreading out in exquisite strands of fire, a nagging reminder that he wasn't whole, that he had limitations, that he was a cripple—a fact he tried to deny every day of his life. When he stood on his crutch that morning he winced and adjusted the brace so that it wouldn't dig into his groin.

"You all right?" Lhaye asked. She watched him adjust the strap and then pull on his coat and hat.

"I'm going out. I'll be back for lunch."

He never complained. To his friends and coworkers he was a bull, strong, with thick arms and a square neck, a wrecking ball of a man, impervious to pain and determined not to let his infirmity get in the way. But with Lhaye he was different. He was comfortable enough with her to be himself. He trusted her to accept his infirmity and not to try to do too much for him, not make a weakling out of him, which was how he felt on mornings like this.

On Sundays Zev liked to go down the street to the upholstery shop and argue with that lackey of capitalistic decadence, Reb Avner Wissotzky. Reb Wissotzky had owned Wissotzky and Sons for most of his life. It was a small shop with only three employees, but it did a brisk business before the war. Now with the textile shortage he had trouble filling his orders. The ones he could fill paid him a premium, so although he worked less, he was still able to pay his employees and provide a decent living for his wife and three daughters.

When Zev walked in that day he spotted Wissotzky in the back at his battered desk, going over the company's books. Even though it was Sunday, the shop was busy. The workers were Jews and since their Sabbath ended at sundown on the previous night, they were expected to come in and work. With the help of his crutch, Zev dragged his leg through the shop and passed two workers who were tying padding onto a sofa frame and a third worker who was in the corner, cutting fabric on a long work bench. The floor was littered with scraps of material and overhead discarded chair frames hung from the rafters. There were piles of foam padding and bags of down feathers stacked up against the walls and specially designed heavy-duty sewing machines sat on a few tables around the room.

Zev nodded to the workers, calling them by name and asking about their families. He had tried to organize them once, but they wanted none of it. Wissotzky paid them a livable wage and they worked only ten hours a day. They got off for Passover and the high holidays, without pay of course, but once a year they were all invited over to Wissotzky's house for blintzes and schnapps served in ruby red glasses with thin gold rims. Zev didn't have any real hope of organizing them. He just did it to aggravate Wissotzky and, in that, he was wildly successful.

"Have you seen this?" Zev asked, throwing down a crisp one-hundred-*karbvanet* note, newly printed by the fledgling Ukrainian state.

"Ya, so?"

"So look at it, right there." He pointed to a line in Yiddish that read HUNDRET KARBOVANTSES. "There, see? Official. Even the government is saying that Yiddish is the official language of the Jews."

With the fall of the czar in March 1917 and the rise of the Kerenskii government, a liberal democratic regime, Jewish allegiance wavered between the Provisional Government in Petrograd and the Ukrainian Central Rada in Kiev. At first it looked like an easy choice. The Jews had always thought of themselves as Russians. They had more in common with the Russian intelligentsia than with the Ukrainian peasantry. But as the Provisional Government began to falter in the summer of 1917, Jewish sentiment began to shift to the Rada. By the time the Kerenskii government fell to the Red Guards on the night of October 25th, the various Jewish factions were embroiled in ideological minutiae over how best to implement the autonomy that had just been granted to them. There were the socialists, who refused to deal with the bourgeoisie; the secularists, who wanted to keep the rabbiniate in their place and the Torah out of secular life; the Bund, Poale Tsion, Folkspartey, and the Fareynikte parties, who wanted Yiddish as the official language; and the Zionists, who favored Hebrew. While all this bickering was going on, reports of scattered pogroms in the west went largely ignored.

Wissotzky picked up the money and stared at it. "The Rada tells you what language you speak and that's it? Now it's Yiddish. Done. Just like that. How long do you think this government will last? Till suppertime . . . till morning prayers?" He wadded up the bill and threw it back at Zev. "You think I care what they print? What they say about *my* language? And who will be printing next, the Germans, the Bolsheviks? Maybe the czar will return—may an onion grow out his navel. Now you listen to me, Mr. Know-it-all, Hebrew has been the language of the Jews for over five thousand years. So don't come to me with this horseshit about the official language. The official language is Hebrew. It always has been, always will be."

Wissotzky was a slight man with a generous moustache that hung down nearly past his chin. His black hair was streaked with gray. His eyes were small, amber, and shot with flecks of gold. He was a religious man, but not as religious as some. He wore no beard, just the moustache, his coat was cut short, no side curls, and his tzitzis was tucked under the waistband of his pants. When he was fuming, as he was now, he slapped the back of his hand against the palm of the other, enumerating all the reasons why he was right and Zev was wrong.

"*Nu*? What are we speaking now? I don't hear Hebrew. Maybe my ears are plugged or my brain stopped working, but what I'm hearing is Yiddish."

"That's because you're an ignoramus and you don't speak Hebrew."

"Right, me and everyone else."

"There are plenty of people who speak Hebrew."

"Oh yes? Where? Here in the shop? On the street corner? Hey, Pincus, you speak Hebrew?"

The man looked up briefly from the cutting table and shook his head. He was too smart to get in the middle.

"People speak Yiddish because it's the mother tongue. Everybody speaks it, unless they're in shul or a pompous ass like you. If you weren't such a stubborn fool, you'd see what I'm talking about. It's the new order. The new order . . . the twentieth century, Wissotzky, wake up!"

"Feh! New order! What kind of an order doesn't respect God's language? Doesn't respect the Torah? You can keep your new order."

They went on like that for some time, their impassioned voices filling the shop despite the hammering and the clatter of the sewing machines. Even though these two disagreed on most everything, there was one thing that they could agree on, and that was the pleasure of spending every Sunday morning proving that the other one was a witless fool and that everything he believed in was unreasonable, unlikely, or just plain wrong.

They were so absorbed in their argument that they failed to see three soldiers dressed in the uniform of the Kuban Cossacks standing in the doorway of the shop. One of them had a bolt of fabric wrapped up in burlap on his shoulder and was discussing with the other two the merits of stopping at this shop or going on to the other one down the street.

"What is it?" Wissotzky called out in Russian, when he looked up and saw them standing there.

"You interested in brocade?" asked the one carrying the fabric. He seemed to be the one in charge. He was young, somewhere in his twenties. His blond hair, shoved under the tall lambskin *papakha*, was tangled with bits of leaves and twigs as if he had been lying on the ground. His beard was unkempt and his filthy gray coat was missing one of the red shoulder boards.

"Depends . . . what color?"

"Red. Is there any other?"

Wissotzky shrugged. "Let me see."

The leader led the way through the shop, tracking in mud and snow and picking up scraps of fabric that stuck to the soles of his boots.

"Lay it out here," Wissotzky said. He cleared a worktable of newspapers and dirty cups and the Cossack set the bolt down, slid off the burlap, and rolled it out on the table.

"I used to work in a textile factory," he said. "This is quality. I know what I'm talking about. This was made before the war."

His companions hung back, slouching against the worktable, eating sunflower seeds and carelessly dropping the shells on the floor. Neither of them was handsome like their leader. He could have been an artist's model, poising on horseback for a bronze monument, the mythic Ukrainian hero.

Wissotzky examined the fabric, feeling the thickness of the embossed floral design between his fingertips. Despite his efforts to look unimpressed, Zev saw the excitement on his face. To Zev the material looked like any other in the workshop, but apparently, judging by Wissotzky's reaction, this was something special. Zev watched him chew on the end of his moustache and run his tongue over his thin upper lip while he struggled to appear bored and even annoyed by the intrusion. Zev had known him a long time and he knew that Wissotzky didn't excite easily, which went a long way to explain why Avner Wissotzky would buy stolen goods from men like these.

"How much?"

"Sixty."

Wissotsky snorted. "Forty, and that's more than fair."

"Forty? It is an insult."

"Not for stolen merchandise. All right, forty-five, but not a kopeck more."

"Stolen? I bought it, free and clear. I even have the bill of sale. Fifty-five."

"Fifty and I won't go to the police."

"Fifty and you'll take back the lie."

Wissotzky examined his thumbnail. "All right, so you didn't steal it. Maybe you found it. Am I asking questions?"

Wissotzky sighed, heaved himself up, and went into the back room for the cash. When he came back out, he handed it to the leader, who counted out the bills, grunted his satisfaction, and pocketed the money. Then the three of them left without closing the door.

When they had gone Wissotzky called Pincus over. "I got the Guchkov fabric," he said. "Stop whatever you're doing and start on the sofa."

"But I haven't finished the Maretsky order."

Wissotzky gave him a look.

Pincus sighed. "Yes, yes." He picked up the fabric and took it back over to his worktable.

The Cossacks returned shortly after that. This time they burst through the door and stormed over to Wissotzky's desk. The leader threw down the money. "I want it back. Where is it?"

"We had a deal," Wissotzky protested.

"Not anymore. Rosenblatt offered us sixty and I want it back."

"It's gone."

"What do you mean gone?"

"I mean cut up into pieces, gone. See for yourself."

Pincus had been working steadily on the order since they had left and already the fabric had been cut up into several large pieces. When the soldiers went over to the table and saw what had happened, the leader whipped around. "Cheating *zhyd*," he sputtered. "Keep it then. But I want the rest of my money. Ten rubles plus another ten for trying to cheat me."

"I don't have that kind of money."

"Liar!" he shouted. "I want it or I'm going to take it out of your hide." The Cossack grabbed a sewing machine and held it over his head ready to smash it on the floor. "I mean it. You have three seconds."

Pincus and the other workers had stopped what they were doing and were watching in growing alarm.

"Hold it!" Zev said. "Just hold it a minute."

"Sixty rubles . . ." the leader shouted.

"He's crazy," Wissotzky said with a wave of his hand. Wissotzky was famous for being pigheaded. His neighbors had stories.

"Calm down now. We're all brothers here," Zev said. "The laboring masses, workers and soldiers, a brotherhood. Comrades, please.

The leader held the sewing machine up higher. "Sixty . . ."

"I told you I don't have it. Give me a year and I still wouldn't have it." He crossed his arms and jutted out his chin.

"Wait!" shouted Zev.

The leader hurled the sewing machine down on the floor. The bobbin and bobbin case went flying across the room. Pincus and the others ran out the door. Zev struggled to his feet. "Wait, wait," he shouted. He took a step toward them, but his leg gave out, pitching him forward. He ended up on the floor.

For a moment the soldiers stared at him and then, forgetting their anger, burst out laughing.

Wissotzky tried to help him up, but Zev pushed him away and fought to get up by himself. When he was nearly on his feet, a soldier pushed him down again, delighting in the new game. This time Wissotzky shoved the man aside and went to help his friend. Zev looked behind him and saw that the leader had grabbed a chair leg and was whipping it back over his head. "No!" he screamed. Before Wissotzky had time to react the soldier brought it down on the back of his head, caving in his skull and breaking his neck. Wissotzky collapsed forward, landing on top of Zev, blood gushing out of the wound and soaking through Zev's coat. The soldiers watched in fascination as Wissotzky's blood ran in a rivulet down the floorboards.

Zev laid him gently aside and struggled to pull himself up. When he got to his feet he smashed his fist into the face of the soldier standing next to him. He felt the small bones of the man's nose turn to mush and heard the gurgling sound of blood bubbling down the man's throat.

The other two turned on him. He swung wildly at them, twisting at the waist, weighed down by the brace and his withered leg. It was easy for them to walk around and come at him from behind. The leader picked up a mallet from a worktable.

"SURA, open your mouth."

"I don't want it, Mameh." They were in the bedroom and Sura was sick in bed. Berta had brought in a bowl of soup on a tray. "Please, Sura, a little more."

"I'm not hungry."

"The doctor says you must eat. It has meat in it. He says you must have meat."

"All right, but I can do it myself. I'm not a baby."

Every time Sura got sick and ran a high fever Berta told herself that she must work harder and make more money. She must move out of this place and into a better neighborhood where her daughter could get well. She was living in her own apartment now, but all she could afford was the one next to Lhaye's, with the same rats and the same toxic miasma rising up from the sewers. The air was fetid and carried a filth that infected Sura's lungs. It made her cough without letup, a telling sign that Berta was failing to keep her children safe.

To make more money she would have to go out to the countryside and be a house Jew to the kulaks and the wealthy estate owners, filling their specialty orders and bringing the hard-to-find merchandise directly to their doors. But it was dangerous out there. The countryside was overrun with bandits and deserters who preyed on Jewish townlets and travelers. So she kept putting it off, hoping that Sura would get better. For a time it seemed that she did, but then winter came and with it more illness, more fever and the cough that exhausted them both.

"Berta!" It was Lhaye screaming from next door. "Berta, it's Zev!"

Berta jumped up and ran to the door. She pushed it open and nearly tripped over a bag of beets and a tin of cooking oil that hadn't been there before. Lhaye was running past her on the landing.

"What is it? What's happened?"

"They beat him up."

"Who?"

"He's at Wissotzky's. I don't know if he's alive."

"Wait, I'll come with you." She went back for her coat and told Samuil to stay with his sister. Then she and Lhaye ran down the stairs and out into the street. They raced together to the upholstery shop where they found a crowd blocking the entrance. Lhaye pushed her way through and rushed into the shop. There she found Zev lying unconscious in a pool of blood. She screamed and sank to her knees by his side. "Zevi! Zevi, wake up!" she sobbed.

Berta crouched down beside her. "Look, he's not dead. He's breathing."

His chest was rising and falling and there was still a little color in his face. Berta looked up at the confusion of faces that surrounded her. She recognized most of them—neighbors, the Jewish wine seller, the tinker, the bristle sorter, the barber, the horse trader—and others she did not. They were young men and not so young, serious, concerned faces, milling about, whispering to one another and glancing over at her from time to time. They carried revolvers like the kind she found in Hershel's suitcase—identical Browning automatics, spitters, as he called them. They fingered them self-consciously, not knowing quite what to do with them.

In a little while, the doctor arrived with a stretcher and two attendants from Nahman Bialik Jewish Hospital. He knelt down beside Wissotzky. After a moment he stood. "Bother about him later," he said to the attendants. Then he moved on to Zev. He checked for a pulse, examined his pupils, and parted his hair to look at the head wound. "This one is still alive." He nodded to the bearers, who lifted him onto the stretcher. Soon they were out the door with Lhaye hurrying to keep up.

It was decided that somebody should walk Madame Alshonsky home. The general consensus was that she didn't look so good. The kosher wine merchant offered and since nobody objected he gave her a few moments to gather herself together and then helped her to her feet. Once outside he escorted her past the crowd, holding himself erect, with an air of self-importance, his revolver tucked into the waistband of his pants for all to see.

"You do not have to worry, Froy Alshonsky. You are safe with me." He patted his gun. "Not to brag or anything, but Pincus came to me first because I'm the best shot in the neighborhood." They were walking under clotheslines of drying laundry that stretched out from the second-story windows. "That is how I got there first. Wissotzky was already dead and Zev would have been too. Once they saw me they ran away. It didn't take much. Your husband always told us it wouldn't take much and he was right."

Berta looked up at the mention of Hershel. "My husband?"

"Reb Alshonsky, a fine man, a righteous man, a real *tsaddik*. You can tell him I said so. Tell him Shammai Eggel said he is a real *tsaddik*. He'll remember me, I'm the sharpshooter. That's what he used to call me, the sharpshooter."

THAT NIGHT Berta got word from Lhaye that she would be staying all night at the hospital, so Berta brought the children over to her apartment, fed them, and put them to bed with Samuil. She put the kettle on for tea and brought the chair over to a little table by the window so she could sit and look out on the street. The shops were closing. The shopkeepers were bringing in what little merchandise they had to sell and lowering the shutters. She was watching the hardware store owner roll in a barrel when her attention drifted to a young man. He was lanky, with stooped shoulders, and greasy blond hair hung in clumps from under his lambskin cap. He was holding an overcoat and carrying a bag and didn't seem to be in a hurry. He didn't look before he crossed the street, sidestepping a passing sledge and walking in the direction of her building.

A few moments later she heard someone on the stairs and knew it had to be the stranger. She could hear him coming up slowly, taking care to be quiet, and stopping on the landing to listen. She went over and put her ear to the door. Taking the knob in her hand, she turned and held it. When she heard him right outside, she yanked it opened and startled him. He jumped back. In one sweep she took in the bag on the doorstep and the coat on top of it. It was Zev's coat. It had been cleaned and pressed. The bag contained potatoes.

"What are you doing here?" she asked.

He didn't answer her. Instead he turned and started back down the steps.

"Wait. Why are you doing this?" She hurried after him and grabbed his sleeve. "Who are you?" There had been a steady stream of little presents left on her doorstep since that first tin of kerosene.

"Nobody," he said tonelessly, yanking his arm free.

"No, wait, please. I want to thank you."

"No need," he said over his shoulder.

She leaned over the railing. "Did you know my husband?" This time he turned back reluctantly and looked up at her. "Met him once."

"Did you work with him?"

"Once."

"Won't you come in?"

"No."

"Please. I want to thank you properly."

"I told you. There's no need."

She noticed that the index finger of his left hand was missing. "Then at least come in and have a cup of tea. I would like that very much."

He considered it for a moment and then halfheartedly turned and followed her back up the stairs. Once inside, she showed him to the little table by the window. "Sit here. I'll get the tea. We have to be quiet, because the children are sleeping." He sat down heavily and surveyed the street outside. She kept an eye on him while she made the tea to make sure he didn't leave.

When she came back in with the cups and a plate of buns, she set them down in the center of the table. She took the other chair and handed him a bun on a plate and a cup of tea. He began to eat in silence, his jaw working as he chewed. She could see that he took no pleasure in the food. He was only there because she had insisted.

"How did you lose your finger?"

He shrugged. "Frostbite."

"Do you know where my husband is?"

He shook his head.

"He didn't send you?"

"Of course not."

"I thought he might've sent you to take care of us."

"No, I've been away. When I got back, they said he went to America and told me where you lived."

At first, she thought he looked like he had spent his childhood in the factories and had gotten prematurely old through hard work. But when he spoke, she knew she'd been wrong. Even though he only said a few words, she could hear that his speech was cultured. He had been educated. He wasn't a worker, although judging by his creased and calloused hands and weathered face he had been doing hard work.

"Would you like another bun?"

He stood up. "No."

"Will you come back to see us?"

He nodded as he put on his coat.

"What's your name?"

He buttoned it up and pulled up the collar. "Pavel," he said, barely above a whisper.

Once he was gone, she went to the window to catch a glimpse of him as he left the building. He looked exhausted as he walked down the street, his hands in his pockets, his head thrust slightly forward on his neck. A dead man walking among the living through a colossal effort of will.

Chapter Sixteen

February 1919

THERE WAS a restaurant in Kamenka, a large town not far from Cherkast, where Berta usually stopped for a bowl of soup and bit of bread whenever she was in the area making her rounds. The restaurant was situated on an island in the middle of the square in the Jewish neighborhood. It was a squat building of peeling plaster with a rusty tin roof and tall windows flanked by broken shutters. When Berta climbed the steps that day she was tired and hungry. She wore a tangled bunch of cheap beads around her neck. This was what remained of her inventory after spending the morning traveling around to the farmsteads and trading them for potatoes and beets, and bundles of feathers, flax, and pig bristles to sell to the merchants back in Cherkast.

Berta knew the proprietress of the restaurant. She was thin with a loose flap of skin under her chin and practically no breasts on a sunken chest. She liked to brag about her two sons who were getting rich working for the Polish estate owner down the road. She was an indifferent cook but kept the inside of her restaurant in spotless order by scrubbing the tables with salt and mopping the floors with carbolic soap. The odor from the soap often overpowered the food and made everything taste bitter and clean.

It came as a surprise when Berta pushed open the door and found the place in shambles. There were dirty dishes all over the tables, broken plates on the floor, chairs overturned, and the contents of a soup bowl splattered on the wall. At first Berta didn't see the little woman slumped in a chair in the back, her clothes stiff with dirt, blending into the chaos. The old woman's eyes were dull and staring out of the hollows in her skull, her stringy hair framing a vacant face. She sat motionless, her gaze fixed on the crusty bits of dried soup on the wall, her flat chest barely rising and falling.

"What happened here?" whispered Berta.

The old woman didn't move. She didn't seem to know that Berta was there.

A younger woman came in through the kitchen door and stopped when she saw Berta crouching beside the proprietress. "We're closed," the woman said, looking Berta over with large suspicious eyes half hidden under a fringe of brown hair.

Berta asked, "Is she all right?"

"Of course she's not all right. Look at her. She's half dead."

"What happened?"

The woman shrugged and turned away. She walked over to a table and started to gather up the plates.

"It's all right. I'm a friend."

The woman hesitated, then said, "There were eight of them. Soldiers, but they weren't in uniform."

"Hryhoriiv's men?"

"No. They were Reds."

Berta was surprised. Of all the factions fighting in the countryside, the Red Army of the Bolsheviks seemed the least likely to kill Jews. The White Army, composed of a loose affiliation of anti-Bolsheviks including the Cossacks; the Volunteer Army of General Denikin; the anarchist Black Army; the Ukrainian army called the Directory; and a long list of bandits headed by atamans or chieftains all waged brutal pogroms against the Jews, slaughtering them by the thousands and destroying their *shtetlekh*. But the Reds nearly always showed restraint.

"Reds? You sure?"

A bitter laugh. "Of course, I'm sure. I was here, wasn't I?"

"What did they want?"

"They wanted to be fed, what else? And naturally there was no question of payment."

"Did she feed them?"

"What else is she going to do? But her sons were out in the back putting away some wood and they came running in. She begged them to go away, but they wouldn't listen to her. Stupid boys. What could they do against those men? They didn't even have guns. The soldiers took what they wanted and shot them in the head." She held a finger up to her forehead. "And the whole time this poor woman was standing there watching."

The woman sighed, shook her head, and took the stack of plates into the kitchen. Berta picked up the saucers and cups and followed her in. "After they shot her sons they told her they'd be back for lunch the next day. That was yesterday, only God help me it seems like a lifetime ago." They put the dishes in the dry sink and went back for more. "She buried her sons this morning. And then they came back just as they said they would and she fed them soup. One of them didn't like it." She nodded to the splatter on the wall while clearing the second table. "They took everything, all the food and the bread, everything from the kitchen, and left. After that she sat down in that chair and hasn't moved since."

Berta helped the woman clear the tables. When they had washed and put away the dishes they got the old woman up and walked her back to the bedroom. It was a neat little room off the kitchen with a clean coverlet over a straw mattress, a coat and a good dress hanging on a hook on the wall, and a pair of shoes in the corner. They undressed her and pulled a nightdress over her head and shoulders. Her arms remained limp at her sides, her face blank, her eyes flat and black like dirty coins. Her will was gone. She had retreated into her own world where the dishes were always clean, the floors smelled of carbolic soap, and her sons were out in the yard stacking firewood for her oven.

The woman found some bread that the soldiers had missed and gave it to Berta. "Be careful on the road," she said at the door, as she watched Berta shoulder her bundles. "Three men disappeared yesterday. So stay off the main road and look out for yourself."

Berta nodded. But on the way out of town she wondered how she was going to get to where she wanted to go if she didn't take the main road. So she stayed on it, passing the outlying houses and taverns, the deserted yards and the brittle sticks still standing in the frozen kitchen gardens, until she came to a cart track that led off through the snowy fields.

The going was slow because she was carrying her bundles and

wearing a pair of men's boots stuffed with newspaper to make them fit. The sun was past its zenith, a raw globe behind the clouds and not much brighter than the moon. The wind was picking up and she clutched the bundles to her chest to block it. She had one last delivery to make and wanted to hurry so she could get back for the early train. The farmstead wasn't far, but it would be hard to find because of the mist that clung to the hollows and spiraled up through the trees. She had never come this way before. She kept thinking that out here it would be easy to freeze to death. Be only steps away from the house and never know it.

Ihor Kochubey's son was getting married and this meant that gold chains had to be bought since it was the custom among the kulaks to cover their brides in gold. Because Ihor Kochubey had already married off two sons the previous year, this bride would have to be satisfied with a necklace and perhaps a bracelet or two. For this reason she would not be the youngest or the prettiest of the eligible girls, but then Ihor Kochubey's son was not exactly a catch either. He was slow-witted and often seen talking to himself.

Berta had borrowed several chains from a jeweler and had sewn them into the hem of her skirt. As she walked through the deep snow across the fields she could feel the soft thud of their weight hitting against her leg. It wasn't easy walking. She had to curl her toes to keep her feet from sliding around in the boots while shifting her bundles from arm to arm, trying to find a comfortable way of carrying them.

Finally she came to a drive that she thought might lead down to the house. It was smoother than the surrounding fields and lacked the undulating corn row pattern beneath the snow. There was a frozen stream beside it that looked familiar, though she couldn't be sure, since she had always seen it in the summer, when it came crashing down from the hillside or in the fall, when the water was nearly gone and barely covered the gravelly bottom. Now it was covered with a thick layer of ice imbedded with bits of leaves and twigs. She crouched down and peered through the milky ice and saw the water flowing beneath it like long, blue fingers. Wedged between two rocks was a clump of human hair trailing in the gentle current. The shock of it knocked her back off her heels. When she came back to take a closer look she told herself that it had to be some strange river reed. Fear was playing tricks with her mind.

On her way down the drive she thought about a warm fire in the stove, sipping a mug of hot tea, and sharing a loaf of bread and salt. They would want the news before they got down to business. They wouldn't want the usual gossip. The goings-on of their neighbors held little interest for them now that the war was over and the Germans had left.

A year ago, in March of 1918, the Congress of Soviets ratified the Treaty of Brest-Litovsk, which gave Lenin peace with Germany, something he had to have if he wanted to stay in power. In return he signed away half of Russia's western domain. Under the treaty the Germans were given the Baltic provinces and the nominally sovereign provinces of Poland, Georgia, and the Ukraine, which, in fact, were not sovereign states at all, but German-controlled protectorates. Under German rule the fledgling Ukrainian state enjoyed a period of peace and a certain measure of autonomy. This continued until the end of the war, when the Germans were driven out, taking any semblance of law and order with them. Now, no one wanted to hear about gossip anymore. All they wanted to talk about were the troubles on the farmsteads, in the cities, about the fighting between the Reds and Whites, about the warlords and the Directory troops who took what they wanted from farms like theirs and moved on. Of less interest were the widespread pogroms that were raging in the *shtetlekh* and in the cities like Kiev and Poltava and the frequent attacks on Jewish travelers on the trains and roads.

She would give them all the news she knew and in exchange they would buy her gold. They would haggle with her and she would pretend to lower the price, but it would be the one that she had been after all along. They needed the gold as much as she needed to sell it, so she was confident it would end well and all this anxiety, the uncertainty, the agonizing slog through the snow would be worth it.

She didn't have far to go before she caught a glimpse of the house through the bare branches of the trees. It was the Kochubey house;

the fancy blue shutters and wide porch were unmistakable. She pushed on with the expectation that soon she would be hearing the dogs bark and see smoke curling out of the chimney. So she was surprised when she reached the bottom of the drive and found the yard empty and the chimney cold, the barn door open and the house deserted and dark. Ihor Kochubey was a careful man and wouldn't leave his barn door open on a day like this. There should have been children out in the yard, bundled up in felt boots and sheepskin jackets. There should have been women in the kitchen and chickens clucking in the coop. Nothing was right about Ihor Kochobey's farmstead and for a moment she wanted to drop her bundles and run. Instead she stood in the snow and waited until the panic subsided. Then she told herself that there were no signs of violence. There were no bodies, no blood in the snow. The house was intact. It was only the quiet that was frightening her. She crossed the yard to the barn, sidestepping a mound of frozen horse manure, and stepped into the darkness of the gaping doorway.

"*Kto-nibyd yest*?" she called out.

The stalls were empty and the hooks were bare where the harnesses usually hung. Her heart sped up. She turned and walked back across the yard. The windows of the house were blank. She walked up the steps and peered in through one of them, but could see nothing but the edge of a curtain and the cold fireplace across the room. She called out again, even though it was considered rude to call out over the threshold.

She waited for a few moments and then tried the doorknob. It turned easily in her hand. She called out once again before stepping inside. It was freezing in the kitchen. It smelled of a dead fire and spilled kerosene. The chairs were pushed back from the table as if the occupants had shoved them out in a hurry. There were wooden bowls of kasha on the worn planks with spoons frozen in place. Next to the bowls sat mugs of frozen tea. A cupboard stood across the room, open and empty. Beneath the table was a glass jar of canned peaches that must have rolled under and then been forgotten. She hesitated before picking it up and then shoved it into one of her bundles.

She checked the other rooms: a bedroom with several unmade beds and another one with a wardrobe and a straw mattress covered in a blanket. She was about to turn and leave the house when she heard a rustling from the back room. This time she didn't call out. She was sick with fear as she crept down the hall to the half-closed door. Behind it was a small room that smelled of mold. There were benches against one wall, a pair of felt boots in the corner, and a few goat hides tacked to the plaster walls, a feeble baton of light straying in through a tiny window. A chicken stood in the middle of the room plucking at something in the dirt. It was a clump of blond hair. This time it was unmistakable. Some of the strands ended in tiny points of blood as if it had been pulled out by the roots.

She turned and ran back down the hall and out into the kitchen. She grabbed her bundles and made for the door, stumbling down the steps and out into the yard. She blindly pushed her way through the snow, no longer thinking, no longer seeing her surroundings or where she was going, but lurching ahead, scrambling back up the drive until she realized that she had missed the track and was thoroughly turned around.

When she set out across the snowy expanse of corn rows she had no idea how to get back to Kamenka. The wind had picked up and now it was whipping across the fields, sending vapors of snow swirling up into the air. It sliced through her clothing, cutting her face; her eyes teared and her lungs ached. There was no cover in the fields. She was a dark figure in a blinding white expanse, easy to spot from horseback, a moving target against a sweeping counterpane.

When the field ended at the base of a craggy hill, Berta decided to climb it to get a better a view of her surroundings. It was a steep climb, over icy ground, and she kept sliding back down. She realized that if she threw her bundles up the slope and grabbed hold of a tree branch, she could drag herself up to the next handhold. In one steep place a bundle came sliding back down again. She tried to catch it, but it tumbled past her and came to rest in a tangle of ice-covered branches below her. She had to climb back down to retrieve it and then struggle back up again.

Finally she pulled herself up to the rocky summit and stood unsteadily in the howling wind. The view was disappointing. She turned first in one direction and then in the other, looking for a break in the fields, for any hint of a road beneath the snow. She was beginning to think that she would have to go back to the farmstead and start over again, when the clouds parted and for a brief moment a shaft of sunlight lit up the horizon. There she saw a spot of gold winking in the sunlight. She recognized it as the dome of the Church of St. Damian the First Called, a famous landmark in Kamenka. Now, as she half slid, half walked down the hill, at least she could comfort herself with the knowledge that she was heading in the right direction and with luck might make it back before nightfall.

It didn't take her long to find the cart track and she followed it back to the main road. Fortunately, only a few passing sledges broke the solitude of the road. No one stopped to offer her a ride. It wasn't safe to help strangers or to request help for that matter. Everyone knew you were on your own. No one expected kindness.

Not far from town Berta came to a large oak whose heavy branches hung over the road and were laden with snow and ice. The finer branches higher up were strung with icicles and etched a confused pattern against the colorless sky. When she got closer, she let out a yelp and sat down hard in the snow.

Hanging above her from a rope around their necks were three Orthodox Jews in belted caftans. They were stiff and blue, their blackened tongues hanging out of their mouths. Eyes open and glassy. Beards thick with snow. Two of them had been robbed of their hats and shoes, the third wore a visor cap and boots that weren't worth stealing. For the moment she could do nothing but stare up at them, at the frozen agony on their faces, the straining rope, the bulging eyes, and the black hands and feet swaying in the wind.

That night when Berta came out through the doors of the Cherkast train station, she found a crowd outside in a tight circle fascinated by something in the street. It was dark and bitterly cold. She pushed her way through the crowd to see what was keeping them from their beds. In the center of the circle was a compulsory labor detail clearing out the snow and horse manure with shovels. Since the Bolsheviks had come to power, it wasn't unusual to see details of ordinary citizens forced into labor. It was unusual, however, to see one like this, made up entirely of men and women in evening clothes. The men were wearing starched white shirts and cutaway coats. The women wore crushed velvet dresses, furs, and long gloves. Berta recognized one of them. She was a customer. She was a young woman and beautiful. Her evening slippers were soaked through, her hair hanging limp and wet beneath her once elaborate headdress. She was shoveling snow, but making a bad job of it. She tried to take too much with each shovelful and lost most of it on the way to the gutter. She glanced up at Berta and a light of recognition came into her eyes. For a moment Berta thought she was going to say something. But then a soldier, who had been trying to light a cigarette, looked up from his cupped hands and ordered her back to work.

Berta turned her back on the crowd and started up the hill toward home. She was exhausted and longed for her bed on the stove and her children in her arms. Just before she reached her room she saw a man wearing a silk dressing gown under a heavy greatcoat, moving through the street like a phantom. He clutched an icon under his arm, his hair was matted with ice, and his cheeks were flushed from either the cold or a fever. He threw one wild glance in her direction and in that moment she recognized him.

"Aleksei Sergeevich," she said in surprise. It was Alix's husband. He didn't seem to recognize her. "What are you doing out here?"

"It's all gone," he said, to no one in particular.

"What is?"

"All gone."

The Bolsheviks had nationalized the banks, factories, and railroads and had even started expropriating the houses in the Berezina.

"Where is Alix?" Berta asked.

He kept on walking.

"Aleksei Sergeevich . . . where is Alix?"

He didn't turn around.

"Lenya!" She called after him. She stood there a moment longer and watched him shamble into the night.

Part Four

The Border Stealer

Chapter Seventeen

December 1919

IT WAS STILL early in the afternoon when Colonel Svegintsev, the commander of the Drozdovskii Battalion, ordered his private train to stop in the middle of a snowy field about ten versts northwest of Cherkast. The men in the infantry sledges couldn't understand it. The Cossacks in their blue caps, gray-green belted tunics, and blue breeches with the red stripe up the side couldn't understand either, nor could the ladies in the commander's private cars who wore black hoods like the nurses but did little nursing. The battalion was supposed to be in retreat. In fact the whole Volunteer Army was in retreat, running from a newly formed Communist cavalry that was swift, skilled, and seemingly unstoppable.

The Drozdovskii Battalion was in the rear of this retreat. So why then were they ordered to take Cherkast? It didn't make sense. Since nobody in the battalion was in a position to question the young commander, the train stopped, the horses were unboxed and saddled and the supply sledges loaded up. It didn't take long for the battalion to assemble in front of the commander's car. Soon the vast snowy field held a collection of armored trucks loaded with machine guns, a repair truck, a battery of eighteen-pounders supplied by the British, a battery of 4.5 howitzers, ammunition sledges, and five *tachankas*, sledges outfitted with Vickers or Lewis machine guns also supplied by the British. Flanking on the left and right were the two companies of Don Cossack cavalry, their razor-sharp swords at their side, their famous *nagaiki*, short-handled whips, hanging from their belts. These were special whips, laced with wire so they could flay the skin off a man's back even through five layers of shirts.

Commander Svegintsev was the youngest officer to ever take

command of the Drozdovskii Battalion and had only just been appointed because General Otlanov, the previous commander, had died of typhus. Svegintsev didn't have much experience, so he didn't really deserve the command or the private railroad cars that were put at his disposal. He should have been satisfied with a sledge and a tent.

Svegintsev was an ardent monarchist. He took the death of his czar and the czar's family very badly. He simply could not believe that God would want the red devils to rule Mother Russia while he, his family, and all his friends were condemned to wander the world as penniless refugees. He was young, not yet twenty-five, and not willing to surrender, especially now that he had a battalion to command. His plan was to take Cherkast, then move on Kiev. He reasoned that once he sent word to General Wrangel, informing him of his victories, he would surely be forgiven for disobeying orders and granted all the honors due a hero. Fortunately for Commander Svegintsev, the men hadn't seen as much as action as the other units. Their horses were still somewhat fresh and there was enough enthusiasm among his junior officers to give credence to his plan.

The young commander stood on the top step of his carriage and surveyed the battalion that stretched out before him in the undulating snow. The men stood in silence, scraping the snow into little piles with their boots or leaning on the butt of their rifles or shielding their eyes with a hand. He thought, *This is Russia, her might, her pride. These are the heroes who will take her back and make her whole again*. And he, Vladimir Arkadyevich Svegintsev, will be the greatest hero of all. He will be remembered as the man who saved Russia even after it appeared all was lost.

He spoke simply to the men that afternoon, his strong voice carrying to the far reaches of the field. He considered himself a good orator and fancied that he had a way of reaching down into the souls of his men. His mother and teachers had always told him that he could be a great leader someday and he was certain that day had come. He told his men that the army was in retreat and that they had been ordered to give up and go home. They were running away like beaten dogs, their eyes always on their backs, waiting for the next blow. "Is that what you want?" he shouted to his troops. "To run back to your wife and mother and hide under your bed? Is that your fate?" He looked into the faces of his men. "No! I say no! I say we stand up to the enemy! Beat him back! Show the Bolshevik dog what the Drozdovskii Battalion can do." He shouted this above their heads, sending his words soaring up into the blue sky yet unmarred by clouds or smoke. "If we stand together and fight like Russian bears *we will prevail*! God won't desert us. He doesn't want us to give up. He wants us to save Mother Russia. *Victory will be ours!*" He shouted this last as a battle cry and waited for the crowd's thunderous reply. Instead, he got only a halfhearted cry of *Na Moskvu*. To Moscow.

The advanced guard rode out against a sky layered with ribbons of orange and pink. It consisted of a company of infantry in their sledges and a squadron of Cossacks, who rode out in two patrols. Behind them came the *tachankas*, swooping over the snow like heavy waterfowl, their occupants holding on to the sides of the sledges to keep from falling out. Following in their tracks came two batteries of field artillery and then the main force, their ponies kicking up snow and dirt as they thundered off across the fields.

About three versts from Cherkast they ran into a small unit of Red cavalry who fired on them from a stand of willows with a sledge-mounted maxim machine gun and would have engaged them if they had bothered to stop. Instead they kept going, spurring their horses up the hills and letting them have their head going down, careening nearly out of control over the windswept snow. Then just outside the city, they ran into three machine gun emplacements situated above the trenches that ringed the perimeter. At the first sign of opposition they turned their horses around and rode back up the hill. There they waited just out of range while their howitzers and eighteen-pounders got into position.

Berta sat down on the pallet next to Sura, took up her daughter's fingers, and brought them to her lips. Sura was bundled up on the straw mattress on the floor in front of the stove. She was propped up on pillows to make it easier for her to breathe. The air smelled of herbal rubs and smoke from the dried white pulp of elderberry branches thrown on hot embers. Berta examined her child's fingers in the faltering light. The fingernails were white and the flesh around the cuticles was a pale blue. She kissed her daughter's moist forehead and looked into her face. Her eyelids were transparent, the tracery of veins plainly visible beneath the skin. Her lips were white and there was a burbling in her lungs with every breath she took, a constant reminder that her lungs were failing, that they were filling with fluid, and that something had to be done.

When Sura was five Dr. Egglostein said her lungs were weak but that she would grow out of it in time. Now she was ten. Her honey blond hair had turned brown, her arms and legs were getting too long for her torso, and still she had bad lungs. Every few months the air in the neighborhood would make her sick and send her to bed with a cold. But this time was different. Berta could see it in her pale lips, her eyelids tinged with blue, the way she struggled to breathe.

Her eyes fluttered open. "What is that, Mameh?" The words came in tortured gasps. Off in the distance there was the thunder of big artillery pieces.

"The guns, my darling."

"Are they going to blow up our house?"

"No, they're far off. We don't have anything to worry about."

Lhaye came in and stood by the sink. She dipped a cloth into the washbasin and brought it over to the bed, where she laid it across Sura's forehead. The two apartments were one now; the doors were always open and the adults and children wandered back and forth without consideration. Lhaye looked over at her sister. "You better hurry," she said, her voice barely above a whisper. The two sisters exchanged a look.

It was only half past three when Berta left the building, but already the sky was growing dark. There were still some people on Dulgaya Street, but no one seemed to be in a hurry. Cherkast had changed hands so many times recently that people took the shelling in stride. It never lasted long, because of the scarcity of shells; targeting was wildly off, and besides, the buildings that were far from the perimeter were rarely hit. Only the children were absent from the street, having been herded inside by their mothers.

Out on the street Berta looked for Samuil in all the familiar places, in the alley where he liked to play with his friends and down at the grocery. She had to hurry, but she couldn't leave until she knew he was safe inside. She called out for him over and over again but got no answer. Finally, when she was on the verge of tears, she heard him calling down to her. She looked up and saw him on one of the upper floors of the bombed-out building across the street. It had been shelled some months ago and stood empty and broken. The wall facing the street had been blown away, revealing the rooms behind it. There was a dry sink hanging over a hole in the floor and several window frames with shattered glass where tattered curtains ruffled in the breeze. The roof had collapsed in a few places, while the staircase never made it to the second floor, stopping in midair. Samuil was standing at the edge of one of the rooms on the upper story. He looked down at her and even from that distance she could see that he knew he was in trouble.

"Samuil!" she shouted.

"I just wanted to watch. You can see everything from up here."

With her heart pounding in her throat, she watched him slither down a post that had fallen at such an angle that it had become a bridge from one level to the next. After that he squeezed through a hole in the floor and climbed down a chimney, jamming his feet against the corners of the bricks and finding purchase on the outcroppings. He shimmied down another broken beam and ran down the last steps of the ruined staircase and came over to her slowly with his eyes on his shoes.

"I thought I told you never to go up there." Her voice was even and contained, but she was furious and he knew it.

"I know, Mameh. But we just wanted to—"

"Go upstairs and help Mumeh Lhaye. She's with Sura."

"Where are you going?" He was twelve, not tall, but wiry, more like Berta than Hershel. There was a shadow of a moustache on his upper lip. His voice was still high, but now and then it dropped down into an unfamiliar register.

"To get the doctor. Now go."

He sighed heavily and turned back to the doorway. He muttered something under his breath but did as he was told, dragging himself up one step at a time.

She ran to the corner and waited while a Red cavalry unit galloped past, halters jingling, rowels on the spurs clinking like a pocket full of silver rubles. Then she crossed the street and ran on to the hill that overlooked the Jewish neighborhood. As she climbed she could hear the dull thud of the incoming shells, and once she reached the top, she saw fighting on the other side of the Lugovaya Market. It seemed closer than it was. She could see the flashes of fire from the field artillery and the exploding shells and hear the sharp crack of rifle fire and the short bursts of machine guns. A detachment of female Red Army troops came up behind her and ran down the other side. They were hurrying to get into position, struggling with rifles that were taller than they were. Two of them were dragging a machine gun through the snow and stopped to argue about the best way of doing it. A third came over, slung her rifle over her shoulder, and stooped to help the others carry it along.

Berta ran down the hill toward the fighting. She heard the whine of an incoming shell and dropped to the ground, covered her head with her arms, and rolled into a ball. It landed just up the street but didn't explode. Instead it sent a spray of snow and dirt high up into the air, sprinkling her with clods of black earth instead of shrapnel. When she realized she wasn't hurt, she got up and wiped away the few unconscious tears of fright. Shells were falling on the neighboring streets. A house blew up behind her and she saw a roof collapse in a rising cloud of dust and fire. Farther down the street someone was screaming. Someone else was calling for help. She kept running, past a burning building and a woman lying facedown in the snow.

At the end of the street she ducked into a doorway and stood there trembling and panting, locked in with fear, too scared to think. She could see the doctor's house on a low rise above her, silhouetted against the sky between the two houses of wealthy businessmen. All three were still intact. But to get there she would have to run through an empty field where there would be no cover from falling shells and shrapnel. In the twilight she could see the pockmarks in the snow left by recent explosions and tried to gauge her chances of making it. Her legs felt rubbery. She didn't know if she could count on them to carry her across.

She took advantage of a lull in the shelling and ran out into the field. She was nearly across when the guns started up again. But they were falling mostly on the other side of the market now. Once across she made her way to Dr. Egglostein's drive and started to climb up to the house. She found that all the windows were dark except for the few that faced north and reflected the fires burning in the market. She picked up the brass knocker and pounded it against the front door. She could hear it echo throughout the house. She waited for a moment and when no one answered, she pounded again, this time with her fists. "Dr. Egglostein!" she cried out. It hadn't occurred to her that he might not be home.

An upstairs window opened a crack and a voice called out. "Who is it? What do you want?" It was the doctor's housekeeper.

"It's me, Froy Saltzman. Berta Alshonsky."

The window opened wider and Froy Saltzman leaned out. "What are you doing out there? They're dropping bombs on us. You're going to get yourself killed."

"I have to see the doctor."

"He's not here. He is with a woman in Krupin. Come inside, I was just about to go down to the cellar. We'll be safe down there."

"Where in Krupin?"

"You're wasting your time. The woman is in labor. He won't leave her."

"I have to know where he is."

"*Meshugeneh!* Who runs around with bombs falling out of the sky? Come with me to the cellar. He'll be back in the morning. Then you'll see—"

"WHERE IS HE?" Berta shouted so loudly her eardrums popped.

Froy Saltzman stood there and gaped. This woman was no doubt out of her mind. "He's at Ya'akov's, the mailman's. Between the community center and the synagogue. But you're going for nothing," she called after her. "He won't come. They're shooting people over there."

Berta half ran, half slid down the rise, the snow soaking through her stockings and piling up in her boots. Back on the road she met more ambulances and a horse pulling a cart, transporting corpses back up to the textile mill by the river. Whenever rival forces fought over Cherkast, the mill became a morgue where they lined up the corpses on the floor and let them wait for the fighting to end and the ground to thaw.

Up ahead she could see the sky above the Lugovaya Market. There was a dull glow over the buildings from the many fires that were burning there. Here and there chimney pots poked up through the greasy canopy of smoke like bare flagpoles. As she got closer to the bridge she saw a wall of fog and smoke lying across the road. It was impossible to see more than a few feet in any direction. She was worried about wandering off the road and getting lost, so she was relieved when she recognized the stone arches of the bridge. She ran across it and on to Podkolokony Street, where she nearly stumbled into a deserted stall and tripped over the remnants of an old army tent that had been left behind by the people who lived on the curb. Farther on she came to a blackened crater in the middle of the street. There were several bodies lying nearby, killed by shrapnel. One woman lay with a hole in her head, draped over the smoldering coals in an old metal drum. The flesh on the inside of her right arm was black where it had been slowly roasting over the dying fire.

Just beyond the market and over another bridge lay Kupin, where the real fighting was taking place. It had been a Jewish townlet once before Cherkast grew up around it and swallowed it whole. Now it stood on the west shore of the Dnieper at the very spot where the Cherkast sewers emptied into the river. The spot was marked by a churning brown effluent that fouled the air, permeated every house, and even made the food unpalatable. Ordinarily a town like this would be of no value to anybody, but it also happened to stand at the hub of seven roads that spun out from its center in all directions. For this reason. if one wanted to take Cherkast, one first had to take Kupin.

Berta crossed the little bridge and ran into the townlet, taking cover in the first house off the main road. The roof was gone and all that was left were four walls around a square filled with rubble. There was a chimney in the middle of the rubble shaped like an inverted Y. Once this had been a nice house, maybe even an impressive one by Kupin's standards. There had been two fireplaces. Now it was just a pile of plaster, burned timbers, and the brown branches of thistles half buried in the snow.

A burst of gunfire drove her to the back and to the privy that was still standing despite the devastation. She stood just inside the doorway covering her nose with her hand, but the smell was so bad she couldn't stand there for long. She picked her way over the rubble until she was back on the main road. It was then she realized that the smell was still with her. It wasn't just the privy that stank of sewers and corruption; it was Kupin and the air all around it.

She darted from house to house, taking cover wherever she could, although her concern was speed, not caution. She kept to the main road, feeling confident that it would take her to the synagogue. Kupin wasn't a very big place and it should have been easy finding the most prominent landmark in town. But the air was even thicker here than in the market and all she could make out were the vague shapes of buildings on either side of the road.

More explosions. A report of machine gun fire. A woman ran past carrying a kid goat that was struggling to get free. Berta called to her: "Where is the synagogue?"

The woman turned back briefly. "You're standing in front of it. What's left of it."

Berta spun around and for a moment considered the building behind her. It didn't look like a synagogue. In fact it didn't look like much of anything. The timbers were blackened and had collapsed in on each other. All that was left was a line of squat windows in the cellar and the archway over the main double doors. Then she saw the community center on the other side and the house between them. She ran through the gate in front of the little house and past the remains of a kitchen garden, a dry tangle of vines and frosty cabbages rotting in the ground.

The man who answered the door seemed too old to have a pregnant wife. Ya'akov was middle-aged, pale with worry, and kept wiping his beard with his hand. He opened the door without question, probably thinking she had come to assist the doctor. "They're down in the cellar," he said anxiously, stepping aside to let her in. He showed her the way to the steps. "We moved her down there. It wasn't safe up here. You better hurry. I don't think it'll be long." He called after her as she climbed down the steps: "Take care of her. I lost the first this way. I couldn't stand to lose this one."

Berta found the doctor with his hand placed firmly on the taut belly of a very pregnant woman who lay writhing in a tangle of sheets on a straw mattress. The room was low beamed with dirt walls and a floor glistening with damp. It was lit by several kerosene lamps to give the doctor as much as light as possible. The young woman was calling out in pain. She was surrounded by several women, one of whom might have been her mother, since the matron held her hand and was singing her a lullaby.

The doctor looked up in surprise. "Froy Alshonsky."

"I have to speak to you," she said breathlessly.

He looked doubtfully at his patient, but she had stopped writhing and was between contractions. "All right. Just for a minute."

She followed him up to the foyer. The mailman was pacing the floor in the front parlor. He stopped when he saw the doctor talking to the woman who had just arrived and watched them narrowly. He didn't like this woman who had taken the doctor away from his wife.

"I've come to get you," Berta whispered. "Sura's sick again and this time it's bad."

The doctor shook his head. "I can't leave now."

"But she can hardly breathe."

"There's nothing I can do for her. I told you that. She has pleurisy. There's nothing anyone can do. You just have to wait and see."

"But you saved her last time."

"She saved herself. Or God saved her. It wasn't anything I did."

The young woman screamed out in pain. Her mother called out for the doctor. "I have to get back."

"No, wait." She grabbed his arm. "You must come. She's dying and I don't know what to do." She was trembling and couldn't stop.

He twisted his arm free, put both hands on her shoulders, and looked into her face. "Listen to me, you have to calm down. Now go back to her. She needs her mother. Keep her warm. Keep her head up. Other than that, there is nothing to do."

He started to turn back and she grabbed his arm again. "No, no, you can't," she said, sliding to her knees. "She'll die. I know she will. She doesn't have a chance without you." The other mother was calling to him, her voice rising with hysteria. A shell fell in the garden outside the house, but didn't explode. The mailman was shouting, "Go to her. She's calling for you. What are you waiting for?"

"Please," Berta was sobbing and holding on to his arm. "She's only a child. You can't let her die."

"Take this one next door," the doctor said to Ya'akov firmly. "Take her to the community center."

Without another word the mailman picked Berta up and carried her to the front door as the doctor headed back down to the cellar. She struggled to get free, but the mailman held her fast while he opened the door and shoved her out. He slammed it behind her and turned the lock. She pounded on it and begged to be let in, but soon the light from his lamp moved off from the window and disappeared down the cellar steps.

She was standing in front of a dark house. A shell exploded down the street in the square. Her ears were ringing and the ground jittered beneath her. She knew if she didn't leave now, she would never make it back, so she turned from the door and ran out through the yard and up the street toward the bridge. She heard a thud, a high-pitched scream, and a deafening explosion. She turned just in time to see the community center blast apart into a roiling cloud of fire, smoke, and debris. Pieces of it fell on the mailman's house and soon it too was ablaze. She thought she could hear screams coming from inside, although that may have been the timbers screeching in protest as they came crashing down, one on top of the other.

Not long after that, she was running up Podkolokony Street. Explosions, mortar fire, sharp report of rifle fire, and shouting from every side. She was by the clubs and the artists' lofts. A child was screaming. A brief stutter of machine gun fire and a reply from another. She was in the middle of it. It was all around her. She dove for a doorway and crouched down low. Bullets hit the doorjamb and bits of flying wood and glass rained down on her. When she looked around she found that the lock on the door had been shot away and the door was swinging open. She crawled into the building over broken glass, cutting her hands and knees, too frightened to stop. Once inside she dashed over to the stairway and climbed up the stairs, ducking as bullets raked the wall above her head.

At the end of a short hallway on the second floor she found a loft fronted by floor-to-ceiling windows. Some of the windows had been shot out and the wind was blowing in a light sprinkling of snow and the acrid smell of smoke and gunpowder. On the other side of the room she saw three men crouched down behind tables that had been turned on their sides. One man was fully dressed, the other one was wearing a coat but no shirt, and the third was nearly naked. Berta crawled over to them.

"Were you out there?" asked the shirtless man.

She nodded and struggled to catch her breath.

"Lucky to be alive," he said to the others.

"Lucky and stupid," said his fully dressed companion. "Who are they?"

"I don't know. Reds and Whites."

"What difference does it make?" said the shirtless man. "The bullets are all the same."

"I had a customer tonight," groaned the nearly naked man. He was shivering and his lips were turning purple. "Now I'm going to freeze to death."

Berta noticed their ink-stained fingers and saw sheaves of blank paper blowing around the room. She guessed that they were copyists, waiting all day and night by their tables for lawyers, playwrights, and professors to come by with papers to copy. Business was never very good and now with the fighting it had to be worse. She imagined them selling a shirt or a pair of shoes in the morning to buy bread and then waiting all day for a customer so they could buy it back by nightfall.

"Help me out, citizens. A blanket, a shirt, anything," the nearly naked man was saying with chattering teeth. "You're not going to let me freeze to death, are you, brothers? Not after all we've been through?"

"Is there another way out?" asked Berta.

"You're not going back out there?" asked the fully clothed man.

The nearly naked man shivered violently and wrapped his arms around his knees. "Please, I'm freezing here. You're not going to let me die. A scarf, a hat, a scrap of anything. Comrades, I'm begging you."

The shirtless man said, "There's a back door. You go down the hall to the other stairs. It's one flight down."

Berta crawled across the room and out through the door. She followed the hallway across the landing. It was dark and difficult to see, but she thought she could make out a water barrel and several pairs of boots lined up by a door. It smelled of mold and rat piss and there was pile of rotten boards and chunks of plaster in the corner. She found the stairs and took them down to a back door that opened out onto an alley. It was foggy and dark. She could just make out a line of overflowing trash cans across the dirt track. It seemed safe, but she didn't trust it, so she found a rag lying on the floor, balled it up in her hand, and threw it out the door. A loud report drove her back among the bags of garbage and old newspapers.

As she crouched there in the dark, her thoughts became increasingly frantic and disjointed. *Sura will live. She will not. God will watch over her. There is no God. Tonight there will be a God and he will watch over her.* She made bargains with Him. She begged her dead mother to intercede. She thought about leaving Cherkast. If only she had the money, she would go to America, even if Hershel were dead, which she now believed he was. She would bring her children to a place where they could be safe. Tears rolled down her cheeks and soon she was sobbing silently into her hands, hopeless, terrified, and filled with rage at the men who were keeping her from her child.

Sometime later in the night she heard a shot and a man scream and after that she could hear him moaning out in the alley. He called out to his comrades to help him and later, in his delirium, to his mother. He whimpered for mercy, begged for release; another shot and then nothing.

When the sky began to lighten, the shadows evolved into distinct shapes: a garbage can, a sledge, an old bed frame lying on its side. With the coming dawn a breeze blew in from the river and the fog began to lift. Berta heard shouting through the doorway and saw men running in from all directions. They were Reds. They jumped on each other, slapped each other on the back, playfully punched each other, and laughed. She stopped a man in a black leather jacket wearing a visor cap with a red star on the front.

"What is it? What's happening?"

"No Whites! They're all dead or on the run. We've been firing at each other all night. The goddamn fog had us all turned around. Yankovsky!" he yelled to a comrade holding a coffeepot. "Save me some of that."

Berta ran on through the city, slipped on the ice, and broke her fall with a bloody hand. People were coming out of their cellars. Some were picking through the smoldering rubble; others were searching the streets for missing loved ones. There was a sobbing woman crumpled over the mangled body of a man. A boy led a roan mare down the street, talking to her the whole time. Farther on two men were unloading mangled corpses from a cart and laying them out in a neat row in the snow.

Soon she was climbing the hill that stood between her and the Jewish section. At the top she paused to catch her breath and searched the landscape below for Dulgaya Street. She thought she could see it through the haze of the smoking chimney pots. She imagined that the light she saw burning in one of the windows was from the lamp in the kitchen. She took it as a good sign for no other reason than she needed a good sign.

Then she was on the street a few blocks away. As she came closer she saw a man hiding in the shadows of her building. It wasn't light enough to see his face, but she had already made up her mind to kill him if he tried to stop her. She had just picked up an iron bar from the rubble of a bicycle shop, when she saw the figure step into the light. It was Pavel.

"I was just about to look for you," he said.

"How is she?"

He hesitated and then she knew. She threw down the iron bar and ran upstairs, flinging open the door and rushing into the kitchen. Lhaye was sitting beside Sura, holding her hand. She got up when she saw Berta come in and tried to put her arms around her sister, but Berta pushed past her. She scooped up her daughter and lay down on the bed. Sura's skin was cold and clammy. Her face was white and tinged with blue. Already the muscles in her face had begun to relax and her cheeks were beginning to sink into her skull. Berta rocked her and prayed, not to God, who had betrayed her, but to Sura, *keep breathing.* Pavel came into the room and crouched down in the corner. She barely noticed him. She only knew that her daughter was struggling to live, her breath coming in jagged gasps that had no rhythm.

Her eyelids fluttered open and for a moment Berta thought she could see a glint of recognition in the feverish black eyes. "Sura, it's Mameh. It's Mameh, *maideleh*. My darling girl. *Tsatskeleh der mamehs.*" Sura looked up at her and struggled to move her lips. They were dry, cracked with fever, and blue. Not a sound escaped them, but the word they formed was plain enough.

Mameh.

A few minutes later the mournful cry could be heard up and down the hallway. It spilled out into the street and mixed with the first stirrings of the morning. By the time the day began in earnest—the women hunting in the rubble for anything salvageable, men loitering on the curb looking for odd jobs, the children off to heder or playing cross tag in the ruins—everyone on Dulgaya Street knew that Berta Alshonsky had lost her daughter.

Chapter Eighteen

December 1919

BERTA LAY on a pallet in the bruised light of morning with her daughter in her arms. She could feel the warmth from Sura's body ebb away as she lay there trying to find the strength to do what must be done. Pavel had been sent away and now only Lhaye remained with her. She came over and closed Sura's eyes and then lifted her body so that Berta could get out from underneath it. Together they lowered her back down on the bed and laid her arms gently by her sides. Her features had changed so much since death had taken her that now she looked like a wax effigy. Berta kissed her one last time and pulled a clean white sheet over her head and together she and Lhaye placed candles all around the bed and lit them.

There was a knock at the door. "It's the *shomer*," Lhaye said, coming back to the kitchen.

"Tell him to go away. I don't want him here."

"Who will stand guard over her?"

"I'll do it myself."

"But you are the *nihum avelim*."

"I said I will do it myself."

That evening, Berta and Lhaye washed the body and wrapped it in a tallis. The man from the burial society came and told her that if she did not have the money for a funeral, they would provide her with one. He was a thin man, all angles, with a bushy beard that nearly covered his lips, leaving only a thin line of flesh where the words came out. Berta didn't have the money, so she was grateful for the help.

"Don't worry, Froy Alshonsky. Everything will be taken care of. It's a nice plot, under a tree. A chestnut, I think." She started to cry. He was used to this and stood there quietly while she pulled herself together. Then he went over a few details, telling her when they would pick up the body and the time of the service.

"I don't want any official mourners," she said, thinking of Aviva Kaspler and her partner.

"She doesn't need them," said the man. "There are plenty of people who will mourn her."

That night she brought her pallet into the front room next to Sura's body and stretched out on it. Lhaye wanted her to come out into the hall to eat something since it was forbidden to eat or drink in the presence of the dead, but Berta shook her head. She only wanted to be left alone. So Lhaye went back to her apartment and her children. Berta could hear them through the wall: little Rivke pleading for her shoe, Vulia teasing her, Lhaye admonishing him. It was the normal clamor of life and it caused her a momentary pang of jealousy. She rolled over and stared at the flickering candlelight. Then she closed her eyes and saw its dark afterimage. She lay there for some time and waited for sleep to come. Her thoughts became half dreams of disjointed images. She felt as if she had been cut into pieces, her limbs severed, her face halved. She could no longer feel her lips. She wondered if she could move at all.

After the funeral, Lhaye and Froy Wohlgemuth, the old lady from down the hall, came over with bread and hard-boiled eggs. This was the first meal of shiva, the seven-day mourning period. Then the neighbors began filtering in with more food and condolences. Berta sat on her pallet and did not move, did not get up, neither washed nor changed clothes nor greeted visitors. These were the rules of shiva. Even if they hadn't been, she would have still followed them. She could do little else. She could hear the comings and goings of others from far away, like a child sent to bed before the guests arrived. But she was in another room and the door was closed. She was no longer a part of the world.

NOW THAT there was no one to tell Samuil that he couldn't go across the street to the bombed-out building and climb up to the second floor, he went up there whenever he wanted to. He liked it up there. He liked sitting on the edge where the wall had once met the floor, with his feet dangling over the piles of rubble below, and watching the housewives in the alleys trade used goods for wood and food. Since he wasn't going to school, he had plenty of time to make himself comfortable. He staked out two rooms that overlooked the street and furnished them with an armchair that was missing a cushion, two packing crates from the deserted poultry market, and a charred table. These were the rooms that he shared with Sasha Riabushinsky and Moses Sforim, who came by after school to play cards. They would stay up there until their mothers called them down. Since there was no one to call Samuil down, he stayed up there long after they left.

There was another room that he had recently claimed. It was in the back and looked out across an empty lot to the back porches of several houses. It was in the corner and out of the way and had a door that closed. He didn't tell Moses or Sasha about it. There was no furniture in there, only three walls and a mantel that jutted out from a chimney that seemed to hang in the air.

On top of the mantel he kept his most secret things. There was a broken comb that he found under a cart. It was decorated with bits of sparkly glass and it glittered whenever he held it up to the light. There was also a scrap of lace that he found fluttering from the ragged edge of a fence post and an old silk flower from Mumeh Lhaye's sewing basket. Yesterday he cut a hank of his little cousin's hair. It wasn't much. She didn't mind. It was the wrong hair from the wrong girl, but the color was right and he put that on the mantel next to the comb. He was always on the lookout for these things. His prized possession was a ceramic cat with a broken tail that looked like Masha. That morning he made a drawing of Arabian horses grazing in a pasture. He balled it up because the horses looked like dogs and threw it off the edge, watching it bounce off the pile of rubble below.

He was supposed to be sitting shiva, but whenever he got the chance, he climbed up to this room and fingered his secret things. That morning he had cried and it scared him. It was so intense that he thought his insides were pouring out of him. At first he couldn't breathe, poised on the edge of something impenetrable and overwhelming. Then he tumbled down into it, his shoulders juddering, his breath ripped from his lungs in big, gulping sobs. Afterward he felt a little better and wiped his face on his sleeve. Even so he didn't want to do that again. It could easily get out of control and no telling where he'd end up if it did.

The idea of the mantel came to him the day after Sura died. He thought if he gathered enough things that she liked, she might come back to look at them. He told himself that he wouldn't be scared. He wanted her to come. He wanted to say that he was sorry for not reading the titles to her at the moving pictures. If he had it to do over again, he would've read them to her. Every word.

He waited for five days but nothing happened. Then on the sixth day, just as he was about to climb down the beam to the second floor, he heard someone walking in one of the rooms down the hall. Footsteps. He listened. "Who's there?" he called out softly.

Silence.

"Who is it?"

Silence.

He listened again. The sound came from his room, the one in the back, as if someone had crossed the floor from the window with the jagged glass to the mantel. Her mantel.

He stood by the hole in the floor, barely breathing. He told himself that if he heard another footstep, he would investigate. Part of him wanted to hear it. The other part wanted to run out of the building. But he forced himself to wait in the gathering darkness. At first he only heard the sounds of the street below, then the sighing of the wind through the charred bones of the building, and then nothing. He waited for a few moments more and then climbed down the beam.

Once outside on the street he didn't go home. Instead he did what he always did when he was bored or when he wanted to be taken out of himself—he used the shadows, trees, doorways, garbage cans, anything that could give him cover to spy on his friends, neighbors, and strangers. From these vantage points he heard about mysterious ailments, unwanted pregnancies, the theft of a pair of shoes, a feud between brothers, and all about loss: the loss of a sister, a husband, a business, a job, a home. It seemed that all of Dulgaya Street had lost something. The whole neighborhood was suffering from a broken heart.

That night, Samuil became a lamppost, the wheel of a cart, and a barrel. He heard about a cheating husband, a colicky baby, and a boil that wouldn't burst. He melded into an old oil drum and heard two peddlers complaining about the new edicts outlawing private enterprise and the black market. They were strangers to Cherkast because he had never seen them before. Both wore long gabardine coats that looked as if they had been bought and sold many times. One wore a pair of battered shoes with flapping soles and the other had a thick black beard and wore shoes that bent up at the toes.

Samuil knew about peddling, about how you had to keep your wares hidden in your pockets and under your clothes, or risk getting shot as a speculator. How you had to hide buttons, soap, suspenders, pots and pans, rope or cooking oil, anything you could trade for food in the countryside to sell in the city. He liked to listen to them because they traveled from town to town and brought news from the rest of Russia and sometimes even from Poland or America. There were stories of pogroms and battles between the Whites and Reds, starvation in Petersburg and Moscow, farmsteads looted, kulaks shot, suspected counterrevolutionaries shot, speculators shot, ordinary people shot for no other reason than they were on the wrong side of the street or wearing a warm coat or boots that looked new. *Better to execute ten innocent people than spare one who is guilty.*

"They pulled him from the train," one peddler was saying to the other. "He had sacks of bulgur in his pants. He was so scared he peed himself and one of the sacks broke and the grain ran down his leg."

"What did they do to him?"

"You really want to know?"

The other nodded.

"What do you think? Shot him. He was a speculator."

"Right there, in front of the whole train? Was it just him?"

"No, there were others. As a reminder, they said. There was a woman with three plucked chickens under her skirt and others, I forget."

They stood in silence. They may have been wondering how long it would be before they suffered the same fate. Then the one with the flapping shoes asked: "*Nu*, you looking for someone?"

"Selensky. You heard of her? An old woman from Spasova."

The other one shook his head.

"Her son is looking for her. Big reward. You hear of her, you tell me. We'll split the reward."

The peddlers were often looking for lost family members. There were families in America and Europe who offered big rewards to anybody who located their relatives. They passed the word from one to another and in that way the search extended beyond the borders and spread throughout the Pale. Samuil was never much interested in missing relatives. He was about to move on when he heard the one with the turned-up toes ask, "*Nu*, what about you? What do you have?"

"A woman and two children."

"There are lots of women and children."

"This one lives in the Berezina. She has a girl and boy. A pretty woman. Lives in a big house on a hill. You heard of her?"

This stopped Samuil and for a moment he didn't know what to do.

"A Jew in the Berezina? This shouldn't be too hard to find."

Samuil jumped out from behind the drum and asked, "What's her name?"

The peddlers gasped, startled by his sudden appearance, and the one with the turned-up toes snapped: "Hey, you little *pisher*, you don't sneak around like that. You could give a person a heart attack."

"I just want to know her name."

"What for?"

"I just do, that's all."

"You know this woman? A big shot like you. You're acquainted with a fine lady from the Berezina?"

"Maybe."

The peddlers laughed. The one with the flapping shoes rubbed his hands together to warm them. "So how much you going to pay me for this information?" Samuil looked at him in confusion. "You expect it for free?"

He shook his head, thought for a moment, then dug into his pocket and pulled out a pearl button and a piece of hard candy that a woman in his building had given him because his sister was dead. The button belonged to Sura and he was going to put it on his mantel, but then he thought his mother might miss it so he was bringing it back. Now he had another change of heart and held out his hand. The peddler took the button and turned it over and over. Then he looked up at Samuil. "Debishonki. Her name is Debishonki."

"Debishonki?"

"That's right."

Samuil thought for a moment. "It couldn't be Alshonsky?"

"It could. But Debishonki is what I heard."

"Who is looking for them?"

"The father. He lives in America. I forget where."

That's all Samuil had to hear. He ran home and found his mother as he had left her that morning, lying on the straw mattress in front of the stove in the kitchen. She had been like that since Sura's funeral, curled up with her knees to her chest, staring at nothing. She was dressed in the same blouse she had worn that day and her hair was unwashed. The only light in the room came from the gaslight flickering outside in the street. The room was cold and the fire had gone out. He heard scratching in the walls and tried to remember if he covered the bread that morning. He was hungry and was counting on it for supper. He didn't want to have to go next door and lie to Mumeh Lhaye about where he had been all day.

"Mameh, wake up." He squatted down beside her and shook her gently. She stirred and opened her eyes.

"Not now, please, Samuil."

"I heard two peddlers talking."

"I'm tired, let me sleep."

"They're looking for a woman and two children. She lives in the Berezina."

"I don't care."

"But it's us, Mameh. They're looking for us."

She closed her eyes again and rolled over. The straw rustled beneath her and a few feathers that had escaped the quilt floated effortlessly on the currents in the room. "Go next door. Mumeh Lhaye will feed you."

"It's Tateh, Mameh. He's looking for us."

"Tateh is dead," she said dully, pulling the quilt up over her ears. "Now, go away."

"No, he isn't. He's looking for us. They say we have to go to Warsaw."

She laughed softly without opening her eyes. "Warsaw, is it? What name did they give?"

"Debishonki."

She rolled back and put her arm under her head for a pillow. Her eyes were open now and dull in the half-light. "Debishonki is not Alshonsky, my son."

"But they always get it wrong. You know how it works. One person hears something different and the next a little more and so on. By the time it comes all the way across Little Russia, it's been changed. Debishonki, Mameh, it's just like Alshonsky."

"I don't think so."

"They're looking for a rich woman with two children who live in the Berezina. That's us, Mameh. That's where we used to live. And he doesn't know about Sura, that's why he's looking for two children. Can't you see I'm right? Mameh?"

But it was too late. She was gone and there was no reaching her. He stood and looked around for the bread. It wasn't until he was eating it at the table that he realized how much he wanted company. So he wrapped it up and put it into a heavy pot with a lid to protect it from the mice and went next door. There he was fed and fussed over. After dinner he lay down between his cousins and, comforted by the warmth of the litter, drifted off into a dreamless sleep.

THE NEXT morning Berta lay on her side staring at the floor. It was dark beneath the stove and there were wispy clouds of dust laced with mouse droppings and the dried husks of roaches. She thought that if she ever got up again, she would clean under there, and took this as a good sign. There was an implication of life after Sura's death in that thought and, although she still didn't believe it, at least she had begun to consider it.

Outside she could hear Froy Wohlgemuth's shuffling step in the hall. She would be bringing Berta two pieces of bread on a chipped china plate and a glass of tea. She had been bringing this every morning since shiva had begun and today, the last day, was no different. Berta heard her at the door trying to turn the knob. Her hands were bent with arthritis and it took her a while to open it. She considered getting up to help and thought this too was a good sign.

"Wake up, *mein teier*. Wake up, *mein faigeleh*." She always called Berta *mein faigeleh*, my little bird. She walked into the front room and put the glass and plate on the table.

"What is it?"

"You must get up. The peddler is downstairs. He is looking for you."

"He's not looking for me."

"Oh, yes he is. He is looking for a woman and two children from the Berezina. How many Jewish women are from the Berezina? Come now, it's time to get up." Froy Wohlgemuth tried to help Berta up, but the old woman wasn't very strong. She had thin arms, a prominent hump on her back, and one hip was noticeably higher than the other.

"You have it all wrong. He is not looking for me. He is looking for another woman by a different name."

"Ah feh! It's always the wrong name. He is looking for you. Why is that so hard to believe? Your husband is alive. He has sent for you. This is happy news. Now come and eat. *Essen*, my brave girl . . . you need your strength." She grabbed Berta's forearm with her twisted fingers and attempted to pull her up.

Berta resisted at first, but she knew Froy Wohlgemuth was right. It was time to get up. There was no food in the house and no money to buy it. She had to find something to sell, something she could trade out in the countryside for food. She couldn't keep relying on Lhaye and Pavel and neighbors for food. She had to start living again. Gathering her strength, she crawled out of bed and stood on the cold, damp floor.

When Berta had finished dressing, Froy Wohlgemuth helped her down the stairs and together they went out into the bright sunshine to see the peddler with the flapping shoes. They found him leaning up against the building watching two housewives argue in the street. He straightened when he saw them coming and studied Berta for a moment. Maybe he was trying to picture her as the grand lady from the Berezina.

"You lived in the Berezina?"

"Yes, but my name isn't Debishonki."

"It's Alshonsky, close enough. The names always change from one mouth to the next." He studied her a moment longer. "You could be her. Fixed up a little, you could definitely be her."

Froy Wohlgemuth clapped her hands. "See? What did I tell you? This is very good news."

"He's just guessing, Froy Wohlgemuth. He doesn't know. They're probably looking for someone else."

The peddler said, "I don't think so. I've been looking for a long time and you're the closest I've come." He examined a callus on his thumb. "You know, there is one way to find out for sure."

"And how is that?"

"Go to Poland."

She laughed without mirth. "I could just as easily go to the moon."

The peddler shrugged. "It's not impossible. It can be done. If you go, then you go to Warsaw. To the American embassy. You give them your name and you give them this." He handed her a grimy piece of paper. "It's got my name on it and an address. It's important, otherwise I don't get paid."

Berta had stopped listening because she had spotted a young girl standing across the street with a baby in her arms. She was waiting for her mother to finish buying potatoes. The girl was only a child, all arms and legs, looking bored and impatient with her baby brother on her hip. Her mother ignored her and continued to take her time picking through the sack. When Berta became aware that the peddler was still going on about the best way to cross the border, she interrupted him and told him that she wasn't the woman he was looking for, that she wasn't going to Poland and, in fact, she wasn't going anywhere. She thanked Froy Wohlgemuth, turned back to the stairs, and went back up to her room, where she lay down on the pallet and stayed there for the whole day and a few more weeks after that.

Berta opened her eyes and for a moment she had no idea where she was. Then it came to her that Sura was dead and she had spent the night on a bench in the Bogitslav train station. It had been a few months since Sura died and still she woke every morning to the shock of her daughter's death. It always took her a while to steel herself against the coming day. But this morning was different. This time she bolted upright because she remembered her bundles and wanted to make sure that none of them had been stolen while she slept. They were all there, tucked under her arms and legs for safety, except for the one that she had been using for a pillow.

To the casual observer her bundles looked like a jumble of old rags. In reality they were sacks of potatoes and beets hidden under lengths of fabric. In one were hidden three bottles of homemade vodka, the favorite currency in Cherkast. In another was a roast chicken wrapped up in newspaper; and in the third, a bag of kasha and a bag of dried white beans. She had spent most of yesterday trudging the muddy roads around Bogitslav, trading yard goods, soap, and tobacco for the contents of the bundles. It had been a long day, spent mostly with her skirt hiked up to her knees, trying to stay out of the sucking mud or else pulling her shoe out when she misjudged a step. Now that she had her vodka and food, she wasn't about to lose them to thieves.

She was only twenty versts outside of Cherkast, and yet it would take her three days to come out and go back again. The station had started to fill up sometime during the night and now most of the benches were taken. There were muzhiki playing cards and smoking *makhorka*, peddlers with their bundles of contraband, and a few soldiers on the bench in the corner playing cards or dozing. Among the waiting passengers were three women in long skirts and heavy plaid shawls who had become friendly during the night and had staked out a bench in the middle of the room by the stove. Now they were sitting in a row like crows on a wire, their bundles at their feet, drinking tea and discussing the merits of magic against pogroms. One of the women, younger than the rest, with a dark complexion, long nose, and large black eyes, was passing around an amulet.

"I'm telling you, it saved my life," she was saying to the others as she watched it pass from hand to hand. She tossed a glance in the soldiers' direction and lowered her voice. "I was caught with a dead rabbit in my bundle. He was a Red and he said he was going to shoot me. You should've seen all the people they shot that day. I was doomed. I knew it. So I prayed and held on to the amulet. And I got down on my knees and begged for my life, but he wouldn't hear any of it. He pointed his rifle at my head and pulled the trigger." The amulet came back to her and she turned and handed it to Berta, to include her in their circle.

"He pulled the trigger?" said another woman with a look of incredulity.

"The rifle jammed."

"Jammed?"

"A miracle. Just like Rabbi Rollenstein said. "A miracle from God."

"He didn't try it again?"

"Oh, he was about to, but then someone called him out. Apparently he was late for a meeting with his unit. He told me not to move. He would deal with me later."

"Did you stay?"

"Are you joking? Of course I didn't stay. How much can you expect from one amulet. No, I was gone in a minute and I've never been back."

For their midday meal the women decided to pool their food. Everyone put out a dish and they shared evenly. Someone put out kasha, someone else bread, someone had a bowl of pickled beets, and another boiled potatoes. Berta only had the chicken. She thought about it for a while before she put it out. But she figured by the time she got home it wouldn't be fit to eat anyway and besides she always had the vodka to trade for another one closer to home. The women were overjoyed when they saw the chicken. Everyone agreed that she should have a larger share, but she said she would be satisfied with the same as everyone else.

During lunch there was talk of relatives in America searching for loved ones. The shy one who smiled too much said she'd heard that a son was looking for his mother, who lived in Spasova. "Her name is Silverstein. She's old. He lives in a big American city and wants to bring her over. Anyone heard of a Silverstein in Spasova?" she asked. She looked at her companions, but no one had. She thought for a moment. "Could be Selensky. Maybe it was Selensky."

The sharp-nosed woman spoke up next. "I heard they found that other woman. What's her name?" Her mouth was full of beets and she had to swallow hard before continuing. "You know. The one from Frampol."

"Hannah Bokser."

"That's her. I heard they found her in Bar."

"Bar?" said the woman with the raggedy scarf. "I was just in Bar. I was asking for Hannah Bokser and nobody heard of her."

"Apparently somebody did. A man named Helleck found her the other day. Big reward."

"Isn't that just my luck," she said, stabbing a boiled potato with the fork. "By rights I should've found her. I was there first. She should've been mine."

The young woman with the amulet now safely nestled between her breasts said, "I heard they're looking for a woman in Cherkast." At this, Berta looked up from her bowl and glanced over in her direction.

"There are lots of women in Cherkast, my friend," said the one with the raggedy scarf.

"Yes, but this one is Jewish and lives in the Berezina," said the young woman.

"Then she shouldn't be too hard to find," offered the shy one.

"That's just what I was thinking."

After that the talk meandered on to their families and to their hopes for the future. Two of them had relatives in America and were hoping for passage if they could find a way to slip across the border. The third had a brother in the party. She had been trying to reach him, but so far he hadn't answered her letters.

When the train finally came thundering into the station in a cloud of fire and smoke, the four travelers rushed outside like everyone else, squeezing through the door and fighting for a good place on the platform. It was a short train made up of third-class carriages without seat cushions and stuffed to suffocation with peasants, soldiers, refugees, and Jews and all their belongings. Boarding the train meant pushing and shoving, elbowing and kicking, anything to get a place, even if it meant a place on the floor or on the roof or on the steps outside. Berta was lucky. She was able to fight her way to the top of the steps. From there she could see the three women from the bench below her, jostling one another, their friendship all but forgotten as they fought for a seat on the train.

ONE MORNING, not too long after Bogitslav, when she still had a bottle of vodka left to trade, she took it up the hill to the neighborhood just below Davidkovo Street. Most of the shops were closed for good, but there was still a brisk business going on in the alleyways and behind the buildings. People were trading all sorts of things for food. On any given stretch one could find embroidered towels, fine crystal, brass samovars: once the precious belongings of the well-to-do, now worthless, except if they could be traded for potatoes or cabbages or the rare piece of real meat, not dog or cat.

It was hard finding the building on Sofiyevskaya. Many of the numbers were missing from the doors and she had to ask her way. When she found the building she walked up the wide stone steps only to find the door was locked, so she went around to the back, where she found one open. This had been a respectable place once with large, airy apartments and a doorman in a red caftan. Now the apartments had been divided up among three or four families and the foyer had been left to molder. The carpet was spongy and smelled of rot. She heard voices on the upper floors. A door slammed. A woman called to a child. There was an apartment to her left with a strong smell of Sterno coming from the open doorway. An old woman sat on the floor in front of a camp stove perched on an apple crate. She sat back on her heels, stirring a small pot of fish-head soup with a wooden ladle, while she watched Berta with tiny, suspicious eyes.

"Do you know if Madame Gorbunova lives here?" Berta asked. The woman studied her for a moment and then nodded to the back of the apartment. "May I come through?" She shrugged and went back to her pot. So Berta walked through the old woman's section that housed her few belongings. There was a sheet at the back that was draped over a rope and acted as a divider. Before parting it Berta called out, "Madame Gorbunova?"

"Who is it?" came the reply from the other side.

"It's Berta Alshonsky."

"Who?"

"You came to my house once for a—" she was about to say *séance* but corrected herself—"communion."

There was a pause and then a short laugh. "That must've been a long time ago."

Berta heard footsteps out in the hall and turned to see two men carrying out a young girl on a stretcher. The blanket fell from one of the girl's arms, revealing a fiery rash. She had typhus and they were taking her away to the hospital to be quarantined. It occurred to Berta that the whole building would soon be quarantined.

"May I come in?" she asked.

"I suppose," came the indifferent reply.

She parted the sheet and saw a much-changed Madame Gorbunova sitting in an armchair by the window, covered in a blanket. She had been a stout woman when Berta had seen her last and, although she was still somewhat thick, she had lost a lot of weight. Now her flesh hung in meaty flaps from her chin and jowls. Her eyes flitted over Berta's shabby clothes and she smiled wryly. "Madame Alshonsky . . . how you've changed."

"Everything has changed."

"Ah, but for the better, don't you agree?" Madame Gorbunova looked pointedly at the sheets that divided her little corner from the rest of the apartment. They could hear coughing on the other side and a low conversation.

"Oh yes, I quite agree," Berta said for the benefit of the others. "It's much better this way. So much was wasted before."

Madame Gorbunova's little corner was packed with furniture and clothing that had once occupied the entire apartment. Everything was piled up in a jumbled testament to happier times. There were two tables shoved up against the wall, one on top of the other, legs sticking up in the air like the stiffening corpse of a dead horse. There were two armchairs standing on the tables with a pile of clothes thrown over them and on the very top was a brass floor lamp, stiff and weighty, crushing the dresses beneath it. On the other side was a rumpled bed, dirty plates, and a camp stove. In between, taking up every available space, was a set of gilt chairs piled up in twos, a dying fern on a stand, a pile of drapes, old newspapers, and a settee set up on its end.

"I must apologize, Madame Alshonsky. I'm waiting for a delivery of wood. You'll have to excuse the cold."

"That's all right."

"And I can't offer you anything. I seem to be out of Sterno. Why don't you push those newspapers aside and take a seat and we'll have a little chat."

Berta thanked her and sat down on the only other available chair. She saw Gorbunova eyeing the bottle she had brought. "So, why have you come?" she asked, shifting her gaze from the vodka to Berta.

Berta paused to steady herself and then said evenly, "My daughter is dead and I wish to speak to her."

Madame Gorbunova nodded slowly and offered her condolences. Then she hesitated and smiled awkwardly as if she had just been presented with a bill she couldn't pay. "I'm sorry. You haven't heard."

"Heard what?"

She took in a breath. "It seems my gift has left me and I am no longer able to contact the dead. The prince has abandoned me. Probably for another woman, if I had to guess." She laughed at this, but it was forced and the smile quickly faded. "I was reduced to using tricks for a while, mirrors and such, but I wasn't very good at it. I was caught on a number of occasions. Very unpleasant. Won't do that again."

"Maybe if you try, your gift will come back."

"I've tried, believe me. It's no use. It's never coming back."

"How can you be so sure?"

"I'm sorry, Madame Alshonsky. I cannot help you."

"Please, it's very important to me. You have no idea. Look, I've brought you this." She held up the bottle.

Madame Gorbunova eyed it again. Then shook her head. "No, I can't."

"Think of it as a down payment. I'll get you another one as well."

"And what if nothing happens? You will blame me and be disappointed."

"I won't. I promise."

"Oh yes, you say that now."

"All I ask is that you try."

Gorbunova thought for a moment and glanced out the grimy window. "Well, perhaps the prince will be merciful today. One never knows with him. He's very capricious. Why don't you open the bottle and pour me a little. They say it frees up the pathways."

Berta opened the bottle and looked around for a glass.

"There should be one over there somewhere. Look under that pile."

She found a glass under a pile of old shoes. She wiped it out with the hem of her skirt and poured a little in the bottom. Gorbunova tossed it back. Coughing, she said, "It's not bad. Where did you get it?"

"Near Vjazovok."

"They know their vodka out there. Thank God for that, eh?" She reached for the bottle and helped herself to a little more. She drank it down and wiped her mouth with the back of her hand. "Oh, how I wish I had a little caviar. You haven't got any, I suppose?" Berta shook her head. "Pity. A little caviar on toast, wouldn't that be lovely. Well, I suppose we must start. Do me a favor and close those curtains. It always works better in the dark."

When Madame Gorbunova was comfortable, she sat back in her chair and closed her eyes. After a while her breathing slowed and she seemed to relax. Long minutes passed and nothing happened. Berta told herself not to worry. After all, it took a while on the night of the séance. She would have to be patient.

More time passed and just when she was beginning to think that nothing was going to happen, Madame Gorbunova's eyes began to move beneath her lids. Berta watched her closely. Gorbunova remained slumped in her seat, silent. Then her mouth opened slightly and she began to snore. Berta sat back trying to decide what to do. Then she reached out and shook her.

"What happened?" Gorbunova asked, her voice sounding thick and sleepy.

"You fell asleep."

She sat up and smoothed her hair. "Sorry, sometimes that happens. No word from the prince?'

Berta shook her head.

"Well, that's it then," she said and reached for the bottle.

"Aren't you going to try again?

"Why? Won't do any good."

"Please, just once more."

Gorbunova frowned at Berta. Then she sighed heavily and looked greatly put upon. "All right, but you have to be satisfied with whatever happens."

"Yes."

"I mean it. The last time."

"Yes, yes, I understand."

With an exaggerated effort she folded her arms over her stomach and closed her eyes. She didn't seem to be concentrating this time, possibly just waiting it out until she could open them again and tell Berta to leave.

Then something happened. Berta wasn't sure what, except that in the next instant Madame Gorbunova's eyes flew open and she sat up. "Someone is trying to reach you."

"Sura?"

"I don't know." Madame Gorbunova closed her eyes again and waited. "I can't see anything. It's all black. Like down a well."

"Is she there?"

"I don't know. There's no one here."

"Then she's gone?"

"I suppose. I can't be sure. I'm not getting anything. Wait . . . no, I thought . . . oh no, it's nothing." She opened her eyes, her lips compressed into a line of frustration. "It's no use. I'm sorry. It's hopeless without the prince. I don't know why I try, it only upsets me."

"No, no, you've been very helpful. I can't tell you how helpful you've been." She took Gorbunova's hand, kissed it, and held it to her cheek. "This has meant everything to me. I'm very grateful."

The old woman looked relieved and visibly lightened after that. Perhaps it felt like her previous life had returned to her. They chatted for a while and then took their time saying good-bye. Berta parted the sheet and left the way she came.

THAT NIGHT, after Samuil went to sleep, she sat up at the little table, with Sura's locket wrapped around her fingers. The street was deserted because of the curfew. A jagged edge of moonlight sliced through a section of the alley and illuminated the soggy rubbish that had recently been resurrected after the first melt. Berta closed her eyes and whispered: "Sura, it's Mameh. Where are you?" The wind outside blew the papers about and scattered the clouds across the sky.

"Try, *maideleh.* Try to talk to me. It's Mameh."

Night creaks of an old building.

Are you there?

Scratching in the walls.

She sat for some time, listening for a response. When none came she concentrated very hard, closed her eyes, and imagined the words flying out the window on the wind. She saw them flying on the currents over the earth, over Little Russia and off to Europe. Now, they were riding a gale over the ocean, now on a wind rippling the sands of a desert. She saw them all jumbled up on a gust over the glassy surface of a lake and tumbling back into order over a swollen stream. Finally they came drifting in on a breath.

Are you there?

"*Yes,*" came the answer. Clear and strong.

But it wasn't Sura who answered the question.

It was Hershel.

Chapter Nineteen

March 1920

BERTA SAT on the top step of the stoop, cleaning a chicken. It lay across her lap, its head drooping over her knees, her fingers straining with the breast feathers as she pulled them out and stuffed them into a sack. Lhaye would be grateful for them. There wouldn't be many, but someday, if more chickens came her way, she would have enough for a pillow. Pavel was sitting a step below her watching the children playing war in the street. The battle consisted of lobbing small chunks of rubble at each other accompanied by the sounds of explosions, running, hiding, and dying dramatically.

Pavel had come over late in the afternoon to bring her the chicken along with a fresh loaf of hard-crusted bread and a box of sugar. She invited him for supper. She had no idea where he got these things and never asked. She figured he was a thief or maybe some big *macher* in the black market, although he certainly didn't act like one. He didn't brag or throw his money around, and he rarely talked about himself. Mostly they talked about Moscow in the old days. She was older by at least ten years, but they knew the same families, rode and skated in Petrovka Park, sledded down the same hills, and summered at neighboring estates. Once he told her he had been in a labor camp and was freed after the Kerenskii revolution. He never gave her any details, not even how he lost his finger, and she never asked, though she wanted to know.

As she worked to clean the bird she told him about the peddlers, about the woman they were looking for from the Berezina, and what Gorbunova had said about someone trying to communicate with her. She didn't tell him about the answer she received the night before, because now, in the light of day, it seemed ridiculous. Like one of her mother's stories.

"I want to go to Poland," she said, struggling with a stubborn pin feather.

He looked up at her and then back at the children. "It's dangerous. They're shooting people at the border. How would you get across?"

"I thought maybe you'd know. I've heard there are people who take you for a fee."

"Yes, and sometimes they take your money and dump your body in the middle of the river. There are always bodies washing up on shore drowned or shot in the head. And what about Samuil?"

"What is there for him here? What future would he have? I just buried one child, I won't bury another."

Pavel reached up and grabbed a feather that was floating away. The oldest boy in the street ordered his younger brother away. He didn't want to go, so the bigger boy dragged him to the curb and told him to stay put, explaining in detail what would happen to him if he didn't. Then the bigger boy returned to the battle, while the younger one watched from the curb. His coat was threadbare and one sleeve hung by a few threads. His nose was red and the cold had turned his knees purple.

"You'll need some money," Pavel said. "I can give you what you need."

"I can't promise to pay you back. I'll try, but there's no guarantee."

He let the feather float away and then stuffed his hands in his pockets. "I won't need it back. When do you want to leave?"

"As soon as possible."

"I can get you a travel permit."

"Will it look good?" She assumed it would be a forgery.

He laughed. "It won't have to. It'll be official."

"And how will you do that?"

"I'll do it."

They sat there talking while she finished cleaning the bird. She didn't want to think about what lay ahead so they talked about Moscow, about Kartsev's chocolates in the Upper Trading Rows and about

Elizaveta Fedorovna's wedding, which they had both attended, she, as a guest of the bride, he, as a little boy. Their talk meandered to other families, to summers in the country, to picking mushrooms and making wild strawberry jam, and never once did they mention the revolution, the labor camps, the prisons, the mass shootings, the hunger, or pogroms, or the journey she was about to take.

LHAYE HAD been sitting at the little table for most of the morning watching Berta tack up the fabric to make it look like blouses and then stuffing it into bundles to disguise it as old clothes. Inside the lengths she hid soap, candles, matches, and pouches of tobacco. Lhaye had been arguing with her ever since she found out that Berta was going to Warsaw. No matter how many times Berta tried to explain it to her, she couldn't understand such foolishness. They were shooting people for nothing. What made her think she could get across the border? Why would she risk Samuil's life to go to Poland because of what some peddlers were saying? It was crazy. If she wanted to leave, she should have gone with Hershel in the first place. Now, it was too late.

"And even if you do manage to get across, you don't speak Polish and you mustn't speak Russian. They shoot Russians in Poland." Her voice was brittle with anxiety and incipient tears. It was nearly time for Berta to leave.

Berta stopped what she was doing, came over, and took up Lhaye's hands in her own. "We've been through all this. Please don't worry. I know where to go. I have enough money. We'll be all right."

Lhaye could smell the kerosene that Berta had smeared on her neck, wrists, and ankles as a safeguard against lice. She walked over to the window and looked down into the street. Samuil was already there waiting with Pavel. "And what if you do manage to get there and you find out that Hershel's not looking for you? What if he's dead? What proof do you have that he's even alive?"

"I'm not going to argue anymore."

"Berta, think about it. You'll be in Warsaw with no place to go. You won't know anyone or even speak the language. You won't have any money. Can't you see how dangerous this is?"

"Come down with me. I want to say good-bye down there."

Lhaye's cheeks flushed and she started to cry even as she struggled against it. Berta came over to her and put her arms around her shoulders. The smell of kerosene was overpowering.

"Lhaye . . . *mein teiers*, we'll be all right. You'll see. Please, let's not argue anymore. We have so little time."

"I'm afraid," Lhaye sobbed, holding her sister close. "I don't want you to go."

Berta stroked her hair and brushed her forehead with her lips. "I know. I know."

When Lhaye had collected herself, she walked Berta down the stairs and out to the sidewalk. There she said good-bye to Samuil, telling him to take good care of his mother. She kissed him and hugged Berta one last time, swallowing hard to keep back the tears. She said nothing to Pavel, because she blamed him for Berta's reckless decision. After all, he had provided the money and the travel permits. As she watched them walk away, her dear ones, the last of her extended family, Berta turned back once and waved to her. She was crying. Lhaye couldn't wave back. She could only stand there until they disappeared in the crowd.

THEY FOUND the station empty except for a few wounded soldiers on cots in the corner, an old woman and two young children, and a nursing mother sitting on a bench near the door. Berta knew they had just missed the train. Then, as if to confirm this fact, the passengers that weren't able to find seats began trudging back in from the platform. Most were grim faced because they had been waiting for days and now they were going to have to wait even longer for the next one.

"You don't have to stay with us," Berta said to Pavel. "We'll be all right. We'll find a seat by the door and wait there."

"No, I'll take care of it."

He left her standing there and walked over to the two militiamen by the platform door. They were dressed in greatcoats and lambskin *papakhas* emblazoned with a red star. At first she thought he was going to bribe them and was apprehensive because she had never bribed a

Red Army soldier before. So it took her by surprise when, before he could say anything at all, they jumped to attention and saluted him smartly. "Comrade Commissar!" they said, nearly in unison.

"I want to see this woman on the train," he said, glancing back at her.

"Yes, Comrade Commissar."

He motioned to Berta and Samuil and they came forward and followed him out through the open doorway to the platform. Berta was dumbfounded. Clearly she had been wrong about Pavel. He was neither a thief nor a black marketeer. Now she didn't know what to think about him.

Outside the air was frigid and smelled of smoke and grease. The rafters were filled with pigeons that wheeled overhead and fought over places to perch. Behind them the militiamen followed at a respectful distance; ahead the train idled on the tracks, a deep-throated rumbling coming from the engine. People were everywhere, sprawled on the roof and on the bumpers; every stair was taken, as was every seat inside.

"You are a commissar?" she asked, as they walked down the length of the train.

He looked weary and slightly annoyed. "I suppose I am."

"Of what?"

"Does it matter?"

As they approached the last carriage, the militiamen went on ahead. The muzhiki saw them coming and moved off the steps so they could go inside. Berta could see them through the windows ordering two passengers out of their seats. They were peasants dressed in belted sheepskin coats. They got up without an argument, at first searching for another place to sit, but seeing none, gave up and left the train. The militiamen came back to report that the seats had been cleared. Samuil climbed the steps and went inside, while she stopped on the first and turned back to Pavel. But he was already walking away—looking as he always did: sour, exhausted, a disappointed man.

She saw him signal the engineer in the locomotive as he passed. A moment later the whistle blew, steam blasted out over the tracks, and the train lurched forward with such force that it sent the passengers in the aisles tumbling into each other. As the train began to move out of the station she climbed into the carriage and found her seat by the window. Soon the wheels were clanking over the switches and smoke was pouring out of the stack. She saw him through the glass, standing on the siding just beyond the platform. He was searching for her among the passengers at the windows. She thought he must have seen her. For in the next instant, Pavel Ossipovich Lepeshkin raised a hand to say good-bye.

SHE SPENT that day seated next to Samuil, looking out the window at the passing fields and farmhouses still wrapped in winter corn husks. The fields had lost most of their snow, revealing black patches of bare earth sparsely sprinkled in new green shoots. Occasionally, she would see a muzhik, his sturdy pony and his family struggling to free a cart that had gotten stuck in the mud. The roads were mired in it, as were the yards around the houses. The sun was getting warmer and the whole region seemed to be waiting for the fields to dry out so planting could begin.

The train stopped at every country station along the way, sometimes for hours at a time. The peasants were trading freely at these stations despite the new edicts. It took only a few steps around a corner to trade a length of fabric for a meat pie or a pouch of tobacco for a chicken or roasted hare. During one long wait Berta and Samuil got off the train, took a stroll through the little town, came back, brewed some tea, and made a picnic in the park by the depot.

That night Berta had a hard time sleeping. She and Samuil had made themselves as comfortable as possible, using their bundles for pillows, drawing their coats up around their shoulders, and settling in for the night. Samuil fell asleep easily, but Berta was kept up by an old man across the aisle whose choking snores rose above the clatter of the wheels. Finally she threw off her coat and got up. She stepped across the aisle and nudged the old man until he shifted position and quieted down long enough for her to fall asleep.

It was near dawn when the train suddenly lurched forward with a piercing screech and stuttered to a stop. The passengers were thrown into the seat backs in front of them, while those on the floor were sent tumbling into each other, their bundles and suitcases torn from their hands, women screaming, men grunting, children crying out in shock and pain. Berta hit her head on the seat back. Samuil flew against the window. The train came to a dead stop in the middle of an expansive field. Outside all was quiet except for the muffled cries of the passengers that sounded like the faraway roar of a river. Inside Berta and Samuil scrambled to their feet and started to retrieve their things. Others were also struggling to get up, calming children, rubbing elbows and heads, dazed and searching for their belongings.

"What happened, Mameh?" Samuil asked, once they had taken their seats again.

People in the carriage were beginning to ask the same question. One old man seated across the aisle held up a bloody rag that he had been holding to his nose. "It might be the Directory," he said, referring to the Ukrainian troops.

"Or Hryhoriiv's army," said another voice from the back.

The Jews in the carriage fell silent at the mention of this name. Nykyfor Hryhoriiv was the bloodiest of the warlords. His army was notorious for the kind of pogroms they waged. If they had stopped the train, then the men would be dragged off and shot, their bodies mutilated and thrown into a ditch. The women would be raped until they died or went mad, and their children killed for sport.

A young man dressed in the uniform of a commercial high school student jumped to his feet. "I'll go and see what I can find out."

"Me too," Samuil said, jumping up.

Berta grabbed his arm and pulled him down. "You'll wait right here," she said severely. He lowered his eyes and gave her a look of reproach. She had humiliated him in public. He was still too young to see the difference between humiliation and death at the hands of Hryhoriiv's army.

While the student was gone, the passengers strained to hear what was going on outside. Someone said it was too quiet for Hryhoriiv's army. Someone else said they may have hit a cow.

The student returned and struggled with the door until it swung open, bringing with it a rush of cold air. He was a particular young man and made sure the door was properly closed before he turned back to the anxious crowd.

"Well? What is it?" asked a woman sharply. Her face was stiff and pale with fear.

"The Reds. They're clearing the train."

"We have to get off?" asked the man across the aisle.

"Here?" asked a woman incredulously. She had two young children.

"But there's nothing out there," said Samuil looking out the window anxiously.

"Hush," said Berta. "It's still only a rumor."

A line of passengers trudged past their window carrying baskets and bundles. Shortly after that, the carriage door opened and two soldiers and a Red Army officer walked in out of the cold. They were bundled up in greatcoats and wore caps with a red star on the visors. The officer had dark, closely cropped hair and a pockmarked face with round cheeks like a rodent. He stepped forward, looked around at the anxious faces, and said, "Comrades, this train has been requisitioned. You are all ordered off immediately. It is needed in the heroic struggle against the counterrevolutionary imperialist forces. Anyone who makes any trouble will be considered a counterrevolutionist and shot on the spot." He stood there a moment longer as if to drive the point home, then turned and left with his fellow soldiers.

At first no one moved. Then a peddler in the back rose and started to gather up his bundles. A couple got up after that and then a few muzhiki and soon the entire carriage was on its feet getting ready to leave. There were so many questions: Where would they go, how far to the next town, where could they stay the night, how long before the next train? Everyone wanted to know the answers, but no one was willing to ask.

Berta and Samuil gathered up their bundles and followed the line of passengers out the carriage door and down the steps. Outside, the air was cold in the frayed half-light of dawn. Vaporous trails of mist swirled up from the rich black earth. They were standing in the middle of a large field surrounded by birch trees, their papery bark curling around their thick trunks, the undergrowth around them softened into a blur of muted colors by the morning fog. Up the track they could see the railroad workers uncoupling the locomotive. Ahead of that was an armored train stretched out on the tracks, silent and dark, an ancient monolith in the gathering light.

"What are they doing, Mameh?"

"Taking our engine."

"Why?"

"They probably ruined theirs. Or maybe they ran out of wood."

The passengers milled about on the track bed, talking in low voices, hands in pockets, looking lost. Nobody knew which way to go. Some were for finding a farmstead and asking the way. Others were for following the tracks. One man, a Jewish blacksmith holding a cloth bag containing his tools, told the others that he knew of a town about half a day's walk.

"What kind of a town?" asked a muzhik, his eyes narrowing.

"A Jewish town."

"A *zhydy* town?" What good is that?" He spat on the ground and walked away.

"What's the name of this town?" asked a man in an expensive topcoat. He could have been a doctor or perhaps a lawyer.

"Lipovec," said the blacksmith. He was a spare man with muscular arms. "It's small, but it's on another line. There's a chance we could catch a train from there. Anyway, I'm going. Come or stay, it's all the same to me."

He picked up his tool bag and started off across the muddy field. Some of the passengers, Jews mostly, followed behind him. Berta and Samuil were among them. The others chose to wait for the Reds to leave. Then they planned on climbing back into the cold dead carriages and waiting, for what, they did not know.

It was difficult getting across the field. A fine mist had begun to fall, gentle but insistent, adding more water to the muddy troughs between the furrows. Soon the water had soaked through Berta's shawl, droplets dripping down her back and onto her face. It was impossible to stay out of the mud. Only by stepping on clumping weeds or skirting the deeper quagmires between the furrows were they able to make any progress at all.

The going got easier once they reached a stand of birches that stood between the field and the road. There the path was solid as it wound under the chartreuse leaves fluttering in the ripening morning. Names were carved into the thick creamy trunks. Names like Mykola and Ostap spelled out in dark bark that had grown up through the knife marks.

Once on the road they avoided the mud by walking on the shoulder or along the middle where newly sprouted grass had just begun to grow. The going wasn't difficult and they made good time, although it turned out that Lipovec was farther than the blacksmith had remembered. They entered the town square that afternoon, worn out, mud up to their shins, and looked around at the shops that were all closed. Something was wrong. Even with the new edict, something should have been open. The street was deserted and the houses were shuttered. There was a visor cap in the middle of the street and a laundry basket full of wet clothes near the pump. There was a wheelbarrow on its side by the grocery and rakes and hoes still out on display in front of the hardware store.

The passengers began to disperse, some going off down one lane or another looking for lodgings and something to eat. Berta and Samuil went down one cramped lane where the houses were all one story, peeling plaster over brick, with steep sloping roofs of rusty tin or crumbling shingles. The windows on all the houses were either shuttered or boarded up and many of the front doors had been reinforced with planks. They went from door to door, balancing on the boards that had been placed over the mud, calling out, but receiving no answer even though they could see smoke drifting out of the chimneys.

"Where is everybody, Mameh?"

"I don't know." She looked up at a ruined castle on a hill above the town and thought it might be Polish. She wondered if they would have to spend the night there without shelter from the rain or cold. Then she saw a woman in a checkered shawl running lightly over the boards a few houses up. She was small, half buried in her shawl, and she ran with a certain grace, keeping her skirts well up over her ankles and her boots relatively clean. She was carrying a loaf of bread under her arm and a sack of potatoes in her hand.

"Mother, is there a place we could stay tonight?" asked Berta coming over to her.

The woman looked annoyed. "I'm no one's mother and no, there isn't."

"Our train's been requisitioned and we have no place to stay."

"Well, that's not my problem," she said, about to go on.

"All we need is a sofa, a rug, a place on the floor. I'll pay."

At this the little woman turned back. "How much?"

"Five rubles."

"That's not very much."

"Imperial rubles."

Her eyebrows flared and she considered the offer. The imperial ruble was the only money left in Russia beside the *kerenki* that had any value. "Just the two of you?"

Berta nodded.

She shifted the potatoes to her hip. "Well . . . I suppose I could use the company." Berta started to thank her, but the woman held up her hand. "Just pay me in advance. That's all I ask. The words you can keep."

The woman led the way to a low house with peeling whitewashed walls under a sagging tin roof. It was fronted by a picket fence that had lost a few posts and was listing badly. From the street they crossed on several boards that led up to a stone step and a front door that had been reinforced like the others. There were six small windows on either side of the door, all shuttered and secured with pieces of scrap lumber that had been hammered into place with big square nails. When the woman reached the door, she shifted her packages to one arm and stuck a key into the lock. Then, after looking up and down the street, she opened the door. "Hurry up. Get in," she hissed, holding the door open.

The interior was dim, the only light coming from the slats of the shutters. Once a lamp was lit Berta could see that they were in one big room that served as both kitchen and parlor. There was a stove and a faded sofa covered in a silk shawl, and displayed on the walls and side tables were framed photographs, posters, and memorabilia from the Yiddish stage. White suede gloves lay next to a vase full of palm fronds that had been painted gold. Sequined slippers sat under a bell jar, and hanging on a hook was an opera cloak decorated with jet beads and ostrich feathers. The photographs showed actors in dramatic poses, heavily made up against painted scenery. The posters announced the productions of various Goldfadn plays: *A Little Letter to a Bride*, *The Daughter of Jerusalem*, *Koldunye*, and others.

The woman watched as Berta and Samuil examined her treasures. "You like my mementos?" she asked, smiling for the first time.

"Is this you?" Berta asked indicating a photograph of a woman, dramatically lit, dressed in a shroud and heavy black eye makeup, rising up from a coffin.

"Yes, I was Leah'le in *The Dybbuk*. *An electrifying performance*, that's what they said. *Breathtaking* was the word they used. And here I am as Sappho and that's Lev Polgar, very famous in his time. I'm Pessel Landau, you've heard of me?"

They looked blank.

"No?" she sighed. "And here I'm Dina in *Bar Kokhba*. It was before we were allowed to speak Yiddish. Before your time I imagine." She looked at the photograph and smiled. "I remember we were in Zemkhov or maybe it was Kitai-Gorod and the gendarmes came and we all had to speak gibberish so they'd think we were speaking German."

Pessel Landau was small with jet-black hair and large, heavily made-up eyes. In the gloom she could almost pass for a girl with her little steps and the coy tilt of her head. On closer examination it was easy to see that her hair was dyed and that she wore too much face powder and rouge. Even in the subdued light one could see the sag of her jawline and the hardness around her mouth. She went over to the sideboard to light the samovar and Berta asked, "So why are all the windows boarded up? What's everybody afraid of?"

Pessel blew out the match with her red, red lips. "You don't know?"

A FEW HOURS later as the sky clouded over and heavy drops began to fall, a squadron of the Petliura Brigade of the Zaporozhian Cossacks, Third Haidamak Regiment, rode into Lipovec at a gallop, eager for the battle that lay ahead. There was no resistance, no battle. The inhabitants were in hiding, but this didn't keep the corporal from proclaiming a victory over the revolutionary scum and ordering a "celebration" to follow.

There was a proclamation that was nailed to the door of the main synagogue. It demanded that all the Jewish men come to the town square by sunset. The residents of Lipovec had not avoided two pogroms by following such an order. Instead the men stayed in their homes and Rabbi Dimanshtein of the Stambulski Synagogue, carrying a Torah and wearing a satin caftan, a prayer shawl, *shtreimel*, and phylacteries, led fourteen of his most pious congregants into the town square. There they presented the corporal with a Torah scroll, a souvenir plaque written in Hebrew commemorating the acquittal of Mendel Beilis, and three thousand rubles. The plaque looked like gold but it was only brass. "What's this for?" the corporal wanted to know. He hadn't even bothered to get off his horse. He just slung one leg over the saddle and leaned down to accept the gifts.

"For the hard life of a soldier," said the Rabbi in Russian. "Please take them with our gratitude and our prayers for your good health and prosperous future."

The corporal opened the bag of money and began to count. There had to be at least a few thousand rubles, which was not a great sum, but more than he had ever seen in his life. He liked the idea of having a few thousand rubles all to himself; he had already decided not to share the money with any of his men. He was the corporal after all, and could make these kinds of decisions.

The problem was his commander, Otaman Semesenko, a twenty-year-old farm boy laid up in Proskuriv with what he thought was influenza but was really the tertiary stage of syphilis, had given him precise orders not more than two days before. They were not to take bribes, not to loot, not to rape or anything else that would bring dishonor to the regiment. They were only to kill Jews. The corporal wanted to do what was right, but a few thousand rubles was a lot of money. It was a dilemma. How could he take the money and the gold plaque and still be true to his orders? The answer didn't come to him until well after they had left the town and were nearly halfway to their next destination. What law said he couldn't keep the rubles and still kill the Jews? He was the corporal after all. He could make these kinds of decisions.

It was late by the time the Cossacks rode back into Lipovec and most of the town was sleeping. The rain had stopped and the clouds were beginning to move off. Before going into "battle" they took the usual precautions, which included smearing black grease paint on their faces. In the cold light of the moon their glistening skin looked decidedly blue.

Their first stop was the Howling Dog Tavern on the outskirts of town. It was so far out that no one heard the screams of the tavern keeper's wife when they threw her out of the second-story window. The tavern keeper tried to comply with their orders, but his hands were shaking so badly he couldn't insert the key into the lock of his storeroom. So they hung the little man from a spindly oak at the side of the tavern. Even though he was barely five feet tall and as thin as a whip, the branch broke under his weight and he and the rope tumbled to the ground. The Cossacks took this as a sign from God that the little *zhyd* should be spared from hanging, so they shot him in the head and turned on his four daughters and young son, whom they had found hiding under the beds.

WHEN PESSEL heard the first screams of the pogrom, she grabbed several pots of water, the bread, and a bowl of boiled potatoes. She told Berta to bring the kerosene lamp and an empty bucket and follow her down to the cellar. There she led them to a pile of moldering fruit crates that lay among the rubbish on the dirt floor.

"Help me," she said, putting down her things. She and Berta flung the crates aside until Berta could see by the light of the lantern that there was a trap door half buried in the dirt. Together she and Samuil pulled on a heavy iron ring at the top of the door until it rose up on its hinge revealing a hole in the floor.

"My uncle had it built after the '05 pogroms. He liked to be prepared."

Pessel threw down a rope ladder and went down first. Then they handed her the supplies and came down after her. Berta pulled the crates back over the door and covered it with more rubbish as she lowered it into place.

The hole was no more than six feet square. The walls were slick with water and the floor was damp and cold. Even so, they sat down on the bare dirt and shivered as the cold crept under their clothes, numbed their legs and buttocks, and seeped into their bones. As soon as they were settled Pessel blew out the light and they sat in the dark, shivering, wishing they had brought their coats, and listening to the screams of the pogrom that came in through the cellar window.

AT THE bakery, the Cossacks helped themselves to meat pies and bread. At the cobbler's, they took the hides and shoes. At the silversmith's, they took sacks of solid silver goblets, platters, and candelabras, every bit of the silversmith's inventory. Yet they didn't take his greatest possession until they climbed the stairs and found his fourteen-year-old daughter hiding in an armoire with her two younger brothers.

They took the girl into her parents' bedroom and threw her down on her mother's faded comforter, a wedding gift from a long-dead aunt. She struggled at first, but after the third Cossack, she settled down and even stopped screaming. After the fifth her eyes became fixed on the faded roses in the wallpaper that were splattered with her brothers' blood. During the sixth something broke inside her and she died before the farm boy was finished.

SOMETIME during the night Berta heard the loud screech of boards being pried off the front door. It didn't take long for the Cossacks to break it down and soon she heard the tramp of their heavy boots on the floorboards overhead. Moments later there were boots on the stairs, then in the cellar directly above them, kicking the crates about and rooting through the garbage.

"Well?" another one shouted from above.

"Nothing. And it smells like shit down here." His voice sounded like it was in the hole right next to them.

"Look again. Look for fresh dirt."

"Nothing. Just some old rubbish."

"You sure?"

"I'm coming up. It stinks too bad down here. Something's dead."

He climbed the stairs and for a while longer there was more clumping about, glass shattering, and the heavy scrape of furniture. Then there was silence in the house, broken only by the sounds of destruction going on in nearby streets.

The pogrom continued for another day and into the night. By then the slop bucket was overflowing and the smell was overpowering. They had run out of water and food and Berta was worried about Samuil, who had begun to cough. "I'm going up," she said, after the screams and the gunshots had drifted to another part of the neighborhood.

"No, Mameh. I'll go."

"Are you crazy? You're just a boy. You stay here."

"Why? I can hide and I'm fast."

"You're not going anywhere."

"Maybe you should let him go," said Pessel.

"I'm not letting my son go out there." She struck a match and lit the lamp so she could see the ladder.

"But, Mameh, I can do this," he insisted. "I'm better at it than you are." His skin was pale in the lamplight. It was covered in a moist sheen like the underbelly of a frog.

"You're not going."

"I've been doing it my whole life."

"No, and that's the end of it."

"I have to go. You'll get caught and I won't. You know I'm right."

She stopped on the first rung and looked at him steadily in the eye. "You can really do this?"

"Easy."

"No, not easy. This isn't spying on the clockmaker's wife. If they catch you, they will kill you. They will hack you to pieces."

"I can do it."

She sighed wearily and then climbed back down. "All right, but don't leave the house. Just empty the slops, fill up the water pots, and bring back a little food. It shouldn't take you more than a few minutes."

"Yes, yes," he said impatiently, climbing the ladder.

Pessel said, "There's a jar of pickled eggs in the cupboard and a box of biscuits on the top shelf. They might have missed them. It's hard to see up there. They'll be stale by now, but they'll have to do."

Berta reached up and touched his leg as he crawled through the opening. "Be careful. Here, take the bucket. No, leave the door open."

"What if they come?"

"You'll need it open."

Samuil climbed up out of the hole and stood on the dirt floor breathing in the musty air of the cellar. It smelled like an ocean breeze compared to the air in the hole. He turned back and pulling his shirt up over his nose he picked up the bucket and climbed out of the cellar. The house was in shambles. It smelled of urine, whiskey, and smoke. The boards over the two windows had been ripped off and the front door dangled by a hinge. Nearly every piece of furniture had been smashed or thrown out the door into the street. The photographs lay in pieces on the floor, the contents of a costume trunk scattered over the wreckage. Through the broken windows, he could see the part of town that was burning. There was a dull glow over the houses and ash was raining down on the muddy lane. He carried the slop to the back door and standing on the steps poured it slowly into the dirt so it wouldn't splatter. Then he stood on the porch listening to the sporadic *pop*, *pop*, *pop* of rifle fire.

He went to the water barrel and plunged the scooper into the cold water and drank his fill. Then he poured some over his hands and on his head and filled the water pots. He hunted for food, but found nothing, not even a raw potato to ease the hunger pangs. He climbed up the counter and checked the top shelves, but there was nothing, only a few rat droppings. He took the water pots and the empty slop bucket back down to the hole and handed them down his mother.

"There's no food in the kitchen. I'm going out to look for some."

"No!"

"I'll be right back."

"Samuil, no!" she cried out.

"Don't worry, I'll be all right." Samuil climbed up the cellar stairs and ran out of the house into the street. He could hear his mother coming after him, but he had a head start and he was faster.

The lane was lit by the glow of burning houses and littered with clothing, broken furniture, and household goods that had been thrown out the windows into the mud. The air was charged with the sound of gunfire and the smell of smoke. He heard a woman's scream that was cut off abruptly, like lifting the needle off a phonograph record.

He ran along on the boards, sometimes using sofa cushions and pieces of furniture to keep from plunging into the sucking mud. He hugged the houses until he found an open doorway or window, and if the house didn't look too damaged, he went inside to hunt for food.

In one house, he found a generous parlor and a dining room. It had probably been the home of a prosperous merchant. Now everything was gone, the doors and windows, the floors were bare, and even the wallpaper had been stripped from the walls. In the kitchen he found all the cupboards open, not a crumb left. He was about to leave when he saw a figure lying on its side facing the wall near the stove. He didn't want to look at the body, but something drove him to it . . . perhaps a desire to make sure the man was really dead.

When he turned the body over he found a middle-aged man whose throat had been cut. The man's sightless white eyes stared up at him and his gaping wound and open mouth were black with dried blood. Samuil's stomach turned and there was a sweet sticky taste in his mouth. He started to sweat and his legs began to tremble. Before he could faint he turned from the body and ran out of the house. He darted down the middle of the lane, forgetting about his attempts to stay hidden, leaping from cushion to tabletop to bureau drawer, to whatever would keep him from sinking into the mud. At one point he stepped on something soft that gave way and when he turned he saw another body, a woman whose ears were missing.

He raced on blindly down the street until he came to the little grocery at the corner that stood open and vacant. The windows had been broken, the door was gone, and there were smashed bottles and barrels out in the street, spilling their contents into the mud, mixing pickles and mushrooms with the eclectic brew of annihilation. He ran in and almost slipped on the sticky mess that covered the floor. It smelled like molasses and cooking oil.

He wanted more than anything to run back to the hole, but there in front of him were jars of herring, boxes of biscuits, smoked salmon, and crackers. He was starving—hungrier than he had ever been in his whole life and for the moment the gnawing in his belly trumped everything, the black blood, the gash in the throat, the lolling head, even the urge to run.

He gathered up what he could and stuffed it into a potato sack. He was about to dash back into the night when he heard the drunken cries of the Cossacks coming down the street. Without thinking he ran to a barrel and lifted the lid.

"Go away!" a young boy snapped. He was crouched in the barrel, standing on a layer of wheat flour, nearly doubled over so he could fit inside. He reached out and pulled the lid back down over the opening.

Samuil tried a cupboard, but another child was hiding there. Another barrel was filled with pickles and vinegar and another one was nailed shut. The Cossacks were on the front steps. There was a high shelf, but no time to reach it . . . potato sacks in the corner . . . too late even for that. The first soldier tramped in shouting to the others that there was food inside. His blue face glistened in the square shaft of moonlight streaming in through a window. There was only the corner now. Samuil dropped to the floor and melded into the stucco wall. His heart was stuttering and he had a tremendous urge to pee. He didn't know if this would work, if he could stay hidden. He had never become a corner in a room before.

Chapter Twenty

March 1920

BERTA'S BOOTS shattered the icy puddles as she climbed up the steep path; her nose prickled from the cold; her fingers were stiff because she had lost her gloves. She could see a tree with white leaves at the top of the hill, silhouetted against the dawn, its thick roots gripping the ground like the talons of a bird. The grass beneath it was cluttered with what appeared to be boulders.

Down in the street she could hear the shul *klopfer* calling the men to morning prayers. Someone was chopping wood and from various quarters came the clamor of carpenters working full tilt to fill the coffin orders. It had been four days since the squadron of Zaporozhian Cossacks had pulled out, leaving twenty dead and the town in ruins. It was getting warmer and there were still bodies lined up on the synagogue floor that wouldn't wait another day. Even at this hour the town was alive with people laboring for the dead: the gravediggers, the shroud makers, the men at the sawmill. All working to put the dead to rest.

The tree was festooned with scraps of paper that quivered in the early morning breeze. Berta had brought her own scrap and worked to tie it to a branch using a small piece of twine. On it she had written a few lines from a woman's prayer, an ancient plea for her dead child, addressed to a god she didn't believe in. The tree was alive with fluttering prayers: Some were for children, others for husbands and parents; some were for luck or simply for the gift of continued life. They looked like butterflies poised on a branch, ready to fly up to heaven with their messages on behalf of the dead and the ones who were left behind to mourn them.

She turned and joined the other women who had come up before her, who were sitting on the grass together and yet apart. No one spoke. No one had to because they understood each other, why they had come and why they were together. Their shawls were pulled up over their heads and their skirts were splayed out around them, solid women, easily mistaken for boulders in the predawn light. Berta pulled her shawl up too and sat among them, her skirts spread out all around her, giving her the same look of solidity, another sad boulder on the scruffy winter grass. She lowered her head and closed her eyes, but instead of a prayer she hummed an old Tartar song about horses on the steppes that she used to sing.

Stop pretty one and let me up
Let me up and we will ride the wind
Ride the wind around the world
Just you and me around the world
Sura and the horse around the world

When Berta came back down she found Pessel running out of the house with laces untied, her coat thrown over her nightdress, wearing a kerchief over her wild hair that fell in disarray down her back. She ran along the boards that lay over the mud, extending her arms out for balance and calling out to Berta. "A merchant has come," she said, nearly bursting with the news. "I just heard it from the old woman in the back. I know him. He lives near Zhvanets."

Pessel knew all about Berta's destination and her intention to cross the river into Poland. "Why are you just standing there?" Pessel asked impatiently. "Go, go. You'll miss him."

"What do you think he'll charge?"

"He'll be fair. He won't take advantage. He isn't like that. He's harmless." It was the highest praise Pessel could give any man.

Berta found the merchant in front of the stable harnessing his horse to a cart that was filled with sacks of potatoes. "Are you going to Zhvanets?" she asked.

"Eventually," the merchant said, glancing up briefly.

"Will you take me and my son?"

This time he studied her more closely before shaking his head. "I cannot. Sorry."

"Even if I pay you?"

"That's not it. I can't overload Esther. She won't have it." The chestnut mare looked around when she heard her name. "Yes, you, my beauty, I'm talking about you." He kissed her nose and stroked her flank. "She won't pull a heavy load over these roads. I know her. She'll be cross and make everyone miserable."

As it turned out, Mottel Fichmann was able to sell a lot of potatoes that day. He gave a pood to the rabbi for the destitute and sold several more by midmorning. By the afternoon, his cart was considerably lighter and this caused him to reconsider. He asked around for the whereabouts of the pretty widow and her boy and was told they could be found at the actress's house.

It only took a few minutes for Berta and Samuil to pack up their things and say good-bye to Pessel. She hugged them and gave them each an autographed picture of herself as Fanitshke in *Mentshn*. The photographs were dull with dirt and creased by the many boots that had ground them into the floor. Still, they were a good likeness of her.

They went to the stables and found Mottel Fichmann already loaded up and ready to go. He moved over so there would be room on the bench. Once they were settled in, he gave Esther a flick of the reins and a string of endearments designed to get her moving. After that, they moved along so slowly that soon Pessel grew tired of waving her handkerchief and went home even though they were still well in sight.

Mottel Fichmann was a Jew who looked like a peasant in a scruffy sheepskin coat and felt boots. He seemed bigger than he was because of his broad shoulders and the way he planted his feet firmly on the ground. Because he had a deep appreciation for his own voice, it wasn't long before he was telling them about his life in Zhvanets, about his lovely wife and their five children, about his travels and his get-rich schemes and anything else that happened to pop into his head as they plodded along over the muddy roads. When he wasn't talking, he was singing to Esther, or stopping for the night with an obliging widow, of which there seemed to be an endless supply from Kiev Province to Podolia.

One afternoon they wound down a steep embankment and came to a small tributary of the Buh River where several women were washing their clothes on the rocks. The women stood in the shallows with their skirts hoisted up and tucked into their waistbands, their brown arms glistening in the sunlight, their hair tied up under white kerchiefs. They beat the clothes against the rocks while they laughed and gossiped, oblivious to the approaching potato cart.

When Fichmann saw the women he pulled Esther up and announced, "It's Shabbes. We're stopping here."

"Can't we go a little farther?" Berta asked. "It's early. The weather is fine. The roads are drying out. We can make some real progress today."

"Travel on Shabbes? But it's against God's will."

"It's only noon. Sunset is hours away."

"Still, no sense in pushing it. We might as well call it a day. We'll stop with Froy Katzenberg, lovely woman, and such a cook as you never saw."

Berta and Samuil exchanged a look. It had become apparent that Reb Fichmann was not fond of pushing it. It didn't matter to him if their journey took an extra day or an extra week as long as there were plenty of widows along the way to make him a hot meal and give him a place in their bed.

Before long they came to a little townlet on the river. The town had only one road running through it, so it wasn't too difficult to find Froy Katzenberg's house, a cobbled-together structure that was only standing because there were two other ramshackle houses on either side holding it up. Even before he had a chance to get down from the cart, the front door flew open and a shapely woman came running out to greet him. She had a thick dark braid twisted into a bun at the base of her neck and two bright spots of color on her cheeks where she had just pinched them. Her chin had a deep cleft like a fist and her round head stood straight and firm on a long stalk of neck.

"*Gut* Shabbes!" he cried, opening his arms and encircling her in his sheepskin coat, tenderly kissing her cheek, her neck, and her lips.

"I didn't think you were coming."

"Not coming? Of course I'm coming. Why wouldn't I come to see my little swallow?" He called all his widows this, indulging them, flattering them, and, most of all, giving them the affection and attention they sorely needed.

When the widow noticed Berta and Samuil, she cooled visibly until Fichmann introduced them as his paying fares. After that she relaxed and invited them all in for tea. They sat in her front room, on rickety chairs, eating stale poppy seed cake with their fingers and drinking glasses of hot tea. The widow was talking about her late husband, whose hand-tinted photograph hung over the chimneypiece and showed him in the uniform of the infantry.

"Killed at Brest," she said with a sigh. "Or at least he was shot there. They wouldn't treat him at the front, because he was a Jew. He had to be transported to another hospital and they said he died on the way. Such a genius with a violin. Such a gentle man." Her eyes misted over as she stared up at his photograph.

Seeing how his widow had suddenly turned glum, the potato merchant jumped in and in a hearty voice that was more peasant than Jew, he asked, "So, my little sunshine, what have you got for me today? I'm in the mood for work."

"Oh, Mottel," she said, looking at him with tender affection. Then, like a general in the field addressing her troops, she rose and announced to the assembled that first they'll clean and then they'll cook.

Berta could see that a timely departure was impossible. The widow was determined to make this a special Shabbes and soon she had Fichmann carrying the front door, the armoire, and the kitchen table down to the river so she could clean them properly. When she wasn't scrubbing furniture, she was cooking soup or baking a pie. She put everybody to work. Samuil gutted and scaled the fish. Berta plucked the chicken until her fingers bled.

During dinner, the potato merchant was especially attentive to his widow. He touched her lightly on the arm to make a point. He kissed the back of her neck when he thought no one was looking and held her hand under the table. The widow soaked it up and her cheeks flamed with pleasure. After dinner, the Shabbes goy came to set the kitchen right and the four of them sat by the stove and listened to Fichmann's stories about his travels and how he outsmarted the Cossacks by pretending to be a deaf mute peasant so he wouldn't give himself away with his thick Yiddish accent.

When it got late, the widow gave Berta a few mats and some blankets and said she and Samuil could sleep by the stove. Then she and the potato merchant climbed the stairs and closed their door. Samuil was asleep before the sounds of their lovemaking drifted down from above. Despite Berta's attempt to drown them out by pulling a blanket over her head, she could still hear, quite plainly, that Fichmann was making his widow very happy. This was unfortunate. She thought if the widow didn't sound so enthusiastic maybe they wouldn't have to spend all of Shabbes with her. Fichmann wasn't particularly religious. Berta could persuade him to travel on Shabbes provided there was a monetary incentive or better yet a fresh widow at journey's end. But this current one sounded so passionate, so ecstatic and grateful, that Berta thought it was very possible they could be stuck there for weeks.

To drown out the widow's pleasure, Berta pulled her coat over her head on top of the blanket. Still she could hear the moans, which were worse than annoying—they were arousing. They reminded her of her own drought, of the steady metronome of loneliness, a sparse existence, where her needs went unmet year after year. It had been so long since she had been with Hershel that she had nearly forgotten what it was like. She put her hands over her ears and closed her eyes. She didn't want to remember, not now, not in this way.

By Sunday morning, Froy Katzenberg was hinting at a more permanent situation for her and Reb Fichmann. She was serving him breakfast at the little table in the kitchen, kasha and eggs, his favorite. Berta was out on the porch with Samuil, sitting on the steps, soaking up the sun, and pretending not to listen to the conversation going on inside.

The widow was saying that she thought it might be a good idea if he started keeping some things with her, a change of clothes perhaps or an extra harness for Esther. Just in case. Maybe they should make plans, have a few set visits when she could expect him. That way she could have his supper waiting for him when he arrived home. She tossed off the word *home* as if it had already been decided that he lived there.

The potato merchant paused for a moment to appear that he was giving it some thought. "Let me sleep on that, my love," he said, pouring milk over his kasha. "I love the way you cook the little kernels. The way the little hard bits are mixed in with the softer ones."

As soon as the widow mentioned set plans, Berta knew they would be off soon. Right after breakfast, the potato merchant announced that there were hungry people waiting for his potatoes and he couldn't, in good conscience, keep them waiting another minute. As much as he wanted to spend his days with his beautiful peach blossom, he had to say good-bye and get back on the road, even though he knew it would break his heart.

After a tearful good-bye, he turned Esther around and soon they were heading out of town under a pale sky. They made good time that day because the roads were dry and Fichmann was tired and not in the mood for widows. They stopped several times for Esther's benefit, but mostly they plodded on in the fine spring weather, keeping an eye out for Hryhoriiv's army and Directory troops. Fortunately Fichmann knew all the roads and kept to the less traveled ones, the ones that were little more than cart tracks and wouldn't have been passable even a week ago.

That night they shared a room at a little inn in a townlet that the potato merchant jokingly referred to as Ganaiden, Garden of Eden, because of the open sewer running down a trench in the back. There was a wedding in town and every room at the inn was booked. Even so the innkeeper didn't want to pass up an opportunity to make a little more coin, so she offered them her room, saying she could sleep at her sister's over the bakery.

The innkeeper's bed was a lumpy straw mattress that was only big enough for one. Fichmann insisted that Berta take it, saying that he and Samuil could spread blankets on the floor. At first it was hard to sleep because of the wedding party downstairs, but they were so tired that not even the music and drunken laughter could keep them up.

Later Berta woke up in the middle of the night to find a hand moving up her thigh. "What are you doing?" she asked, pushing his hand away.

"I thought you might be lonely," Fichmann whispered. He had

squeezed into the bed beside her and was lying on his side, holding on to the headboard to keep from falling off. His other hand came back, gently brushing the inside of her thigh and moving up with purpose. "I'm good with widows, very gentle and kind, just what the doctor ordered."

Berta couldn't be angry with him. He saw himself as a champion of the ladies, devoting himself to their service, doing his best to make them happy in a bitterly unhappy world. "But I'm not a widow," she whispered. "I have a husband in America."

"I didn't know," he said, making no attempt to remove his hand.

"That's all right," she said, turning away from him and leaving his hand behind, naked and lonely under the coverlet.

"And you're going to him?"

"Yes."

He took his time thinking about this. "When was the last time you saw him?"

"Eight years ago."

"That's a long time. Do you miss him?"

She pulled the quilt up over her shoulder. "Yes," she said, vaguely.

She lay there facing the wall, listening to the sound of Samuil's breathing. He was snoring softly in the corner. Then she turned back and lay on her side to give Fichmann more room. They were lying face-to-face, close, but not touching. His breath smelled of the beer he had with dinner. "I heard it from the peddlers," she whispered anxiously.

"What?"

"That he is looking for us."

"So?"

"So, it didn't come in a letter. It wasn't official. It came from them."

"And this worries you?"

"I think I made a hasty decision. I should have thought about it longer. I think I made a terrible mistake."

"What do you mean?"

"What if they got it wrong? What if he's not looking for us and we're in Poland and there's no way of getting back? What will happen to my son?"

The potato merchant thought it over and then said, "The peddlers are often right, not always, but often enough. I've heard plenty of stories of wives reunited with their husbands because of them."

"You have?'

"Many times."

"And they're true?"

"I've always believed them to be."

They lay there together while she thought it over. Then he rolled on his back and extended his arm out as an invitation to her. She moved over to him and curled into the warm crook of his shoulder, letting the atavistic comfort of his presence seep over her, quieting her fears, softening the raw edges.

After a while, he got up without her having to tell him, kissed her on the cheek, and returned to his blanket on the floor.

BERTA HAD no idea what a border stealer was supposed to look like. He could've been a Polish count or the heir to a Polish estate. His clothes were clean and there was a ring on his little finger that glinted in the lamplight. He was a wiry man with thick ropy arms and thinning blond hair. He wasn't big, but his chest was muscular and his neck was thick. It was as if the top half of his body had been meant for someone else.

They met at an inn in Zhvanets, a town located on the north bank of the Dniester River. It was bordered on the west by the Zbruch River, which separated it from Galicia, now under Polish rule. There was an attempt at respectability at the inn: curtains on the windows, a little vase of roadside flowers on wooden tables that had been freshly scrubbed with salt. Fichmann handled the bargaining: so much for a river crossing, so much now, and so much when the woman and boy got across. The fact that the Pole never looked at her, not once, made her uneasy. She wanted him to think of her as a human being, not as a load of household goods to be picked clean and dumped into the river. She remembered Pavel's stories of bodies stripped naked, battered by rocks and currents, washing up on slices of river sand. But Fichmann swore he knew this border stealer. It was said that he had the best boat in town and knew every inch of the river.

She watched him eat his bread and salt and down his vodka. His cheeks were flushed with the heat of the stove. His hair was plastered to his forehead and he kept twisting the ring on his little finger with his thumb, while his eyes slowly traveled around the room, finally coming to rest on her. He eyed her with a speculative look, authoritative and appraising.

When it came time to pay the first installment, Berta stepped outside and went around to the back. There was a man relieving himself in the clearing behind the inn who seemed unconcerned by her presence. When he was finished he buttoned up his pants and as he passed her he said some pleasantry that was lost in the clamor of the inn.

When she thought she was alone, she picked up her skirt and tore the thread away with her teeth and let down the hem. She took out the money and was counting out the sum when she happened to look up and see the border stealer, standing in the shadows not too far off. His back was to her and he was relieving himself, seemingly more concerned with the arc of his stream than what she was doing. Still, after that, she found a new hiding place for her money. She hid it in the heel of her shoe despite the discomfort it caused her and the feeling that one hip was higher than the other.

Two nights later, they met the border stealer down by the river near the place where the women bathe and wash their clothes. It was a dark night with no moon, only a scrim of stars winking overhead in the mist. He was standing by a heap of boulders in a little clearing; behind him the river was a disembodied roar through the trees. She expected him to have an electric torch or a lantern, but he had nothing to light the way.

"How will you see?" she asked him, as he led her and Samuil down to the shore. He walked down the darkened path as if it were broad daylight, while they stumbled after him, tripping over tree roots, their clothes snagging on the bushes and low-lying branches.

"I don't need to see. I was born on the river. I only need to feel."

The border stealer led them down to where the boat was tied to an aspen standing on a small spit of land that jutted out into the river. He untied the painter and held the boat steady while they climbed in. He joined them, picked up the oars, and let the current take them out into the middle. The river was swollen with melted snow and stunningly cold. Occasionally a wave broke over the bow, soaking Berta's clothes, numbing her legs and hands, and forming a pool in the bottom of the boat.

She watched the border stealer using one oar then the other, sometimes rowing backward, sometimes forward, cursing the river and searching the water for signs that only he could read. At one point he got up and her heart stopped. But it was only to find a small bucket, which he handed to her so she could start bailing. Even so she watched every move he made, especially when they got farther out into the river. There he maneuvered the boat along the current, around boulders and half-submerged logs that came up so fast she didn't see them until they were nearly past. Soon they were in a wider part and the river slowed down. It grew quiet and she could hear the water slapping against the boat and against the boulders that lined the shore. She was aware that he was watching her in the dark. Once when he shifted position, she tensed and gripped the sides of the boat.

He laughed: "I'm not going to murder you, woman. You don't need to be worried about me. It's the river you should be worried about . . . and the border guards." He nodded up ahead and she saw searchlights raking the waves, illuminating the trees along the shoreline, and lingering over a pile of boulders that sat in the middle of the river.

"Will they see us?"

"Probably."

"What should we do?"

"You're not going to do anything. You're going to sit there and let me do my job."

The border stealer guided the boat to a place in the water where the river was squeezed into a frothy tumult between two granite cliff faces. There he let the current carry them past the searchlights, rowing furiously first with one oar and then the other, in an effort to keep off the rocks that threatened them on either side. Only once did the light fall on them, but it was only for a fraction of a second. Even so, she could hear the impotent crackle of rifle fire behind them, answered by similar fire from the Polish side.

The current carried them swiftly along past beaches and coves that seemed like suitable places to pull in. When she asked the border stealer about them he only grumbled "patrols" and kept rowing. At an unlikely place he rowed into a rocky cove and guided the boat up alongside a fallen log. "All right. Here you are," he said, tying the painter line to the log and returning to his seat.

"Here?" she asked looking at the jagged rocks that acted like a fortified barrier around the shoreline. "How are we supposed to get in from here?"

"That's your problem. But whatever you do, you better be quick about it. There'll be patrols up and down here looking for you. You'll have a little more time because of the rocks. They won't think to look here. They won't think you're stupid enough to try, so you better get going."

Berta had no choice but to pay the man. She took off her boot, counted out the money, and handed it over. He counted it quickly and pocketed the bills. "The best way in is through there," he said, pointing into the gloom.

"Where?"

"You'll see once you're in. Now off with you. I have to get going."

She took off the other boot, tied them together, and hung them around her neck. Samuil did the same. Then she stood a little unsteadily in the rocking boat and climbed over the side, lowering herself into the frigid water. Samuil followed and she could hear him sucking in his breath as he let go of the side of the boat. They couldn't touch bottom yet and had to feel their way along the slithery bark of the log. Soon Berta was fighting the current, grabbing on to a boulder while reaching behind with her free hand for Samuil. But he had caught his own boulder and didn't need her help. They scrambled over the rocks, over a mossy outcropping, a crevice, the roots of a dead tree, moving from one slippery surface to the next. In some places the rock faces were serrated and spiky, in others smooth and slippery. Berta led the way, shivering in the cold, picking her way in the dark. She was careful to keep her footing, changing direction only when she had to, but always keeping an eye on the shore and adjusting their course whenever she could.

They crossed a place where the rocks were piled on top of each other, their sharp, ragged-toothed outcroppings jutting out in all directions. Her fingers were numb and stiff and it was hard to get any strength out of them. She was about to tell Samuil to be careful when she heard him grunt, his feet scrambling to find purchase, and a splash.

"Samuil!" She whipped around in the dark and lost her balance, falling forward and landing on the sharp edge of a rock. She broke her fall with her hands, but sliced open her leg just below the knee.

"Mameh!"

She turned back and dislodged her foot that was wedged in a crevice. The water was nearly up to her hip now and icy cold. It numbed her leg so she didn't realize how deep the gash was, how it cut through muscle and tissue nearly to the bone. There was hardly any pain so she assumed that it was warm water running down her leg and not blood.

Chapter Twenty-one

March 1920

BERTA DIDN'T want to lean on Samuil. She didn't want to appear sick or injured because it might draw attention to them. She wanted to walk off the train along with the other passengers, one foot in front of the other, down the steps, and into the station. So she waited until they were nearly alone in the carriage and then stood. The pain was so intense it made her dizzy and she had to sit back down.

"Mameh?"

"Shush, keep your voice down. I'm all right. I'm just going to have to lean on you a little."

Fichmann had told them where to go once they crossed the river—to a shtetl and a house, whose occupants were part of the rabbinical underground. The rabbi's wife cleaned the wound and bandaged it, gave them dry clothes, changed their money, bought them train tickets to Warsaw, and taught them how to say *Warsaw* and *American Embassy* in Polish without accents. All along the border and in the larger cities there were houses like this one, sanctuary for fleeing refugees on their way to America. They were funded by those already in America through a variety of organizations with names like Relief of Jewish War Sufferers and European Jewish Appeal.

Samuil helped her off the train. It was hard getting down the steps. She had to lean heavily on the railing and put most of her weight on the other leg. Once they were out on the platform, she limped over to a post and leaned against it, waiting to catch her breath.

"Warszawa?" she asked a porter who happened to be passing by.

He hardly gave her a glance. He was bored by her ill-fitting second-hand clothes, her dirty bundles, and the shoes the rabbi's wife had given her that were so big she had to shuffle along to keep them on her feet. Without a word he nodded to a nearby platform and walked on, stooping to pick up a coin dropped by some passenger hurrying to catch a train.

Since the train wasn't due for another hour she decided to find the *pol'za*, the facility, where she could clean the wound and change the bandage. She found it in a little alcove off the main thoroughfare. It was for ladies of a certain class, expensive women who traveled with maids and nannies and were married to men in industry or in respectable positions in the government. It was late and so it was nearly empty. An older woman, expensively dressed with a cigarette between her fingers, looked up when Berta came in and watched her with curiosity through a haze of smoke. A seamstress was at the woman's feet pinning up the hem of her dress that had most likely gotten caught on her heel.

An attendant in a starched black cap and jumper and white shirtwaist stepped over to Berta and pulled her aside. She put her lips to Berta's ear and whispered sharply in Polish so as not to make a scene. Instead of leaving, as she knew the woman wanted her to do, Berta reached into her pocket and brought out a handful of coins and dropped them into the attendant's hand. The attendant looked at them and then up at Berta. She was confused. Berta nodded to the porcelain sinks and to the stack of clean Turkish towels that sat on a little table by the door, motioning to them and then to herself. The attendant asked her a question in Polish and Berta nodded without knowing what she said, but guessing she was clarifying Berta's request to use the facility. After that the attendant poked at the coins in her hand, probably thinking that she could get fired for something like this. But in the end she pocketed them, waved Berta in, and led the way through the room, grumbling the whole way in Polish.

She stopped in front of a door marked by a sign that Berta couldn't read. The woman reached into her pocket, took out a key, and inserted it into a lock. She motioned Berta inside. It was a little room for the employees. It had a stove with a rusty tea kettle, a table, and a few chairs, and in the corner was a stained sink, a castoff from the other room.

By now the attendant knew Berta didn't speak Polish and motioned with her hands, palms down, to indicate that she should wait there. Then she left and came back shortly after that with a towel and soap. She threw them down on the counter and stood there waiting for Berta to use them. Berta tried to explain that she wanted privacy and when the attendant finally understood, she left, complaining loudly in Polish but closing the door behind her.

Berta went to work. She propped up her leg on the sink, carefully removed the bandage, and examined the wound. It was torn and inflamed. There was pus oozing from beneath a flap of skin that was beginning to smell suspicious. The surrounding tissue was red and painful, but it had stopped bleeding. She filled the basin with hot water and soaked the towel in it. Then she wrung it out and put it over the wound gasping at the first touch of heat. It was painful, but it felt good. It felt clean. She wanted to keep it there as long as she could and brought over a chair so she could sit and be moderately comfortable.

The attendant came back after only a few minutes and walked in without knocking. When she saw Berta with her leg propped up on the sink she ordered her to get dressed and get out. Berta ignored her and reached into her bag for a bottle of antiseptic that the rabbi's wife had given her and poured it over the wound. She winced and her eyes watered. The attendant took a good look at the gash, sucked in her breath, and grimaced. She watched Berta wind the fresh bandages around her calf and when she was done, the woman took away the soiled bandages without a word and waited while Berta got ready to leave. This time the attendant helped Berta shuffle out past the woman who was standing in her corset, watching the seamstress sew up her hem. On the way out the attendant turned and slipped something into Berta's hand. It was a bar of soap.

SAMUIL HELPED her off the train at the Warsaw station. She was too weak to walk without his help. He held her arm as she limped past the darkened ticket counters, out through the brass doors to the curbside and the waiting cabs. She knew they should walk to the back of the line, where the cabs were cheaper, but her leg was throbbing and she felt hot all over, so she took the first one they came to. After she and Samuil climbed in she instructed the driver to take them to the American Embassy in almost perfect Polish with only a hint of an accent.

Although it was hours before dawn, they climbed the steps of the embassy and lay down against the doors, gathering their bundles in around them and huddling together to keep warm. It began to rain and across Ujazdowskie Avenue she could see dark sheets of water falling on the locust trees. Fortunately the portico was deep enough to keep them dry so there was no chance they'd freeze to death. The *rebbetzin* had told them that once they were on the steps of the embassy they were never to leave no matter what. "You're in America as long as you're on those steps. You wait there for the doors to open. Nobody can hurt you there. Nobody can say a thing."

Berta couldn't sleep, so she lay there listening to the sounds of the sleeping city, the rain on the pavement, the occasional automobile splashing through the puddle at the intersection and the rhythmic *drip*, *drip*, *drip* from the rain spouts, which seemed to underscore the rhythmic throbbing of her leg and head. She eventually fell asleep and dreamed about Fichmann and about the river, not the one they had to cross to get to Poland, but the gentle tributary by the widow's house. In her dream he was trying to coax her out of the water, but she didn't want to leave. The water was cool and she was hot and thirsty, and it felt good against her skin. She woke to find a soldier shaking her shoulder and speaking to her in a language she didn't understand.

"It's open, Mameh," Samuil was telling her. He was on his feet and trying to help her up, but she didn't want to get up. She wanted to stay in the river.

The soldier pulled her to her feet and held on to her until she was steady enough to stand on her own. He kept motioning to the street and speaking in a raised voice as if she were hard of hearing. She told him she had business in the embassy and couldn't understand why he didn't step aside. It took her a moment to realize she was speaking Russian and he was an American. Samuil gestured that they had business inside and finally the soldier understood and let them go in.

"You have to look healthy, Mameh," Samuil whispered anxiously, as he helped her through the heavy glass door and into the marble foyer. "They won't let you in otherwise. They won't let sick people into their country."

She knew that well enough. She knew that she had to appear in good health, so she smoothed out her clothes and brushed her hair with her fingers. She straightened her back and looked straight ahead, even though she still had to shuffle to keep her shoes on and couldn't put much weight on her bad leg. Because of this it took them a long time to cross the great expanse of marble to the reception desk.

A girl in her twenties sat behind the counter typing at a desk. She was copying a list of names and telephone numbers from a handwritten list on a pad. Her red lacquered fingernails flew over the keys, while her eyes kept traveling from the list to the keyboard and back again. Another girl about the same age was talking on a telephone at a nearby desk. Both were smartly dressed in suits with long straight skirts, crisp white blouses, and ties. Their hair was cut in the same bob and they wore the same red lipstick that matched their nail polish, despite the fact that both were expressly forbidden by the foreign service dress code.

Berta couldn't understand the telephone conversation because it was in English, but she could tell it was a personal call by the way the girl cradled the receiver between her ear and shoulder and picked at her freshly manicured nails.

"Mademoiselle . . . *S'il vous plaît.*" Berta held on to the desk for support. She was dizzy and feeling nauseous. Her words came out in a breathy rush.

The girl's eyes slid over to her and she held up a finger. She chatted on for a minute more and then with exaggerated reluctance put the receiver back in its cradle and regarded Berta with undisguised annoyance.

"Yes?"

"*Mon nom est Madame Alshonsky. Pouvez-vous m'aider à trouver mon mari.*"

"Oh, French." She sounded disappointed. "I'm not very good at French. I don't suppose you speak English?"

Berta shook her head. "*Son nom est Alshonsky. Il habite en l'Amérique. Pouvez-vous m'aider à le trouver.*"

"Look, I have no idea what you're saying." She turned to her friend, who had stopped her typing and had been following their conversation with interest. "Francis, don't we have someone here who speaks French?"

"Iris, wait." Francis pushed back her chair and stood up. "You're not listening to her. Did you hear what she said?" She came over and considered Berta from across the counter. "Did you say *Alshonsky*?"

Berta hesitated because she had thought she had heard her name, but it was so badly mangled that it was nearly unrecognizable. "__," she said, dropping the French. "__, ___ ___*Alshonsky*." Her heart was pounding in her chest. There was a sickly sweet metallic taste in her mouth. Black shapes drifted down through her field of vision.

"Now what is she speaking?"

"Russian, I think. But, Iris, listen." And then to Berta she repeated: "Alshonsky."

"*Oui*," said Samuil hopefully. Then under his breath he added: "Open your eyes, Mameh. They're watching you."

"Iris . . . it's that woman and her son."

"No."

"*It is.*"

"But she had a daughter too."

"I'm telling you. It's her."

Iris turned back to Berta. "Alshonsky, right?" Samuil nodded vigorously. "Oh my goodness, we found her." And then to Berta: "Mrs. Alshonsky, we've been looking all over Europe for you."

Berta held on to the counter and tried to stop the room from spinning. Samuil caught her arm just as she was about to slip to the floor. "Look healthy, Mameh," he whispered fiercely. "You have to look healthy."

"Oh God, she's ill. She's going to faint." Francis rushed around the counter and took her other arm.

"She is fine," Samuil said in French. "She is healthy."

"I'll call a doctor," Iris said, reaching for the phone.

Francis was already helping her to the bench. "No. She's burning up. Call an ambulance."

Across the hall a crowd of hopeful émigrés lined up at the windows, waiting to get their papers stamped. Their faces turned to watch the boy help his mother to the bench. They stared openly, not bothering to hide their interest. It didn't seem to matter. The woman was obviously beyond caring. Her face was sickly white, glistening with sweat, her eyes bright with fever, and she was shivering, even though she was wearing a coat.

"Mrs. Alshonsky," Francis said in her flat American accent. She crouched down in front of Berta and took her hand. "Hang on there, Mrs. Alshonsky. We're calling an ambulance."

"It's no good, Mameh. They know you're sick. They're not letting us in," Samuil said plaintively.

With a great effort of will Berta opened her eyes and for a brief moment she saw the concern on the girl's face. She knew Samuil was right. It was hopeless. She didn't know what to tell him. She didn't know where he should go for help or how he was going to get there. There was no money left. The girl kept talking and, although Berta didn't understand a word, she knew this young woman meant well. She could hear the sympathy in her foreign words.

"You're going to be all right, Mrs. Alshonsky. We're taking care of everything. We've been waiting for you. Your husband has been looking all over Europe for you."

She seemed like such a nice girl and she wasn't that young. Surely, she could take care of a child like Samuil. He was so smart and almost full grown. How hard would that be? Maybe she wanted a boy to take care of. Maybe she would be willing to be Samuil's mother. In time she would love him. How could she not? She would see how special he is and eventually he would grow fond of her too.

"Do you understand, Mrs. Alshonsky? He's been looking for you. He left word at all the embassies around Russia. You are an American citizen. You're safe now."

Berta leaned back as the blackness swirled behind her closed eyes. She could hear nothing now but the slowing beat of her heart. Samuil was in good hands, she could see that. This woman would take care of him. It would be all right. He was safe. She could sleep now. She didn't have to fight anymore.

"What's wrong with her?" the young woman said in clumsy French.

"She's fine. She's healthy," Samuil answered desperately.

The last thing Berta heard was the woman replying, "No, she's not fine. She's not fine at all."

And then she was riding in an open sleigh with Sura by her side. They were sailing down Petrovka Street, bundled up in furs and leather blankets, coming home from a party at the Kokorevs'. She could smell the signal bonfires at the intersections and hear the sleigh bells and the whoosh of the runners on the hard-packed track. There was a candle burning in one of the upper-story windows of a large house. It melted the frost on the glass in a perfect semicircle.

Are you happy, Mameh?

Very happy.

Sura looked up into the sky and closed her eyes. She let the snow fall on her face, icy and wet, thudding down on her cheeks and lips with down-feather softness. Berta put an arm around her daughter and breathed in the smell of her hair and felt her silky cheek, wet and cold against her own.

Epilogue

May 1921

THE FLIVVER was parked in front of the Hoenig Brothers hardware store and undertaker, a brick building adorned with new awnings and wrought-iron chairs that sat out in front. Painted on the side of the building was a huge sign proclaiming in big block letters THE FARMER UNION BETS ON *YOU!* Up the road, a work crew labored to lay down a new wood-block road. Hershel had talked the other business owners into pitching in for it. *It will be good for business*, he had told them. *New roads for a new day*.

Once they were settled in, Hershel pulled out the carburetor choke, pressed the starter button, and when she caught he released the brake. They drove out past the business section, which was still composed of mostly empty lots, but here and there were clapboard and brick buildings fronted with signs that said simply FURNITURE; LUMBER; SINGER SEWING MACHINE.

At the edge of town they passed bungalows with wide covered porches known by the names of the families who lived there: the Bronfstead house, the Kilbourn house, the Kempers'. Set back from the road was a large clapboard house hidden by a screen of bare branches. It needed paint and the widow's walk was boarded up. This was the Leinenkugal house, husband and son killed in the war.

They drove on past the cemetery with its starched rows of white crosses. Here the farm boys of Barron County were laid to rest after the Great War. The war to end all wars. A few American flags had survived the snows of Armistice Day and were still stuck in the ground next to vases of dead flowers.

Since Hershel discovered that the power of the engine and the feel of the road could take him out of himself, he pressed down hard on the accelerator and kept his foot there, turning onto Highway 48 because it had just been graded and strewn with hay to keep down the dust. Soon they were doing nearly thirty on the straightaways, passing lines of mailboxes with Norwegian and Swedish names on them like Korvold, Vicklund, and Sjodahl. Occasionally, he glanced over at his son and was gratified to see how much he was enjoying the ride. He seemed to take everything in while he trailed a hand out the window, holding it stiff against the oncoming wind. For years Hershel dreamed of afternoons like this. Only he had thought there would be two children in the car.

To rid himself of this thought he stepped on the gas and they sped around a curve going too fast. He had to focus to bring the car back to equilibrium and that brought him out of his reverie, back to the road, to the day, to the rolling pasturelands and the puckered surface of a passing lake.

Eventually 48 got bad and Hershel had to slow down, but he was still content to ride along and listen to the drone of a well-tuned engine. They had the windows down and the split window shield open despite the gathering clouds. Soon there was a chill in the air that hadn't been there before and the smell of fresh earth and rain. Fat drops began to fall on the windshield, mixing with the dust and insect splatter. Hershel pulled over to close the windows and thought about turning around, but just then the sky opened up again and brilliant rays of sunshine shot through the layers of clouds. They seemed to illuminate a part of the landscape not too far off. He took it as a sign that the rain was moving on. That they could keep going.

"What should we do, Son? Should we turn around?"

Samuil shook his head. "Let's keep going." They spoke mostly English now. It had been more than a year since Samuil had come to Rice Lake and already he was fluent.

IT WASN'T unusual for Hershel to take his son out for a drive in the coupelet on Tuesday afternoons. They usually started out from the dealership on South Main and rode out of town on 53 to Haugen or 48 to Cumberland, depending on the condition of the roads. That day

Samuil came over after school and Hershel told his partner, Marty Zelig, a fancy dresser from Lithuania, that he was going home early. Zelly made a face, but what could he do? Hershel was a full partner and could go home whenever he damn pleased.

When Hershel first arrived in Wisconsin, he lived with his sister, Rachel, in Cumberland. She and her husband ran a grocery and set him up with a cart and sundries to peddle to the local farmers. It didn't take him long to see that, just like the muzhiki in Little Russia, the farmers didn't want to buy from him; they wanted to sell. So he and his little mare traveled the countryside buying up rags for the paper mills and pelts for the furriers in Green Bay and Chippewa Falls. He was personable. He spoke English and told stories about the goings-on in town and on the neighboring farms. It wasn't long before he had four carts working for him, a nice house on North Wilson Avenue, and a membership in the chamber of commerce. He wanted to join the Masons, but he was a Jew. Lines had to be drawn, even in Rice Lake.

One day he watched the Ford dealership go up on South Main Street. He had his eye on it even before it opened with balloons and flags on the Fourth of July. He knew the future when he saw it, but he also knew that the future was not easily abided in Rice Lake and that there would be stumbles and perhaps a fall before it finally took hold. He waited for the fall before approaching Martin Zelig with an offer to buy in as a full partner. Zelly put him off for a while, but in the end he took it because he had no choice. Since then they built it into a growing concern, and Zelly, who still complained that he had been cheated, never regretted his decision, not for a minute.

FOR A WHILE the rain stopped, but the sun didn't come out. In fact the sky darkened again and the wind picked up and soon they were driving through a hail of white and pink blossoms from a stand of hawthorns. A heavy branch landed on the hood and careened off the windshield. It startled them so much that Hershel had to pull over and wait until his heart stopped hammering in his chest. Peering out through the windshield he saw a flash of lightning that shattered the sky and then a crack of thunder that seemed more like an explosion.

This time Hershel put her into gear and drove on, looking for a widening in the road so he could turn around. The branches in an aspen grove were thrashing about in the wind, and the grass on the verge was nearly flattened to the ground. When he came to a bend, he slowed, turned the wheel sharply, and gave her a little gas until he made the turn and was heading back the way they came. It started to rain, not splashes on the windshield, but a deluge so dense that they had to pull over and wait. Lightning streaked across the sky and Hershel sat there watching it, afraid to admit how nervous he was. The hair on his arms was standing on end from the static electricity. He wondered if the tires would ground them or if they would end up a blackened crisp for some farmer to find. He looked over at Samuil, who sat very still, his face a white mask.

Staring out at the sky, Samuil asked, "Will the tires ground us?"

"Yes."

"You sure?"

"Yes," he said, without hesitation.

WHEN THERE was a break in the storm, Hershel pulled out the carburetor choke and pressed the starter button: She coughed and sputtered, but didn't catch. He reset the hand spark and the throttle lever and pressed the starter again. This time she started on two cylinders, coughing pitifully.

"Please God," he whispered, giving her a little gas. She coughed again and then, as if sighing in relief, she caught and roared into life. He let out a breath that he didn't even know he was holding. Then he touched the dashboard with two fingers and brought them to his lips as if he were kissing the Torah.

"Let's go home, Papa."

He gunned the engine a few times, threw her into gear, and eased her out into the roadway, avoiding potholes full of water and mud.

When they walked into the comfortable house on North Wilson Avenue, Hershel could hear the sound of an English language record drifting down from upstairs. He heard a precise voice on the gramophone saying *I would like to go to the library.*

Samuil shouted up the stairs. "Mama, we're home."

Berta appeared at the top of the stairs and leaned over the banister. "You're home! Thank God!" Then as usual, whenever she was overcome by emotion, she lapsed into Yiddish. "Hershel, you took him out in this storm? Out on those roads?"

"English, Berta. Speak English."

She sighed. It was frustrating having to put all her thoughts and emotions into a foreign tongue. "You want he should burn up? With all that . . ." Flicking her fingers in the air.

"Lightning, Mama."

"Ya, lightning. What were you *tinking*?"

"It's all right, *mishka*. I was watching out."

"Watching out? Watching out for lightning? And then what? You were going to catch it in your hand?" Berta could no longer sweep down the stairs but she managed her limp by holding on to the banister.

"Can't we have a little fun, Mama?"

"Fun, yes. But this? *Ach*, such foolishness." She took Samuil's face in her hand. "Do me a favor, *boitshikel*. Stay away from lightning. Now, take off your shoes. Olive just mopped the floor."

She took their coats out to the porch to shake off the water.

"You should've seen it, Mama. It lit up the sky. It rained so hard I thought it was going to break the—"

Hershel waved a hand in front of his face to shush him. "We'll just go up and get ready for supper," Hershel said quickly, to change the subject. "What's for dinner?"

Berta came back in with the coats and hung them in the closet. "Chicken and *knedla*."

"I like *knedlas*."

"So tell me something I don't know."

Their house was located in the best neighborhood in town. Their street was wide and divided by a median strip where maples and oaks grew among the serviceberries and dogwoods. It had a wide covered porch and tall windows to let in the light. There were two bathrooms, one upstairs, one down; a velvet settee in the parlor; and a Quick Meal porcelain stove with four burners and an oven in the kitchen.

HERSHEL STOPPED at the linen closet on his way to the bedroom to get a fresh towel. Berta was always complaining that he used so many that Olive couldn't keep up. Usually the closet was filled with them and bedsheets too, except when Olive got behind with the laundry. Today there were only three left, so that when Hershel took one out he could see all the items stored in the back. There was his old Homburg that he knew he would never wear again. There was Berta's yarn bag filled with needles and skeins and the beginnings of a chenille throw that had been started with enthusiasm but quickly abandoned. There was a photo album belonging to his sister, Rachel, and beneath that was the box.

The box had come shortly after they had arrived from Poland. Lhaye had sent it through Pavel, because it was difficult to get things out of the country. It was a simple pine box with green curlycues around the perimeter of the lid. It wasn't large or heavy. When Hershel lifted it out of the closet, he could hear several items rattling around inside. He didn't like to look at it. He wished that Berta had found some other place for it, possibly among her things in the armoire. It would have been nice if she had stored it away in a place where he never had to lay eyes on it. Of course, he never mentioned this to her. She wouldn't have understood.

Hershel had no idea why he reached for it. Usually he went out of his way to avoid it. Maybe it was the dangerous storm that unsettled him and the fact that Samuil had been there with him. Berta was right. He shouldn't have taken Samuil. It was no place for the boy.

He took the box to the bedroom, sat down on the bed, and opened the lid. Inside was a toy horse, beautifully rendered, tenderly cared for, with a long flowing mane that was still in good shape despite the fact that it had journeyed from the Berezina to Dulgaya Street and then all the way to America. There was a pair of gloves with violets on the cuffs. They hadn't fared so well. They were dirty with holes in the fingers. There was a bell and a hair clip etched with violets, pink ribbons, and a silk bow. Hershel examined the contents, picking up the bell and ringing it and then quickly silencing it so that Berta wouldn't hear. All these items were nothing but a little girl's treasures and yet they had such an effect on him. Shame, grief, and, above all, a hectic restlessness to get away.

HE HAD TWO schnapps before dinner and another one with the chicken. He could tell that Berta noticed by the way she looked at him, surprise at first, then with feigned disinterest so as to not embarrass him. Usually he was careful with his liquor. It was already a year into Prohibition and good liquor was not so easy to come by in Rice Lake. When he came up to bed, he saw that the linen closet door was ajar. He opened it and found that the towels had been rearranged to hide the box. For an instant, he felt an immense rush of tenderness for his wife. The ferocity of it caught him by surprise. She was already asleep when he crawled into bed beside her. She lay on her side, away from him. He wrapped himself around her and drew her close. She murmured something unintelligible in her half-waking state. He fell asleep with his face buried in her hair, smelling the rose petal soap she favored.

HE AWOKE around four in the morning, got dressed, and left the house. The night was clear and clean after the storm. Tangles of downed branches littered the street and a torrent of water still ran in the gutter. Water droplets rained down on him whenever the wind rattled the branches. The air was surprisingly warm.

He walked down North Wilson to South Main toward the outskirts of town. He passed Dick Hamilton's brother-in-law, the one who came back from the Marne whole in body but not in mind. The two men glanced at each other as they passed on the wooden sidewalk. The young man was wearing his bedroom slippers and singing "America the Beautiful" in a loud voice as he shuffled along. When he stopped singing, Hershel glanced back to see why and caught him peeing in Mrs. Bronfstead's camellias.

Hershel took a dirt road that led into the hayfields and cut across a pasture. He sloshed across the sodden meadow, coming within touching distance of the grazing cows. They stopped when he approached and watched him suspiciously. Once he had gone a fair distance he turned back to them: unmoving hulks, cardboard cutouts against an inky sky.

When Hershel reached the edge of the pasture, he saw his destination: a grove of aspens crowning the hill. He welcomed the climb out of the muddy field. The mud and water had come in over his shoes and now his socks were soaked. He started up the trail just as it was getting light enough to see the buttercups growing at the base of the rocky outcroppings. When he reached the top he found a suitable boulder among the many strewn about and sat down. There were tiny pools of water caught in the depressions of the rock that soaked through his pants.

After a while he took out several pieces of paper and a pencil and sat there thinking about what he wanted to say. By then the sky had turned to a delicate blue. Red and pink ribbons banded the horizon. He didn't want to write a prayer; he didn't believe in God. Instead he wrote only short notes. He talked about how much he missed her, about her childhood, memories of Masha the cat, the park, riding on her pony. He wrote about coming to America, his regrets, his remorse in leaving her, stupid and unforgivable. He kept on writing, slowly draining the reservoir of shame, until he ran out of things to say. Then he hung the strips on the low-hanging branches, along with the bell.

When he was done, he sat back and watched them tremble in the morning breeze in concert with the new leaves. They reminded him of a quilt of butterflies, newly emerged from the cocoon, fanning their wings to dry them. The bell rang softly, and he listened as it mingled with the sound of the brook at the base of the hill.